PRAISE FOR THE SUMERIANS TRILOGY

"A wonderfully evocative novel... whisking the reader away to ancient Sumer with its dry humour, atmosphere and complex characters."
GRIMDARK MAGAZINE

"The kind of original, exciting, sexy, funny, ambitious storytelling that the world simply needs more of."
CAROLINE O'DONOGHUE,
New York Times bestselling author of *All Our Hidden Gifts*

"I love it! Spectacular storytelling, vibrant prose, wonderful handling of multiple narrators, and genuinely gripping. I haven't read a historical novel this good for years: it's reminiscent of Rosemary Sutcliff at her peak."
JOANNE HARRIS

"*Inanna* may take Gilgamesh as its source material, but it is wholly its own creation. In this richly rendered world of gods, mortals and monsters, the pace never falters, and neither does the sense of an epic being constructed – like the temple to a new divinity – before your eyes. The most enjoyable novel I have read this year."
LUCY HOLLAND, author of *Sistersong*

"Beautifully crafted and elegantly told, I was carried away to a world both famili...
Inanna has an enthralling...
CLAIRE NORTH, World Fantasy Aw...

Also by Emily H. Wilson
and available from Titan Books

Inanna
Gilgamesh

NINSHUBAR

A Novel

EMILY H. WILSON

TITAN BOOKS

Ninshubar
Print edition ISBN: 9781803364445
E-book edition ISBN: 9781803364452

Published by Titan Books
A division of Titan Publishing Group Ltd
144 Southwark Street, London SE1 0UP
www.titanbooks.com

First edition: August 2025
10 9 8 7 6 5 4 3 2 1

This is a work of fiction. All of the characters, organizations, and events portrayed in this novel are either products of the author's imagination or are used fictitiously. Any resemblance to actual persons, living or dead (except for satirical purposes), is entirely coincidental.

© Emily H. Wilson 2025

Emily H. Wilson asserts the moral right to be identified as the author of this work.

No part of this publication may be reproduced, stored in a retrieval system, or transmitted, in any form or by any means without the prior written permission of the publisher, nor be otherwise circulated in any form of binding or cover other than that in which it is published and without a similar condition being imposed on the subsequent purchaser.

A CIP catalogue record for this title is available from the British Library.

EU RP (for authorities only)
eucomply OÜ, Pärnu mnt. 139b-14, 11317 Tallinn, Estonia
hello@eucompliancepartner.com, +3375690241

Printed and bound by CPI Group (UK) Ltd, Croydon CR0 4YY.

For Jenny and Andy

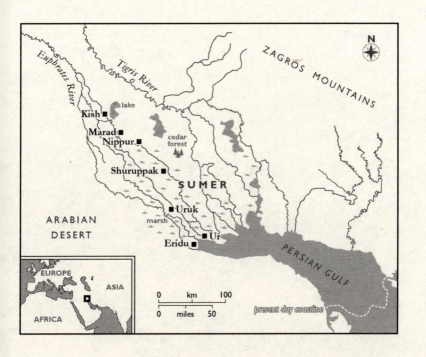

Ancient Sumer in 3999 BC

DRAMATIS PERSONAE

The Anzu, High Gods of Heaven
Tiamat | queen of Creation
Apsu | first lord of Creation
Ninlil | princess of Creation, daughter of Apsu and Tiamat
Nergal | son of Ninlil and Enlil
Qingu | the Bull from Heaven

The Anunnaki, High Gods of Sumer
Inanna | goddess of love and war
An | king of the gods
Nammu | queen of the gods
Enki | lord of wisdom and water, son of An
Enlil | lord of the sky, son of An
Ninhursag | former wife of Enki
Nanna | god of the moon, father of Inanna
Ningal | goddess of the moon, mother of Inanna
Ereshkigal | queen of the night, Inanna's sister
Utu | god of the sun, Inanna's brother
Lugalbanda | Gilgamesh's father, *sukkal* to An
Ninsun | Gilgamesh's mother

The Half Gods
(immortal children of the Anunnaki and humans)

Dumuzi | god of sheep, son of Enki
Geshtinanna | daughter of Enki
Isimud | Enki's *sukkal*
Osiris | lord of Abydos, son of Enki
Isis | lady of Abydos, daughter of Enki
Damkina | wife of Enki

The Humans

Gilgamesh | mortal son of Lugalbanda and Ninsun
Harga | former stone man
Enkidu | the wild man
Amnut | Inanna's childhood friend
Della | mortal daughter of Enlil, wife of Gilgamesh
Shara | son of Gilgamesh and Della
Lilith | high priestess of Uruk, lover of Ninsun
Akka | King of Kish
Inush | Akka's nephew
Shamhat | priestess in Shuruppak
Biluda | royal steward at Kish
Dulma | priestess at the Temple of the Waves
Adamen | leader of the marshmen
Tilmun | son of Adamen
Sagar | the old marshwoman
Userkaf | Egyptian boat captain
Tallboy | one of Harga's crew
Shortboy | one of Harga's crew

Demons and Other Creatures

Ninshubar | a new god, *sukkal* to Inanna
Marduk | formerly known as the Potta, a Sebitti
Bizilla | soldier of Creation, first amongst the Sebitti
Enmesarra | leader of the lost Sebitti
Galatur | the black fly
Kurgurrah | the blue fly
Namtar | priest-demon of Ereshkigal
The *gallas* | demon warriors of the underworld
Neti | gatekeeper to the underworld

PART 1

"When skies above were not yet named,
Nor Earth below pronounced by name,
Apsu, the first one, their begetter
And maker Tiamat, who bore them all,
Had mixed their waters together...
When yet no gods were manifest,
Nor names pronounced, nor destinies decreed,
Then gods were born within them."

From the Ancient Mesopotamian
creation myth known as "Enuma Elish",
as translated by Stephanie Dalley

CHAPTER 1

HARGA

In the marshes north of Eridu

They say there are days in the deep marshes, in high summer, when the frogs boil alive in the shallowest stretches of water.
I had never believed it.
Until now.

We were making our way, in crushing heat, through a wilderness of reeds and narrow waterways. It had become my duty, in the months since the fall of Sumer, to patrol the marshes that had become our hiding place.

I was in the first canoe with the boys and the dogs. Behind us came our marshmen allies, in their own carved-out canoe. As I turned to look at them, all eight of the marshmen turned their eyes to me, like a pack of panthers hunting as one.

My black robes and turban were soaked through with sweat and the air was so humid that I could get no relief from it. Clouds of insects swarmed at my mouth and cheeks. Every muscle in me strained to flap at them or even to throw myself into the murky water, just for the brief release of it. But there could be no flapping or leaping with the hard eyes of those marshmen on me.

They were all so deadly serious. Everything was deadly serious to a marshman. Even when they drank and danced, or tied up a sandal, you would think their lives depended on it.

I turned back to my study of the reed beds ahead of us. Reeds that might at any moment reveal a hut, a fisherman, or a boatful of enemy soldiers.

My two Uruk boys were stood at the front of our canoe, poling us along with reasonable dexterity. They pushed on their long wooden poles, silently pointed out crocodiles to each other, and flashed each other smiles, quite as if neither was aware of the heat or the insects.

The Uruk boys had come to me in the usual way.

I first saw them begging in the main square at Uruk. Both were missing teeth and fingers, and I could tell that they were starving. They looked like trouble, but then they also had that look to them, that they might flourish if shown kindness.

I added the two of them to my crew and soon enough they had a bit of flesh on them, although nothing would ever make them pretty. The short boy, we named Tallboy, and the tall boy, we named Shortboy. Such were the heights of what passed for humour in the barracks at Uruk.

When the city fell, there was not much time to be worrying over my gang of boys, but I kept those two close to me, them being the newest of my crew and the least likely to survive out on the wind.

As for the boy in the back of our canoe, he did not come to me in the usual way. He was not the usual sort of boy, if indeed he was a boy at all.

I turned to glance at Marduk.

He was a tall young man, extremely unusual to look at, with skin so pale you could see his veins through it and hair the red of a setting sun. He had daubed his ghostly face with marsh mud for the purposes of our expedition, and he now sat with his muddy chin resting on the head of his Akkadian dog of war. Behind him were his pair of high-bred court dogs, with their black coats and razor-sharp ears. They had once belonged to a half-god called Dumuzi.

I had told Marduk not to bring the dogs, but he was an impossible boy to deal with.

Marduk turned his dark blue eyes to mine when he felt me looking at him.

"Harga, I have been dreaming about her again."

I did not need to ask who he meant by "her". "Whisper," I said.

"It is the same dream over and over," he said, more quietly. "Always with us sitting by a campfire together. So vivid I know it to be a vision, not a dream."

What could I say to him? Ninshubar had been dead six moons, cut down by the war god Nergal on the banks of the Euphrates. She was lost forever. So, I said nothing.

"We will find her, Harga," Marduk said. "I am certain of it. I don't know the how or the why of it, but we will see her again."

At that moment a flamingo lifted off and the two court dogs began barking. The dog of war at once joined in with her short, rasping bark.

My cheeks burned with the humiliation of it; that this appalling breach of discipline should be witnessed by the occupants of the boat behind.

"Control them," I hissed at Marduk.

The dogs quickly stopped with their barking, only to stand

with their front paws on the edge of the canoe as they stretched out their snouts after the now-distant flamingo.

"Marduk, you are going to get us killed," I said. "Keep them quiet or I will put them over into the water."

We travelled on in grim silence. The shame of what had happened slowly seeped into my bones.

At last, Marduk whispered: "I am so sorry, Harga."

I rolled my shoulders but did not answer.

"The dogs are all very sorry too," he said, which was patently untrue.

I took a round pebble from the leather pouch at my waist and began rolling it around between my fingers.

I once had a dog. A good dog, clever and alert, who would not have started barking when I was out on a hunt. How I loved that dog. But that was when I was very young and had not learned the cost of loving something.

Oh, the memory of that good dog, and how he trusted me.

Marduk put a cool hand on my right shoulder. "What is it, Harga?"

I rolled my shoulders and he took his hand off me.

"I thought you said something," Marduk said. "You made a noise."

"Just keep a look out," I said. "And keep those dogs quiet. Perhaps there is some deaf old man here, many leagues distant, who has not yet heard us coming."

"Smoke!" whispered Shortboy, turning back to us. He pointed left. "A hut."

I nodded and tipped my head left, and the two Uruk boys pushed us over and straight into the reeds. I felt the lurch and bite of the canoe sliding onto mud.

The marshmen came swarming up beside us. I made eye contact with the leader of the marshmen and he twitched his eyebrows at me by way of agreement. This was definitely the place, then.

"Knives out, lads," I said to my crew, voice low. I took two more pebbles from the leather pouch at my waist. "Keep your ears open. I want every single one of them dead. Man, woman, goat. Everything here dies today."

Tallboy gave me his gap-toothed grin. "Everyone dead, sir."

The boy Marduk stood up behind me and, with a bronze axe in each hand, leaped out of the canoe with godlike lift and poise. The eyes of every marshman followed him as he soared and landed, knees softly bent, upon the island.

The three dogs leaped out after him onto the muddy bank.

I pulled my sling shot from my belt and made the secret signs on my chest.

"May the gods of Sumer look kindly on us," I said.

CHAPTER 2

NINSHUBAR

Lost

I was standing on a plain of new spring grass with a soft blue sky arching over me.

Low hills rolled away from me like waves upon an ocean. The sun, a pale yellow, stood directly overhead.

For a heartbeat, the rolling green hills flickered. For a heartbeat, there was darkness and I could not breathe.

A heartbeat, and the light was true again. The grass was soft and damp beneath my bare feet. The wind was cool and sweet.

I was wearing a simple red robe fashioned from one long piece of cloth. It fell, glowing and soft, to my knees; the spare cloth was thrown over my left shoulder. It was the same red cloth we had used, in my own country, for celebration feasts and deep-cave ceremony.

I had a beautiful flint axe in my left hand and a fire-hardened spear in my right. I had my bow and quiver over my left shoulder. All these objects were familiar to me. I had made them all myself.

I put the back of my left hand to my throat. My eight-pointed ivory star was missing. And where were my *mees*? My arms had been heavy with the weapons of the gods when… when it happened.

When the thing happened that I could not quite remember.

Again, the dark flicker, the threat of something being very wrong indeed.

The thought wormed its way to the front of my mind: *Am I dead?*

Once allowed in, the thought took hold of me.

I breathed in deep.

I had no idea where I was or what had happened to bring me to this rolling grassland.

I sat down, heavy, on the ground. I laid down my axe and my spear beside me and took off my bow and quiver, laying them over my lap.

Was I dead?

Fragments of memory sparked bright in my mind. Rolling, locked in violent embrace, with the Lord of War and Chaos upon the banks of the Euphrates. I had been trying to kill him. *It was a fight to the death.*

The image of Inanna lying close to me, bloody and battered. Her black eyes on mine.

Half a memory – a sliver only – of terrible pain.

Did the soldier of Creation break my neck?

If I was dead, this rolling grassland, these weapons I could hunt with, made sense to me. When my father and brothers were killed by lions, the shaman talked of them hunting in the afterlife. Perhaps I would meet my father and brothers out here on this undulating plain.

For a few heartbeats, I was overwhelmed with emotion. If I

was dead, I had failed to protect Inanna. I had failed to protect my son, the Potta. I was a fool and I had failed.

I rubbed a tear from my cheek with the back of my right arm.

Harga's face came to me then, his mouth pinched in amusement.

What would he think if he could see me sitting there, weapons down, wallowing in my failure, when I had not even made sure of the area? I laughed out loud at myself.

Yes, I must make sure of the area. There could be enemies in all directions. This might not be death. This might be something else entirely. What might be over the horizon? If I could cry and laugh, what else could I do? I would find out. Inanna might be out there on the rolling plain.

I picked up my weapons and I climbed back onto my feet.

I paced down the rolling grassy hill into the gently curving valley below, and then up the hill on the far side, before scanning the horizon very carefully. All I could see was the steady roll of the hills, going on in every direction without change or feature.

I walked down into the next valley. The memories of what had gone, of who I was, were slipping into order.

I was *sukkal* to a high goddess. I was a child of the red moon. A creature of war. Whatever was out there in this vast grassland I would find it and if necessary, wrestle it to the ground.

Axe in one hand, spear in the other, I kept on walking, my bare feet strong upon the fresh green grass.

I said to myself the running words.

One step and then the next.

CHAPTER 3

GILGAMESH

North of Uruk

Once this had been Sumerian country and I had ridden the land as a prince and a king.

Now it was Akkadian territory and we kept to the forests and the marshes until it was time to put our heads up and strike.

The moon goddess and I, along with our gang of irregular soldiers, were camped out in a stand of date palms somewhere to the north of Uruk.

I had volunteered to go into town for supplies, it being a long time since I had put myself forward for such a chore. I had disguised myself as a trader; one of those men who bring coracles of goods down from the mountains. And so, in a heavy robe and wrapped headdress, I limped my way through the mud-brick town and into the central market.

Yes, there I was, large basket in hand, pointing at fresh-baked bread, soft cheese with flecks of rosemary in it, and some very good-looking peaches. Just by chance, I suppose, the baker, in his leather apron, said to me: "Did you hear they killed Gilgamesh's wife?"

I had to remember to breathe.

"No," I said, keeping my face still and my voice soft. "I had not heard."

I took a deep breath in and a deep breath out.

The baker nodded at me as he passed me my warm loaves. "They threw her off the moon tower at Ur. With her baby boy in her arms." He shook his head. "These people," he said, by which he meant the Akkadians.

I took my loaves and put them in my basket, and nodded and even smiled at the man. "That is certainly how they kill people in Ur," I said. "I have watched people make the fall."

The market and its busy throng seemed to swim around me, the faces blurring into each other.

"Gilgamesh will go mad, when he hears his son is dead," the baker said. "He did not care much for the girl, but a man cares about a son."

"No doubt you are right," I said.

I bought two large jars of the local spirit at the next stall. I drank the first jar sat in the dust in an alley behind the market, my bad leg stretched out in front of me. A lone chicken pecked around me as I drained the jar. It was a long time since I had had a drink.

"That was for my wife Della," I said to the chicken. "This one is for my son, Shara." I raised the second jar to the ragged-looking bird and took my first swig of it.

The bird looked so thin and dirty.

I put a loaf of bread down in the dust for it and watched as it pecked at the crust. It did not make much progress, so I tore apart the loaf and let it peck at the soft stuff inside.

"My family is dead," I said to the bird. "My mother, the goddess Ninsun, was cut down in battle outside Uruk. I did not see her die, but afterwards the men there showed me pieces of her, so I am certain she is dead."

I downed the second half of the second jar. "My uncle Enlil, who I loved more than anyone perhaps, is also dead. He had his head cut from his shoulders." I nodded to the chicken. "Enkidu, who I knew such a short time, died in the loft of a flea-ridden hostel, dead to poison, all my fault. And now my wife and child are also dead. Thrown out to their deaths from the Temple of the Moon. And that is my fault too."

They said my father, Lugalbanda, was still alive inside Sippur, although the city was besieged and no one could be sure of what was happening inside it.

Did Harga count as family?

I wondered if my boy was frightened as he tumbled from the moon tower. I wondered if Della managed to keep hold of him as she fell or whether she let go of him and he died alone.

I pressed the tears from my eyes with the heels of my hands.

I was going to need more alcohol.

Somehow, at some point, I made it back to our camp, although I remember nothing of that part of it.

I woke up in the early dawn, face down on a sweet-scented bedroll. My head was split in half with pain. I was no longer in the main camp; I was down by the water hole beneath the date palms.

It took a while for me to remember about my wife and child, and I lay still while the memory of it sliced through me. Only then did I realise that there was someone lying behind me. I could feel their warmth along my spine.

I did not, at that moment, very much care what I had done the night before or even what might follow after. It was not the first time I had woken up, after too many cups of wine, to find some man or woman lying next to me and with no memory of how they got there.

The secret was to slip away before they awoke. If they found you already gone, the subject might never be spoken of.

I sat up, quietly, my head thumping. Very, very carefully, I stood up, putting all of my weight into my good knee, the other having been ruined during the siege of Uruk and what came after. Even standing up carefully was agony.

I glanced down at my bedroll partner: a young woman with dark curls, face down.

My belly turned over. It was not a woman: it was a goddess. An ancient goddess, although she looked no more than twenty years old. It was Ningal, goddess of the moon, once high goddess of Ur. Oh, and mother of the goddess Inanna, who I had once lain down with in private.

Well, did it matter? The goddess and I were both adults. Inanna was long gone, more than likely lost forever. Perhaps she was high up in Heaven and looking down from there at this squalid little scene.

Probably, it did not matter.

A flash came to me, of Ningal pouring me wine. She was a beautiful woman. Another flash of memory: me, crying in her arms.

I had always thought her beautiful. Looking at it from that angle, perhaps it had always been going to happen.

So yes, probably it did not matter. Yet it was not my first disaster and this smelled, faintly but distinctly, of disaster.

I limped quietly away, in the direction of the camp, careful not to stand on anything that might snap and make a noise.

It did not matter who I had woken up with. She would forget it. I would forget it. We would go back to being comrades in arms again.

After I had forced down my breakfast porridge and a skin of water, I found a scrap of shade and laid myself down again.

I woke with an even worse headache and someone gently squeezing my right arm.

The moon goddess, Ningal, was sitting cross-legged next to me with a cup of water held out to me.

"It's my fault," she said, her voice low and soft. "I knew it would end in trouble, the moment I accepted a drink from you. But I did it anyway."

She looked as if she had slept a full night and woken entirely refreshed. You would never have guessed at anything else from the soft bloom upon her skin.

I sat up, groaning out loud as I moved my left leg, and took the cup of water from the goddess. "I am very happy indeed for it to be your fault," I said. "In general, I find people prefer to blame me for everything."

I could not quite look her in the eye.

"I have felt your eyes lingering on me, time and time again," she said gently. "Presumably it was your intention to lie with me. And yet now you cannot even look at me. I forget how very young you are."

"I'm not sure that intention is the right word," I said, sipping at my water. "Certainly, I have noticed how handsome you are. Who could not?"

She sighed out. "Well, I am not often a drunken fool. Or have not been for many hundreds of years. I suppose I must count this as adventure."

We sat in silence for some moments.

"There's a supply run going up to the Kur," I said. "I'm going to join them. They need extra muscle." I smiled at her. "I can still throw an axe."

She sat up straight. "Are you going because of last night?"

"I'm going because I'm too slow to be out here. I'm too slow in a fight. Maybe I can be of more help up at the Kur." After a short pause, I said: "Of course, you are very welcome to join me."

The last part was untrue. Added to that, I knew very well that she would never willingly spend time with her father, Enki, who was currently camped up at the Kur.

Ningal put on her temple face: austere, without emotion.

"I will rejoin Isimud," she said, "and do what can be done down here by the river."

She stood without saying anything more.

I felt sorry for the whole thing as she walked off, but no doubt I would forget soon enough. The shame would die just as it always did.

It was then I remembered again about my wife and son. An icy rush of sadness passed through me and I sat there, only breathing, until it died down.

I would have liked to have known my son.

How I hoped that he had died painlessly.

CHAPTER 4

NINSHUBAR

Lost

I walked across the rolling grassland, and I made my calculations.

The sun was directly above me and there it stayed as I climbed up countless, gentle hills and down into countless, gentle valleys.

The sweet wind kept on blowing, never changing.

The grass was soft and lush beneath my feet. Not a thorn in it. Not one bare patch of earth, or flower, or sapling.

I walked for what must have been hours, yet I felt no tiredness, no hunger, no thirst. Only a sprightly vitality; a pleasure in my movement.

Would this day ever end? Would the sun ever set? I stopped walking on the brow of a hill exactly like all the others. What if there were no edges to this world?

More and more, it seemed unlikely that I was alive, yet here I was, in a strange world with different rules.

I stood and shut my eyes a moment. Where did my instinct

lead me? I realised I did have a preference as to my direction. I did not know why, but the path I was on felt right to me.

I broke out into a run, fast at first then slow and steady: the hunter's run. I found I could keep running without effort. I ran as strong and clean as I had as a young girl on the savannah of my childhood.

For hour upon hour, I kept on running, never tiring, never sweating, never needing water or food.

I emptied my mind of everything except the running.

Thoughts bubbled up. Would I simply run on forever, on a hunt that would never end? Would I ever see my son again? Would I ever find Inanna? Would I ever go hunting with Harga again and watch him skin a rabbit?

I examined the thoughts and let them go, and I kept on running.

I said to myself, over and over, the running words.

One step and then the next.

Something changed.

I dropped down into a valley like all the other valleys, but when I looked upwards, I found myself at the bottom of a hill far larger than all the other hills I had climbed. How had the hill grown larger?

I climbed it, of course, but at the top of the rise, I froze.

Below me, close enough to shout down to, two figures stood together on a grassy plain: one very small, and one very large.

The small figure was Inanna. She stood with her chin lifted high… looking up at a huge, black dragon.

I had seen images of dragons scratched on cave walls. I had thought them a fantasy, but this creature was real. A giant, many-headed lizard, with heavy wings furled upon its back and a powerful, swinging tail. I counted its heads: it had seven.

The black dragon towered over Inanna, six times her height at the shoulder.

Tiamat.

It was Tiamat. I knew it in my gut.

As I watched, the creature dipped its fanged jaws down towards Inanna and Inanna stretched up her right hand as if trying to touch one of the creature's black-scaled heads. Why was she not afraid?

"Inanna!" I shouted.

I think she heard me and was turning to me.

I ran down the hill at a sprint. For a handful of heartbeats, I lost sight of them in a curve of the land that had not been there before. When I saw them again, Inanna was stepping forward towards the night-black monster.

And then they were gone.

When I reached the spot where they had been standing, I could smell sulphur in the air and, for some heartbeats, the noxious stink lingered. Then it was gone and there was nothing to suggest that Inanna and the dragon had ever been there.

I bent over to touch the grass. It was soft and lush. There were no marks on it.

Everything flickered around me: for a heartbeat, everything went dark.

I had to keep hold of what I knew to be true. I was dead. That was probable. Yet I felt very alive in that vivid world.

Only heartbeats before, Inanna had been there.

"I will find you, Inanna," I said out loud, to the grass, to the unchanging sun, to the soft wind. "This is the sacred promise of a goddess. I will find you and I will help you get back home."

CHAPTER 5

INANNA

In Heaven

I sat with my friend Amnut in the ochre room at my mother's temple in Ur. We were playing the game of twenty squares, with the ancient board set out between us on a small ebony table.

"Inanna, tell me again about your mother stealing the *melam*," Amnut said.

I looked up at her in surprise. "Did I tell you about that?"

Amnut was dressed in her crimson dress and matching cape, and she was looking at me very seriously, a frown upon her lovely brow. "You said that your mother could not bring a baby to term until she had eaten all the *melam* she could find. That she devoured all the *melam* your father had and all the *melam* that your grandfather Enki had too. And only then did you begin to grow strong inside her."

Her eyes were such a brilliant blue.

"My father could not forgive her for taking the *melam*," I said. "Even though I was the result of it. That seemed to bring him no comfort."

Were Amnut's eyes always blue?

"Amnut, something is wrong," I said.

The room was moving around me.

My chair collapsed beneath me and I cried out in pain and shock as I tumbled to the floor.

"Amnut, help me," I said.

But I was falling into the dark.

I stood with my hands upon a stone wall, my fingers pale against the blocks of dark rock. There were black marks on my forearms, about the size and shape of fingerprints, and I was cold and all of me ached, even my fingers, even my skull, even the skin on my forehead and my eyelids when I blinked.

I had to be dreaming. Why else was I standing with my hands on a stone wall?

A memory came to me, very clear, of a tall, dark-skinned woman with an axe in one hand and a spear in the other. She had been shouting out to me and I knew that whatever she was shouting was important. But I could no longer remember what she had said.

I realised that I had no idea who I was or what was happening, and panic rose up in me. My heart hammered hard against my ribs. There was something around my neck: a thick loop of metal, too tight for comfort. I pulled at it, but it would not come off.

I realised there was someone behind me. In terror, I slowly turned around.

And saw the tall, golden figure by the door.

She was so familiar to me. Her short hair was flame red, her skin strangely pale. She turned her dark blue eyes to me.

Bizilla.

It was Bizilla. I could breathe again. My heart began to slow. She did not mean me harm.

"Bizilla, what is happening?" I said.

We were in a small, windowless room with stone-block walls and a heavy wooden door.

Bizilla was stood with her back to that door as if at sentry. She was dressed in a coat of golden scales, with a blocky, gold belt around her waist.

When she did not answer me, I said her name again. "Bizilla?"

"Get back into bed," she said.

I had not noticed the bed, but there it was along one wall. A wooden bed with a thin mattress and a grey blanket upon it. Next to the bed, on a small wooden table, stood the large, flickering candle that was our only source of light.

"Why am I in this room?" I said.

"You always ask that," Bizilla said.

"How do I know you?" In that moment, I could not be sure I really knew her at all.

"You always ask that. And I always tell you: I am Bizilla."

"You are very familiar to me," I said.

I walked over to the bed, careful of my aching feet upon the stone floor.

"Where is this?" I said, putting my hands down to the mattress.

"Nowhere good," said Bizilla.

I sat down upon the bed too quickly and pain shot up my spine. "How long have I been here?"

She closed her blue eyes, just for a moment. "Long enough for you to stand over by that wall and put your hands on it perhaps two hundred times."

I was naked. How had I not noticed? My whole body was

covered with the bruises that looked just like fingerprints. I pulled again at the metal band around my neck.

"Bizilla, what has happened to me? I think I am hurt."

"It's not time yet for your medicine," she said. But then she looked over at me again. "I don't really see what difference it will make," she said, coming to sit beside me. She drew a small glass bottle from her sleeve, poured some clear white liquid into the lid of the bottle, and passed it to me to drink. It tasted of vanilla.

"Bizilla, I have seen someone just like you before," I said. "I am certain of it. A boy. A young man."

"You've seen me every day here," she said. "You have seen some of my comrades too, although you may not remember it."

"Is one of them young? Does he have a dog?"

"We don't have dogs here," she said. "Except in stories." She frowned. "The medicine has confused you."

"Bizilla, I think something bad is happening. I think I am in the wrong place."

"No doubt that is true," she said. "Now go back to sleep."

Again, the darkness came for me.

CHAPTER 6

HARGA

In the marshes north of Eridu

I climbed, stiff-legged, onto the wooden jetty at the Refuge. As I reached down for a rope, I realised I had torn the muscle in my right shoulder again. Perhaps in that day's fighting, perhaps before that without noticing. It was an old injury, from when I carried Gilgamesh out of Ur, and it didn't need much to make it flare up again.

I thought to myself, *I am too old for this*. The same thing I always thought, these days, when I got out of a canoe.

I was old and I was dirty, befouled with marsh mud and other people's blood. The boys were no cleaner and the three dogs were worse.

Tallboy took the rope from me when he saw me grimacing and the three boys made sure of the boat, tying it up close to the jetty. "We'll get you a bucket of water, sir," said Tallboy.

"Bring it to my hut," I said.

As the two Uruk boys trailed off along the shoreline, giggling over something, the priestess Lilith appeared. She put her hands on her hips and placed herself as a firm block on the path that led to the heart of the Refuge. Her long soft waves of hair were gone, shorn off after the death of her lover, the goddess Ninsun, but she was still a beautiful and imperious woman even in a ragged apron and wooden clogs.

"Did you find the alleged spies?" she said.

"Who knows what we found." I shrugged and winced again at the pain in my right shoulder. "But anyway they are all dead."

I made to walk past the priestess, but she put a flat palm up to me.

"You should swim and get clean," she said, lifting her chin at both me and the god-boy Marduk, who was by then stood behind me, fussing over his dogs. "You will attract rats. You will terrify the children. Swim first."

"The boys are fetching me water," I said. I was bone tired by then from the day's heat and the savagery and I could not summon a smile for her.

"I don't know why you don't just swim," she said.

A mosquito landed on my cheek and I slapped one exhausted hand at it. "There are swamp sharks here and they are hard to see coming, being all covered in green slime. And then also there are the crocodiles."

As I said the words, Marduk began stripping. A moment later he dived naked off the end of the jetty, a pale streak against the red sky and the green of the reed beds. The dogs leaped after him, paws outstretched, into the brown marsh water.

"Marduk, there are more sharks at dusk," I shouted. "Think of the dogs!" I turned back to the priestess, frowning. "It is not safe, Lilith."

"Is that a cut?" she said, reaching for my blood-encrusted left arm.

"It's a graze."

"Harga, let me see it."

"No."

For some moments we glowered at each other, and then the priestess said: "Did the marshmen fight well?"

"Oh yes, most viciously. They are the very pattern of good allies." I cast a glance out at the pale god-boy, who was laughing and splashing with the dogs in the slimy and fetid marsh water.

"We are not taking the dogs again," I said.

"You should not have agreed to it."

"You took Marduk's side! Anyway, he did most of the killing, impossible as he is. He moves so quickly now it can be hard to keep your eye on him."

"Do be careful of him, Harga," she said. "He is not like your other lost ducklings."

"I do not have ducklings," I said, pulling myself more upright. "They are soldiers, not ducklings."

At that moment my two young soldier-ducklings returned with heaving wooden buckets and armfuls of cleaning rags. They had washed their faces and looked very young as they made their way towards us through the gloom. But that was neither here nor there.

The boys dipped heads and knees to the priestess and set the buckets down before me. When the priestess seemed not to be moving anywhere, I went to pull down my long under-trousers.

"All right, I will leave you to it," she said. "I will have some lamps sent down for you all."

"I'll see you in the Palace after," I said.

The priestess threw me back a smile. "Your curls are growing back, Harga," she said. "But there is silver in them now."

I ran my hand over my head. "I will shave it again tomorrow."

It had not yet been a year, after all, since Enlil and the others had been killed.

A long time before, in a war that only the gods remembered, Enki, the lord of wisdom, had created a secret hiding place in the deep marshes north of Eridu, his home city. He fashioned his hiding place on an island you could walk around in one hour, but it was solid mud at least in a land of floating islands and constant flooding.

For centuries after, Enki kept the island stocked and garrisoned, in case one day the land, and his city, were invaded.

We called the island the Refuge and it was a clever place to hide. First off, why would an Anunnaki, a lord of the Earth, choose to build a village in the most awful place imaginable? You could not look at the water without getting gut cramp. The frogs made so much noise you could not sleep. The island, such as it was, was home to rats as big as dogs and deadly snakes and everything was thick with fleas.

Then there were the marshmen, who would kill you if they didn't know you, but if they did know you then they would certainly kill you. Perhaps because of something your grandmother once said to their grandfather. Not to forget the marshwomen, who were twice as dangerous as the men.

Lilith, once high priestess of Uruk, once lover of Gilgamesh's mother, was now self-appointed queen of the Refuge. At one point we had had Enki's wives, past and present, on the island, but neither of them found the fleas to their taste, and they had ceded the ground to Lilith.

At the very centre point of the Refuge there stood a long reed hut that served as our main gathering place and that had come to be known as the Palace. It was built of reeds rolled together into logs and then fashioned very ornately into a high-ceilinged building.

"You do not believe the stories about spies in the marshes?" Lilith said to me as we ate our bowls of crocodile stew in the Palace that night.

"I don't think Adamen knows how to tell the truth," I said. Adamen, the leader of the marshmen, was someone I had disliked on sight.

"Adamen's brother was a good man, his father too."

"Yet somehow they are dead and he is who we have to deal with."

We were sitting together, cross-legged, on the rug at the centre of the Palace. The heat and the smoke and the fleas were just as thick upon the rug as in any other part of the Palace, but the rug had once been in Enki's palace at Eridu, and so by common consent was left for Lilith and her most senior counsellors.

On that muggy evening, with most of our ruling council away from the Refuge, the rug was ours alone.

All around the edge of the Palace sat a crowd of priestesses, orphaned children, and courtiers who had escaped the Akkadian slaughter.

"Adamen wants us to believe that there are spies creeping into the marshes," I said to Lilith, chewing determinedly at my crocodile. "That's about all I can be certain of."

Lilith put her bowl down. "These marshmen are warlike and murderous, it is true, but who in Sumer has been more loyal to the Anunnaki and their servants? I do not think there are any tricks here."

"This crocodile is inedible," I said.

"It's snake," she said. "Giant water snake. It's all the boys could catch today."

"Oh," I said, peering closer at it. "I did not think they could be eaten."

Lilith began to thread an ivory needle, holding it up to the dim light of the fire as she did so, her tongue between her teeth.

"How can you see to do your darning in here?" I said.

"I'm no god, but I have good eyes even in dim light. And anyway, I'm not going to darn, I'm going to sew up your arm, so pass it over."

"No."

"Quickly, Harga."

"I do not see why you are in charge of me," I said. But I moved over, sullen but obedient, and rested my arm on one of her knees.

I looked down at her neat stitches as she sewed and tried hard not to wince or flinch.

"I'll help your girls with the new garden tomorrow," I said.

Marduk arrived, stooping to pass beneath the reed lintel. His red hair was still wet from his swim but he had put on a clean smock. A moment later all three of his dogs were leaping on me. The dog of war put her snout into my bowl, rendering it instantly empty.

Marduk tipped his head to me in greeting. "I'm going out looking for Ninshubar tomorrow. I would like it if you came."

"I've got business here. I've said I'll help with the garden."

"Please come, Harga," he said.

"Oh, Harga," said Lilith. "We can do the garden without you."

Marduk cast his very beautiful smile down at her and then turned back, shining, to me. "I will do all the paddling," he said. "You can sit at the back of the canoe like a king."

I gave out a sigh. "The dogs must stay here." But I said it with no fight in me.

"We will find her," the god-boy said as he dropped down to sit beside me.

What was the point in arguing with him?

Much later, before turning in, I went to say goodnight to Lilith.

She was sitting out in front of her small sleeping hut, looking up at the full moon.

"Sit down then," she said, when she saw it was me. "I have some secret wine that I bought off a marshwoman, if you'd like to share it with me."

"I would like to wash the giant snake out of my mouth." I settled myself cross-legged beside her. "I have eaten all kinds of snake, but never one so unpleasant."

"I think this will certainly clean your mouth out," she said, sniffing the wine before she poured.

We touched our cups together and drank.

It tasted like concentrated urine, or perhaps fruit that had been left on the ground to rot.

"Can that really be wine?" I said.

"The heat must have turned it."

"Such heat," I said, shaking my head.

When we had both drained our cups and she was refilling them, I said to her: "So how are you?"

"I am no better." She tipped her face back up to the bright night sky. "I go on because the children here deserve to be looked after. And because I think, what if Gilgamesh comes back and has need of me? He no longer has a mother except me. So I go on. But it is an effort, even sitting out here with you, who I count now as an old friend."

"I'm old, certainly. I feel it more each time I meet the enemy."

"How old are you exactly, Harga?"

"We don't celebrate birthdays in the stone country. But I think thirty-six perhaps, or thirty-seven."

She laughed. "Old then. But not as old as me." She gave me an appraising look. "Do you grieve for her, Harga?"

I sat up straighter. "For Ninshubar?"

"Yes."

I gave a shrug.

"But you had feelings for her?"

"I learnt better than that a long time ago."

"I thought you had hopes of her. That's what people say."

"No," I said, more firmly than I meant to. "They are wrong to speak so. I did not have hopes of her. And I do not have hope now of us finding her, as that foolish boy does. Hope is what kills you. Hope is what rots you out from the inside."

She looked at me sternly, her face silver in the moonlight. "Maybe it's better to fight hope than to have none at all."

I leaned over and kissed her stubbly head. "I'm very sorry for your loss, Lilith," I said. "Ninsun was a fine soldier."

"She was also a fine lover, in the time that she loved me."

"She will always be remembered," I said. "If that is of comfort. They will still build temples for her."

"Perhaps," said Lilith. "Perhaps when the Akkadians are gone."

I took a deep breath in. "I lost a lover, a long time ago." It was strange to even say it out loud. "It occurred to me today that with the god Enlil dead, perhaps I am the only one alive in the world who remembers her."

"Who was she?"

"My wife," I said. "And I lost my son too, the same night. And a dog, although it feels foolish to mention him. In my early days with Enlil, when I was not much more than a boy, he let me have a family."

"How did you lose them?"

"In the great flood. Our house was washed away in the night and for a while we were all together. But in the morning I was alive, caught up in a tree, and they were all gone. Somehow I lost hold of them in the darkness."

"I'm very sorry for your loss, Harga. I did not know."

"It was a long time ago."

"I'm sorry all the same."

"After they died, I realised I did not have the strength to lose anyone like that again. I thought, it is not enough to say I am from the stone country. I must be a real stone man. With a heart only of stone. I must be stone all the way through. And that is how I live now."

"That is how you think you live your life now?"

I nodded. "Stone all the way through."

She poured us more of the terrible wine, one eyebrow raised.

"I do miss Enlil, though," I went on. "And I miss Ninshubar, too."

Then we sat there in the muggy dark, we two old humans, and listened to the infernal frog noise, and looked up at the moon, and thought about those forever lost to us. I wondered if they were somewhere out there in the infinite dark, or instead just entirely extinguished.

CHAPTER 7

NINLIL

In Heaven

My white-robed body servants knocked at the door to my bedchamber and came in without waiting for an answer, as they were used to doing. They brought with them the freezing air of the palace corridors.

In the days before I was snatched away from Creation, my bedchamber seemed enormous and thrillingly luxurious. Most importantly, it had been mine. I was allowed to choose the pink velvet curtains and the thick white rug that lay in front of the fireplace. Bizilla, my holy *sukkal*, helped me hang my attempts at artwork upon the pale pink walls. On warm days the curtains would be pulled back and the huge window opened, and I would look out on fountains and, beyond, an avenue of flowering bushes, and I would breathe in the sweet scents of the gardens. Once, with Bizilla's blessing, I climbed out of the window, jumping down onto the stone terrace.

Now the curtains were brown with age, the rug was thin and worn, and the pictures I had painted were so faded I could no longer make them out. The window behind the ancient curtains had long been boarded over and the room did not seem spacious with all my servants crammed into it.

I stood passive, my arms raised, as they sewed me into my white dress and knotted diamonds into my hair. They were focused entirely on the cloth, on the fit, on the sparkle.

None of them said to me: "Why did you come back?" They must all have been thinking it, though. After all, who would willingly return to this palace of darkness and pain?

In fact, my son and I were chased through the gate to Heaven by the goddess Inanna. But before that... the truth is that I had chosen to climb the staircase to Heaven. I had thought I was doing the right thing. Facing old demons, facing up to my responsibilities.

More and more, that seemed like a terrible mistake.

At last, the dressers draped a heavy white fur cloak over my shoulders and clasped it at my neck. They sank into deep curtseys and were gone.

I was alone, in the bedchamber of my early childhood, for perhaps a minute. For that minute, I stood completely still, my eyes on the coal that burned in the grate.

Another knock and two white-clad footmen entered the room, bringing another blast of iced air with them. Their job was to deliver me to the banqueting room at exactly the right time and with the right amount of pomp, and this they would do elegantly but without fail.

When I first returned to Heaven, I fought against the nightly dining ceremony. I told everyone who would listen that unless they brought me my son, Nergal, I would not go along with any of it. I sat myself down with my arms folded tight across my chest when the body servants came. Soldiers came then to strip me, dress me, and carry me to table. They were happy to tie me to my dining chair. I learned that there was no point in fighting, because in the palace of Creation dinner would go on, just as it always had, and I would be there at it regardless of how much fuss I made.

"Are you ready, my lady?" one of the footmen said, when they were all in the correct position in the corridor.

"Quite ready," I said.

I moved out into the corridor and then we began our sombre, very formal procession to dinner. I walked with thirty footmen in front of me, all in white and with white ribbons in their hair, and with another thirty footmen behind me, all equally splendid.

The corridors we slowly paced along were dark, dirty and decaying. The windows had been blocked up to keep out the snow and the jagged storms, yet the cold quickly sank into my bones.

To reach the banqueting hall we had to pass along the vast, central hall at the heart of the palace. The alcoves were full of refugees, camping out on the cold flagstones, and they turned desperate faces to me as I walked by.

There were Sebitti everywhere, gold in the gloom.

I glanced up and noticed that one high-up window had not yet been boarded over. Through that one small rectangle of transparent mica, perfectly framed, I glimpsed the Star of Creation. A dim, pale, fading sun. I paused a moment, absorbing the shock of how familiar it was to me and yet how strange, after four hundred years spent in the glare of Earthlight.

"My lady?" said the footman behind me. Obedient, I walked on. Far above my head, barely visible in the low light, huge dragons decorated the vaulted ceilings. Great monsters, breathing out fire, with streams of smaller creatures spilling out behind them.

We reached the towering basilisk entrance to the banqueting

room. I paused a moment as Sebitti pulled the enormous doors open, and then continued my stately progress.

The central table was carved from black stone and lit by scores of candles. Each of the four walls of the hall had its own fireplace, heaped with burning coal, yet it was even colder in that dining room than in the cavernous hallway outside.

My father was already there at the head of the obsidian table. The great Apsu, lord of Creation, lord of Heaven, had all-but-died before I was born. It was said that he could no longer bear to be alive in a realm with my mother in it.

The years of barely being alive had left him mummified, his flesh welded to the rusting chair he sat in. Over the years he had been rather knocked about, despite everyone's best efforts. He had lost two fingers and much of his hair, and now he sat with his balding skull drooping almost to his lap. If he was conscious, it was many turns of the Wheel of Heaven since he had given any sign of it, but all the realms forbid that the first lord of Creation should miss a family meal.

I wondered what would happen if I put my healing hands upon him. But then I knew that he had chosen his fate, a very long time ago.

I sat down upon my black stone chair, some distance to my father's left, and my servants arranged my clothes just so, tucking my cloak around me. Then my footmen retreated to the wall behind me, the lucky amongst them with their backs to the fireplace.

My brother Qingu was next to arrive with his fleet of red-clad footmen behind him. He was a big man, dressed in a white fur cloak much like mine, and while I had been away in the realm of light he had grown the curving, black horns of a bull. The tips almost met about an arm's reach above his head.

I wondered how heavy his skull must feel, but he seemed to move it very naturally, as if the horns made no difference to him.

"Sister," Qingu said, as he sat down opposite me, his black bull horns glistening in the firelight. He picked up the golden goblet in front of him and raised his voice for the servants. "Do I have to beg for wine?" He waved his cup in the air. "Is it too much to ask that my wine be ready for me?"

Behind him, there was a kerfuffle amongst the red-clad footmen; a moment later one of them came forward with a golden jug of wine. He filled the golden goblet and Qingu immediately drained it. "You can leave the jug there," my brother said, and poured himself more. He drank it straight down again and only when he had his third goblet in hand did he look back over at me.

"Has she told you what she's doing?" he said.

One of my white-clad footmen was at my shoulder, offering me wine. I shook my head at him before answering my brother. "Who?"

Qingu grinned, exposing his sharpened teeth. "Don't be so dull, little sister. What is our mother up to? You know perfectly well what I mean."

"I have no idea," I said. "If she let me touch her, perhaps I would. But she won't."

"She ought to be giving birth to Sebitti," he said. He tipped his thick horns at me. "But instead of giving birth to soldiers she is gestating something else." He raised both eyebrows at me. "You must have noticed."

"I want to see my son," I said. I kept my voice calm and low.

"Ugh!" he said. "Enough with that. You'll upset Father."

We both turned to look at the dried-out body of the lord god Apsu.

I would have said something, but the great doors to the dining chamber were slowly creaking open.

A fog of sulphurous gas swept over us and before we could see her we could hear her: the groans and deep grumblings of the dragon queen.

Qingu put down his goblet and composed himself, his face growing stiff and distant. I shifted in my seat and sat up straighter. It was important not to anger her. Things were bad enough when she was calm and there was no need, I had learned the hard way, to make things worse.

When the doors at last stood fully open, the Sebitti, my mother's private army, began to enter. They were tall, pale-skinned, red-haired, and blue-eyed, and all dressed in the gold-scaled coats that their lineage gave them the right to. As they entered the room their gold scales, moving in unison, gave out a shimmering metallic rustle.

Behind the Sebitti, came the dragon.

She was huge, yet agile, her heavy black scales sliding over each other. Each of her seven sharp-fanged heads was set with a pair of brilliant blue eyes. Her chest was wide and powerful, her tail long and heavy, and her oily, feathered wings lay furled upon her scaly back. My mother was perhaps the weight of forty men, and the height of four large men stood on each other's shoulders, but I knew she had the strength of a whole legion of Sebitti.

With the low, grumbling noise that she always made while settling, she squatted down into her place at the top of the table, directly opposite her husband, my father, who I had only ever known as a husk.

The Sebitti arranged themselves behind the dragon, their hands on their golden weapons belts, their dark blue eyes turned to the floor. Seventy of them stood guard over her at dinner. Ten groups of seven, because seven was the holy number.

"Hello, Mother," said Qingu. He tipped his horns to the dragon.

"Hello, Mother," I said, my voice small in that huge space.

In the wall behind my brother, a small door opened and I caught the flicker of something pale approaching. It resolved into a long line of attendants carrying gold tureens.

The food was served out to us in golden bowls of various sizes. A trough for my mother, a generous dish for Qingu, a small dish for me that was no larger than one of my hands. No dish for my father.

Qingu was allowed to point at what he wanted, before being served. I had to accept what I was given, and that night I was served a quivering lump of pink flesh, too large for my small plate. Blood at once began to seep out onto the gold and the black stone of the table. There was skin on one side of the meat. Smooth, tanned, skin.

Hungry as I was, the nausea rose up in me.

Perhaps it was only pig.

"I wonder who it is," Qingu said, grinning at me. "See if you can guess."

My mother was looking intently at me: all seven heads trained on me, all seven sets of jaws gaping.

"Thank you, Mother," I said in a whisper.

I tried to cut into the meat with my knife and fork, but it was too rare for utensils.

I picked the meat up in my hands, hot and slippery though it was, and took a bite. As I swallowed the meat, I tasted the terror in it. The anguish.

The awful memory came back to me, of eating my own husband's head. I had done it to honour him, after Nergal killed him. But I had tasted pain and shock then too.

"It's quite the rush, isn't it," said Qingu, "when the meat is really fresh."

I ate. I kept on eating.

I had worked out that my choice was stark. I must kill myself, thereby abandoning my son forever, again, or I must eat my food every night and stay strong for my son. Keep the healing sea inside me alive. Be ready for whatever lay before me.

I chewed the meat down, blood streaming down my chin and onto my beautiful white furs.

It was probably a pig. A terrified young pig.

My mother had always liked to watch me eat. She had always said I needed to put meat onto my bones. Now her seven heads swayed back and forth as I chewed and swallowed, and sometimes retched, and then swallowed again. My mother the dragon made the strange groaning noise that she only made when she was happy.

Qingu grinned at me as I ate. "Nothing is too good for the heir of Creation," he said. "Nothing is too much for the woman who will one day rule over us. This is why you came back, isn't it, for all of this?"

"I did not come back to usurp you," I said to him, putting the meat down. I turned to my mother. "I did not come back to claim anything."

"Yet it is all about the female line," said my brother. "And so, you are elevated, having done nothing to deserve it." He glanced at our mother. "Of course, I am happiness itself to see you returned."

One of the dragon's seven heads swayed closer to me, pushing my hand back towards my plate.

"Eat up, eat up!" said Qingu. "Before the blood stops pumping."

CHAPTER 8

GILGAMESH

At the site of the Kur

In ordinary times it would have been a journey of only a few days up into the Zagros mountains, but with Akkadians running amok in the land, we were obliged to take our train of pack mules by the hard and boggy back ways, fording the Tigris in the midst of wild forest. It was a long two weeks, therefore, before the men and I emerged onto the high plateau.

Once, there had been a neat stone hut on that stretch of flat land, and behind that hut, the path up the side of the crater in which the Kur sat. The Kur, the underworld, Ganzir... the Anunnaki had many names for it. In temple, when I was growing up, they taught us that the spirits of the dead went to the Kur, but that was something I could no longer believe in.

Now the plateau was an ocean of fallen rock with no hut and no crater wall in sight, but in the distance I caught the red-blood flash of Enki's tents.

I drew up my mule and signalled to the others to halt, before carefully dismounting, putting my weight on my good leg first.

We would have to pick our way over the rubble on foot, leading the mules behind us.

I had been to the site of the Kur twice before. The first time, what felt like aeons before, I went there to help resurrect the goddess Inanna.

The second time was not long after the fall of Sumer. I went up with Enki to try to work out what had happened there. We found no sign of Neti's hut or the crater or the Kur itself, only this wilderness of fallen rock. Since then, I had been all over Sumer, doing what I could against the Akkadians, but Enki had stayed up on the mountain.

Now, as we made our way across the rubble, we passed Enki's teams of diggers, their pickaxes swinging. The lord of wisdom emerged from beneath a leather sunshade to stand hands on hips as we drew close. Inanna's lionesses were lain down in the shade, but they lifted their yellow eyes to me in greeting. We had found them roaming the mountain when we first visited after the fall of Sumer; it seemed Inanna had chosen not to take them with her into the Kur.

"I did not expect you," Enki said, the sun catching the gleam of bronze in his shorn hair.

"Yet here I am," I said.

Enki and I sat together beneath his sunshade and drank mountain tea together. The god seemed older and more tired.

"There is some bread in that basket next to you and fresh cheese. Also, some figs, if you don't mind getting sticky."

I helped myself to a fig. "Delicious," I said. "I do not fear getting sticky."

"Pass one will you?" said Enki.

He was a strange creature, the lord of wisdom. He had fastidious manners and always made me feel welcome at his table or in his tent. Yet I could not say I really knew him, even after many weeks spent together. In times of war you get to know a man, or woman, for that matter. I thought briefly of the moon goddess and my cheeks burned.

Yes, you get to know a person, through and through, yet Enki's deeper nature eluded me. His leopard eyes passed over me as I ate my fig and I could not tell what he was thinking or what his deepest motives were. I had never known a person so hard to read and also so hard to conquer even when I set out to charm him. Sometimes I saw flashes of something so ancient and rotten in him that I would briefly recoil. And then there would be the vibrant enthusiasm that I found hard to resist.

"I'm close to giving up," he said. "We have dug down in fifty different places and still found no sign whatsoever of the Kur."

"Do you think it's not here?" I said. "Could it have flown away?"

"No, no," he said. "I have spoken to witnesses out of Susa now and the residents of a mountain village an hour's walk from here. Some things I can be certain of. The mountain opened and swallowed up the Kur."

I stretched out my bad knee. "What else can you be sure of?"

"That my son Dumuzi and my daughter Geshtinanna went into the Kur and did not come out. That my granddaughter Ereshkigal, and Nergal, a soldier of Creation, also passed into the Kur and have not been seen since. The same for Ninlil, my dead brother's wife, and Utu, my grandson. And of course Inanna, with her blue lightning. All went in and none came out before the Kur was eaten by the mountain."

"What about Tiamat, this dragon queen you have been fretting over? Is she no longer a threat?"

"I can only be sure that Tiamat sent Nergal here to murder my brother, to fetch back Ninlil, and to find the master *mee*. It is natural that she wanted her daughter back and that she wanted my brother punished for taking the girl. But the fact she also sent her soldier to fetch the *mee* means that Tiamat may have greater plans for this realm. The *mee* is both a key and a navigation device. If her plan is to come here, everything we have here is at risk."

"And so, you keep digging," I said.

"And so, I keep digging. I must find out if Tiamat intends to come here."

"And also, you want to rescue your missing relatives," I said, smiling at him.

"Oh, that," he said, with a wave of one hand.

I took my turn at one of the dig sites. The sun seared my bare back as I swung my flint pickaxe into the mess of rock and earth. The hope, of course, was that somewhere just beneath us we might find the red rock outline of the Kur. But all we were finding was rubble.

When the pain in my left knee was so severe that I thought I might collapse upon it and embarrass everyone present, I made my way across the ruined mountainside, one careful step at a time, to rejoin Enki beneath his sunshade.

"Anyone can see that the digging is agony for you," Enki said. "Why make such a martyr of yourself?"

"I thought it might help morale."

"Not my morale." He poured me a cup of wine.

"It's hard going," I said to him. "We think we are making progress but then the pit collapses and the ground shifts beneath us."

NINSHUBAR

Enki emptied his own wine cup. "What are you really doing here, Gilgamesh?"

I could not say, *Oh, I lay with your daughter the moon goddess and now I am hiding from her.* So I said: "I feel bad about Inanna." It was true, or partly true, but it did not sound very true to me as I said it. "I said I would protect her, yet I failed."

Enki's eyes flicked over me. "I also feel bad about Inanna," he said. He stared at his feet.

I gave out a laugh, I was so surprised. "I did not think you a sentimental man."

He shook his head, unusually gloomy. "You know when the master *mee* is used on you, it leaves footprints. And Inanna certainly used the *mee* on me."

"What does that mean?"

Enki shook his head. "All that's irrelevant," he said. "What is relevant is that if the Kur is lost, then we can presume Tiamat cannot come here. That's good." He lifted his chin. "It also means that we Anunnaki are here forever now. Citizens of the realm of light."

"I thought you loved it here."

"Oh, I do," he said. "Of all the Anunnaki, I am the one who loves this realm best. But one likes to know there's a way out if it came to it. It is strange to think there might not be. Unless..."

"Unless what?"

"When we fled Heaven, it was our intention to come directly to Earth. We were told there was a gate here. Instead we found ourselves up in the Kur, up in the stars, and had to fly it down here to reach Earth."

"Oh," I said, understanding dawning. "So there could be another gate? Down here on Earth?"

"Of course. My mother and I spent years looking for it and

never found it. Why do you think we spent so long wandering the world?"

"I suppose I thought for the adventure of it."

Enki turned to look at me. "I should go to Abydos."

"Oh?" There had never been any mention of a trip to Abydos.

"In Egypt," Enki said.

"I know where it is, Uncle."

"There is still a small chance that there's a gate there. Small, but I think worth making sure of."

"What makes you think that?"

"Your friend Marduk had a tattoo of a lion-headed bird on his arm before he was struck with lightning. He said he got the tattoo in Abydos. That bird is the totem of the Anzu, the first family of Heaven. They live in a land called Creation and all the other lands of Heaven bow their heads to them."

"Marduk told me they worship Tiamat in Abydos. But they worship her in other places too."

"There is also the fact that my mother was in Egypt but never told me about it. I only found out recently."

"In Abydos?"

"I think so."

"Surely your mother would have found the gate, if it was there?"

He shrugged. "I may be wrong, but it's a scab I want to scratch at."

"Because it could be a way in for Tiamat?"

"That exactly," he said. "I ought to be sure. It could be a way in for Tiamat or a way out for us."

I examined his bronze-sheened profile for a hint of emotion, but could find none.

"I'll come with you," I said. "Although I'm not as good in a fight as I used to be."

"You're still good for some murder," he said with a lean smile, "and for some after-dinner stories." It was the closest he had ever come to jesting with me.

"So that is what I'm good for now," I said. "Stories and bloody murder."

"Don't underestimate the combination." His smile faded. "Stories and murder have kept the Anunnaki in power for four hundred years."

"Should we take the men with us?"

He lifted up the jug to pour himself more wine. "Let's send them back to Isimud."

"Enki, what if we're wrong? What if we are only a few cables from the Kur and there are still people inside it?"

"I suppose they will die down there," he said. "I think we have done what we can."

CHAPTER 9

ERESHKIGAL

Inside the ruins of the Kur

I was fat, filthy, and ill. My gut was horrifically distended and my back was in agony. Yet I had to keep digging because who else was going to rescue Nergal?

Once I had had an army of demons. How I loved them, each and every one of them! They would have dug through this landslide in hours. But all of them were dead, murdered by my foul and black-hearted sister.

Alone, weeping, I lifted each rock and threw it aside, my fingernails stained with the mud of the underworld, my dress ragged, my feet bleeding. As I dug, the stars above me slowly blinked out of existence and it grew darker with every hour that passed.

When it all became too much for me, I lay on my side in the rubble and cried.

I did not have enough time with him.

"Ereshkigal?"

I sighed out hard but pushed myself up into a sitting position. "What?" I said.

Dumuzi stood with one foot up on a rock and his hands on his hips. "What a sight you are, Ereshkigal. Now look, you need to come with me."

"I will not," I said. I tipped myself slowly forward onto my hands and then climbed, with a groan, to my feet. "If you will not help me, just go away."

Dumuzi shook his finely cut nose at me. "Have you noticed that the stars are going out?"

There was a time when I had found him very beautiful. Delicious to look at, even more delicious to touch and taste. Now I was so angry with him for refusing to help me that I was almost repulsed by him. He and his useless sister had insisted on trying to dig their way out towards the realm of light. But it was Heaven we needed to get to!

"The stars, Ereshkigal," Dumuzi said, his voice raised higher.

I could not help but glance upwards. There were still some stars above me, but huge patches of the night sky were a blank. "What of them?"

"Well, you tell me," he said. "We are inside your creation. Why are the stars going out?"

"You don't understand how it works."

"But that's the point," he said. "It's not working. And there's another thing. The wind is no longer blowing."

For a moment, I think my heart stopped.

"Oh?" I said, very casual.

"There's been a breeze blowing," he said, gesturing back towards the Dark City, and beyond it, to his rival dig site. "The wind has been blowing steadily all day every day. It smelt of forest. But today when we got out to the dig site, there was no breeze. Come see for yourself."

I wiped my filthy hands on my damp, muddy skirts. "I will come see if you come and help me dig here."

"That will not happen," said Dumuzi, his jaw tight. "I'm putting my foot down, Ereshkigal, and it is not only for my own sake. Look at you!"

I burst into tears. "I will come to see about the wind," I said. "Even though you are so horrible!"

"Come on then," he said, sounding tired, and began to make his way back along the ruined road towards the city.

I followed him, my mind alive with worry about the wind. If the wind stopped... I did not want to think about it.

Dumuzi kept turning to look at me as I limped along behind him. "Are you still nauseous?"

"Of course I am!" I shouted. "I am terribly sick! And you have done nothing at all to help me!"

I put my hands upon my ruined, bloated belly, and wept and wept as I walked.

Dumuzi took a great breath in, and another out, and came back to walk next to me. "Please let's not do this all again."

"If you had any feelings for me, you would be helping me get to the eighth gate so that I can get through to Heaven. You would not be digging at another site entirely against all my wishes and pleas."

He put out a hand to me and I slapped at it.

"Ereshkigal, please, everything we have done has been in your best interests. We care for you, whatever you may think. We need to get you out into the world of light before the Kur collapses in on itself. I think in your heart, you do know that I'm right. I think that you know you are running out of time."

"Nonsense," I said, but then I thought again of the breeze stopping and a shard of fear went through me. My guts began twisting and jabbing at me. Never mind the underworld dying. I was dying from the inside out! Not that anyone cared about my condition. I put my hands on my belly for a moment until the disgusting squirming stopped.

Dumuzi held a hand out to me again. "Lean on me, Ereshkigal. You cannot do all this alone."

"But I am alone," I said. "Entirely alone." My feet looked very swollen upon the dark-slabbed road. I no longer had my little dresser-demons to come and put slippers on me in the mornings and somehow, I had forgotten to put any on. But then I could not remember how long it was since I had been back in my bedchamber in the Dark Palace. I had fallen into the habit of sleeping at my dig site so that I would lose no time at my digging. Sometimes Dumuzi's sister, the girl Geshtinanna, would come to find me with a basket of food and water. She would force me to eat and drink before I went on with my rock moving. She was a horrible traitor for not helping me with my dig, but sometimes she was very kind to me.

Beside me, matching my slow pace, Dumuzi said: "If the wind no longer blows, how long have we got?"

"The wind still blows. You have made a mistake."

He sighed out heavily. "I do hope you are right."

"I am going to check on the wind and then I am going to go back to my dig site and I am going to get through to Heaven and rescue Nergal."

"You cannot help Nergal if you are dead. This insanity must stop, Ereshkigal. I am heartily sick of telling you this."

I plodded on, my hands on my belly, and I continued to weep. For Nergal, my one true love, forced through the eighth gate by my terrible sister. For my demons, all murdered by Inanna. For my silver *gallas*, now standing motionless, refusing to be awoken. I even wept for the gatekeeper, Neti, who was nowhere to be seen. And every day there was new evidence that the Kur was dying or already dead.

Geshtinanna stood waiting for us at the bottom of the steps to the Black Temple. She was twisting her hands together as she did when she was very anxious.

"Oh, Ereshkigal!" she said, rushing down to me to take my arm. "How are you, my beloved?"

"Just help me up the steps," I said.

I gave her my right arm and I gave my left to Dumuzi, even though neither of them deserved such an honour.

"Did he tell you that the wind has stopped?" said Geshtinanna. "Are you well enough to come out to our dig site and see for yourself?"

"That's not necessary," I said. "Take me to the holy of holies."

As they helped me up the huge temple steps, my legs grew heavier and heavier. Was it my imagination or was it already hard to get sustenance from the air?

We passed into the Black Temple. Not so long before, on very special occasions, we would light a thousand candles there. Now only one dim-burning firebowl cast out light along the avenue of dark glistening pillars.

Geshtinanna lit a candle, dipping it into the firebowl. I took it from her and limped around behind my blackthorn throne to the door to the holy of holies. It was the small room in which we kept the tablets that recorded the sacred lore pertaining to my dark realm.

"Shall we come in with you?" Geshtinanna said.

"I must commune with the spirits alone," I said.

"What spirits?" said Dumuzi. "You do talk nonsense, Ereshkigal."

I stepped into the room, my candle raised, and pushed the door shut behind me.

Careful not to spill wax, careful of my belly, I sat down on the rug at the centre of the room.

For a while I just sat there, alone, and very gloomy indeed.

There had been a vent in this room with fresh air pouring in day and night. The air then went up through the pipes in the ceiling and in that way fresh air was pumped around the temple and the palace.

Now the air in the room was still. Indeed, it was already stale. My guts twisted deep inside me, jabbing out at my muscle and skin.

I did not need any magical spirits to tell me that our situation was desperate. The Kur was running out of air and it would not be long until we were all dead.

I thought of Nergal again, his face turned to me as we lay together.

I did not have enough time with him.

CHAPTER 10

INANNA

In Heaven

I awoke with the almost-memory of a dream. Someone had been calling to me across a grassy plain. A tall woman with weapons in her hands. She had called out my name. But what name did she call?

I opened my eyes and cried out. A strange woman was standing over me. She had skin so pale she might have been a ghost and a coat of shining gold scales.

I could not understand who she was, and the back of my head was very painful, as if someone had dropped me onto a hard surface.

My heart began beating almost out of my chest.

Oh, but then I remembered her and took a great breath in. "You are Bizilla," I said. She was familiar to me. I was certain of it.

"Yes," she said.

"Who are you?"

"I'm Bizilla. You already know that."

I lifted my aching head a fraction. I was in a small, stone-walled room.

"Where am I?"

Bizilla moved away from my bed, to stand as if at sentry at the heavy wooden door.

She was so intensely familiar to me, but I could not work out why. "I have met someone who looks like you," I said. "He was young, but very tall, just like you."

"You are confused."

"No, I am certain," I said. "I only met him once, but I am certain. A boy not so much older than me."

"No," she said. "You are mistaken."

I pushed myself up into a sitting position and realised I was naked beneath my thin grey blanket. My body was covered in small dark bruises like fingerprints and I had a round metal bar around my neck. It would not come off.

Panic rose up in me.

"Bizilla, what is happening?"

"Over and over and over." She sighed out, closing her deep blue eyes for a moment.

"Please, what is happening?"

She tipped her head up to the stone ceiling but did not answer.

"I don't think I should be here."

"No one should be here. But that's not up to me."

"Who is it up to?"

Bizilla gave out another sigh. "If I tell you the name of the one who keeps you here, you will have forgotten by tomorrow."

"But I know your name. I know you."

"Yes, you've got my name. You do remember that. I'm not sure why. My name. And you think you have seen someone like me before. Although it seems very unlikely."

She came over and offered me a bottle cap full of liquid. "It will help you sleep," she said. I noticed she was wearing a gold bracelet; the shape and size of it were familiar to me.

The liquid tasted of vanilla.

Amnut and I were walking along the ramparts at Ur. There were no guard rails to keep us from falling and far below me I could see city streets thick with merchants and shoppers.

Amnut turned to face me. Her eyes were such brilliant blue. Were her eyes always blue? I had an idea they had once been yellow.

"Be careful you don't fall," she said.

But I was falling.

As I fell, I heard a woman shout out "Inanna!" I turned my head and caught a glimpse of her, but I kept on falling, into the black.

I woke in complete darkness. Had I just heard the noise of a door closing?

I was in bed. I ached all over. I had the strong sense that I had forgotten something; something desperately important. But what? I had woken in the middle of a dream. I had the faintest memory of a woman calling out to me. A tall, very dark-skinned woman with a bow over her shoulder. As I reached for the memory, it slipped away.

There was a hard band of metal around my throat and I could not get it off.

I thought I heard voices, and then came sounds like bolts being pushed or kicked aside. "Nothing works here any more," a woman said.

The door opened and standing there with a small candle held high, was a tall, very pale-skinned woman in a knee-length gold coat.

Bizilla. It was Bizilla. The relief of it.

She closed the door behind her, pushing it shut with one shoulder, and came over to light the large candle beside my bed.

As she leaned down to do it, I put my hand out and grabbed at her gold-scaled sleeve.

"Bizilla," I said. "What is happening?"

She tried to take her arm away, but I held on to it for my life.

"Bizilla, what is happening?"

"Oh, just let go," she said, and pulled her arm roughly away.

"You look like the Potta," I said.

Her face was hard in the candlelight.

"What did you say?"

"I met a boy called the Potta. And he looked like you."

"Where did you meet this boy?"

"I don't know," I said. "I think he is called Marduk now. But he used to be called the Potta."

"You don't know what you're saying," she said.

The metal band around my neck was too tight; there was no obvious clasp on it.

"Can you help me get this off?" I said.

She did not move to help me. "What do you remember about the boy?"

"I saw him," I said. "I'm so sorry, I can't remember where. Bizilla, where is this? What is happening?"

She reached into her coat and pulled out a small glass bottle. She poured a little liquid into the lid. I noticed she had a gold bracelet on her right arm. "Drink some of this," she said.

It tasted of vanilla.

"Go to sleep," she said. She blew out the candle next to my bed and I listened to her going back out through the door, knocking on it first, and noisily slamming it behind her. Again, I heard bolts being forced into position and the muffled sound of Bizilla cursing.

In the darkness, I breathed through my mouth, trying to calm myself. All of me ached and my limbs did not feel right. I worried that my bones were crumbling.

A cry burst out of me and I wept for a while, taking great ragged breaths, although it hurt my ribs to do so.

For a moment, in the absolute black, I imagined two faint figures beside my bed, their faces hooded. Men sketched out in the faintest light. One black, one very dark blue. They stood with their hands held in prayer before them. I stopped crying and stretched my left hand out towards them.

A moment later they were gone, and I was alone in the dark once more.

CHAPTER 11

MARDUK

In the marshes north of Eridu

Seven moons had passed since my mother Ninshubar's death, but I refused to believe she was truly gone. Every time I went out into the marshes, every time I plunged my paddle down into the water, I would lift my eyes to the reeds. Looking for something, not her perhaps, but a sign of something that might lead to her.

Sometimes we would go out into the marshlands only to look for Ninshubar. Mostly though, we went out looking for spies. Or at least, people the marshmen said were spies. Today we were four boats in all; our group from the Refuge, and then three boats full of marshmen. I waved over at my marshman friend Tilmun, who was in the boat just behind us, and he lifted his chin at me and smiled.

Although we were there for spies, still, with every stroke of my paddle, I kept on looking for Ninshubar.

Harga, who hated the marshmen and most particularly Adamen, their leader, sat in front of me in our canoe, my dogs filling his lap, glowering at all around him.

We were right at the edge of the marshes, where the tangled web of waterways gave way to neat farmland and then the sacred Euphrates. Ahead of us, I could see a stand of palms and the reed-bundle roofs of a village.

Harga turned to me, one heavy finger to his lips.

I had been a soldier, by then, for some time. I had fought up and down the Euphrates, under Gilgamesh's command, doing what we could to damage Akkadian supply lines. During my time as a protector of our people in the marshes, I had fought numerous actions. I was not some newborn, about to stumble helpless and foolish into battle. But still Harga lifted his finger to his lips and scowled at me as if I needed to be told to be quiet when we were creeping up on the enemy.

I smiled at him and gave him a wink, which I knew to be infuriating to him, and then I climbed out onto the clay shore. I quickly crouched down to kiss Moshkhussu, and then so that the other dogs were not jealous, I also kissed them.

Harga frowned at the sight of me kissing the dogs. He lifted his right forefinger to his mouth again, although I had been making no noise at all.

Tilmun arrived at my side, we smiled at each other, and then we crept forward elbow to elbow, Moshkhussu a pace ahead of us, the two black dogs, the Uruk boys, and Harga just behind. The reeds made a crackling noise beneath our feet however carefully we placed our steps. When the skin drew back from Moshkhussu's fangs, I knew we were close. I raised one axe at Harga. He turned to the marshmen, who were creeping close behind us, and raised his chin in warning.

The noise reached us then. It sounded like cheering.

Ahead of us, through the reeds, I could see the huts and a sorry-looking cow. And there, a crowd of marshmen. The men were stood with their backs to us, shouting out and laughing. We need not have been creeping so quietly.

At the centre of the small crowd of marshmen, two men were teetering, locked together.

A heartbeat later, a small village dog charged us, lifting its throat to bellow as it ran.

One more heartbeat and Moshkhussu had it by the neck. She thrashed it to death. By then the knot of marshmen ahead was dispersing; they were picking up weapons. They were running at us.

A kind of thrill rose up in me; a delight for what was to come.

Harga slipped away to my left. He liked to stay at the edges of a fight, picking off his targets. That was not my style. I had not been a fighter for as long as he had, but I already knew that I was quicker than a normal man or woman. I had learned to run straight at the enemy. It worried people when you ran straight at them with no apparent fear and with two axes raised.

I gave a smile to Tilmun and then I ran forward, fast. At the very last moment I leaped into the air so that I could come down on the enemy from above. Then I began the killing. In the beautiful, stretching frenzy of it, I thought only of their eyes, their weapons, the shifting of their bodies, and the arcs of blood that lifted through the air.

I lost all sight of Harga, with his stones and his catapult, and of Tilmun and my two Uruk friends, Tallboy and Shortboy. I even lost sight of the dogs. That was how it was for me, since my rebirth in lightning in the mud beside the Euphrates.

And then it was over and the frenzy slowly died in me.

The dogs ran at me, tails wagging. Harga stood with his back to a large clump of papyrus, lecturing the boys. Tallboy was nursing a cut arm and Harga was looking down at him and saying, very sternly: "You should stay at the edges of a fight. Never get caught in the middle of things." He gave me a glance, checking me for signs of injury. He turned back to Tallboy: "Never mind what Marduk does. He is something different."

"Are you hurt much?" I said to Tallboy, stowing my axes as I walked over to him.

"It's not deep," he said, holding his hand over his wound and looking a little tearful.

"Collect up the enemy's weapons," Harga said to us, and then he went off in the direction of Adamen.

We three boys, as Harga called us, picked over the bodies. It was work I didn't like. I didn't mind the killing, the feeling of it, the precision, but I didn't like the gore and the twitching. I didn't want to look at how young some of the dead were.

Tilmun came over as I wrestled an axe from beneath one of the bodies. He was the firstborn son of Adamen, leader of the marshmen, and he would be a great man one day. For now, however, he was only twelve.

"What was that you were doing?" Tilmun said to me. "Were you trying to dance with them or kill them?" He gave me a wink.

"I did not see you there at all," I said to him, winking back at him. "Were you hiding in the reeds?"

Tilmun wiped his bloodied face on his robe. "I suppose you did distract them, worm-lord." He looked over at his father, who was engaged in tense conversation with Harga. Tilmun was always watching his father.

He turned to me and was about to speak, but closed his mouth on it.

"What?" I said.

"Nothing," he said, smiling.

We moved over to stand beside Harga and the marshman king.

"If these men were spies…" Harga was saying.

"They most certainly were spies," said Adamen. He said it flatly and without any politeness.

Harga gave him a long look and then said: "If these men were spies, then these marshlands of yours are riddled with spies." He had blood on his cheeks and hands. "We are within sight of Akkadian country. How can the Akkadians not already know we are here?"

Adamen gave a shrug so casual that it bordered on open insolence. "If the Akkadians come into the marshes, we will be ready. There is no need to be fearful, Harga. We have lookouts from here to the great river. And a hundred canoes standing ready to spirit you away if it comes to it." He lifted one hand and fluttered out his fingers towards the open water.

Harga did not look happy to be accused of being fearful. Nor did he seem comforted by Adamen's fluttering fingers.

I walked back towards the boats with Tilmun at my side. I would have asked him for his views on the men we had just killed, but his eyes were on his father's back, so I said nothing.

In the canoe, on the way home to the Refuge, I said to Harga: "You think the Akkadians are coming for us?"

"I'm certain that they are. And sooner rather than later."

"You don't trust Adamen?"

"Do you trust him?"

"I like his son."

Harga slowly rolled his shoulders. "The father is not the son."

I realised then that Harga's arm was bleeding. His old wound had opened up. "Are you all right, Harga?"

He shook his head at the question. "You were dancing about in there today," he said. "You were lucky not to get hurt."

"No one touched me."

"You danced," he said. "You need to take this more seriously."

"Perhaps this is how the Sebitti fight," I said. I said the name of the Sebitti slowly and carefully. I was still getting used to it.

"So Enki may say, but I struggle to believe that you are some creature of Heaven when I have seen you pick your nose and eat what you find there."

I laughed at that and then I breathed in deep on the sultry marsh air, and looked out over the wilderness of reeds, shaking the killing off me, shaking off Harga's mood, shaking off my worries about the way Tilmun looked at his father.

"We should go out looking for Ninshubar tomorrow," I said.

"You must let her go," said Harga, without looking at me.

"You know I see her in my dreams," I said. "You know it is a vision."

"I know no such thing."

After my mother Ninshubar was killed, I went mad for a while. I lay in the mud of the Euphrates with Moshkhussu in my arms and thought I would die there. But then lightning hit me. It was not just ordinary lightning, but the blue lightning drawn down by the goddess Inanna. Since then, I had not only been myself, but also something different. New powers had grown in me and new ways of thinking that spoke to something deep inside me. But Harga did not want to acknowledge it.

"I know the difference between a dream and a vision," I said. "And since the lightning hit me, I have had visions."

"No one has visions," said Harga. "Dreams don't come true. And we don't know what kind of lightning hit you, if indeed it did hit you. And we have no idea at all what it has woken up in you or not woken up in you. Enki has filled your head with useless nonsense."

"Go easy, Harga," I said, as Tallboy and Shortboy cast worried eyes back at us.

Harga turned to me and was not easy. "I want you to grow up, Marduk, before you make mistakes that lead to some very hard lessons indeed. You need to let this foolishness go and look to your solemn duty."

We paddled the rest of the way home in silence.

There was no point arguing with Harga when he was in one of his moods.

I knew he did not mean to be so harsh. But then I wondered if he was right; if my confidence in my mother being alive was nothing more than fantasy. I wiped the tears from my cheeks, before anyone could catch a sight of them.

CHAPTER 12

ERESHKIGAL

In the Kur

The Dark City, my home for one hundred years, was running out of air.

I sat on my blackthorn throne in my glittering black temple with my hands on my swollen belly. Dumuzi and Geshtinanna stood at the steps that led up to my throne, each with a candle in hand.

"We need to leave," Dumuzi said. "Please, Ereshkigal, turn your mind to helping us."

"I don't know," I said, shaking my head. "It means giving up on Nergal."

The dark paintings of my ancestors looked down at me with hard eyes.

"I have never been loved by anyone before," I said. "Except by my demons and they are all dead."

"So, this is the problem we have," said Dumuzi, his most earnest self for a moment. "I believe it is simply impossible for us to get through to the eighth gate in the time we have left. You must abandon your plan of getting through to Heaven."

"I am so sad," I said.

Geshtinanna reached for one of my hands and covered it with kisses.

"But then again," Dumuzi continued, "we seem to be making no progress at the other site. We can find no trace of the walkway that used to lead up to the seventh gate. It's all just a mess of rubble out there."

"And it's so dark there now," said Geshtinanna. "But, my lady, perhaps if you came to help us, you could tell us where to dig? No one knows this place better than you do."

I put my hands on my warped guts and breathed in as they twisted beneath my hands. "If we abandon the Kur," I said, "we may never get back in."

Geshtinanna knelt on the top step, next to my throne, and took both of my hands. "My lady, first let us ensure your safety. Then we will plot a way to save your Nergal. We have only had your safety in mind when we went against your wishes. Please believe me, my lady."

With one last shuddering sob, I said: "We will need more candles, if we are to get out. And some lanterns."

"We have ample candles and lanterns at the dig site," said Dumuzi.

"Oh," I said, avoiding his eye. I sat myself up straight. "No, I did not mean that." I waved a hand in dismissal. "It would be easier to get out via the holy of holies."

Dumuzi's mouth grew hard and flat.

His chest rose and fell.

It was several moments before he spoke.

"Ereshkigal, we have spent months and months digging through rubble, in dreadful circumstances."

I sniffed back my tears. "We have all been digging," I said.

"Ereshkigal," he said. "Are you telling us that there is a way out to the realm of light from inside this temple? A way out that you have known about all along?"

I looked over at Geshtinanna. "Tell him to be nicer!"

"I do not think I have ever been so angry with anyone in my life," said Dumuzi. "To think that all this time you knew of a way out and did not tell us."

Geshtinanna shook her head at her brother and then helped me stand up. "Just show us the way out, Ereshkigal. He will not be cross once we are out in the Earthlight. All this will be forgotten then."

"I'm really not sure it will," said Dumuzi.

I climbed down from my throne, my nose held high, and led the pair of them back to the entrance to the holy of holies.

Dumuzi and Geshtinanna both leaned into the small room, peering down at the flagstone floor.

"No," I said, pointing up at the low stone ceiling. They both looked up at the square of heavily inscribed stone there. "We can take this way out," I said. "If it is the Earth we are headed for. We need to climb up two or three floors and then there is a way out. Or that is what my demons told me."

"Months and months we have been digging!" said Dumuzi.

I lifted my nose at him. "It is very good of me to tell you about it now," I said. "Now that you certainly need it. And anyway, the hatchway is clearly marked."

They both peered back up at the panel of inscribed stone.

"Are those marks upon it writing?" said Dumuzi.

"It is how the old gods wrote," I said. "The whole Kur is full of it. What sort of a queen would I be to live here one hundred years and not learn to read the markings?"

"And what do these markings say?" said Geshtinanna.

"They say, 'this way to go out'," I said. "So you see I have not been hiding anything from you. Now I must go and fetch my belongings. You go fetch anything you wish to take. We should leave very soon."

I trudged along the dark corridors to my bedchamber, a flickering candle held up in my right hand. The corridors were all so familiar to me. So loved. The dust of the dead no longer fell, but it lay in drifts along the walls.

In my dim bedchamber, I held my candle high and looked around at the piles of furs on my bed. At the pieces of the Kur, that I had collected over the years; the small handles, knobs, pieces of strange substances that I could not understand. Also the secret finds that I knew to be valuable. There by the wall, my little demons' beds were all still laid out, but now full of dust.

This would be my last time in my bedchamber.

I looked at all my clay tablets. All my histories, that had taken me so long to write. I knew they were too heavy to take, and I wept for them. Then I wept some more for my demons, who I missed so much.

When I had stopped weeping, I went to my secret hiding places and took out all the different *mees* that I had collected over the years. Some were Anunnaki, some were Anzu, and some, found in the depths of the Kur, were far more ancient still.

I pushed as many *mees* onto each arm as I could, found a pair of old woollen slippers that would fit my swollen feet, and then made my way back to Dumuzi and Geshtinanna.

They were standing outside the holy of holies with a candle and a small leather bag each.

"We will need something to stand on," I said, lifting my chin to the hatchway.

Dumuzi fetched himself a chair. "I'll go first and try to help you up. Although I do not think you should be standing on chairs in your condition."

"What condition?"

"Oh, Ereshkigal." He shook his head. "The nonsense."

"If you had cared about my condition, you would have helped me at my dig site!" I shouted. I calmed myself down. "We are all going to have to climb and crawl," I said. "This way out is not the proper way out. It is only for dire emergencies."

Dumuzi stood on the chair and managed to pull the hatch down towards him, ducking his head out of the way. He carefully peered into the dark space above. "Pass another candle, will you?" he said to his sister. His head disappeared up through the ceiling.

"It's just a room with another hatchway leading upwards," he said, his handsome face tipped down to us. "I think I can get up, but then I don't see how anyone else will be able to pull themselves up and I certainly can't see how we can get Ereshkigal up."

"Do not talk about me as if I am not here!" I shouted up at him, my hands on my belly.

"I will get more things to stand on," said Geshtinanna.

In the end they stacked three temple pews at awkward angles and I was able to climb, very nervous, up through the hatchway. Geshtinanna and Dumuzi held on to my arms and legs and pushed and pulled me. Our reward for all our effort was to find ourselves all three crammed into the tiny loftspace above the holy of holies with three candles in small dishes between us.

By the flickering light, Dumuzi began fiddling with the next hatchway.

"I think you need to close the other one, below us, before the next will open," I said.

"How do you know that?" he said.

"It is common sense," I said. "It's how the seven gates work when you come in from the outside. You have to close one behind you before another will open in front of you. To keep the Kur sealed."

"So where does this lead?" Dumuzi said, once the lower hatchway was shut. "Ereshkigal. Tell us where this goes."

"It just goes out," I said. "My demons explored and they told me it leads all the way to the roof of the Kur and out into the world of light. Although," I frowned up, "of course my demons never went through the final door, because I feared they could not survive on the outside. But they got to the outer edge of the Kur and saw the door that leads directly out into the Earthlight. They read the signs on the door and it was clear what it was."

"Brother, let us hurry," said Geshtinanna. "The air tastes stale to me now."

"Even when we are out of the Kur we may still have a long way to dig," I said. "The Kur has sunk deep into the mountain."

"We will all dig together," said Geshtinanna, "if we have to dig."

Dumuzi managed to get the second hatch open. He stood up into the space above, holding his candle up above him. "Another space, almost the same but much smaller in height and with two ways out, I think. One in the roof, one in the wall."

"That's wrong," I said.

"You better come and look at the markings on the doors," he said. "I think the markings on each door are different."

I crawled over to the trapdoor and stood slowly up.

There was another trapdoor in the ceiling in the room above

us. But there was also a small door set into the wall to my left. Both of them bore inscriptions.

With Dumuzi's and Geshtinanna's help, I dragged myself up into the space so that I could look closer at the markings. Dumuzi put his head up into the room. "Surely we should just keep going up in the same direction. If we are heading for the roof of the Kur, then let's go up."

I was sitting cross-legged, my belly in my lap, breathing hard, my back against the cool wall, my brain working overtime.

There was the hatch in the roof just as there was in the two rooms below. But to my left there was a new door that should not have been there. Not unless my demons forgot to tell me something and that would not have been like them.

Oh, my beloved demons, how I missed them!

I frowned from one door to the other as Dumuzi and Geshtinanna climbed up into the tiny space.

The markings on the trapdoor in the roof were wrong. They should have been the same as on the two hatches below. Simple marks that meant "this way to the light". But now the markings in the roof square did not say "this way to the light". The marks read: beware.

The door to my left, meanwhile, should not have been there at all. I had had no report of it. It was covered with marks that seemed to glow in the candlelight. I only recognised one of the marks and it was the sign the Kur made when it meant to say my name.

"This might be a message for me," I said, pointing to the door to the left.

"What does it say?" said Dumuzi.

I shrugged. "I cannot tell."

"You don't know what it says or you won't tell us what it says?"

"Speak softer to her, brother," Geshtinanna said.

"I will speak to her just as I choose."

I breathed in deep, waiting for the vile lurching inside me to die down. "We must go through this door to my left."

"But that's not what you said before," said Dumuzi. "You said we must keep going up and up into the roof of the Kur."

"Something is wrong," I said. "The Kur has changed the markings. There is something wrong with the passage out."

"Perhaps there is too much rubble above us if we have sunk into the mountain," said Geshtinanna.

I was getting no goodness out of the air. "Geshtinanna, put your candle close to this wall, please."

I still could not read it properly. "There is energy in this door," I said. "It is still glowing. It is still working when the rest of the Kur is dead or dying. Perhaps it created this door for us in its last moments. Perhaps it is a gift to me."

"We cannot go through the top door if the Kur is warning you against it," said Dumuzi.

"We have no choice then," I said. I put my hand out, palm first, and laid it on the door in the wall.

CHAPTER 13

NINSHUBAR

Lost

I stood on the grass plain, in my strange afterlife, and I made my calculations.

Inanna and the black dragon had vanished from the very place I stood, using magic unknown to me.

So.

It was hard to think coolly and clearly.

I looked about me and all I could see was the green grass, rippling in the soft wind, and the good blue sky with the pale yellow sun that never moved.

I paced around in wider and wider circles, but could find nothing remarkable about the spot. I had been in a land of undulating hills. Now it was only a flat, grass plain, stretching in all directions. I forced myself to be calm and strong.

Then it came to me, in a blast of certainty. I must dig. There was something unusual about this spot, but it could be hidden beneath the grass. So, I must dig. I had my good flint axe. I would use it to dig.

It was not a perfect plan, but it was a plan and I knew the value of a plan, and so I began to dig, one axe-worth of earth and grass at a time.

My progress was excellent, although my axe was designed for battle rather than hole-digging. My arms remained strong and fresh, my waist a willow tree; I felt I could dig forever. Soon I was standing almost up to my chest in the hole I had dug, with heaps of dirt and turf on all sides.

Slowly, though, my confidence began to wane. The soil I was digging through was unchanging in colour and texture. There was no sign of me working my way through layers and perhaps to something hidden beneath. Would I dig here forever, as once I had thought I would run forever?

For a while, I lost all sense of time.

I kept on digging.

A sharp cough, and a shape against the sky. I almost leaped out of my own body in shock.

A man was peering down at me from the edge of my pit.

How had I allowed myself to be crept up on?

I shielded my eyes to look up at him. Could it be Neti, the gatekeeper of the underworld?

He certainly looked like Neti. He was dressed in a cherry-red outfit; I had never seen him dressed like that. The cloth was not dissimilar from the cloth I wore. But it looked exactly like him: the face that could not quite be aged, the features that were hard to remember.

I almost laughed to see him there, so very out of context. It was surely a good sign, him being a person so entwined in Anunnaki business and history.

"Ninshubar," he said, peering down into my hole.

"Neti?"

"What do you think you are doing?" he said, his voice neutral, his expression plain.

"I think you are trying to tease me, Neti, because you can see very well that I am digging a hole."

"Are you, indeed?" he said.

I climbed slowly up out of my pit, looking him over for weapons. Neti seemed taller than he had been; not by much but there was a difference. He almost came up to my shoulders. I stood a few paces back from him, since I had no idea what he really was.

"Where is this?" I said to him, dropping my muddy axe back into its leather sheath. "And what are you doing here? What is happening?"

"Three different questions," he said, tipping his face up to the sky and frowning.

"Inanna was here," I said. "And Tiamat. I think it was Tiamat. A black dragon with seven heads. They were here not very long ago. It's why I started digging." That sounded rather foolish, when said out loud, so I added: "I thought perhaps they might have gone downwards."

"Are you sure they were here?" he said, looking down into my pit.

"I am certain of it."

"And you believe they were here a short time ago?"

I paused before answering. "I can't be sure of that." I realised that in fact I had no idea how long I had been in the pit. I looked down into it and realised it was vast, perhaps thirty paces across.

"You are certainly bound tight to Inanna," he said. "How

else could you have got here? I suppose it's the nature of the *sukkal* ceremony, all that formal swapping of blood. The *melam* clinging to its own."

"So, she was here?"

"Possibly," he said. "The structures between the realms are complicated. People have added things, over the millennia. Superstructures, substructures. Ways to get through the system more quickly."

His words meant nothing to me. "Neti, can you help me find her?"

"This is a lot of trouble now." He smoothed down his red suit. "Things are being stirred up that should not be stirred up."

"I am only trying to find Inanna," I said, taking a step towards him. "I'm not causing trouble."

"If only that were true," he said, lifting his fingers to the sky.

"Neti," I said. "I do not want to have to threaten you. You should help me."

"I owe you nothing, *sukkal*. Nothing at all."

"Very well then, I am asking for your help."

"I've already given you help."

"Have you?"

He lowered his hands. "I've already given you a push. Better that than have you careering around here, making all this noise, shaking the spiderweb and attracting who knows what. Better you return to the land you know and make all the noise you like there. Yes, I have given you that push, although I owe you nothing and just as easily could have ended things for you."

"I don't understand you."

He sighed out, long and heavy. "Ninshubar, I think you have been spun about."

"What does that mean?"

"You are digging down," he said, pointing down into my pit. "But you should be digging up." He pointed straight up at the sky.

"Up?" I looked up at the pale yellow sun that never moved. "You want me to dig up?"

"Perhaps I should have ended it," he said, sounding weary.

"Ended what?"

"Your pain, Ninshubar. Your pain." He seemed less solid than he had been, as if he was slowly fading.

"What do you mean?" I said. "Explain yourself better."

"You need to go up," he said, one finger pointing to the sky. Why was he suddenly so close to me?

A heartbeat later he was gone.

Then it was only me again, next to my huge pit, beneath the soft blue sky and its unchanging, unmoving sun.

I climbed down into my huge pit. What had Neti meant when he said I was digging in the wrong direction?

I looked down at the earth. For a heartbeat, everything flickered. Everything was dark and I could not breathe.

Light again, the pale sun.

Was the darkness that snapped in and out of focus, the darkness that tickled at the hairs on the back of my neck, was that darkness the truth?

I had thought I was making sure of the area. Exploring my environment. But was all this nothing more than a dream and a distraction?

On an instinct, I lay down on the earth at the bottom of the pit and shut my eyes. I remembered Neti saying that he had already helped me. Given me a push. What did he mean by that?

Or had I only dreamed him?

I opened my eyes, one last time, to that diffuse blue sky. I breathed in, one last time, the smell of the sweet, clean earth. And then with no warning at all, I plunged down deep into the terrifying darkness.

To the truth of what was happening to me.

CHAPTER 14

NINLIL

In Heaven

Bizilla came to visit me in my bedchamber. I sat on my narrow bed and she sat in my old rocking chair beside the crackling fire, and we listened together to a storm that shook the palace walls. "I am sorry I could not come before," she said.

"Why is your hair so short?"

"I cut it when you were taken," she said. "And I have kept it short ever since."

The heir to Creation is given a *sukkal* while she is still in her cradle, so I did not remember the day that Bizilla swore herself to me. But I knew she had been with me every day of my childhood until the day of my kidnap.

"I let myself believe that you were happy elsewhere," she said. "That there would be no need for you to ever return to all this."

"In many ways, I was happy on Earth. Yet one bears the scars of one's past."

Bizilla leaned forward and took my hands in her own. Her

touch sent a wave of shock through me. She was so very, very full of pain.

"Why come back, Ninlil? You should have kept your son with you in the realm of light."

"My mother is planning to invade the Earth," I said. "I knew I had to face her sooner or later."

"Have they spoken to you of the exodus?" She sat back in her rocking chair, taking her hands from mine.

"They have told me nothing directly," I said. "But I can see that everything is crumbling. There are refugees everywhere. Everyone is whispering to each other. My brother quizzes me about every aspect of the realm of light."

"They say the exodus will be peaceful," said Bizilla. "That there is plenty of room in the realm of light even if hundreds of thousands of us pass through the gates."

"Perhaps," I said.

"If indeed we ever go. Your mother is stalling, and no one can be sure why." She paused for a moment, her eyes cast down. "I can never forgive myself," she said at last.

"Only my brother is to blame, Bizilla."

"He tricked me," she said. "Tricked me into letting him take you for a walk without me. Yet I must bear full responsibility for what happened."

"My brother tricked you and he tricked my Anunnaki kidnapper, too," I said. "He addled Enlil's brain with the master *mee*. He used the *mee* on me too, ensuring my part in it all. None of what happened is your fault. He did not like giving up his place as heir and that is all there was to it. He did not care who he hurt."

"So what will you do now?"

"I hope to stop the invasion if I can."

"Ninlil, you cannot stop your mother." She said it with heavy sadness.

"But I intend to try."

"The entire realm is collapsing in on itself," said Bizilla. "Thousands of new refugees arrive each day. Your mother may be stalling but very soon she will have no choice but to leave this place."

"But she could go anywhere. There are other realms. There are many gates. She need not follow the Anunnaki through to Earth."

"She knows the realm of light is safe for her. She knows that because you and Nergal both survived it. She knows that because Qingu tortures the girl Inanna, day after day, in order to wring from her every detail of the realm she was born in. The realm of light is going to be our new home and there is nothing you can do to stop it."

"I am going to try," I said. "But first I must see my son."

"If I can find a way to get you to him, I will," said Bizilla. "But your brother has me standing guard over Inanna day and night."

"I will try my brother again," I said. I looked around my childhood room and thought of Inanna, and how very young she was. "If there is something you can do for the girl, will you do it?"

"If I can," said Bizilla. "If you ask it."

"I do ask it," I said. "I do not think her bad."

"Then I will do what I can for Inanna," said Bizilla. "You have my word."

CHAPTER 15

GILGAMESH

At Swenett, in Egypt

Enki and I went south from the site of the Kur on mules, with Inanna's lions ranging out alongside us, taking down game where they could. When we reached the coast we took passage on a merchant ship heading west, although the sailors made a fuss about the lionesses until we had agreed to double their payment of gold.

A week later, with the summer winds behind us, we were dropped off in a desert town on the coast of Egypt. There we bought camels and supplies and set off across the desert, heading for the famous River Nile.

It was eight days in all across the great sands, all of it very hard upon my bad knee, but at last we reached the Nile city of Swenett. There, the god Enki and I sat at a long trestle table, above the tumbling river, and drank cool beer. I sat with my bad leg up on a wooden bench and for a while the pain did not bother me.

"They must cool the beer in the Nile," Enki said, pouring us both more.

It was hot but the air was damp and sweet and there was no dust: what a perfect place it was.

Enki leaned over to the lions, who sat, panting heavily, on the grass beside our table. He kissed each on the head. "They are bringing water for you, sweet girls."

"I have never tasted anything so delicious," I said, looking down into my golden, frothing beer.

"I agree absolutely." He downed his second mug of beer. "These past months, since the death of my brother Enlil, I have not felt myself capable of happiness. Now a mug of beer leaves me overwhelmed with joy."

"It is exactly the same for me," I said, taking up my mug. "I thought I would never know joy again after the death of Enlil and my mother and…" I found I could not yet mention my wife and son, so I only paused and then said: "Now I feel that this beer and the thought of the food coming is all that any man could hope for."

I breathed in deep on the moist air. "That is the desert for you," I went on. "I was lost once in another desert and attacked by lions. Not friendly lions like these two." I looked down, dubiously, at Inanna's lions. "I still remember my first drink after the desert. It was only water, but it was the sweetest water I had ever had." I remembered, too, that I had fought and killed the man who had given me that sweet water. But I was not sure how well that reflected on me and so I let the story end there.

The white-robed innkeeper emerged from the cookhouse with a fleet of small boys in his wake. Between them they carried bowls of water for the lions, two large jugs of the cool beer, and huge platters heaped with spiced beans, goat stew, battered river fish, and grilled venison.

We passed a plate of fish down to the lions and then began to eat even before all the dishes had arrived.

Enki waved at the innkeeper with his spoon. "We have changed our minds. We will try your lamb parcels and also the fried cheese you spoke of."

"And the palm heart salad," I said.

"And we will have the same again of the river fish and the beans, and four portions of the goat," Enki said. "Actually six portions. The lions love goat." His sunburn blisters seemed to have healed already; that was the *melam* in him.

"If I ever get back to Uruk, I am going to have them prepare me fish just like this," I said to Enki.

"Once you have evicted the Akkadians and rebuilt the city," he said, one eyebrow lifted.

"Oh, yes, yes. Or do you doubt that will ever happen?"

"Oh, we'll get it all back," he said. "The Anunnaki will rise again. Not that there are many of us left."

"How many is it?"

Enki frowned, thoughtful. "Me, of course." He held up one finger. "You don't count, being mortal. We must consider those who went into the Kur as lost for now. So I will not count Inanna, or Ninlil, or Utu, or my granddaughter Ereshkigal, so-called queen of the underworld. Geshtinanna and Dumuzi are only classed as half-gods, so I will leave them off. Your mother is dead, of course, and I am sorry for it." He rubbed his hands through his shorn hair. "And there's my brother Enlil." He looked down at his food for a moment, then raised up his fingers again. "So that leaves me, the moon gods, your father, and the lord god An, if they are still actually alive inside Sippur. And possibly my ex-wife, Ninhursag, although she is in the wind. My mother, Nammu, I think died in her prison cell in Akkadia. So that makes six Anunnaki left in the world, and maybe fewer."

"Not many," I said.

"My point is," he said, beginning on another fish, "that we few Anunnaki will see the Akkadians fall. Whether *you* are alive to see it, of course, is another thing entirely."

"I don't need reminding of my mortality."

"It's that knee that's going to kill you," he said, blandly but with conviction. "Not your lack of immortality. The knee is poisoned. Anyone can see that. You should have the leg taken off."

"I will not do that."

"Any ordinary man would be dead by now. But there is only so long even a child of two gods will be able to stave that off. The black rot will creep up towards your heart."

"I am not going to have my leg taken off."

We were both silent a moment.

"Well, perhaps some of the lost Anunnaki will return," said Enki, pouring more beer. "Inanna has already survived one death."

I caught an odd expression on his face as he said the goddess's name. I remembered what he had said to me about the master *mee* leaving footprints.

"Inanna took all your *mees*," I said. "You must have been very angry with her."

He looked up at me. For a moment I thought he was upset. But a moment later he said, very polite: "No, no, she and I are quite good friends now, I think."

When we were round-bellied and greasy-faced, and the lions were laid out flat on the grass, Enki called the innkeeper back over.

"We are looking to travel by boat now," Enki said to him. "We plan to travel north to Abydos. Do you know someone who might be able to take us? We have camels to trade."

"I can most certainly find you a boat," the innkeeper said.

"Indeed, I am the owner of the very best ships in Swenett."

"Well, we would like one of your very best ships," Enki said. "My companion here is done with riding."

"It will be my pleasure," said the innkeeper.

A short time later he returned to us with a small boy close behind him. "My lords, this boy is my eldest son and a very fine captain of boats. He says he will take you down the river to Abydos." He lifted both hands, very apologetic. "Of course, your camels, while very fine, will not cover the whole cost of a ship down river."

The boy, although dressed in no more than a slave's tunic, nodded his head at that in a serious manner.

The innkeeper bent low from the waist and the young boy at once copied him, while also trying to keep one eye upon us.

"Perhaps one of those bracelets you are wearing," the innkeeper said, from the depths of his bow, "might be something you would be willing to add into the trade for the food and drink you are enjoying, and also for the services of this boy and the rental of my best ship."

"You cannot have my bracelets," said Enki.

I glanced down at the lions. Each of the sleeping beasts wore a golden collar set with expensive-looking red gems.

"They need their collars," Enki said, following my glance. "I had them especially commissioned."

"We would also accept the lions themselves," the innkeeper said.

"That will not be acceptable," said Enki. He cast a glance at my bronze axes, which I had laid out on the table while I ate.

"I'm not giving up my axes," I said. "But I have armour with me. Of the highest quality." I gestured towards my leather backpack.

My own armour had been taken from me a long time before, on the battlefield outside Uruk. The armour in my backpack, taken from some dead Akkadian, had no sentimental value for me, but it was good bronze and worth something.

"We would like to see this armour," the innkeeper said.

He and the boy both bowed deep again.

"We'll need some new clothes as well," said Enki. His blood-red robes were in tatters, after nights spent sleeping on outcrops of sharp rock. "Perhaps some simple white robes like your own," he added to the innkeeper.

"When we have seen the armour we can certainly talk about new clothes," said our host.

When the deal was done, Enki and I walked in our fresh, white robes down the steep, tree-shaded street that led down to the river. I had my axes strapped to my back, my sword on my hip, and had it not been for the agony in my left knee, I might have felt rather pleased with myself.

"May I ask, my lords, what your business at Abydos is?" said the innkeeper as we walked. He glanced again at Enki's *mees*. "Is it possible you know the gods there?"

"I have children there," Enki said.

"You do?" I said.

The innkeeper looked from one to the other of us. "Children?" he said, smiling. "May I ask their names?"

"The boy is Osiris and the girl is Isis," Enki said. He lifted his shoulders a fraction. "Half-gods."

"You have children in Abydos?" I said.

"I have children everywhere," Enki said to me, with a shrug. "It did not seem important."

The innkeeper stopped walking. "My lord, are you saying that Osiris and Isis are your children?"

"I am saying that," said Enki, pausing mid-stride, "because they are."

The innkeeper slowly climbed down onto his knees. He put his hands up to Enki in supplication. "My lord, I had no idea. Of course, there will be no payment for the food or the ship. The armour will be returned to you at once."

The man bent his head. He seemed genuinely frightened.

"When I see my children, I will tell them how pleased I was with your service to me," Enki said, frowning. "Now stand up and let's get to our ship."

The innkeeper stood, but walked well behind us as we made our way down the curving road to the river docks.

"They are unafraid of me and yet they are terrified of my two half-god cast-offs," Enki said to me, his voice low.

"I suppose it depends on the nature of your so-called cast-offs," I said. "I am amazed you have never mentioned them to me in all these long days of travel."

"Oh," he said, waving my words away. "The boy was trouble, you know. Perhaps he would have grown out of it, but my Anunnaki brethren made me throw him out. He took the girl with him. I thought they might die in the desert, but they have made something of themselves here. One hears news now and then."

"Does one," I said.

Swenett was built at the point where the rocky upper reaches of the Nile flowed out onto flat and open riverplain. The city docks consisted of a dozen jetties bustling with boats and goods and people.

At the first of these jetties stood the most beautiful sailing ship I had ever seen. She was fashioned from cedar and acacia, long and thin, with the most extraordinarily high bow and stern. There was a small cabin in the centre of the ship; it was already full up with sacks and barrels. Indeed, the ship looked ready to let slip.

"Our very best ship," the innkeeper said, ushering us onto the jetty. "There are plenty of supplies aboard for you."

"That was quickly done," I said, beaming at the innkeeper. "When it cannot be an hour since we asked you for a ship."

"We are a quick people, here in Swenett," said the innkeeper, bowing.

Enki and I climbed on board and the lions leaped on after us. Our small captain whistled and up came five more boys from the crowds, all smaller than him and more ragged. "These boys will work the oars," he said. My armour arrived from the inn in the hands of two young women and was passed reverently up to me on board the ship.

We all lifted hands to the innkeeper and minutes later we were out in the middle of the great brown river as it spread out onto the plains. It was wider than any river I had ever seen, and more quickly than we could have imagined we were out of the town and in open countryside, with a pleasant breeze playing over our ship.

For leagues either side of us stretched drowned fields.

"The river is very high now," our young captain told us. His Sumerian was even better than his father's. "We need all of this water and the rich soil it carries to sink into the land so that when the river goes down, the crops can grow."

"We use canals in Sumer," I said.

"Of course, we use canals as well, and reservoirs," said the boy. "On a vast scale. Everything is better and bigger in Egypt." He gave me a kindly nod.

⁓

The boy's name was Userkaf and as we slid down the Nile, the current pushing us on, he had plenty to say to us about the manifest wonders of Egypt.

"My family are the most powerful family in this part of the country," Userkaf said, "because we control Swenett and all access to the upper Nile. Of course, the gods sit above us, but in terms of human families, we are at the pinnacle."

"You do not dress like the son of a fine family," I said.

"In Egypt, we know that wealth is hard won and poverty always close by," Userkaf said, with great complacency. "Why would I wear fine clothes that might tempt someone to steal from me?" He gave me a kind smile. "You carry bronze axes, my lord. Now who am I to tell you it is unwise? You are a great lord in your country. But if you were a normal man, I would advise you against carrying such axes on your back when bronze is very precious here. Egypt is better than other places on Earth, but it is also more dangerous. It is the most dangerous place on Earth."

"There are more dangerous places," Enki said, with flat finality.

"You are wrong there," said Userkaf, most politely, and with an air of even greater finality.

Enki laughed. "Have you travelled the world?" he said to the boy.

"I do not need to travel the world to know the truth about my own country," he said.

"Well, we are very lucky to have found you and this beautiful ship," I put in.

"Our spies have been tracking you all the way across the desert," Userkaf said, with a dismissive wave of one hand. "We have been preparing this ship for a week. Let us hope that our friends in the north do not yet know of your arrival."

"Who do you mean by our friends in the north?" I said. I rearranged my bad leg, very carefully, on the deck before me.

"The gods of Abydos," he said. "Who you claim as your children," he added, with a nod to Enki. "If you were to ask my advice," Userkaf went on, "I would tell you to stay out of Abydos."

"Are these gods so bad?" I said.

"Very bad, my lord. Very evil." He nodded at Enki. "If you do not mind me saying, my lord."

"I've done wrong myself," I said. "I would hesitate to call another evil."

Enki gave the faintest shrug. "The boy has odd tastes."

"You may claim them as your children," the boy went on, "but we are taught here that their mother is Tiamat, queen of all the gods."

"Oh, that is interesting," said Enki.

"You know of Tiamat?" said Userkaf.

"I was subject to her once," said Enki. "A long time ago and in a very different place."

On that first night we moored up in reeds at the edge of the great river. The boys threw rocks overboard as anchors and curled up together in the stern to sleep. Enki and I sat on the foredeck and watched the moon rise huge and yellow over the Nile.

"Have you been here before?" I said.

Enki lifted both eyebrows and nodded. "When there were no towns here, only farmsteads and villages, I walked the length of the river all the way to the sea."

"It sounds good to me now," I said. "Walking the world alone, exploring."

"Your walking days are over, Gilgamesh." He said it not unkindly, but as plain truth.

"Yes, I know," I said. "I know." I looked up at the moon and felt very sad indeed.

CHAPTER 16

MARDUK

In the marshes north of Eridu

The whistles rang out across the reed beds. The calls that meant: *friends arriving*.

I recognised them at once, even far out in the channel: it was the moon goddess, Ningal, Enki's *sukkal*, Isimud, and a squad of soldiers. I lifted a hand in delight to them. They would have hours' worth of news from the front and there would certainly be a party.

Ningal, the moon goddess, was first to climb out of the canoes. She wore fighting leathers and had scraped her hair back into a knot. "Can you still be growing?" she said, as she offered me her cheeks to kiss.

"Tell me everything!" I said.

She laughed. "I will save it all for the Palace."

"At least tell me where Gilgamesh is."

"Oh," she said, looking around her as if searching for something. "He is with Enki."

"But well?"

She seemed not to find whatever she was looking for. "Oh yes," she said, turning back to me. "He is quite well."

Soon enough we were all crammed into the Palace, with Ningal and Isimud sat on the rug in the centre of it. The priestesses plied them with clean water, herb tea, cinnamon biscuits, and fresh figs.

Ningal and Isimud recounted the story of their weeks away from the Refuge: the towns they had attacked, the supply lines they had destroyed. But the real news was saved for last.

"King Akka has left Ur and is on his way north with eight barges of soldiers," said Ningal. "He is intent on breaking through to Sippur."

All gathered were quiet a while, absorbing the news. Sippur was the last Sumerian city holding out against the Akkadians. An, the king of the Sumerian gods, was said to be inside the town, and it had come to have great meaning for my Sumerian friends. It gave them hope that it was possible to stand up to the enemy; that it was possible that all of Sumer might one day be free of the Akkadians.

"I'm not sure what we can do for those inside the city," said Harga. "Even if we wanted to help them. What could we do against eight barges of soldiers?"

"But we have to try," said the moon goddess. "Surely?"

Later that day, in honour of Ningal's and Isimud's return, Adamen, the king of the marshmen, arrived with his son Tilmun. We met in council with them: me, Harga, Isimud, Lilith, and Ningal from our side, and Adamen and Tilmun from the other.

I sat and petted my beautiful dogs while they argued.

"If you would lend us two hundred fighters, we could make a real difference in the north," Isimud said.

"We have been over and over this," said Adamen. "My deal with the lord god Enki is that I offer you safe harbour in these marshes and that none of my people lay a hand on you in anger. That is a very different thing from throwing two hundred of my men into a slaughter."

"We are not ungrateful," said the moon goddess, Ningal. "You are the most loyal of all Sumerians and we will never forget it."

Adamen's jaw twitched. I knew he did not consider himself a Sumerian; he believed his people to be more ancient and more important than any city people. But he said nothing.

"King Akka and the north aside, we should speak of our arrangements here," said Harga. "If the Akkadians come into the marshes in force we would be trapped on this island if you did not get to us in time."

Adamen set down his guest tea. "If the Akkadians come, we will send hundreds of canoes and take all of you off into the reeds. That is the plan and it is a good plan. They cannot hunt down hundreds of canoes. It is how we have always done it here. We scatter like seeds in the wind, when the enemy comes to hunt us. This is how we have always survived here."

Ningal smiled at the marshman and then at Harga. "King Adamen, you are a good friend to us."

When we had seen the marshmen back to their canoe, the five of us stood on the beach and watched them disappear into the reeds.

Isimud said: "The men need rest. Let's take some time to think hard about Sippur."

"King Akka could be there by now," said Ningal. "The city could already have fallen."

I took a step forward. "I could go north," I said. "I could go fast alone and find out what is happening and come quickly back."

All four of them shook their heads at me.

"Best we stay together," said Harga. "And start looking for a better hiding place."

"Where could be better?" said Ningal. "There is nowhere else inside Sumer that could hide so many of us. Besides, the marshmen have always been our friends."

"So you keep saying," said Harga.

Later still, there was the party. Venison was roasted over fires; bottles of spirit were conjured up. There was music and dancing on the cleared ground outside the Palace.

Very late on, when I had perhaps drunk more spirit than was wise, I found myself alone with Harga. He was sat by the fire, looking into the flames, apparently oblivious to the merriment around him.

"Are you well, Harga?" I said, sitting down next to him. My dogs wedged themselves between us.

"I'm well," said Harga, pushing one of the black dogs away from his face.

"You seem a little sombre."

"I'm sober and you are drunk. But I am well, nonetheless, I assure you."

"Why not celebrate?"

"Because the Akkadians could attack at any time and one of us should be sober for that."

"Oh," I said, supping on my cup of date spirit. "You make a good point."

It was then that Ningal, the moon goddess, attempted to sit down with us. She stumbled and ended up almost in Harga's lap. Without expression, he lifted her off him and sat her down between the two of us, firmly moving the dogs aside.

"I am so sorry, Harga," she said. "I've drunk more than I meant to."

"It's easily done, with that stuff," said Harga. "It's mostly poison."

"There is something I would like to ask you both," said Ningal, "as two people I trust, for your discretion, but also your wisdom."

Harga cast a wry glance at me. He did not think much of my discretion.

"Go on," I said.

"I will need more alcohol for this story," she said, and so I poured some of my own spirit into her cup.

"At the start of the invasion, I was away with Gilgamesh for weeks at a time," she said. "We were very close." She fell silent, looking down into her cup.

"With all due respect, my lady, it is not much of a story," said Harga.

The moon goddess pretended to swat at him. "Let me finish." She drew herself up and breathed out hard. "I lay with him," she said.

For a moment, Harga's mouth hung open. He closed it and then nodded, grimly. "You lay with Gilgamesh?"

The moon goddess nodded slowly, her mouth turned down. "He had just received the news that his wife and son were dead, and we got drunk and lay down together."

"It could have happened to any of us," I said, smiling at her and patting one of her arms. "I do not see a problem. You are a lot older than him, yes. But what of it?"

Harga and the moon goddess did not seem interested in my views on the subject.

Ningal put a hand out onto one of Harga's knees. "I had an idea when we were in Uruk that Inanna once had feelings for Gilgamesh. Do you think that is true?"

Harga tipped his head to one shoulder and then over to the other shoulder. "I do think that is true."

"Oh," said Ningal. "I was worried about that." She looked deep into her cup. "Should I tell her, do you think? I mean, if she comes back?"

"I would certainly tell her," I said.

"That is one view," said Harga, scowling at me. "But it might blight her relationship with Gilgamesh and it might also blight her relationship with you."

"That is my fear," said the moon goddess.

"Say nothing then," Harga said, with sudden vehemence. "Ever. The one good thing about this is that even Gilgamesh, stupid, loutish, and foolish as he is, would never be such a lunatic as to tell her himself." He breathed in deep and briefly squeezed the goddess's hand. "I do not blame you, Ningal. It is not you I am angry with."

Ningal withdrew her hand from him. "Harga, I am as much to blame for what happened as Gilgamesh is. We were both drunk. We are both adults."

"I don't think Inanna will mind," I put in.

"You met Inanna once and for about ten minutes," Harga said to me. He softened his tone. "But yes, who knows, perhaps in fact she would not much mind at all." He turned to Ningal. "Take all the blame you choose to, but this is not the first time that Gilgamesh has complicated things."

"I understand that," she said. "But I ought to have known better myself."

Harga leaned over and kissed her forehead. "Forget it, goddess. When Inanna comes back, we will deal with it then, if it ever comes up."

Ningal nodded, smiling warmly at him. "It's such a small thing, in the scale of things, with a war going on."

"A very small thing," said Harga, nodding. He caught my eye as he said the words, and I saw he did not mean them. "A very small thing," he repeated.

CHAPTER 17

GILGAMESH

At Abydos, Egypt

Userkaf, the young Egyptian ship captain, insisted on dropping us some way upstream from Abydos.

"This is the normal place to drop people," he said, pointing to the muddy embankment. "Even gods must be dropped here."

All I could see, other than the great river, was green fields in all directions. Although, perhaps, in the far distance, I could make out the shape of palms and low mud buildings?

"Yes, that is Abydos," said Userkaf, following my gaze, and nodding at me. "Very close."

"It looks like quite a walk from here," I said, frowning at the horizon and thinking of my knee. The town looked to be about four leagues down river from us and set back at least a league inland from the Nile.

"It would be remarkable if I went any closer," said Userkaf, with solid conviction. "I do not wish to be remarkable."

"How old are you?" I said, as I followed Enki and the lions off the boat onto the embankment.

"I am ten. I stand on the brink of manhood." He gave me a bow from the deck of the boat, one hand tight on a rope.

"Well, I thank you for your service and all the advice as well," I said.

"Do not mention my name in Abydos," Userkaf said, shaking his head at me. "That is all the thanks I need."

Moments later his crew of small boys were pulling up square brown sails and the boat was pulling away to the south, against the current.

"May the gods of Abydos look kindly on you," Userkaf called back to us, a hand raised, his face sombre. He turned to the workings of the boat and did not look back at us.

"I wish I had his confidence," I said. "I think I used to have it."

"But life crushed it," said Enki.

"Yes," I said. "Exactly that."

We made our way north along the embankment with the lions loping on ahead as the day began to warm. I had imagined the fields to be empty, but a flock of brave children gathered behind us as we travelled, first one small girl and then many others. Some of them danced close enough to touch a finger to our robes.

"Even these children do not fear me," said Enki, scowling down at a small naked boy. "How low I have sunk."

Abydos was indeed set a league back from the banks of the Nile, but with a well-built canal supplying it with river water. We took a turn to our left when we reached the canal and followed the palm-lined road there towards the town. Even before we were halfway to Abydos, it had become clear to us that a large number of people were gathering on the road ahead.

"Do you think they are here for us?" I said, squinting ahead, one hand shading my eyes.

"I think we would make very poor spies," Enki said. "Everywhere we go here, we are expected. Planned for. Nothing we say or do surprises anyone in this country, so sure are they of our movements and intentions."

Enki put the lions on their leashes. I turned to find that the children had been swallowed up by the fields.

I put a hand to each of my shoulder harnesses and drew out my axes.

"Perhaps they will greet us with arms held wide," I said, swinging my axes in slow, careful circles. "Perhaps they will be delighted to see us. The famous hero of Sumer, that being me of course, and Enki, father to the gods of Abydos."

"Perhaps," he said.

"Is there any power left in your *mees*?"

"They are drained and useless. Although I suppose I could throw them at someone."

As we drew closer, we were able to make out the exact nature of our welcoming committee. First came perhaps fifty men on camel-back, dressed in black robes and carrying heavy spears. Behind them came two hundred or so soldiers, all with a copper-capped spear in one hand and a leather-covered shield in the other. These fighting men parted, giving way to a great horde of priests in pointed white hats. The priests made their way towards us waving small metal flails at the sky and chanting something in an unfamiliar language.

We drew up, Enki, the lions and I, to watch this strange assemblage draw close to us along the sandy road. There was something behind the white-robed priests; some kind of gold platform being carried along with the horde.

"I think they have a god with them," I said.

As I spoke, the ranks of white-robed priests parted and we caught our first clear sight of what was coming at us.

It was a huge wheeled platform, glinting gold in the morning sun, and being pulled towards us by ten white oxen. A host of bare-chested oxen-drivers walked on either side of the platform, and on the top of the strange contraption, on a high gold throne, sat a woman who must surely be the goddess.

She was an astounding sight: a vision in see-through red cloth, and with both breasts bare. She had a tall crown of black and gold upon her head and her face was painted so heavily that she looked more like a statue than a woman. Even so, I could see at once, from the flicker of her leopard eyes, that she was Enki's child.

"Isis, I presume," I said to Enki.

"So it seems," he said, his eyes fixed on his daughter.

When we were four cables apart, the priests stopped their chanting and the platform and its large assembly of attendants drew to a halt.

In the hushed silence that then fell upon us, the goddess said: "Hello, Father." Her accent was Sumerian, but with a strange lilt to it.

"Hello, Isis," he said, with no smile. "Is Osiris here?"

"No," she said. "Is it him you came for?" Her mouth turned down.

"I came to see you both," he said. "It's time I did. May we talk in private?"

"Certainly," she said. "When you tell me why you're here."

Enki paused a moment. "I came to see the temple. I think you call it the Osirion. I believe my mother may have been here."

"Oh, the temple. Of course." She nodded, her face hard. "Well, then, you can follow me. If you want to see the temple, you can see the temple."

I put my axes back into their straps. "I'm Gilgamesh," I called up to the goddess. "Son of Ninsun and Lugalbanda. I believe we are cousins."

"Hello," she said, without enthusiasm.

It took some time for the host of bare-chested oxen-drivers to persuade the beautiful white oxen to trace a full about-turn, but once that was done, we followed on behind the extraordinary gold float, with the priests then following behind us. Behind them came the foot soldiers and the warriors on camel-back.

Amidst this grand procession, we passed out of farmland and into the dusty outskirts of the low-built, mud-brick town.

The people of Abydos knelt down for us as we passed, pressing their hands and their foreheads to the dusty street. Everywhere, there were saucer-eyed cats.

"What a strange number of cats there are," I said to Enki. "And with such strange eyes. Does this not all feel very strange to you? And if this is your terrible daughter, where is your terrible son?"

"I suppose we'll find out," said Enki, his jaw set hard.

We passed numerous half-erected temples and grand-looking houses. The workers stopped work and knelt as we went past. Abydos, it seemed, was on the rise.

The Osirion, when we reached it, looked to be a more humble affair. It was a mud-brick building, low and rectangular, set upon a simple brick platform. Yet the doorway to the temple was framed in a heavy, rose-coloured granite.

The float was set down, the goddess helped out, courtiers rushing to keep her red skirts from the dust. As we followed Isis up the steps to the temple, I said to Enki, very quiet: "This all feels quite odd to me."

In the doorway to the temple, Isis turned to look down on us.

She was beautiful close up, even with her features so heavily obscured with paint. She had silky brown skin with a hint of bronze to it, the blackest hair, and eyes that glittered tortoiseshell.

"Welcome to the Osirion," she said.

We turned to find that the priests had surrounded the base of the temple: a three-deep row of white. Behind them, stood the soldiers, three rows deep, and behind them, the men on camels.

If you were a suspicious type, if you were Harga, just for example, you might have thought: *We are surrounded.*

Isis showed us her white teeth and very beautiful smile. "I must insist on you coming inside," she said.

We ducked our heads down beneath the rose granite lintel as we passed into the dark of the temple.

It smelled as if something had died in there.

There were no windows and only a few firebowls arranged around the place. But as my eyes got used to the gloom, I realised the walls of the temple were already lined with more white-robed priests. Isis took a seat on a wooden throne in the centre of the room.

Behind her, rearing over her, was a huge stone statue, very ancient in appearance, of what looked like a dragon from the temple stories. A dragon with seven heads, its eyes set with blue gems.

To the right of this statue, in deep shadow, lay a group of small boys, bound and gagged.

Userkaf was there amongst them. His bright eyes met mine.

A shard of icy anger passed through me. "What are you doing with these boys?" I said to the goddess.

Isis lifted her nose at me. "These are my humans, not yours. What does it have to do with you?"

"Why are they here?" I said.

"They should not have helped you get here," Isis said. "Everyone who has helped you will die for it. That is how the people learn."

"You will not harm these children," I said, my fists clenched. Enki stepped forward then, to stand between me and his daughter.

"Isis, perhaps we could start afresh," he said.

"Let the children go," I said, stepping forward.

"I will do just as I please," said Isis. Again, a flash of her very white teeth. "Do not pass out orders to me, cousin."

"You will not hurt them," I said.

It was then I noticed, behind the statue, a heavily carved stone doorway at the back of the temple.

Isis followed my gaze. "Yes, the very old place is down there. You can both kneel down before me now."

I glanced at Enki.

"Why should we kneel, daughter?" he said.

"Perhaps then I will let one of the children live."

I at once knelt, my bad knee blazing into agony. After a moment's pause, Enki knelt down next to me, holding the lions tight to him. "This doesn't seem very polite, daughter."

Isis smiled down at us. "There's going to be a ceremony now. These priests will cut up these little boys, one by one, and feed their blood to Tiamat. There is nothing you can do to stop them. We are used to people struggling here."

Enki took a deep breath in. "Daughter, may I explain why we are here? I have news that affects us all."

"Why should I listen to anything you have to say, after what you did to me?"

"That was all a long time ago," Enki said. "The Anunnaki wanted you dead. I let you and Osiris live."

"You let him prey on me!" she shouted. "You let my brother despoil me. Ruin me. You should not have let him take me!" Her face crumpled with upset.

I looked from her to Enki.

"I thought you wanted to go with him," Enki said. He tipped his head to the side. "Come back with me now, if you are unhappy."

It seemed a strangely cold response, in the face of her raw upset.

"It's too late now," she said. "I have no one else now. Because of what you did."

"I am…" said Enki. He seemed unable to complete his sentence. "Perhaps I was wrong not to have separated you."

"You were very wrong," said Isis. "And now I am going to have my revenge. When these boys are dead, you and my so-called cousin here are going to be cut and your blood fed to the goddess, too. And to be sure that you can never be resurrected, Enki, every priest here, and me also, is going to eat one very small piece of your flesh. Today is your last day on Earth, Father."

"That seems extreme," said Enki.

"It does seem extreme," I put in, very earnest.

Enki lifted up his hands to his daughter. "Isis, we fear that Tiamat may be moving against us. All of us should be concerned by that. Let us talk it over with you."

"Whatever Tiamat plans, she has my support," said Isis. "Now bring forward that one," she said to her priests. She was pointing at Userkaf. "He will be the first to die today."

CHAPTER 18

NINLIL

In Heaven

On Petition Day, which came once in every turn of the Wheel of Heaven, I knelt with the petitioners in the throne room. By rights it was my mother's throne room, but for a long time the ordinary work of the court had been left to my bull-horned brother.

It had once been a fine room but now the huge windows onto the garden were blocked with stone and the floor was filthy with trodden-in mud and snow. Qingu sat on the central throne with our decaying father, in his rusting chair, alongside him. He conducted his business in a brisk if irritated fashion.

I knelt along the back wall amongst noblewomen who had had their children taken from them by foul husbands, and mothers who had already lost a child to the dragon queen, and had now had another marked down for sacrifice, even though the rule was that you only lost one. Amongst the desperate poor and the desperate rich.

"I am too busy for petitioners today," Qingu said, looking

over at us. He waved us away with one hand. "I have urgent work that must be done. Can someone not move these people on?" He looked over to his guards. "Clear them out."

"Petition Day is sacred," I called, from my place along the wall.

Qingu climbed down from the throne and came to stand in front of me. "It is embarrassing to see you on your knees, sister. Where is your pride?"

"I don't think you are embarrassed," I said. "And I have never been proud."

He laughed. "I suppose not."

"I am heir to the throne, as you keep reminding me, and I come to the court in petition on Petition Day. That is a sacred thing." I had my hands clasped before me as I spoke, raised to him in supplication. All the other petitioners lifted their hands to him, in copy of me.

"Qingu, just let me see my son. Just let me see him once."

He scowled and shook his head. "Kneel there, what do I care? But I don't have time for you. I'm not sure you understand what's happening here, sister."

"I understand that you are planning to invade Earth. Everyone here knows what is happening."

He made a scoffing noise. "That is a strange way of looking at it, Ninlil. As an invasion. Our world here is collapsing. Very soon, everyone here is going to die. So we are going to flee." He looked over at the queue of courtiers in front of his throne. "We are going to flee to a world that by all accounts is well suited to us all. One of those accounts being from your own son and one of those accounts being from you."

"We are too many. We will destroy the realm of light."

"The realm of light and its survival are not my priority," he said. "You may care nothing for the people of this realm, but I do, and we are going to pass over in an orderly and peaceful manner to the Earth, as you call it. All of which involves a great deal of work. So you kneel there, snivelling about your son, and all you others," he waved his hand over the other petitioners, "you keep kneeling and snivelling about whatever you are snivelling about, and I will get on with saving the good citizens of Heaven."

He returned to his throne and waved a nobleman over to him from the queue there. "About the camps," the man said, coming forward.

At dinner that night, while we waited for our mother to arrive, I said to Qingu: "Brother, why is she a dragon?"

"Our mother?" he said, pouring himself more wine.

"Who else can I possibly mean?"

"I think it makes it easier to spawn the Sebitti." He shrugged. "It certainly keeps the nobility in line." He drank down his wine.

"And why is the world dying?"

"So many questions!" He threw his hands out in a wide circle. "It's wobbling," he said, moving his hands back and forth. "The Wheel we live on is stretched out in a great loop around the Star of Creation. It cannot start wobbling without terrible things following."

"Brother, this I do know."

"Perhaps you've noticed the weather, sister?"

"I've noticed."

"In just two turns of the Wheel, all the trees here have died. The structure of the world is breaking down."

"What I meant, Brother Bull, is to ask you for the reason for this wobble. We were told the old gods built this realm to last forever. What has gone wrong?"

He poured himself more wine and lowered his voice: "Of course everyone blames us for our lack of moderation. It takes vast amounts of power to keep the Wheel in position and they say we have been immoderate." He cast eyes over to our mother's place at the table. "They know she has direct access to the central power reserves. They say she has stripped them with her endless wars and extravagances." He slugged back his wine. "I can't see how we could have caused it all ourselves. I think it's Heaven's turn to die, that's all. The families on the far side of the Wheel have already gone through the gates to who knows where. The people of this world are scattering across the realms."

He pulled up his right sleeve and showed me the dark grey metal bracelet there. "Recognise this?"

"My son was wearing it when we reunited."

"Did he tell you what it was?"

"He told me it was a key."

"I would call it a navigation device." He pulled his sleeve down again. "Passing between realms can be very difficult without one of these. You can get trapped between realms and die there. The other families will suffer because of it, but we have this."

"When I first saw that navigation device, it had a gold casing over it and Enlil was wearing it. He called it the master *mee*."

My brother was only silent for a moment. "He stole it."

"We both know that's not true, brother. I have some of his memories now. I honoured him after his death by eating what I could of his corpse."

He waved a hand at me. "Nothing you say can be trusted," he said. "You went with the man willingly, by your own account. You stayed there with him for thousands of turns of the Wheel.

Willingly, by your account. You left your son here and made no attempt to return to him. You are suspect, Ninlil. You might as well drop that old story of how I gave you away to the Anunnaki, because the truth is that you have become an Anunnaki." He went silent then as the great doors began creaking open.

"Please let me see my son," I said.

He bared his sharpened teeth at me. "I never will."

"I have told her what you did," I said. "I will keep on telling her, until she truly understands."

The Bull of Heaven tipped his horns at me and dropped his voice to a whisper. "Sister, I do not think she will care," he said.

CHAPTER 19

ERESHKIGAL

Lost

One moment I was in the space in the roof of the Kur with Dumuzi and Geshtinanna beside me. The next moment bright light enveloped me and I felt that my bloated belly was gone; that the flesh of my abdomen was taut and flat. I felt a sensation of falling and at the same time being lifted up.

A moment later I was lying on my side in absolute darkness. I breathed through my terror as I tried to understand what was happening. It was cold and damp and I was lying on what felt like rock. I tried to raise my head and hit my skull on more rock.

Carefully, I felt around me in the blackness. I seemed to be in a narrow space barely high enough for me to turn over in with my guts as they were.

"Dumuzi?" I whispered. "Geshtinanna?"

No reply came.

It was as if I was in some sort of cave. I could not tell if I was in Heaven or still upon the Earth.

My *mees*! I had always worried so much about wasting their

power, but who could accuse me of being wasteful in such desperate circumstances?

I closed my eyes tight and focused on the feel of them, the little tickles and traces, and my right wrist burst into a blaze of white light.

Yes. I did seem to be in a cave.

"Dumuzi?" I whispered again, in case he was hiding in the shadows somewhere. "Geshtinanna?"

I could hear nothing except the dripping of water.

I looked past my feet and the cave seemed to continue in that direction. Eventually I managed to twist myself around upon the rock so I could crawl forward.

For a while the ceiling of the cavern grew lower and I was frightened I was going the wrong way. I kept crawling, sometimes crying out with the fear and discomfort, and finally the cavern grew a little larger around me.

Was there light ahead? Could I smell incense?

Yes! I scrambled forward as fast as I could manage on my hands and knees, and found myself on a lip of rock, looking down on some sort of flooded temple. Everything was carved out of a rose-pink sort of granite. The altar, sat upon an island in the centre of a rectangular lake, was lit up by candles.

I let the light from my *mee* fade away; there was no point in wasting it.

It was quite a climb down to the lake and there was water directly below me. I could not tell how deep it was, but it was oily, black, and frightening. I wriggled forward to get a better view of the whole room. At the far end, to my left, stone steps led up from the water to a doorway. Perhaps I could climb down, cross the water over to the altar, and then cross the water again to climb up the steps.

I lay there on my shelf of rock, trembling. I was frightened of trying to get down and frightened of what lay beyond that door, even if I could reach it, but I could not stay where I was.

In the end I took off my woollen slippers and set them aside. I would need all the purchase I could get. Very slowly and with great awkwardness, I turned myself around and began to edge myself off the rocky ledge and downwards.

At last, I put one foot down into the cold water and to my surprise, it immediately hit stone. Smooth stone: a ledge. I put my other foot down and stood, only ankle deep in the black water, and very relieved.

I slowly turned around to stand with my back to the stone slab wall. Could I swim across to the island?

Well, there was nothing for it. I put my left foot out and began to lower it deeper into the black water, further and further. Such bravery! I still could not feel the bottom. And then I slipped.

I might have hurt myself very badly. Instead, I found myself standing, very shocked, my arms flailing, up to my bloated waist in water. With flat stone beneath my feet.

The water was only waist deep!

If the water stayed this shallow, I would not need to climb onto the island. Instead, I could simply make my way around the moat to the steps that led up to the door. It was cold, but I could do it. How slowly I walked though, creeping forward, one questing foot at a time. Always thinking I might suddenly plunge into deeper water.

At last I was climbing up onto the steps.

The doorway was covered with the same marks as the Kur used. Some of them meant something like "walk gentle here".

Of course, I had only walked gently my whole life, so such warnings did not concern me.

I pressed my hand on the ancient stone door.

Nothing happened.

I pushed: nothing. I tried to slide it aside... yes! Slowly, slowly, I slid it over to the left and it disappeared into a slit in the rock.

Ahead lay a narrow tunnel. Its blush-pink walls had candles set into them and the corridor climbed upwards before disappearing to the right.

So, up I climbed. Every few cords, I would stop and breathe heavily. The smell of incense grew stronger and stronger.

Ahead: a flight of huge stone steps. I was shaking with exhaustion by the time I was finally at the top.

There I found another doorway. It was covered in ordinary Anunnaki markings and I traced the faint shapes and whispered them out loud as I read: "All praise the goddess Tiamat, Queen of Creation."

Anunnaki language. If I was in Heaven, I must be on Anunnaki land.

The door at the top of the stairs had a hole in it, and when I pulled it... the door slid open.

I peered through.

Gloom. Heavy incense. Priests in strange pointed hats.

There was a huge statue ahead of me, silhouetted against a bright doorway. A statue with seven heads growing out of it on snaking necks. To my right and left, there were bronze firebowls full of embers. How hot it was!

I lit up my protective shield, blasting away the dim shadows, and I felt for my combat *mees*, the ones I had found deep inside the Kur. They still had power in them.

And so, sheathed in white light, I walked out into the temple, my hands on my belly.

There was a disgusting smell, like an animal had died and been left to rot.

Creeping forward, half-blinded by the sunlight from the entrance, I held one hand over my mouth and nose.

Even half-blinded, I immediately recognised my grandfather Enki. He was kneeling in front of a throne and holding two lions. There was a young man beside him, also kneeling.

"Ereshkigal?" my grandfather said, in what sounded like astonishment. The lions bared their fangs at me.

Without pausing to take in the rest of the scene, I blasted my grandfather with one of my combat *mees*. With some satisfaction, I watched him keel over onto the floor, pulling the lions down with him.

Priests rushed forward towards me, but thought better of it. Then I realised there was someone sat on the throne. A woman, dimly familiar to me, in some fine red cloth. I frowned at her.

It was so hot!

I looked back at Enki's companion. He was very beautiful and I found myself breaking into a smile for him.

I looked around further and saw, along one wall, some small boys, all trussed up.

The hard truth dawned on me, in that sweltering room. I was not in Heaven. I was on Earth. I was in some second-rate temple somewhere.

"How very disappointing," I said.

CHAPTER 20

INANNA

In Heaven

Amnut stood over me, her brilliant blue eyes fixed on mine, her black hair falling straight as rain around her face.

I was lying flat on my back and there was something pressing down hard on my ribs; I could not move, not even to look at what was holding me down.

"Amnut," I whispered. "Help me."

For a moment Amnut was no longer Amnut. There was a man standing over me. A man with two huge horns growing out of his head.

His eyes were a brilliant blue. "Answer the question more fully or I am going to keep hurting you," he said.

The pain was too great to bear.

I stood with my palms pressed against a cold stone wall. The air was cool upon my face.

Oh, my ribs were hurting. I looked down and realised that

I was naked. There were small dark marks all over my body: bruises in the shape of fingerprints. I had some kind of band around my throat; a thick bar of metal, perfectly circular. I could not work out how to get it off.

I turned, panic rising in me. A woman was there; a woman in a gold-scaled coat. She was standing with her back to a heavy wooden door. What was happening?

Oh, I knew her! I knew the woman.

Bizilla.

My heart calmed. I could breathe.

I looked around the small windowless stone-walled room we both stood in. There was a bed along one wall, with a candle burning next to it. Was the bed my bed? There was a grey blanket upon it.

"Bizilla," I said. "What is this place?"

She spoke over me, her voice just a little raised. "Oh, for all of Creation, Inanna, just get back into bed."

I kept my face plain, like a dove. She had called me by a name: *Inanna*.

"I am sorry to anger you, Bizilla," I said. I made my way over to the bed. Everything hurt and I was cold. But somewhere deep inside me, a small flame had been lit.

I had dreamed of a tall woman with a bow over her shoulder. She had shouted out a name to me: *Inanna*.

I hugged the knowledge to myself as I sat down on the bed and pulled the blanket around me. *My name is Inanna.*

Bizilla let out a sigh. "I'm not angry with you. You've done nothing wrong."

"Am I dreaming, Bizilla?" My voice felt false to me now, with my secret knowledge burning in me.

"No," she said. "It would be better if you were."

I lay down then, pain spreading across my back, and pulled the blanket up over me. "Why do I hurt?"

She shook her head, her cheek turned from me.

I pulled the blanket up higher around my neck and again felt the metal collar around it. "I don't know what is happening, but I know you."

Bizilla was so familiar to me. Had I once met a boy who looked very similar to her?

"I think I have met someone who looked like you," I said.

"So you say."

"He had a dog," I said. "With huge jaws."

"Now you are dreaming," she said.

I kept looking at her. Something had come back to me.

"We called him the Potta," I said.

"Who is we?"

I went very still. Yes, who was we?

"I don't know."

The pinprick of flame inside me grew brighter.

My name is Inanna. The boy's name was the Potta.

I shut my eyes, and let my breathing grow shallow.

Inanna.

After a long while, I heard Bizilla pulling at the door and swearing beneath her breath in some language I did not recognise. Then came the sound of the door opening and closing again.

The small light inside me flared upwards.

It lit up the dark plain on which I had been stumbling. In the distance, for a moment, I saw the tall figure of that lone woman, a spear in one hand, an axe in the other. "Inanna," she said. A familiar face. But then she was gone again.

Then the truth flooded through me.

My name was Inanna.

Ninshubar was dead. I put my hand over my mouth, to stop myself making a noise.

I remembered An, the king of the Anunnaki, leaning over me when I was only a baby, and whispering to me: *Love and war... do not forget the second part.*

I remembered Gilgamesh leaning down to kiss me for the first time when we lay together in temple.

I remembered Ninshubar lying dead on the grass beside the river. My blazing, all-consuming grief and rage. I remembered the eighth gate and the great claws reaching out for me. Was I in Heaven now?

"I am Inanna," I whispered out loud, wiping at my tears.

A violent burst of white light and two spectral figures appeared before me. Two men, drawn of black light, but one with hints of blue to him. The shadowmen wore long robes, their hoods drawn low over their ghostly faces.

The blue shadowman smiled at the black shadowman. "Brother, she has awoken," he said. He turned to look down on me.

"Hello, Inanna," he said, very quiet. "Do you remember us?"

"Kurgurrah!" I said to him. "Galatur!" I said to his black shadowman brother.

They were my grandfather Enki's so-called flies. Except of course they were not flies; they were ancient beings or something perhaps more mysterious. At times they took the form of small black flying things, and I remembered opening my mouth to let them in, perhaps a long time ago on the banks of the Euphrates, but perhaps only moments ago.

Kurgurrah, the blue shadowman, knelt before me with one long finger lifted to his translucent mouth. "My lady, do not speak out loud, even in a whisper. Only think your thoughts and we will hear you. The Anzu must not know we are here with you and they must not know you have remembered who you are."

Had he been made of flesh I would have gathered him into my arms and kissed him. But instead, trying to make each word very clear in my mind as I traced it out, I thought at him: "You cannot know what it means to have you here with me."

"You cannot know how relieved we are that you have come to your senses," said Galatur.

"How long have I been here?"

"About seven moons, as you measure it in the realm of light," said Galatur.

"We have been dancing around you and trying every trick possible to make you aware of us," said Kurgurrah.

"But to no avail," said Galatur.

I hugged my arms around my aching ribs. "Ninshubar kept saying my name. In my dreams. Then Bizilla said my name and it unlocked something. Am I in Heaven?"

"You are indeed in Heaven," said Kurgurrah. "Birthplace of your whole family."

"You are in Queen Tiamat's castle, at the heart of the Anzu lands," said Galatur. "They call this place Creation."

I had to remind myself not to speak out loud. "I must go home. I should not be here."

Kurgurrah stood up. Together they took a step back from my bed and bowed their heads.

"My lady," said Kurgurrah. "There is nothing we can do to help you while you wear that metal around your neck."

I put both my hands to it. "What is it?"

"They call that band 'the bolt'," said Kurgurrah. "It is designed to contain even the most powerful amongst us."

"Because it is around your neck, it contains you," said Galatur.

"And because we were inside you when they put it on you, it also contains us."

"It anchors us all to this place," said Kurgurrah. "We cannot remove you from this realm with the bolt around your neck."

"You need to get that band off," said Galatur. "You need to convince someone to take it off you."

I nodded, my mind ablaze with all the questions I had. "Why does Bizilla look like Ninshubar's son?" I said.

"They are both Sebitti," said Kurgurrah. "Soldiers of Creation. Born of Tiamat and unable to raise a hand against her."

There was noise at the door and the flies disappeared.

Bizilla pushed her way into the room, her gold-scaled coat gleaming in the light thrown in from the hallway. She pushed the door firm shut behind her before coming over and pouring me a little medicine.

"Thank you, Bizilla," I said. I did not know what else to do except to sip it down: it tasted of vanilla. "What is happening to me, Bizilla? Can you tell me?"

"Just go to sleep," she said.

She blew out the big candle and then in the pitch dark went over to the door. I heard it open and close, and her fiddling with the locks on the outside of it.

The two bright sparks at once danced before me, one black, the other blue. "We are here with you now, Inanna," the blue spark said. "Have strength now, my lady."

And then the black spark said: "But we need the bolt off you and quickly."

I remembered in time not to say my words out loud. "What is the hurry?"

"Oh, Inanna," said Kurgurrah. "You are dying. Can you not tell?"

"I have died before," I said. It was my intention to be funny. But the two sparks dipped low as the words formed in my mind.

The blue spark, Kurgurrah, said: "If you die in this place, you will be forever dead. From this place there can be no resurrections. You would already be dead if it were not for that medicine they are giving you."

I said: "What is it to you if I live or die?"

"Things are in motion now," Kurgurrah said. "This is the part we have to play."

"I am full of sleep," I said. "We must talk more when I awake."

"They are keeping you unconscious," Kurgurrah said. "There is a sleeping draught mixed in with that medicine."

But I was already slipping under.

CHAPTER 21

HARGA

In the marshes north of Eridu

I insisted on a morning patrol around the Refuge so that I could see for myself that all the lookouts were in place. I travelled with the three dogs clumped up between my outstretched legs, although I was the only one who had not wanted to bring them. The Uruk boys were up front as ever and Marduk sat behind me with his paddle across his lap.

My shoulder was sore and I felt tired to the bone. Every fight took more out of me.

"You are always so sunk in your thoughts, Harga," said Marduk. "Why not look about you, lift your head?"

In the front of the canoe, the two Uruk boys widened their eyes at each other.

"Look about me?" I said. I tried to scowl at him, over my right shoulder, but it was too painful to turn, so I shifted around to scowl at him over my left.

Marduk seemed impervious to hard looks. He waved long fingers at the drab and unchanging vista of reeds, fetid water, and featureless turquoise sky. "Look at where we are! The wonder of it. But you are sunk in your thoughts, too sunk to look about you. You are always worrying for us all, worrying for the Refuge, worrying about spies."

"I would be a child if I did not worry."

"But we have doubled the lookouts and we have our evacuation plan. All approved by you. If anything happens the marshmen will come to whisk us away into the reeds. They will bring hundreds of boats. All is agreed. Sworn in Anunnaki and marshman blood."

"All the same, I do not like it." I turned back to face the front of the canoe.

"But it is such a beautiful place," Marduk said. "No signs of the gods' work upon it. No fields, no canals, no disfiguring cities, and all of this wilderness thronging, bursting, with wild creatures. I wish you could take pleasure from it, breathe it in."

I brought my right hand down hard on a mosquito. "That's one less wild creature," I said. But then I looked back at Marduk's luminous face and I remembered that he was alone in the world, except for me and the Uruk boys.

"I should look about me more, Marduk." I attempted something of a smile. "I will try to find the good things in this terrible place."

Marduk laughed. "I love it here. Of course, it is very different from the country that I grew up in, but there is the same simplicity to it. I had not realised how much I was missing the wild spaces when I was forced to be a city creature."

"I've grown to appreciate cities," I said. "I've grown to appreciate four walls and a tiled roof that doesn't let the rain in." The sky, a moment ago so bland and blue, was clouding over quickly.

"Perhaps cities are better if you are a free man," Marduk said. "I have only been a slave in them. First in Abydos and then in Kish."

I felt a spot of rain on my forehead. A moment later it began to pour down. Huge warm droplets of good clean water. All of us threw our heads back, even the dogs, and we let the water wash our faces and fall into our open mouths.

"I can taste my own sweat," said Tallboy, laughing.

"I do like it when it's like this," I said. The marsh water, so black and oily a moment ago, was now a flattened, beaten grey beneath the hard and steady rain. All the heat had gone out of the day and for once the air tasted clean and fresh. "Yes, this I like," I said, turning my face back up to the luscious rain.

Tallboy whistled and threw a hand into the air with his forefinger raised. There was something ahead on the water.

Moshkhussu growled and the fur rose up on her neck.

The rain died and there ahead of us, in the middle of the waterway, was a canoe with a small black-wrapped figure in it.

It was a marshwoman, an old woman, apparently all alone on the water. She raised a flat palm to us and we each raised a palm to her in reply.

As she lowered her hand, the sky cleared, the clouds furling and lifting. She at once produced a paddle and in four or five expert strokes drew up alongside us, turning neatly to match us side on. A baby goat put its face over the side of the old woman's boat and peered at the dogs in alarm. It looked wet and rather sad.

I had had a pebble out in my hand, ready to use it, but tucked it back into my pouch, and instead concerned myself with the dogs, lest they get any ideas about the baby goat.

The old woman pointed her chin at the little grey goat. "A gift," she said. "For the old lady."

There was some silence then, if one ignored the background

barrage of frog song, as all of us absorbed her words, and the meaning of the small goat, and who she must mean by the old lady.

"This goat is for the priestess Lilith?" I said.

The old woman frowned and shook her head. "I mean the ancient one," she said. "Who you call a moon goddess."

"We would be honoured to take you back to our island, if that is what you are asking us to do," I said. "Will you follow us?"

The old woman made a snorting noise. "My name is Sagar and I was born on the Refuge. I will show you the quick way back."

With two short strokes she paddled her way clear of us and set off in a firm line towards a bank of reeds.

"I suppose we follow her then," I said, with a look at Marduk.

He frowned after the marshwoman. "I think she knows something," he said. He plunged his long steering paddle overboard, to turn us after her canoe.

"About Ninshubar?" I said.

"Maybe," he said, without looking at me. The Uruk boys, after a glance at me, plunged their poles into the water.

"How can you know that?" I said to Marduk, but he did not answer me.

I fished out my own paddle from beneath the dogs, and dipped it over to the right, and to the left, building the power of it and ignoring the pain in my shoulder. At least the air was cooler after the rainstorm.

The Uruk boys turned in some surprise when they felt the canoe accelerate.

"Watch how I move my paddle from side to side," I said to them. "And try to copy me. You have both been getting water in the boat."

The lookouts did their work and by the time the marshwoman, Sagar, stepped out onto the wooden jetty at the Refuge, the priestess Lilith was already standing waiting with Ningal, the moon goddess, beside her.

The marshwoman stepped out neatly from her canoe and looped a small rope around a wooden post. She and Ningal regarded each other for some time in silence, each with their hands on their hips.

"Should I know you?" said the moon goddess.

"You will know me now," the old woman said. "This goat is for you." She bowed deep to the goddess. "I saw you once in Eridu," she added. "When you came for the wedding of your daughter."

We all gathered for the visitor ceremony in the hut we called the Palace.

The marshwoman sat at one end of Enki's fine rug, her baby goat in her lap.

I sat at the other end of the rug, with Marduk, Lilith, and the moon goddess cross-legged beside me. The two Uruk boys stood guard at the entrance to the reed hall and

Isimud, Enki's wraith-like *sukkal*, stood against one wall, his hands behind his back. He did not drop his soldier pose even for one minute. But that was Isimud.

The marshwoman sipped at her tea, made from the dried leaves of healing marsh herbs. The baby goat was complimented by the moon goddess, as custom dictated. But then the traditional tea ceremony, with its long pauses and very, very small talk, was cut mercifully short.

"I have drunk enough tea now," the marshwoman said. "I am glad to see people living here again. Also, I am glad that you accept the goat and that now we are hearth friends."

Marduk leaned forward, his hands clasped. "My lady Sagar, I am wondering if you bring news of my mother, Ninshubar?"

"The *sukkal*?" said the marshwoman.

"She is *sukkal* to Inanna, yes," said Marduk.

The marshwoman paused only for a moment before speaking. "Ninshubar was buried in the war graves at Ur," she said. "Stripped of her Anunnaki weapons and thrown into a huge pit with all the other war dead."

None of us spoke in reply.

I kept my hands on my knees and my face still. Nothing had changed. Ninshubar was dead; nothing had changed. But perhaps I had let some small piece of hope creep into my heart, because Marduk had been so certain that we would find her.

It is the hope that kills you.

The marshwoman sipped more tea, her eyes on Marduk. "I met her once, this Ninshubar you speak of. She was strong. She would have done well here in the marshes."

Marduk folded his hands in his lap. "You are certain she is dead?"

"She was recognised," said the marshwoman. "Hundreds went into those pits, and she was amongst them."

"I don't know how you can be sure," he said, lifting his chin.

The marshwoman turned to face the moon goddess. "That is not the news I came to bring you." She bowed her head down, before lifting it again to speak. "I bring news I cannot be proud to bring to you. News that shames me."

We waited in silence.

"My people have betrayed you," she said.

CHAPTER 22

NINSHUBAR

Lost

For a time that I thought would never end, I was not much more than an animal streak of fear. I was in darkness and I was afraid.

Later, I do not know how much later, a sense of self began to return to me. With it came the idea that I was something separate from the solid blackness around me. That I was somehow inside something.

Time passed in the darkness. Perhaps it was days, perhaps weeks, perhaps moons.

Later, I began to understand that I was trapped. That I could not breathe or move or see. Then I was so terrified that I thought I would die of fright.

Later, the pain came. A full-body pain, every nerve in me screaming murder, but the worst pain was in my neck. There I felt a searing, obliterating agony.

For a long time, I was only my pain, but at some point I began to feel new sensations; feelings that gave texture to my pain. My mouth was full of something. Was it mud?

Yes, perhaps my mouth was full of mud, and the mud was full of sharp fragments. I began to imagine that I could taste something rotting in the mud inside my mouth. When I began to retch, I understood that my lungs were also full of the foul and scratching mud.

Oh, the terror I felt then.

Memories began to form.

I had been free, on a grass plain. I had stood, breathing easy, beneath a yellow sun. I remembered cool, sweet air.

Then again came the pain, the bludgeoning, scraping pain, pressing the memories out of me.

A long time later, perhaps days, perhaps weeks, perhaps many moons, I remembered the man in red, looking down on me.

I remembered his words to me. *You are digging the wrong way.*

That was when I understood that I was buried. I was alive, yes. But I was trapped deep beneath the earth, unable to move, unable to help myself.

And I could not tell which way was up.

In the absolute blackness, in the solid, cloying, thick sludge in which I was held, everything might have been down, and everything might have been up.

I became aware that sometimes I was awake and sometimes I was asleep. When I slept, I dreamed of standing on the sea floor, my feet on white sand. I looked up and saw the silver glint of the surface of the ocean, but when I began to swim towards it I found myself upside down, my hand meeting sand. And then true panic would rise up in me, and I would wake, still unable to breathe or move.

If panic could have killed anyone, then I can tell you, I would surely have died.

Which way was up? I could not tell.

Hours passed, or perhaps days, or weeks, or even many moons. I was trapped, panicking, desperate to breathe yet unable, and I could not tell which way was up.

Later the exact words came to me, intensifying my pain, ratcheting up my panic.

Buried alive.

I was buried alive.

I knew I could not last much longer.

PART 2

"If you do not send that god to me,
I shall raise up the dead and they will eat the living.
I will make the dead outnumber the living!"

From the ancient Mesopotamian
poem known as "Nergal and Ereshkigal",
as translated by Stephanie Dalley

CHAPTER 1

INANNA

In Heaven

I woke to candlelight, in my stone-block prison cell. Bizilla was gone, but I could hear muffled voices outside the door.

The two shadowmen flickered into existence, their heads bowed, their eyes on me.

"Are you still yourself, Inanna?" said Kurgurrah.

I sat up, groaning out loud; everything hurt. I was naked and I pulled my thin blanket up around me. "I hurt," I said.

"Only in your mind," Kurgurrah said. "Speak to us only in your mind."

"Oh, I am sorry," I said, careful not to speak aloud.

It was at that moment that I remembered my lions.

"My lionesses," I said to the shadowmen. "I left them near the Kur. I abandoned them. They have never been on their own before."

"They can hunt," said Galatur. "Your lions will prevail."

Another memory came back to me, twisting, nauseatingly,

inside me. "I killed my brother Utu," I said, thinking out each word. "I did it as if it was nothing."

"He betrayed your family," said Kurgurrah. "He kidnapped the lady Ninlil and delivered her to the Kur."

"I did it unthinkingly," I said.

Why did I do it?

I had been crazed with grief. Was that it? But it was not the grief I remembered. It was the feeling of the power flooding through me; of the power being part of me and how invulnerable I was.

Then the memory returned: Ninshubar was dead.

The grief knifed through me.

"Brother, she is very weak," said Galatur.

I tried to steady my breathing. "I am quite well."

"They have had you unconscious for a long while," said Galatur.

I pulled my blanket down so I could look at my breasts, belly, and thighs. I was covered in small bruises. I looked up at the hooded figures standing over me.

"Do you know what they are doing to me?" I said.

"When you are unconscious, we are unconscious," said Galatur. "But you can see there the marks of their hands, pressed into your flesh. They do not go at their work gently."

"They are trying to discover where your power comes from," Kurgurrah said. "They want to know what you can do and why you can do it."

I smiled at them. "I wish I knew."

Kurgurrah frowned at me beneath his hood. "You have been using the power that binds your realm. The power that keeps the wind blowing and the wolves hunting. It is the power that exists to protect your world from destruction. To keep it the sanctuary that it is."

"There was just such a pool of power here in Heaven," said Galatur, "but Tiamat has drunk too long and deep and now this realm is failing."

"I did not knowingly reach for the power," I said. "When those I loved were in trouble, I found it there before me."

"It was the same with Tiamat in the first days," said Kurgurrah. "But you should know that you have drunk from a well that was not meant to be drunk from. Or not by someone like you. You risk losing yourself if you continue."

"What does that mean?"

"That you will lose your humanity," he said. "Your compassion. Your love. You will kill again…"

There was a noise outside the door, as if someone had dropped something.

"You must give no sign to Bizilla that you have remembered yourself," said Galatur.

The shadowmen disappeared.

Bizilla pushed the door open with her right shoulder. She had a bowl in one hand and a cup in another; the smell of hot porridge reached me.

"Sitting up already," she said.

She put the bowl into my hands and the cup down next to the candle. "I forgot your medicine." With a heave and a bang behind her, she was gone again.

The shadowmen at once appeared.

"So, they are torturing me to find out about my power," I said, only thinking the words. "But we don't know what questions they are asking. We don't know where they are doing it or how."

The porridge was bland, but I forced it down.

"Why don't I remember it?" I said. "They must wake me up to torture me, otherwise how can I answer their questions?"

The two shadowmen looked down on me, sombre. "We don't know," said Galatur.

"Perhaps they take the bolt off me when I am tortured," I said.

"We don't know," said Kurgurrah.

"I think that if I keep taking the medicine, there will be no end to this," I said. "No end except my death."

A noise at the door and the shadowmen, solemn, flickered out of existence.

Bizilla entered my cell, holding the glass bottle of medicine.

"Bizilla, what is happening?" I said. "Where is this?" I tried to make my voice very natural.

She seemed not to notice any difference in me as she sat down on the bed and opened the bottle. "This will help you feel calmer." She took my porridge bowl from me and passed me a bottle-lid full of liquid.

She looked down at the bottle just for a moment and I tipped the medicine into the blanket beneath my chin. "Vanilla," I said.

"Is it?" she said, taking the lid back from me. "This was especially mixed up for you."

She gave me back my porridge and waited until I had finished it. Then she stood, and paused, looking down at me. "Get some sleep," she said. "It's better you sleep."

She blew out the candle and then in the pitch dark, she left the room, wrenching at the door.

Kurgurrah and Galatur appeared, casting their spectral light around my prison cell.

"What now?" I said.

"Now we wait," said Kurgurrah.

CHAPTER 2

NINLIL

In Heaven

I had given up hope of ever being allowed to see my son, when one evening the locks rattled and Bizilla was in my bedchamber, a candle held aloft. "I'm here to take you to Nergal," she said.

I pushed back my furs and swung myself from my bed. "Now?"

"We will have to go outside to get round to him. You need to wrap up."

I pulled on my fur-lined boots and my white fur cloak, almost falling over in my hurry. "I'm ready."

We turned left out of the door to find a Sebitti standing ahead, holding up a torch. He nodded to us and stepped aside.

I followed Bizilla down cold stone corridors at a pace that was almost a jog and then with no warning a door opened up ahead of us onto the night, letting in a blast of snow and freezing wind. Another Sebitti held the door for us, a torch raised to the swirling snowflakes.

The night sky; the snow: everything was stained a ghastly pink. Ahead, through the heavy icescape, I saw the blaze of something that looked like molten lava, great clouds of steam rising up into the snowstorm. "What is that?" I said.

"A new volcano," said Bizilla. "Lava is coming up everywhere. Come, Ninlil, we must hurry."

We bent our heads against the wind as we hurried through the knee-deep snow, keeping the dark towers of the palace to our left and the river of burning lava to our right. Bizilla seemed immune to the frozen night, but within moments I was so cold that I had to channel all my healing energy into my ears and cheeks.

In the distance, through the blizzard, lay a tented camp with fires burning between the shelters. "What is that?" I said, raising my voice to be heard over the wind.

"Refugees," Bizilla shouted.

I caught, ahead of us, the glimpse of gold scales; another Sebitti, waving to us from a doorway. Moments later we were back inside the palace and out of the clawing storm. Bizilla knocked the snow from her boots and clasped the shoulder of the waiting Sebitti.

"It's all clear ahead," the man said to her.

We hurried down a flag-stoned corridor and up a short set of stairs to a heavy wooden door. Bizilla pushed her way through and suddenly we were surrounded by bright candlelight and warmth.

And there was my son Nergal, coming to me, his hands outstretched.

I stood and looked at him, my hands hanging.

"Mother," he said.

He put his arms around me. Oh, his good smell, his smell so deep and familiar to me. For a while, I let myself simply be happy, then I let my consciousness creep out into him. He seemed anxious, but well. The huge never-healing marks, that had once been cut into his back and head, had stayed healed since I did my work on them. Relief coursed through me. I kissed his snub-nosed face, a kiss on each warm shaven cheek.

"I could not be sure if you were alive." I burst into tears of relief.

"I am not in favour, but I am not completely out of favour," he said. "Now, I have people for you to meet."

I stood back from him and looked around.

It was a large room with fires blazing at either end of it. There were small wooden beds everywhere, some set against walls, some sat out in the middle of the room. On all these beds, and standing in between too, were pale-skinned, red-headed, blue-eyed children. Some no more than infants, some past puberty.

I turned to look back at Bizilla, who was standing with her back to the door. She nodded at me.

"Sebitti children," I said. "I did not know it was possible. I thought all were born as adults and that all were born to my mother."

"Not always," said Bizilla. "Sometimes a Sebitti woman finds herself pregnant."

Nergal stretched out his hands to the room. "These children are all family to me." He took a deep breath in. "I train them up to be soldiers. To be Sebitti."

I went to the bed closest to me, and sat down, my hand out to the red-haired toddler who sat there. "Where are their parents?"

"We're not allowed to keep our children," said Bizilla.

Nergal came to sit next to me, dropping a kiss onto the toddler's head. "I was a foot slave to the dragon queen, for a very long time. Up close, I learnt many things, including that sometimes the Sebitti do have children, although it is meant to be impossible."

The little boy looked up at him in delight.

"Then one day they brought a Sebitti baby to Tiamat in the main audience chamber." He looked over at Bizilla before going on. "In those days, Tiamat believed that the Sebitti children were hers to do with as she pleased. Hers to consume, shall we say. But I told Tiamat that I would do anything, anything at all, if she would let me take the baby."

"And she let you?"

"Ever since then all the Sebitti children have been brought to me to raise as soldiers. That is how it is done now. The oldest is fourteen." He gestured to a tall, thin boy who was leaning against a wall, and the boy lifted his chin at me. "They stay here with me until they are ready to join a squad of seven.

"Of course," my son went on, "there was a price to pay for the children. And the price was that I had to go to Earth to kill my father and to fetch you back whether you wanted to come or not."

I took a deep breath in. "You know they are planning to go through to Earth?"

"I know everything the Sebitti know," he said.

"Do you think she will take you with her?" I said.

"Let's talk over by the door."

Bizilla, my son, and I stood in small council then, keeping our voices low.

"If things go bad," Bizilla said to me, "stay in your room until one of us comes to fetch you. Do not go wandering around alone."

"What will bad look like?" I said.

"It's going to be chaotic when the exodus begins," said my son. "There will be fighting."

"Many will be left behind," said Bizilla. "What benefit is there for Qingu in thousands of people passing through to this new realm? His plan is to move the Sebitti and the court through first, and then the armies of Creation will go through with the last of the *melam* supplies and other key resources from houses across the Wheel. Only then will the citizens begin to pass through." She raised her eyebrows to me. "I think by then the gate will have been shut."

"Surely the houses will suspect just such a thing?" I said.

"They are negotiating for their position in the queue," said Nergal. "The canny ones will find their own way out, I think, through other gates, to other realms that have not been visited for thousands of years, but that might provide sanctuary now."

"I find myself divided," I said. "I don't want everyone here to die. But I don't want the Earth invaded."

"I am trying to come up with a plan," said Bizilla. "A way to ensure our safety."

"Whatever happens, I won't leave you behind again," I said to my son. I put my arms around him and held him firm.

"Time to go," said Bizilla, tipping her head to the door.

Nergal kissed me on each cheek. "Beware the dragon," he said.

"I think she still loves me," I said.

He shook his head at that. "I think the love has died within her. Keep yourself safe, Mother, until we come for you."

CHAPTER 3

NINSHUBAR

Buried alive

Old memories, long forgotten, bubbled up to me through the rotting mud. For the first time in a long time, I thought about my mother.

When I was very young I took food from the cooking pot before my mother had taken her portion. It was a breach of etiquette, but I thought that she had already eaten and had intended no offence.

My mother ignored my excuses and knocked me hard to the ground.

Young as I was, I climbed back up with both fists clenched and anger burning in my heart.

She watched me stand with a smile on her face. "You climb back up, Ninshubar. But will you always climb back up? Because that is what it takes. You have to get back up every time." She curled her top lip at me. "I wonder if you have the strength for it."

My mother, who in the end hated me so much she tried to kill me. I wondered if she was still getting back up or whether by now someone had put her down onto the ground and made sure she stayed down.

My mother wanting me dead was a pain that I had never faced. Now I remembered her standing out on the ridgeway above our summer camp, calling out the ritual words at me. Calling out for my death.

She was a terrible mother to me. But that did not mean she had always been wrong. I must climb back up. I must climb up and keep on climbing up. It was then that I realised... I was lying face down.

In the horrifying mud soup that I was buried in, I was lying face down.

I began to push a little. I tried to move just a little in the thick mud I was trapped in. It seemed impossible, but I kept trying. I cannot have moved very far, if at all, before my strength was gone.

Later, I do not know how much later, I began pushing again, pushing down with my hands, pushing up with my spine.

Just a little. Just a very little. The smallest wriggle. Up.

Hours passed, or it might have been days, or weeks, or moons.

For a long time, I gave up hope. I gave in to the pain and the panic.

Then again, I would begin to try.

I tried to wriggle upwards.

Everything I had ever failed at came rushing back to me. Had I been right to leave my own people? Should I have stayed and accepted death? Was that the path of honour?

I passed out for long periods. I lost all sense of time.

Then I would remember my mother's face, looking down at me, and I would try again to move, to squirm, to rise.

I forced myself up towards the surface of a remembered ocean.

I pushed my way up towards life. Towards the blue sky that I prayed to all the old gods would still be there.

Slowly then, my mother's curled lip very clear to me, I climbed back up.

Through death, through horror, through pain, through terrible fright, I climbed back up into the world.

I first felt the difference behind my skull. There was less pressure as I pushed myself upwards. It felt like a dramatic change after so long in the heavy, thick mud, yet I did not dare hope. By then I had been wriggling upwards for so long that I could not remember a time before.

My forehead was abruptly free and I felt air on my face. My mouth was uncovered and out of instinct I tried to breathe in.

It was then, as I tried desperately to draw in air, that I felt myself to be choking to death. My lungs and throat were packed tight with sludge.

Somehow, thrashing in wild panic, I got my whole body out of the ground. Somehow, convulsing, I vomited out great gagging lumps of rotten mud. And at last I breathed air into my bleeding, poisoned lungs.

By all the gods, dead and alive, by all the stars, I breathed.

I breathed but I could not see. Was I blind? I put my hands to my face and felt something caked over my eyes. I clawed at the crusty mask until finally I was able to blink my eyes open.

I was outside, lying on my back on the ground, with a glorious night sky arching over me. The stars were as bright as torches to me in that first moment of seeing again.

It took a while for me to process more than that. To be able to feel what was beneath my hands, to turn my painful neck just a fraction and see where I was.

I was lying in soft, sandy soil beneath a velvet sky.

I would have laughed and cried out if I could, but there was no power in my throat, only the deepest of aches.

This was no longer a nightmare. This was real. I must gather myself and be cautious. What did I know? I had been dead, that I was sure of. I remembered the fight with Nergal, a soldier of Creation, on the banks of the Euphrates. I remembered Inanna looking over at me as the war god took my life. Her precious face.

I had walked the grass plains of an afterlife and I had spoken there with Neti, gatekeeper to other realms. Perhaps Neti had helped me escape that grassland; he had spoken of giving me a push. Or perhaps my *melam* had saved me. Either way, I had climbed back up.

So.

I did not yet try to sit up, but I put my hands to my own body. I was naked and unarmed, and my eight-pointed star was gone from my neck. I could feel all my bones through my skin and my hair was heavy with mud and filth and had grown so long that it hung from my skull in bedraggled clumps. I did not want to think yet of what sort of filth it was that covered me, but I knew I had climbed out of a grave and that it had not only been my own stench down there in the pit of death.

The thought came clear: *I must be sure of the area.*

Somehow, I sat and then stood, my legs almost buckling beneath me. I was surrounded by grass-covered dunes, a javelin's throw out from the walls of a huge city. The shape of its walls and towers was familiar to me. Could it be Ur, Inanna's home city? We had sailed past it an age ago; I had seen it in the distance by daylight and from the sea. It could be Ur, but I could be wrong.

On top of the walls, I caught the movement of men and the glow of fires burning. I quickly dropped down onto all fours.

So.

I must make my calculations. If this was Ur, then perhaps the men and women on those city walls were friendly. They would know the moon goddess, Inanna's mother. They would know Inanna, of course, and they would welcome me into the city, therefore, as Inanna's *sukkal*.

If they were friendly, but I could not be sure of that. Uruk had been under siege when I died and the Akkadians had been running amok in Sumer. The land had been in turmoil. So perhaps they were my enemies up there on the walls. And I was weak and had no weapons.

If this was Ur, though, then the sea would be close by. In fact, could I hear waves upon the cool night air? I remembered that Ur stood with one shoulder to the ocean and the other to the great river, and it looked out over many islands. They called the gulf between Ur and Eridu the land of ten thousand islands. If I could get to an island, I could take my time to recover myself.

It was a plan, and any plan was better than no plan.

Slowly, slowly, I crawled across the sand dunes towards the faint sound of the waves.

I breathed in deep on the good air. On the smell of the night. On the smell of the sea. And more and more, on the terrible smell of my own body. At first I had been nose-blind to it. Now the stench of the filth upon my body began to clog up my nose and lungs. I smelled of rotting meat.

I caught the glimmer of starlight on ocean.

Not far out from the shore, I made out the dark shape of an island, and a pattern of palm fronds against the sky. I could see no lights or fires upon the island; perhaps it would be empty.

Well, if you are going to do something, better to do it quick.

I stood, my knees weak, and waded out into the cool night sea. I threw myself out into the purifying waters and I began to swim.

CHAPTER 4

ERESHKIGAL

In Abydos, Egypt

I stood in the horrible, stinking temple, with my grandfather unconscious on the floor and a lot of other people around who I didn't know and didn't want to know.

"Where is this?" I began crying. "I'm so tired."

I made my way past the sprawl of my grandfather, and his lions, and his handsome young friend, to the open doorway. All I could see, in the glare, was a crowd of vicious-looking men and a vista of mud-brick buildings, and I quickly retreated back into the foul-smelling temple, my hands on my belly.

"Hello, Ereshkigal," said the young man as he grappled with my grandfather's lions. He had straight black brows and shining skin and the most wonderful smile.

"May I stand up, my lady?" he said, the lions' leashes by then firm in his hands. "I have an injured knee and kneeling down nearly kills me."

"Just tell me where this is." I blew my nose on my sleeve.

"This is Egypt." He stood up, grimacing. "We are in Abydos, my lady."

I looked round again at the girl on the throne, in her pretty, diaphanous dress, and all the priests in their pointy white hats, and the ghastly dragon statue, and finally, in the shadows, the boys tied up on the floor.

It was all so sweaty and dark and horrid. "Well, I have to go," I said to the handsome young man. "I cannot be wasting time here."

The man came a step closer, holding his lions back from me. "My lady, I am your cousin Gilgamesh, son of Ninsun and Lugalbanda."

"I've never heard of you." I pulled myself more upright, very conscious of my bloated midriff.

Gilgamesh came closer still. He smelled of cedar wood, sweet and warm. "I was born long after your descent into the underworld."

"Are you a god?"

He paused a moment before answering, his tortoiseshell eyes fixed on mine. "I am only a man." His voice dipped a beat lower as he said the word "man".

For a moment, I felt rather weak at the knees.

"Will you not sit down, my lady?" he said, as if reading my mind. He gestured over to the throne and the sulky-looking woman sitting upon it.

"Isis," he said to the woman. "Perhaps Ereshkigal could sit down there? Given the circumstances?" He raised both his eyebrows at the woman.

I saw that she was going to refuse and so I blasted her with a combat *mee*. She keeled over, straight down onto the hard floor, and lay there, moaning quietly, as I climbed onto her wooden chair. Some priests came forward as if to help her, but I lifted my chin at them and they stepped back.

"I do need rest," I said. "It's so hot in here."

Gilgamesh gestured to the priests. "Perhaps someone could fan Queen Ereshkigal? And perhaps fetch her some cool water and some sweetmeats?"

"I would like some sweetmeats," I said, sniffing back tears. My belly was huge in my lap and it was hard to take a proper breath.

"Would you prefer to be somewhere cooler?" said Gilgamesh. "The woman on the floor there is called Isis. She is a daughter of Enki and I believe she will certainly have a palace here."

How nice he was!

"I cannot stay long here," I said. "I need to get to Heaven before it's too late. It may already be too late."

"Just rest a little here and let us talk," said Gilgamesh.

I did feel a little better once the priests were fanning me with peacock feathers. The water they brought tasted delicious and a bare-chested man brought me a tray with cheese, sweet jellies, and slices of melon. I rested the tray on my belly as I ate.

"I have not eaten fresh food for a very long time." I looked down sadly at my bare feet. "Oh, I left my slippers in the cave."

Gilgamesh stood in front of my throne, the lions in hand. The woman, Isis, lay quiet on the floor beside him. Behind them, my grandfather was starting to wake up.

"You must tell my grandfather to stay down and stay quiet or I will kill him," I said.

"Do you hear that, Enki?" said Gilgamesh, raising his voice and glancing over his shoulder.

"I hear it," came the answer from the floor.

"You be quiet!" I screamed at Enki, the old rage flaring up in me. It took a while to calm down. "You know it was Enki who sent me down into the underworld?" I said to Gilgamesh. "It was he who locked me in there. It was because of him I lost my baby."

Isis, unexpectedly, spoke: "He was a brute to me, too."

I looked down at her and noticed how frail she looked beneath her sheer dress. I had a rush of sympathy for her. "He will not hurt you now, my lady," I said, but then I looked around me again, frowning. I lifted my chin at Gilgamesh and gestured over to the trussed-up boys. "What is happening here?"

"This woman you are speaking to so very kindly is about to murder them."

"Tiamat demands human sacrifice," Isis said from the floor.

"Oh, no," I said. "No. I will not have children hurt." I began on the melon slices. "What are you all doing here in Egypt? What is happening?"

"Isis, as I said, is the goddess here," said Gilgamesh. "Enki and I came here to find out if there was a gate to other realms here. And it seems, from your sudden appearance, that there is."

He was so courteous and polite.

"I did not come through a gate," I said, lying out of old habit.

A voice from the floor: "Gilgamesh, all she does is lie."

"Do not speak about me!" I screamed down at my grandfather, my heart and lungs red hot with fury. "You will not speak about me again! I will pluck your eyes out! My Nergal should have killed you! He should have slaughtered you! He killed the wrong brother!"

Gilgamesh was looking from one to the other of us, one wide, strong hand out towards me. "More water, my queen?"

"I would like more water," I said. "And then I'm going to go."

"My lady, may I ask where you came from?" said Gilgamesh. "Before arriving here, I mean."

"Oh," I said, too exhausted, all of a sudden, to be clever in my answer. "I was in the Kur and trying to get out. And then suddenly I was here."

Gilgamesh seared me with his smile. "We were also at the Kur, or at least somewhere above it," he said, very eager. "Enki and I were there together only two weeks ago. We were trying to dig our way down to it. It was only when we had given up all hope of finding the Kur that we came here."

I stood up, one hand on my belly. "Well, I am going. I must fetch Nergal back from Heaven."

Gilgamesh's lovely smile seemed to stiffen just a little. "Nergal killed people I love," he said. "Why do you want to help him?"

"None of you know him," I said. "He did what he did for honour and because he had to. Now I am going." I looked around at the young boys tied up along the wall. "Release those children," I called out to the priests.

Gilgamesh took a step forward. How very appealing I might have found him, if I had not sworn myself to Nergal. "Queen Ereshkigal, I will help you down to this gate you spoke of."

"I would like help," I said. "It was horrible getting up here."

Isis sat up. Her black eye paint was smeared down her cheeks. "There's no gate," she said. "There's only the underground temple and the lake down there. Nammu was down there months and months, and never found a gate."

"Then how do you explain Ereshkigal's appearance?" Enki bellowed. "Do you think she walked here from Sumer? In her condition?" Enki stood up then, his fists clenched. "What are my crimes against you, Ereshkigal? Do you even remember what happened? You were mad then and you are mad now."

I blasted him again with one of my *mees* of combat and he went down like a felled tree.

In the quiet that followed, the priests released the young boys, who at once made their way over to Gilgamesh.

"You should go, boys," Gilgamesh said to them.

"Only to be snatched up again outside?" said one of the boys. "We are staying with you."

Gilgamesh cast a glance at me before turning back to the boys. "All right," he said to them. "Stay close then."

He tied the lions to a stone column, and then limped over to me, the gang of boys close on his heels.

"Lean on me, my lady," he said, and took one of my arms in his. Slowly, we made towards the door at the back of the temple, with the boys clumping up close around us.

"I will come too," said Isis, standing up. She waved her priests back. "I would like to see this supposed gate." Enki remained on the floor, apparently unconscious.

Gilgamesh pulled the door aside and then led me into the tunnel. Behind me came the boys, and the goddess Isis, holding her pretty red skirts up from the stone floor.

"Were you all alone in the Kur?" Gilgamesh asked me, as we made our way down the rose granite tunnel.

I did not like to be questioned, but then he was so very delicious. "I was there with Dumuzi and Geshtinanna," I said, "but now they are lost."

"Just the three of you?"

"I suppose so."

He glanced ahead as the tunnel curved down to the left, and then turned back to me. "And Inanna and the others?"

"I don't know where they are," I said. "I suppose some of them went through the gate. I know Nergal did."

I frowned to myself as we crept down towards the room with the moat and the altar. I had no idea how I was going to make the gate work. If it even was a gate. It had been a portal of some kind. Was that a gate? Would I have to simply crawl back into the cave space? But then what if that simply put me back into the Kur?

I had left the stone door to the altar room open, but somehow it had closed. Gilgamesh put a hand to it, and with pushing and pulling, managed to slide it open again.

Inside, all was exactly as I had left it. The oily, black moat. The huge slabs of stone that made up the walls, roof, and altar. I noticed now that there were inscriptions all along the side of the altar stone.

"I need to get across the moat to the altar," I said to Gilgamesh. "I want to try to read all the inscriptions."

"Can you decipher these marks?" said Isis, from the corridor beyond. "Nammu spent an age trying to read it all."

"I think I can do better than Nammu," I said. "Who was, after all, a traitor to our family."

I put my left foot out into the water.

"Do be careful, my lady," said Gilgamesh, holding on tight to my hand.

"It is not as deep as it looks," I said to him, looking deep into his iridescent eyes.

And then I was plunged into darkness. I had the strangest sensation, of falling, but rising too. I still had my hand on someone, but it was pitch dark.

I willed my protective shield to flare into life around me.

I was still holding on to Gilgamesh by my right hand.

But we were no longer in the Osirion.

CHAPTER 5

NINLIL

In Heaven

My father's birthday was a state occasion. A day of ceremony, singing, and the beating of ancient drums in the echoing, stone chamber that had once been his private audience room.

My mother shifted in and out of the room throughout the day, uncomfortable, angry, growling. Her belly was strangely distended and something was moving around inside her. All day, the Sebitti followed her into the room, and out of the room, faces impassive, their coats glittering in the light of the candles and fires.

My brother and I sat on either side of my father, both very cold despite our furs and the firebowls.

"How I wish I could put my hands on her," I said.

"You would have more luck with our father," said Qingu.

While my mother and her Sebitti were gone from the room, my brother took the opportunity to pace around.

"This is a senseless waste of time," he said to me, rubbing his hands together. His breath showed white against the dark walls and the sea of black-robed priests around us.

My father's head seemed to have tipped even closer to his lap. His courtiers had draped a new piece of black velvet over his head, but it did nothing to disguise the flaps of desiccated skin hanging from his nose and chin.

"I am the last person who can help you with any of this," I said.

Qingu nodded his great horns at me, and then tucked his hands beneath his armpits. "Whatever she's growing in her belly, it is not doing wonders for her temper," he said. "Perhaps you may have noticed."

"I can see she's uncomfortable."

Qingu laughed. "It's rather worse than that, sister. She's been hunting, shall we say, rather indiscriminately."

A chill ran through me, more unpleasant by far than the physical cold. "How so, brother?"

"She ate a Sebitti earlier," he said, his voice low. "Very bad for morale."

I took a deep breath in. "Who did she eat?"

"No, not your precious Bizilla. Just someone who moved too slowly when our mother was getting up out of her fire pit. But I mean, that's the least of it. She was out in the camps earlier wreaking havoc. Then she went through the hunting chambers when no one was expecting her. Killing courtiers alongside the official sacrifices."

Qingu cast a glance at movement amongst the footmen at the doorway and then sat himself back down on his throne. "I think she's coming back."

"Brother, can you do nothing to stop all this?"

He shrugged. "Her priests say she's hungry for certain things. That it's all part of whatever is happening inside her. This mystery pregnancy."

"Do her priests not understand it?"

"I think they do, but very sadly, they do not answer to me."

A group of young dancing girls, dressed in black slips, entered the chamber, nervous eyes upon the row of thrones before them. "Oh, I was wrong," said Qingu. "Only more dancers." The priests drew back to give the girls space to do their dance.

I watched the girls weave between each other, shaking red ribbons at each other. I saw that between them, they were tracing the shape of a dragon. I imagined for a moment my mother ploughing through these little girls and snatching them up high in her seven powerful jaws.

"I wish she would let me help her," I said.

"You must drop that silly fantasy," said Qingu. "Our mother is who she is and will never change. Which reminds me, she wants to eat the girl Inanna."

I turned to face him. "Why?"

He shrugged. "For information, I suppose."

I had only met Inanna once and then in the midst of anguish and violence. But she was Ningal's daughter. A small girl with very black eyes.

"No, Qingu," I said. "Let the girl live."

"The dragon's given out explicit orders," he said. "Or that's what her priests say."

"How can she give out orders when she does not speak?"

"They say she rumbles and paws at the ground and they say they can understand her. Regardless, it's happening. A formal sacrifice."

"You have been torturing the girl, brother. You know everything she knows about the realm of light. Surely there can be nothing new to learn about the Earth."

"Yes, but there's nothing like getting it first-hand, the old-fashioned Anzu way," he said. "You ate your husband. Is that not the same thing?"

"My husband was already dead and I did it to honour him. To save any last memories still in there."

"Inanna had real power on Earth. Perhaps our mother hopes to truly understand that. Either way, if it brings her pregnancy to an end and allows us to begin the exodus, I am all for it. The very ground is breaking apart beneath us. There are new lava flows every day."

The little girls withdrew. Two new groups of dancers came flooding in, one group in blue robes, the other in green. At first, they danced apart, and then they began to weave between each other.

My brother gave out a loud sigh. "It's the mixing of the waters," he said. "How much longer can this go on?" He gestured to one of our father's black-robed priests and the man approached us with his head bowed.

"Yes, my lord?"

"How much longer?" said Qingu. "I have an exodus to worry about."

"Well, it's the Creation origin story," said the priest. "First the mixing of the waters, the two waters symbolising your parents, and then your parents giving birth to all the lesser gods. There are three more acts after this."

"I know what it is," said Qingu, his fists clenched. "I am aware of the Creation story, being myself a high priest of Heaven. What I asked was, how long is it going to take?"

"Perhaps another hour," said the priest.

"Tell them to dance more quickly," said Qingu, tipping his horns down at the man.

The priest withdrew, his head still bowed.

"Brother, what will happen to my son when we pass through the gate?"

"Lots of people will be left behind," Qingu said, his eyes on the blue and green dancers. "I will do what I can to keep order, but the fact is it will be chaos."

CHAPTER 6

INANNA

In Heaven

Without Bizilla's medicine, sleep seemed impossible. My pain grew worse and worse and I could find no comfort. The shadowmen watched me twist and turn, their hands clasped before them.

In the end though, I must have slept.

I awoke to find the candle lit and Bizilla standing over me.

Was I going to be tortured? Was this how it happened?

I realised that I should have been unconscious with the medicine; that I should have been pretending. Now it was too late for that.

"Get up," said Bizilla. "Quickly."

"Why?"

She shook her head at me. "It doesn't matter why."

I pulled my blanket tighter around me, as if it would give me some protection. "I don't want to get up."

She put her hands on her hips and shut her eyes for a moment. "The queen wants to see you."

After a moment's pause, I said: "What queen?"

"It doesn't matter what queen. Get up."

"Why does the queen want to see me?"

"She didn't say. It doesn't matter. You have to go. Now get up."

Bizilla banged her left fist on the door of my prison cell and called out a language I could not understand.

She turned back to me as the bolts shifted. "The less you say or do the better."

"What is happening, Bizilla?" I said. But I sat up in bed, and swung my aching feet to the stone cold floor.

The door opened and six gold-scaled soldiers came through the door. They all looked so very like Bizilla: the same red hair, pale skin, and dark blue eyes.

Bizilla barked out something to her comrades and they passed her a black bundle. She shook it out: a dress. I held up my aching arms so that she could slip it onto me.

Even belted at the waist with a piece of leather string, the thick black dress was too long for me, touching the floor and covering my hands.

Bizilla pulled up more cloth over my string belt, so that my bare feet were free of it, and then put a heavy grey cloak round my shoulders. "It's cold in the palace," she said.

The Sebitti spoke amongst themselves as I was being dressed, their eyes on me. All the while the door to my prison cell stood open and I caught glimpses of a wall of rock beyond.

"Follow me," said Bizilla.

She went out first into the tunnel, lit a torch from the firebowl there, and turned left. I watched her go, standing stock still, until one of the other Sebitti gave me a sharp push in the back.

The tunnel outside looked to have been carved out of solid rock. Lumps of rough stone bulged up through the sandy floor. "Can you not walk quicker?" Bizilla said, turning back to me.

"I have no strength in my legs."

She turned and continued, but at a slower pace.

A few cords along, we passed through a wooden door and out into a man-made, stone-block tunnel with a flagstone floor. The walls were lined with the mounted heads of creatures so strange they could not be real. A giant serpent with fangs as long as my arms. Another creature looked like a man at first, until I realised he had fish scales for skin.

"Hurry," said Bizilla, pulling me on.

We came to a steep flight of stairs. I felt hollowed out, my feet and bones an agony, but I began to climb after Bizilla, with her six gold-scaled colleagues close on my heels.

The stone stairs went up and up. After three flights, I sat down on a step. "I can't," I said. "It's too much."

Bizilla leaned over and picked me up in her arms. She glanced down at me as she climbed and I thought she was about to speak, but she said nothing.

I felt colder and colder, even in Bizilla's hard arms, even with my cloak wrapped around me. My bare feet, poking out of my cloak, grew numb.

At last, we reached the top of the stairs and a wooden door with three metal bolts across it. Bizilla put me down onto the cold steps.

"Can you stand?"

"I think so," I said, putting one hand out to the stone wall.

Bizilla drew back the bolts one by one.

"Keep your eyes down in here," she said to me. "Don't get involved with them."

She pulled the door open and I was almost blinded.

Before us lay a sparkling room, bright with golden mirrors, candles, and crowds of pale-faced men and women in brilliantly colourful costumes. For a moment I thought it was a party; that we were interrupting some fine palace occasion. Then I saw the blood on the floor. The faces turned to us were desperate.

Along one far wall, dead bodies lay in a gruesome heap.

Bizilla pulled me through the crowd, looking neither left nor right. She seemed bigger in the bright-lit room and more dangerous.

"Bizilla," a man shouted out. "Stop!" He was dressed in black; he had blood on his face and hands. "Bizilla, she's gone mad. She is killing at random now. You must do something."

Bizilla did not turn around to look at him. She pulled me on with a hard hand on my right arm towards a black metal door set into the golden, mirror-lined wall ahead.

The crowd followed us. Bizilla's comrades turned to face the oncomers, their hands on their golden belts, as Bizilla pressed her shoulder to the door and then banged both fists on it. "Nothing works any more," she said.

One of the Sebitti left his place behind me to help her. "We should have gone round the long way," he said. Together, they put their shoulders to the door. Long moments later, it swung open to reveal a dark garden beyond.

Bizilla pushed me roughly through and then the gold-scaled Sebitti bundled through after me, shutting the door as fast as they could on the angry shouts behind us.

The garden beyond was heavy with the smell of wet and vegetation. A line of burning torches marked a pathway through dark palms and heavy flowering bushes.

Above us, the vaulted glass roof was clogged with snow. I had only seen snow once before, when it fell upon Ur in one day, but was gone by the next morning. Here it lay in huge heaps on the glass roof and more came twisting and tumbling from the black sky above.

"Bizilla, who were all those people?"

She took me by my right hand and stalked onwards along the mosaic path through the palms and flowers.

"Bizilla, tell me!"

She paused a moment, looking hard at me. "She hunts in those rooms." Then she walked on, pulling me harder.

Something thin and red was moving quickly over the ground, its body rippling from right to left.

"Oh!" I said. "A snake!" But it was gone already.

"We call them serpents here," said Bizilla.

On we went, through the cold garden, and I saw more snakes, a slither here, a slither there. I looked down at my bare feet as I stepped, fearing I might tread on one.

The path ahead was blocked by an enormous tree trunk. Its branches reached all the way up to the glass roof and only when we were close did I make out the small metal door set into the side of it.

Bizilla pulled the door open, stooped down, and was about to pull me through the door into darkness. I took a step backwards in confusion and fright.

Bizilla gripped my hand tighter. "It's not a real tree. It's a doorway."

With the hands of the other Sebitti pushing me on, I stepped through the door. There was no need for me to duck my head.

I emerged into a vast, ice-cold room.

There were people everywhere, some clustered around firebowls, others trying to sleep under piles of blankets.

I had never been in a room so large. As Bizilla lifted her torch, to shut the door behind us, I caught a glimpse of the paintings on the arched ceiling high above us. Many-headed dragons breathed fire and stretched out their wings. They seemed to be birthing other creatures, but I could not work out what the smaller creatures were.

Bizilla took me by the arm and began to drag me forward past the crowds.

"Who are all these people?"

They had bags stacked between them. They all turned anxious faces to us as we passed.

"Who are they?" I repeated. "What are they all doing?"

She stopped to look down at me. "Can you go no quicker?"

"I cannot."

She picked me up again.

"Bizilla," I whispered to her. "Why are you taking me to the queen?"

She kept her chin lifted and did not answer.

I turned my head. Ahead of us I could see huge wooden doors that reached all the way up to the roof; impossibly tall doors, the height of a full-grown cedar.

The stink of sulphur washed over me as the huge doors began to open.

Bizilla put me down. "Time to meet the queen," she said.

CHAPTER 7

HARGA

In the marshes

The marshwoman petted her small goat, in the gloom of the Palace, as we absorbed the news. The plan had always been that the marshmen would whisk us away from the Refuge if the Akkadians entered the marshes.

Now the Akkadians had entered the marshes and the marshmen would not be coming.

Marduk was first to react. "I have fought alongside the marshmen time and time again and trusted them with my life. I would count Tilmun, the marsh king's son, as a friend for life. Surely they cannot break the guest bond?"

"There are other bonds," said Sagar, the old marshwoman. "And besides, they do not plan to attack you directly. They are withdrawing their protection and Adamen argues that there will be no direct breaking of any promises given."

Isimud was standing along one wall of the great reed hut, his hands behind his back. "For two hundred years, all my life, your people have been loyal to my lord Enki," he said. "Why would they break with him now?"

"Where is Enki?" said the marshwoman, lifting her creased face to him. "Where are the Anunnaki?"

"I am Anunnaki," said Ningal, the moon goddess. "I am here." She looked very beautiful, and very honest, but sitting there beside us on the filthy rug, she also looked like an ordinary woman.

The marshwoman shook her head. "Everyone knows that Ninsun of the Anunnaki died at Uruk. That Enlil was beheaded at Nippur. Now they say that Nammu is dead at Kish. The marshmen are not afraid of you, moon goddess. They know you can be killed and that has made a difference to them."

"I would not want to be labelled suspicious or untrusting," I said. "However, the boys and I have made some preparations for just such a time as this." I lifted my chin to the two Uruk boys guarding the doorway.

"You have?" said Marduk, looking up at me in surprise.

I nodded again to the Uruk boys. "We have ten canoes out by the jetty. Tallboy and Shortboy, bring those canoes up on shore and guard them. I don't want them disappearing."

"Yes, my lord," the two Uruk boys said in unison.

When had they started calling me "my lord"?

That point aside, they ran out of the Palace very smartly.

I looked back to the council on the central rug. "I have some more canoes hidden in with the ducks, in that patch of thorns at the back of their enclosure, and some more behind my hut," I said. "Eighteen in all. And there are weapons stashed in all of them."

"Twenty-eight canoes plus mine is twenty-nine," said the marshwoman.

"Maybe six people in each," I said, "more if we put children in.

If we cram them tight." How I cursed myself at that moment for not having done more. It had been hard to get canoes and hide them without anyone noticing. But I should have done more.

"Not enough canoes for all of us," said Isimud.

"Not enough," I said. I took a stone from the pouch at my waist and began rolling it around in my right hand. "When will the Akkadians be here?"

"Very soon," said the marshwoman. "There is no time to fetch more canoes."

I rolled my shoulders. "If they are already in the marshes then we don't have time to get out. We need another hiding place."

"They will know all the hiding places," said Lilith.

We all looked to the marshwoman.

"There is a place I can take you south of here," she said. "Plague killed the whole village and no one goes there."

"For good reason?" I said.

"I've been there and survived. It's two hours away by canoe."

"But we don't have enough canoes," said Isimud.

Marduk looked around at each of us before speaking. "We play a game sometimes..." he said. He trailed off. "Not a game, exactly. It's a sort of exploring thing. No... it's probably a terrible idea."

"Now is the moment for terrible ideas," I said.

He smiled at that. "The boys and I, we just go into the water," he said. "And we sort of make our way. Walking, really."

"How?" I said.

"I can swim, of course, but Tallboy and Shortboy can't. I swim across the wider channels, and they launch themselves across into my arms. The rest of the time we wade where we can or pull ourselves along by grabbing the reeds."

"Can you cover distance like that?" I said.

"You get muddy and it's easy to cut your feet and hands, but yes you can cover distance, if you don't mind the snakes and so forth."

I looked to Lilith. "I say we go into the water right now. Children and anyone who is vulnerable in the canoes. One strong paddler in each canoe. The rest of us in the water. We will walk out of here."

Lilith bent her shorn head to me in agreement. "What should we take with us?"

"Nothing at all except the weapons each person chooses to carry," I said. "The animals must be left."

"Not the dogs," said Marduk, his mouth flat.

I sighed out heavily. "The dogs come," I said.

"And this goat," said Sagar.

"The dogs and the goat come," I said, with a deep breath in, "but everything else must be left. No bags, no supplies, no livestock. Marduk, go now and fetch all the lookouts in. I don't want anyone left behind."

"I'll fetch them back," he said, and was gone, a pale streak with three dogs streaming behind him.

"So, everyone into the water," said the moon goddess.

"Better that than be surrounded here, and all die in a foolish last stand," I said.

Isimud took a step closer to us all. "Or we take the fighters in the canoes and leave the others. The Akkadians will not kill unarmed women and children."

There was a long, stiff, silence.

"We will be following Harga's plan," said the moon goddess, her expression stone-like.

I helped her to her feet.

"Can you swim, my lady?" I said to her.

Her face softened into worry and sadness. "I never bothered to learn."

CHAPTER 8

GILGAMESH

Lost

Queen Ereshkigal lit up the cave around us with the white light from one of her *mees*. Inside that bubble of brightness, I held on tight to her hand. I did not want to be accidentally parted from her in this mysterious and possibly magical place.

That said, the cave looked very like a natural limestone cave of the sort I had explored as a boy. The cavern we stood in was perhaps four cables high in parts and it disappeared away into darkness to our left and right. Great columns of rock flowed down from the high ceilings and the floor was studded with glittering stone columns and piles of loose rock and sand.

All I could be sure of was that we were no longer in the temple beneath the Osirion.

"Enki!" I shouted out, my hand tight on Ereshkigal's. "Userkaf? Isis?"

We were both quiet, waiting for an answer. I could only hear the dripping of water onto stone.

"Who is Userkaf?" she said.

"One of those boys. A fine young man."

We were quiet again.

"Let us look for a way out," Ereshkigal said. She began picking her way across the rough cave floor. She seemed very energetic for a woman in late pregnancy.

"My lady," I said, pulling back against her insistent hand. "My lady, let me help you. You could fall or twist an ankle here."

"You have an injured knee," she said. "You can barely walk."

I bit down on a retort to that; after all, even with my bad knee, I was surely more agile than a woman on the very brink of giving birth.

"Is this the underworld, do you think?" I said. "Could we be back inside the Kur?"

Ereshkigal shook her wild curls at me. "It is not the Kur. I don't know where we are. I feel that we will be lost forever. And all this while they could be torturing Nergal!"

I helped her across a small stand of sharp-looking spikes of rock. "So, your plan is to get to Heaven and find Nergal and take him back to Earth?"

Her face crumpled. "It's all I want."

And then a voice came to us, floating from the shadows ahead.

"Madness," it said.

Ereshkigal and I froze.

We could hear nothing except for the dripping of the water, which now seemed to echo all around us.

When it seemed the silence would go on forever, I said: "Who goes there?"

Nothing.

But then I fancied that I could see light and shadows moving amongst the dark rock formations ahead of us.

I was about to say something when a man in a red suit stepped into sight with a bright oil lamp held up in one hand.

"Neti!" said Ereshkigal, letting go of my arm. "What are you doing here?"

"You," said Neti.

"Hello, Neti," I called up to him. "Do you remember me? From your little hut?"

Neti tipped his head down to me. "I remember you, child of Ninsun and Lugalbanda." He frowned. "Where did you two come from?"

"Egypt!" I said.

"Interesting," he said.

Ereshkigal let the light of her *mee* fade. "Neti, are my demons here?"

"I'm afraid not, Madam."

"Are you here alone?" I called.

"Well, not any more," he said. "Stay there, I will come to you."

As I turned to take Ereshkigal's arm again, I stubbed a toe on something heavy and hard; the shock reverberated through my bad knee. In the silt beneath my feet, there was the outline of a large skeleton. "Bones," I said out loud.

"The caves are full of them," said Neti, as he came to stand with us, his lantern raised. "The skeletons of travellers."

By the light of Neti's lantern, I could make out the outline of dozens of human hands on the walls around us. Beyond, a row of red dots stretched away into the shadows.

"Yes, there are paintings in all the important caves," said Neti, nodding over at the paintings. "Sadly the clues they leave are opaque to me."

Ereshkigal sat down on the cave floor, breathing heavily. "Do you have any food or water, Neti?"

"I have neither," he said. "Which is very soon going to be a problem for you."

I sat down next to Ereshkigal, grimacing, and stretched my left leg out before me.

Neti stood over us with his flickering oil lamp held high.

"So?" said Ereshkigal. "Spit it out, gatekeeper. What is happening?"

"This is an in-between place," said the gatekeeper. "A natural space between the realms. It is in effect a huge cave system. Some of the caves are gates which lead off to other worlds, but which cave leads to what and whether they will work for you is all unclear." He looked down at Ereshkigal and said: "I was thrown in here when you opened the eighth gate to let Nergal through. I presume the Kur thought I would be safer here. So here I am."

"You've been here all this time?" said Ereshkigal. "Alone?"

"Alone except for all the dead bodies, yes," said Neti. "I have been trying to leave, but the caves don't seem to work for me. Or perhaps I have been in the wrong caves."

"No," said Ereshkigal, shaking her curls. "This is wrong. I have been through the gate system. My family and I stepped through the gate on the Anunnaki's land in Heaven and we stepped directly out into the Kur. There was no cave system involved."

"Your family had the master *mee*," said Neti. "The old gods built quicker ways through between realms, but you need a tool to follow them. So here we are, in the original space between the realms."

"How do we get to Heaven?" said the goddess.

"I was once stuck in these caves for ten thousand years," Neti said. "Without a navigation object, you are very unlikely to survive these caves."

I turned to Ereshkigal, putting a hand on her sleeve. "My lady, if what Neti says is true, we should return to Egypt and rethink." I turned to Neti. "We should be able to retrace our steps, don't you think? We arrived very close to here."

Ereshkigal pulled her arm away from me. "I am going to Heaven and I am going to rescue Nergal." She burst into tears. "I did not have enough time with him."

"My lady, it cannot be long before the baby comes," I said.

There was a silence that I can only describe as frozen.

"What baby?" she said. I could not tell if she was lying or joking, or was simply delusional. Or perhaps her belly was the symptom of some strange disease, and I had made a horrible mistake?

Regardless, she began sobbing. "Gilgamesh, Neti is lying to us. He knows the way to Heaven. He is choosing not to tell us."

"Are you lying, Neti?" I said.

The gatekeeper looked to the roof of the cave before wearily shaking his head.

"I have spent the past one hundred years with him," Ereshkigal said. "I can see his thoughts passing across his face!"

"Neti," I said. "Be honest with us."

Neti lifted his lamp higher. "There is something that I have found that you may find interesting," he said. "For all the good it will do you. But it is some way from here."

"Show us then," said Ereshkigal.

By the light of Neti's oil lamp we made our way out of the cavern and into the rocky tunnels beyond.

"Where did you get the lamp?" I said to Neti as we crept along, each with an arm around Ereshkigal.

"I found a stash of them," he said. "Next to a large cluster of skeletons."

At last we came to an unpromising stretch of rock wall that turned out to boast a drawing, sketched in charcoal, that was unlike all the other art we had seen in the caves. Neti put his dim lamp closer to it. It was a dense grid of lines.

"Is it a basket?" I said.

"Personally, I think it looks more like a sketch of a boat," said Neti. "However, by walking back and forth a great deal over the many, many years I have spent in here, I have worked out that it is a map."

Ereshkigal put her nose very close to the drawing. "I have seen maps like this before," she said, "in the Kur." She turned to glower at Neti. "Gatekeeper, where is the gate to Heaven?"

He sighed out. "I don't know exactly, because nothing works for me."

"Just take me to the cave!" she shouted at him. "You are stalling!"

The gatekeeper stamped a foot. "You will make too much noise, Madam!" he cried out.

"Now we get to it," said Ereshkigal, turning to me in triumph. "This is why he tells us all is hopeless. Because he fears we are making noise!" She turned back to the gatekeeper. "I am happy to make a noise," she said. "Let them come and get me, whoever it is you are frightened of."

"You should be frightened too," Neti said quietly.

"Just lead on, gatekeeper," said the queen of the underworld. "Show me the gate to Heaven, or what you think is the gate to Heaven. You will not stop me getting to Nergal."

CHAPTER 9

INANNA

In Heaven

She was a dragon. A many-headed black dragon, squatting over a pit of fire.

Tiamat.

I had dreamed of her. I had glimpsed her in the shadows, reaching for me. Now here she was, very real, in this huge, vaulted, stone room.

She was a broad-chested creature with long, snaking necks and fanged jaws. Her obsidian scales rippled as she moved; her feathers glistened, oil black. Her reptile eyes, a brilliant blue, all turned to me in unison.

Bizilla tried to push me forward towards the dragon. In my terror, I found the strength to resist her. I stood then, anchored, just inside the doorway.

The dragon had seven heads.

There were people all around me. Golden Sebitti, in their sets of seven. Soldiers in black and red. A man in white fur, with huge horns growing out of his head, sat on a golden chair beside the dragon. He had the same brilliant blue eyes. Next to him sat a man who looked to be dead, or near death, and seemed to be tied to his chair.

I saw the birds then, chained up along the far side of the room. Giant, golden-feathered eagles, twice the height of a man, but with the furred heads and clawed front legs of lions.

"You should kneel," Bizilla said to me, one hand on my shoulder.

I knelt onto a black flagstone so smooth and polished it might have been a thousand years old. I was so frightened that all thoughts of escape were pressed out of my mind. I could only breathe and try to keep breathing, my mouth open, my sides heaving.

The dragon climbed up off her bed of flames and began moving towards me, surprisingly quick upon her powerful back legs. Her seven heads reared up over me and, on instinct, I ducked my own head down, my face bowed to the floor. I could feel the heat of her breath on the back of my neck.

In the corner of one eye, I saw the dragon's tail lifting.

And then something hit me from behind, right in the back of the skull, and I went down hard and painful upon the flagstone floor.

I came to and I was hanging upside down from one ankle, black cloth swirling around me, the floor an arm's length below me. I tried to pull the cloth aside so that I could see, and the room spun around me.

The dragon was sat back on her hindquarters and I was hanging from her powerful right forearm. Her claws cut into my ankle.

Somewhere close, Bizilla was speaking: "My queen, does this need to be done?"

A pair of white fur boots swung into my field of vision. "For all the stars, Bizilla, stand aside," he said. "What has come over you?"

I found myself being lifted higher in the air. The dragon's claws cut deeper into my ankle.

"We may need her on the other side," said Bizilla. "She could prove a valuable hostage."

There were men in red around me then, obscuring my view of Bizilla's gold-scaled coat.

"Someone take the bolt off the girl," said the man with the white fur boots. "Mother, you can't eat her with the bolt on."

Abruptly, I dropped almost to the floor and my hands touched cold stone for a moment.

Men in red pulled at the metal loop around my neck. As they wrestled to get the so-called bolt off me, Tiamat's seven heads dropped down and wove in closer to me, blasting me with her hot, sulphurous breath.

It was only then that I truly understood that she was going to eat me.

"My lady, please," Bizilla was saying.

Behind Bizilla, the man in the white fur boots said: "Someone cut that Sebitti down. She's gone mad. Someone run her through."

A clanking noise; the metal was coming away from my neck.

The bolt was off.

A hard, black light burst out around me.

For a moment I was falling and then I was caught, awkward, upside down, in Bizilla's hard arms.

"What is happening?" said Bizilla.

She put me down onto my feet.

The shadowmen blinked into existence. Except they were no longer shadows: they were men of flesh with dark beards and gleaming eyes. One wore a black cloak, the other a dark cloak laced with blue.

"I did say we would show you something, if you could get that collar off," said the man in blue. Kurgurrah.

Around us lay a strange scene indeed.

Everything and everyone was motionless. The central fire pit still shone out red but the flames no longer flickered. Tiamat was frozen above me, her claws reaching out, her mouths agape. The gold-scaled Sebitti warriors stood mid-motion around us. Soldiers in red were caught in the act of lifting their swords at Bizilla. The man with bull's horns and white fur boots was frowning at us, his hands on his hips, but he did not move or blink. The giant lion-birds crouched motionless along the back wall of the room, some with their great wings half-unfurled.

Only Bizilla, the two shadowmen, and I, stood alive and moving in this scene.

"What is this?" said Bizilla. "What is happening?"

"Can you get me back to Earth?" I said to the shadowmen. "Where is the gate?"

Galatur smiled at me.

A square of pure white light appeared in front of us.

"Will this gate do?" Galatur said. He took my hand. "We must go now, Inanna."

I turned to Bizilla. "Come with us. They are going to kill you."

"I cannot come without Ninlil and the others," she said.

"There's no time for this," Kurgurrah said. "It takes unimaginable power to create a gate like this and to hold it open. Come now before we are spent."

"Bizilla," I said to her. "She will kill you if you stay, for what you just did, trying to help me."

Kurgurrah and Galatur shared a glance.

"Time is running out," said Kurgurrah.

"If you come with us, you can come back," I said to Bizilla. "But you cannot help anyone if you are dead."

Bizilla looked round at the red-clad soldiers and gave me a faint nod. "I will come with you, Inanna."

Moments later, on Galatur's arm, I stepped through the door of living light.

CHAPTER 10

NINSHUBAR

Alive

In ordinary times I was a wonderful swimmer, but these were not ordinary times. Having crawled out of my pit of death, I waded into the night-time sea and found myself swimming with all the grace of a newborn gazelle. That is to say badly, slowly, and with the ever-present threat of drowning.

My fingers seemed not to want to close and there was no strength in my arms and legs. I breathed in water and for a moment felt that I was back in my grave.

After I had thought perhaps six times that I was going to sink down forever beneath the black sea, my waterlogged hands finally touched sand. Coughing, crawling, twice tipping face down onto gritty sand, I made my way up onto the island.

I was close to being entirely done, but I had the good sense at least to crawl into undergrowth before collapsing. Yes, no doubt Harga would have made sure of the island before lying down, exploring every hand's breadth of it. The pain and exhaustion I felt would be nothing to him. I smiled to myself, at the thought of Harga seeing me as I was, lying there so naked, weak, foolish, and exposed.

And then, unceremoniously, not caring at all about the thorns and how wet and cold I was, I fell into the deepest, most dreamless slumber of my life.

I awoke to the astonishing and marvellous feeling of hot sun on my skin and I opened my eyes to palm trees and the bluest sky.

A heartbeat later I sensed that I was not alone.

I lay still, breathing gently, listening out with every hair on my body. Then I moved my head just a fraction to take a look around me.

It was agony. I put my head back down on the sand. My neck was still very sore indeed.

I breathed in very deep, and then lifted my head, more carefully. My view was obscured by leaves, but there was someone sitting on the beach between me and the sea. A man with brown hair and a long brown beard.

"I see you are awake," he said, turning to look at me. A highborn accent.

Very slowly and carefully, I pushed myself up into a sitting position.

The man on the sand had a spear in one hand and a shaft-scraping stone in the other.

"I wonder what your story is," he said.

He was dressed in the sort of smock a humble fisherman might wear and he was barefoot. Yet I knew at once what he was. His skin had an unnatural, elemental sheen, as he moved to look back at his spear; the same metallic sheen that all the Anunnaki had when the sun caught them, even my beloved Inanna.

"I am going to guess that you are hungry," the Anunnaki said. He rummaged in the canvas bag that sat beside him on the sand, and then came over to me with a lump of bread and a piece of cheese.

By the time he sat down again to work on his spear, I had already devoured the bread and the cheese, too quickly to taste them. It hurt my throat to swallow, but my hunger overrode my pain.

I tried to make a noise but could not. The Anunnaki understood me nonetheless and came back over to me with a waterskin. I could tell, when I saw him move, that he was a powerful man.

The water did not touch my sides. I shook out the last droplets into my mouth.

"You can come out onto the beach," the man said. "I will not hurt you."

I shook my head, slowly, and I threw him back the waterskin.

"How quickly you are healing," he said. "I can see the difference in you already and it is only moments since you ate."

I gave the smallest shrug. Oh, even my shoulders ached.

"I'll get you some more water," he said. "And what about some more food?"

Slowly and carefully, I nodded my head.

"Come out," he said, as he moved away from me. "You cannot be comfortable there in those thorns."

I carefully shook my head.

"I can just as easily hurt you sitting in that patch of thorns, as I can hurt you if you come to sit on the beach."

That was true enough.

"You don't have to worry about anyone coming at us from the sea," he said. "The Akkadians patrol the waters half a league out. Here, in the inner islands, I see a patrol boat perhaps three times a week. Sometimes they come close and I wave at them and shout out to them in the language of the fishermen on these islands. They have never yet bothered to land here."

Again, I gave a little shrug.

"Well, suit yourself," he said.

He walked off out of sight.

I stood, slowly, and crept over to where he had been sitting. I snatched up his spear and weighed it in my hand. There were many things I could have done with that spear, but an idea came into my head and it wiped out all other ideas: *fish*.

By the time the Anunnaki returned to the beach, carrying a leather pack and waterskins, I was already standing in the waves with his spear raised above my head. Heartbeats later, I caught my first fish. I devoured it raw, standing there naked in the ocean. It was salty, bloody, sweet, and elemental, and I left only the spine and skull for the crabs. I washed my hands in the gentle surf and then I raised my spear to fish again.

All day, I fished, with the hot sun on my bare back. I devoured each fish as I had the first in a frenzy of desperate greed. All day the man watched me from the beach. Now and again I would wade up onto the sand to put my hand out for his waterskin and each time he would hand it over without comment.

When dusk came, I went back to my bed of thorny undergrowth, giving a wide berth to the Anunnaki as I passed him. I lay down again, my new spear next to me, and again fell into a slumber deeper than any I had known.

When I woke it was full daylight and the Anunnaki was on the beach again, this time with a canoe. He was readying it for a journey. "I'll be back before dusk," he called over to me. He came up the beach and deposited two full waterskins near me.

I nodded at him in thanks. As I nodded, I realised how much better my neck was.

The Anunnaki paddled off in his canoe without looking back at me.

I stood on the beach until I was sure he was gone and then I set about searching the whole island. It was not a large island: a hundred or so palm trees, some piles of grey boulders, some dense scrub. It did not take long to search.

At the centre of the island I found a shoulder-high rock surrounded by thorny bushes. It all looked innocent enough except that there were footprints everywhere and what looked like an attempt to cover them over. Then I spotted the piled-up palm leaves that covered the entrance way to a tunnel through the bushes. I dropped down, crawled in, and soon enough I found the burrow.

The Anunnaki had dug himself an underground hiding place beneath that rock at the centre of the island. Inside the damp hole, poorly hidden, I found a bronze axe and two bronze knives, and one can never have too many weapons.

I also found, in the underground burrow, a tar-covered barrel of water and two stone jars of dried foods.

Just outside the burrow, but out of sight from the island at large, the bushes were hung with various provisions and tools. One large bush had been converted into a rainwater collector, with the old sails of a boat rigged up to funnel water down into a pottery urn. It was all neat enough work for a fisherman, although of course the man was not really a fisherman.

In one of the hanging bags I found a long length of red linen which smelled fresh enough. I folded it around me, threw the end over my shoulder, and tied it at the waist with a piece of embroidered leather that I found hanging in the tree.

I sat down then and without ceremony ate a great deal of my host's food. Dried dates and figs, several round cheeses, a large amount of dried venison, and then, after slight reluctance at first, a whole box of dried fishes. My nose wrinkled as I crunched on them; they were meant to be eaten boiled. But I kept eating and downed a dozen cups of his stored water. After that I crawled into his burrowed-out hiding hole and fell into my newfound pit of heavy slumber.

I woke to the dark shape of the Anunnaki peering in at me.

"This does not seem very civilised," he said. "Eating so much of my food, taking so much of my water, breaking into my hiding place, taking that cloth without asking. All this when I have done my best to treat you as a hearth friend."

"Back away," I said, the axe in my right hand, and after a few heartbeats he did so.

I climbed slowly out of the hole, axe still in hand, the two bronze knives tucked into my embroidered belt, and then I crawled out of the tunnel through the bushes.

The Anunnaki was standing well back from the entrance to the hiding place. He had a dead pig on the ground behind him and a great deal of blood on his fisherman's smock.

"I brought you a proper meal that might help put meat on your bones," he said, "although you do not make me very keen to share it."

I stood up to my full height. I was, by quite some measure, taller than him, and I guessed I would be a great deal quicker in a fight. I could see no obvious weapons on him; there were no *mees* on his arms. I wondered what he had done with his.

"Do you want to have a talk about rights and wrongs?" I said.

"Not especially," he said. "Morality in general holds no interest for me." He tipped his head towards the pig. "I thought we could risk a fire tonight."

Later we sat side by side, beneath the star-studded sky, the fire between us, and feasted on roast pork. Across the water, the great ramparts of the city stood tall and dark against the stars.

"Is it Ur?" I said.

"Yes, Ur," he said. "Beautiful Ur."

"And the Akkadians have it now?"

"Well, yes," he said. "King Akka himself has moved in."

"How long has it been?" I said.

"What do you mean?"

"How long since the city fell to the Akkadians?"

"Seven months or so," he said. "Maybe eight."

I had to take some time to absorb that. I had been in my grave for at least seven moons.

"Where have you been all this time?" he said.

"In a grave. Just over the water there."

He looked out over the ocean, nodding. "They had an open pit there for a few weeks after the invasion," he said. "They slung in all the dead together."

I took a deep breath in, pushing away memories of the mud. "You are Inanna's father," I said at last. "The moon god Nanna."

"Yes," he said. He glanced sideways at me. "I also know who you are. The stories of you reached me before the cities fell."

I turned around to face him full on. "Do you know where Inanna is?"

"The story is that she went into the Kur, blazing with blue light. And after that the mountain collapsed on top of the Kur."

"And then?"

"Since then nothing," he said. He poked at the fire with a stick. "No one knows if she is still in the Kur or whether she has passed over to some other realm. No one knows if she is alive or dead."

I remembered the sight of her on that grassy plain in my afterlife. But what did that mean? Perhaps nothing.

"The others," I said. "Do you know where they are?"

"Can you be more specific?"

"My son," I said. "He calls himself Marduk now. Gilgamesh. Your wife, Ningal. A man called Harga. Have you heard news of any of them?"

"Oh them," he said. "I am told your friends have been making sport of the Akkadians up and down the river." He cut himself more pork. "Also, that they are using Enki's Refuge in the marshes."

My heart began to beat faster. "What names have you heard?"

"Gilgamesh. Enki. Isimud. My wife is said to run with them. Also, a pale-skinned god, who is now much spoken of. I think that is Marduk."

"And a man called Harga?"

He shook his head. "I don't know. Maybe."

"How far is this Refuge you speak of?"

"A day's paddle, perhaps two. It's in the marshes north of Eridu. But I'm told the Akkadians have got wind of them and intend to clear them out of there. It may already be too late for them."

"I'll leave in the morning," I said. "Will you come?"

He smiled. "I will not."

"You will stay here?"

"Yes I will."

I did not want to call the man a coward, but I understood now why Inanna so rarely spoke of him.

"It seems extraordinary to me," I said, carefully, "that you can be sitting out here in plain sight and the Akkadians take no notice of you."

"I slipped away from Ur in the night, with soldiers, and we left a heavy trail heading east. Then a long time later I crept back alone in a canoe and set myself up here. The Akkadians see only what they want to see: ten thousand islands full of fisher folk who bring fresh fish to their markets each day."

"It must scratch at you though, must it not, to see them on the walls of your city?"

He tensed at that. "No doubt when I was sapling young, as you are now, I might have thought it strange to be sitting here while the enemy walked the streets of my city. But I have seen things go very wrong before and have learnt how to withstand it when they do. The risk right now is too high. So I must keep on waiting."

"So you will wait until the Akkadians are dead?"

"Dead or gone, I don't care which."

"And then you will swoop in, dressed as a fisherman, and say how sorry you are to have abandoned them but you're back now."

He sat himself up straighter. "Oh, I think I'll dream up a better story than that," he said. "A god is nothing without a good story."

The next day I hunted out his canoe in the undergrowth and pulled it down to the sand, ready to go. I loaded up the boat with all the fresh water and lumps of roast pig that I could find, and I added some firewood and a flint strike-a-light, and some moss to get a fire going. For good measure, I threw in my host's one good blanket.

The moon god stood and watched me prepare to go. He

reminded me very strongly of Inanna, as he stood there. "You might have asked first," he said.

"I am engaged in matters of state," I said. "In acts of duty. Are you? I think I have a better right to this canoe."

He gave me a weary smile. "When honour and duty have killed you, Ninshubar, or rather, killed you for a second time, I will be in Ur, sitting on my terrace, eating a fine supper with a magnificent view of this island. Then we can talk about matters of state and who might have done the best thing for Sumer."

"We will see," I said, as I pushed the canoe out through the first waves and then hopped in very neatly. I had become a fine boatswoman since leaving my own country.

As I was about to plunge my paddle into the water, I looked back to see Inanna's father frowning to himself, as if in indecision. A moment later he came wading out to me. He took a hold of the canoe, holding me steady in the water.

"Ninshubar," he said. "If you see the boy Gilgamesh in the marshes, will you tell him that I think his son is alive?"

I rested my paddle over my lap. "What do you mean?"

"The word went out that Akka had killed the boy's wife and child. But my man in the city says it was a lie. They threw the woman off the moon tower, but they hid the baby in the palace nurseries in case the child might be useful to them later. The baby is still there amongst the Akkadian royal children."

I looked down at my paddle and made my calculations.

"Gilgamesh's father used to be my friend," said Nanna. "I would be grateful if you would pass this on." He let go of the canoe.

I immediately paddled hard for the shore and leaped out onto the sand.

"I have a new plan," I said to the moon god. "I am going to go to Ur. And the exciting thing is that my plan involves you."

CHAPTER 11

INANNA

Lost

I stepped through the gate of light created by the shadowmen, and I found myself in total blackness.

"Kurgurrah?" I whispered. "Galatur?"

A yellow light. It was Bizilla: the gold bracelet on her right wrist gave out soft pulses of light.

We were in what looked like a natural cave. Perhaps one cable across, two cables along, and with no visible way out. The air smelled of wet and rock. There was no trace of the sulphurous stink we had just left behind.

Bizilla was looking hard at me. "Do you know who you are, Inanna?"

"I know."

"Do you know where we are?"

"I do not."

"Where are your friends? Those men?"

"They were not exactly men. They could be here, but in another form."

My ankle was hurting; I looked down and realised it was bleeding. I found a rounded boulder to sit on and tried to staunch the bleeding with my dress. It was then I saw the two obsidian beads gleaming up at me from the floor of the cave. I picked them up and held them tight in my hand, not having anywhere safe to put them.

"Could this be the Earth?" Bizilla said, as she shone her *mee* along the length of one side of the cave.

I shut my eyes and tried to feel my old network of blue light. If we were on Earth, surely I would connect with the lake of shining power? But there was nothing.

"I don't think this is Earth."

Bizilla moved over to another stretch of wall and put her hands on the rock. She lifted her right wrist to cast the light higher up to the roof of the cave. "It all looks natural."

She made her way along the wall, carefully shining her light into every crevice.

"It was good of you to have argued for me, Bizilla," I said. "To have put yourself in harm's way for me."

She paused a moment, looking over at me. "It was an act of madness. And because of it I have now abandoned Ninlil, who I am sworn to."

"You're her *sukkal*?"

"I do not deserve to be," she said. She turned from me, lifting her wrist again. "I think this might be a way out," she said. "How is that ankle?"

I pushed myself up. "Good enough."

We climbed up behind a pillar of flowing rock and through a narrow gap. I had to lift my dress up and bend down low to get through the passage. There were red handprints all along the rock wall.

"Have you ever seen anything like this?" said Bizilla.

"I have not. But at least someone has been here before."

We passed through into a passage tall enough for us to walk upright in, although the floor was rocky and uneven. The cave walls were decorated with a line of faded red dots, each about half the width of my hand across.

We had to edge around a large stone pillar before emerging into a much larger cavern. Bizilla lifted her wrist and we peered around us at the temple-like heights of the new space.

The floor of the cavern was studded with pillars, rock flows, and all manner of obstacles and protuberances.

"I suppose we just keep going," said Bizilla.

I heard something. A rock tumbling, perhaps? I put my hand out to Bizilla and gripped on hard to her arm. "I think I heard something."

We looked at each other, eyes wide, and Bizilla let her *mee* die.

We stood in pitch darkness, holding each other. I tried to breathe as quietly as I could.

Water dripping on rock. Nothing else. Absolute blackness.

Perhaps I imagined it, but for a moment I thought I saw light along one wall.

"I think I saw something," Bizilla whispered. "A shadow moving."

"I did too."

We were both quiet, holding on tight to each other, for what felt like an age. All we could hear was water dripping.

"I'm going to creep forward alone," whispered Bizilla. "If there is someone there, I will secure them."

"I don't want to be left alone," I said.

Ahead of us then, came the unmistakable sound of a woman's

voice. Just a fragment. And then, in a lower register, a man attempting to whisper.

"Who is there?" Bizilla called.

A long pause, a deep silence, in the darkness.

"First tell us who you are," the man called back, his voice echoing around us.

I almost laughed out loud, because I recognised his voice. "Say your names and then we will say our names."

"Inanna?" he said.

A bright white light lit up our cave.

Ahead of us, three cables along, stood three figures.

A woman with wild hair and a huge belly, and a *mee* blazing white upon her wrist… it was my sister, Ereshkigal. Next to her stood a man in red, holding up an oil lamp. It was the gatekeeper, Neti.

With them stood a young man with black brows and the most luminous smile, so bright it might alone have lit up the cave.

"Hello, moon cousin," Gilgamesh called out to me. "How very good it is to see you."

CHAPTER 12

HARGA

In the marshes

The Akkadians were coming, the marsh people had abandoned us, and now the plan was to simply walk out into the reeds.

Within an hour everyone was gathered upon a muddy shore on the far side of the Refuge from the jetty that we would ordinarily leave from. Our idea was to slip away with no eyes on us.

The muggy air was full of anxious murmurs and babies crying as we dragged the canoes through the mud and reeds until there was enough water for them to float. Two of the canoes had holes in and immediately began to sink. That left us twenty-seven canoes in all, including the marshwoman's age-darkened vessel.

In the end we got one hundred and fifty or so people into the canoes, as well as the three dogs and the guest-gift goat. That left sixty-five of us to go into the water, including all of Isimud and Ningal's soldiers. Some of them could swim, but many could not.

"I should warn you it is not only snakes out there in the water,"

Marduk said to me and the Uruk boys, as he lifted the dogs into an already overloaded canoe. I had insisted on the dogs' jaws being bound shut with leather string, and all three looked at me reproachfully.

"There are also crocodiles and hippos," Marduk went on.

"And biting fish," said Tallboy.

"And these little scorpions that really sting you," said Shortboy.

"That's enough, boys," I said.

The moon goddess, in her fighting leathers but barefoot, had taken a place at the front of a canoe with a crowd of young children behind her. "I feel bad taking a place in a boat," she said.

"Paddle hard then," I said to her. I put out a hand to her and we briefly gripped hold of each other. Then I looked about at the canoes, trampled reeds, anxious faces, and those of us about to wade into the foul water, and made the good luck signs on my chest.

"Come then," said Sagar, the ancient marshwoman. She pushed off with her paddle and headed out through the reeds towards open water. "Time to disappear," she said.

I checked that my stone pouch and catapult were bound double to my belt, and that my knives were secure, and into the stinking water I went, following on after Marduk and the two Uruk boys, since it was they who claimed to have marsh-walked before.

Very soon the canoes had pulled well ahead and the rest of us were chest deep in water and thoroughly covered in marsh slime. Sometimes I found myself pushing myself along with my feet, trying to get purchase on whatever nasty undergrowth there was beneath the black water. At other times I pulled myself along with my arms, wincing at the pain in my shoulder.

My fighting leathers were quickly sodden and heavy. I thought about stripping naked, but then thought about all the creatures that might like to take a bite out of me.

How I hated the marshes!

At the outer edge of a reed bed, we faced a gap across to what I suppose amounted to the next island. A gap no wider than a stream, really. The canoes were already across, disappearing into the reeds beyond. Marduk turned to face me, his red hair slick to his head. "I'll go first," he said. He dived swiftly under the water and emerged on the other side. Finding purchase there, one arm wrapped around reeds, he stretched a hand back towards me. "I'm ready to catch, if you will throw, Harga."

I turned to Tallboy. "You first, lad."

I lifted him up and threw him over to Marduk as best I could.

An hour later, clustered in the midst of a thick stand of reeds, we were all exhausted. We were about to cross over another stretch of open waterway, but those of us in the slime needed a chance to get our breath. The canoes floated between us and it was tempting to hang on to one, but they were already all overloaded.

And then we heard a dog's bark, close by.

I looked to Marduk's dogs, but their mouth bindings were holding.

I lifted a closed fist in signal and our floating village moved backwards into the heart of the reeds.

Signalling to the others to stay where they were, I pulled myself slowly forward in the direction of the dog's bark.

When I glimpsed open water ahead, I slowed. I dipped myself fully beneath the water, once, to make sure I stank only of the marsh.

A little further forward, and I had a perfect view. A huge barge was moving across the waterway ahead. Its high wooden sides gleamed a warm yellow as it cut through the dark marsh water, its bronze-tipped oars moving in slow but steady union.

From my low position in the reeds, I could see no one on deck, but then a dark-haired young man in Akkadian blue came to stand at the railings on my side of the barge. He looked out into the distance but did not drop his eyes down to me. The man had lost his nose; the centre of his face was a mess of scar tissue.

A marshman came to stand beside him. It was Adamen, our supposed ally. The shock of recognising him there, with the enemy, quickly turned to fury. I had thought Adamen capable of fleeing or doing nothing. I had not thought him capable of outright treachery.

"Well, where are they then?" the man in velvet blue said to Adamen. Only when he spoke, did I recognise him. It was Inush, King Akka's nephew. The scarring was a gift from my friend Gilgamesh.

It was the strangest thing, to be so close to those two men, close enough to hear their conversation, and yet invisible to them. I sank myself lower in the water so that only my nose and eyes were above the surface, but Inush and Adamen kept their eyes raised, looking out over the reeds I was sheltering in.

"Someone must have warned them you were coming," Adamen said, "but they cannot have got far. They had only a handful of canoes to escape with."

Inush frowned at him. "And you're sure one of them has very pale skin?"

"And red hair and blue eyes," said Adamen. "He is the one who fights like a devil."

"The man I knew was not a fighting man," said Inush, shaking his head. "But perhaps I did not know him well enough."

And then the barge had passed by, as if it had only been some colourful mirage, and we were all dreaming there in the wall of reeds.

I pulled myself slowly back to the others. We had no idea if more boats would come, so we stayed exactly where we were for one long hour, only moving around a little to check that everyone was well. At one point I found myself hanging off Ningal's canoe.

She looked so young and pretty with her curls slicked back and marsh mud on her face, that I could almost understand Gilgamesh lying with her and almost forgive him for it. But not quite.

"Can the water be safe to drink?" she whispered.

"For you maybe. The rest of us will get gut rot."

She squeezed the hand I was hanging on with. "One step and then the next," she said.

It was only then that I remembered, with a sickening lurch, what the marshwoman had told us about Ninshubar. That she had been thrown into the mass graves outside Ur.

I had crept past those open pits dozens of times when we were preparing to enter Ur to rescue Gilgamesh.

I turned my face from the moon goddess, there in that wilderness of reeds, to hide the tears that I could not stop coming.

CHAPTER 13

NINLIL

In Heaven

I sat by the fire in my bedchamber, on my old rocking chair, thinking about my mother, when my brother Qingu opened the door. "Oh dear," he said, looking in. "What a sad little scene."

He dipped his horns down beneath the door frame as he entered. "Our mother has gone into a frenzy," he said. He had on his long white fur coat and matching boots.

I stood up. "What do you mean?"

"Killing, eating, you know how she gets." He peered around at my small bed and ancient drawings.

"Qingu, did you come to fetch me?"

He gave a shrug. "The priests think she's ready to go into labour. They think having you there might calm her."

I pulled on my fur-lined boots and my white fur cloak. "Lead on then."

In the corridor outside, my brother's red-robed guards stood waiting for us alongside a dozen of my own white-robed servants. Half moved off ahead of us; the others followed on behind. Qingu walked side by side with me and I realised we were the same height, if one ignored his horns. He seemed more twitchy than normal, almost anxious.

"Did something happen?" I said to him.

He tipped his huge horns from side to side without turning to me. "The little girl escaped. The girl Inanna." He flicked his eyes over me. "And Bizilla went with her."

I stopped walking. "What do you mean?"

"Bizilla's gone," he said. "Keep walking."

I kept walking, breathing through my upset. "Why has Bizilla gone?"

He shrugged. "They had help from someone. That is all unclear. But it happened in the audience room in front of everyone. Dear Mother was about to eat the girl. It was a scene."

I had asked Bizilla to help Inanna. Had I done right?

"How did they escape? Where did they go to?"

"All unclear. They were there and then they were not. Mother did not like that. Father was knocked over. Not very holy."

At the towering doors to my mother's main audience chamber, my brother said: "It will just be us going in." As he spoke, he took hold of my arm.

Ah, the shock of his hand upon me. Without any conscious thought or effort, I found myself flooding into him. Into the darkness that was his heart.

"Ninlil!" He sprang backwards away from me, pulling his hand from me as if I had bitten him. "Keep your hands off me."

He was shaking. Looking down at my hands, I realised I was shaking too.

The men pulled the doors open for us.

Inside the audience chamber, our mother, the dragon queen, squatted upon a great fire pit. She breathed out yellow clouds of sulphurous gas and roared and grumbled. Her priests, draped in black, crowded around her, their faces pink in the firelight. They lifted their voices to the vaulted stone roof in the ancient birth song of Creation.

The dragon turned one of its seven heads towards us and a moment later her chief priest hurried up to us. "She wants you to sit over there." He pointed to two golden thrones. My father, head tipped forward, was already there in his rusting chair.

And so we sat there, my brother and I, while the priests chanted and my mother roared and shifted in her bed of fire.

"At least finally we can see what the mystery is," my brother said, scratching at one of his horns. He kept his voice low. "The mystery gestation. All very odd and yet so important the whole world must wait for it to happen. Even with our realm falling apart around us." He seemed quite cheerful, but then the minutes turned into hours, and his temper frayed.

I was too far from the fire pit to get any benefit from it and my toes and fingers grew numb. Our mother roared but seemed to make no progress.

Qingu yawned and scratched his horns again. It occurred to me, afresh, just how very silly he looked.

"Why the horns?" I said to him. "They must be so heavy."

"I did it for a party." He smiled at me. "It was a nasty joke on some groom. I stuck him through with them after the wedding ceremony. It was very funny."

I was quiet a moment. "Was the groom injured?"

Qingu put his hand over his mouth to stop a laugh. "He died!"

I took a deep breath in. "How can that be a joke, brother?"

"Oh," he said. "He took the girl from me. It's a long story."

I sat in silence then, nauseous with horror. How had I come to be sitting here in complicity with such people?

Qingu tapped my right knee with his gloved left fist. "Sister, the man was in the wrong. Everyone knew it. But the point is that I decided I rather liked the horns. They are a good story, like Mother's dragon form. I became the Bull of Heaven and she became the Dragon Queen. Stories matter, you know."

"I do know," I said. "I was thinking over what you did to me. Leaving me with Enlil that day. Leaving Enlil with very explicit directions as to what he should do to me, thanks to the master *mee* you now wear again. Did you also use the master *mee* on me, to make me give birth? To make me insist on running away with Enlil? Did you give him the master *mee* with the express intention that he take me to another realm, leaving all here clear for you?"

He laughed, although quietly. He then re-formed his features into kind concern or as close as he could get to it. "I'm not going to admit to anything, sister. However, setting aside the circumstances of your disappearance, I will say it was a difficult time for me politically." The last he said with a serious frown on his brow.

"Should I feel sympathy for you?"

"There was talk about marrying me off to one of the Anunnaki. To the girl Ereshkigal."

I had lost interest in speaking to him. What could be gained by it?

He seemed not to mind my silence. "The point being that with you gone, the Anunnaki gone, all of their lands coming to us, and our mother going mad with grief, I cannot deny things were better for me."

He scratched at both horns at once. A comic sight, had I been in the mood for comedy. "Of course, later, when I realised how much we needed it, I regretted the loss of the master *mee*."

It was then that our mother, the dragon, gave out a roar so deep and long that the whole room shook and all turned to face her.

A movement, a shifting of her tail, and something long, black, and glistening slid out onto the flagstones from between my mother's hind legs.

My brother stood up to get a better view of it. "By all the holy stars," he said.

CHAPTER 14

NINSHUBAR

On an island just off Ur

The moon god and I stood on the beach, squared up to each other, with the canoe between us. I had my spear; he had no weapons on show.

"I am going to take this canoe and I am going to go to the marshes to help my friends," I said.

"I wish you luck there," said the moon god.

"But first there is something we are going to do together." I pointed across the narrow blue strait that lay between our island and the mud-brick ramparts of Ur. "First we are going to go across to the city and rescue Gilgamesh's son."

"No," he said, taking a firm step back up the beach.

I strode forward and in the same movement put the tip of my spear against the soft place behind his left ear. "I don't know Ur and I don't know anyone in it. You will come with me to Ur to rescue the child. Afterwards you can come back and sit on this beach like the coward you are and wait for the Akkadians to die natural deaths."

"No," he said.

I gave him a little jab with the spear, enough to make him leap backwards, his hand to his neck, blood streaming through his fingers.

"You're mad," he said. "We have no hope of getting out alive."

His eyes flicked left towards the undergrowth.

Ah, the *mees*.

He should have kept them handier, for just such a moment as this.

"Let us have a look about," I said, pointing my spear at his guts. "You first."

I made another sweep of the island, with him walking just ahead of me, one hand to his neck wound. Beneath a palm tree on the far side of the island, I saw the marks of someone having covered something over and sprinkled the area with dead leaves. I dug with my axe and quickly found a small wooden box with four shining *mees* inside.

The heavy bracelets felt alive on my arms. *Mees* of protection and *mees* of close combat, two of each.

The moon god watched me from just out of spear range.

"I won't hurt you again," I said, "as long as you do as I say. Now you and I are going to sit and talk."

We sat down opposite each other on the hot sand.

"Tell me how you get information from the city," I said.

"There are some boys who sail an old temple skiff. They use it to carry messages, important packages, sometimes passengers, around the ten thousand islands. The Akkadians use them all the time, but they are loyal to Sumer."

"And?"

"And when I put my tar-covered barrel out on the beach here, the boys come in to pick up a message from me."

"And then?"

"They take the message to my man in Ur and put it into his hand and his hand only. That's the system."

"Put out the barrel," I said, looking down at the *mees* on my arms and enjoying the feel of all they could do.

"If we enter Ur, we will die," he said. "We will be torn into pieces, just as the goddess Ninsun was at Uruk."

"I never met Ninsun," I said. "Although I know her temple in Uruk."

"She died in battle. Like any ordinary soldier. And they scattered her body to the wind, to make sure she stayed dead. They say Nammu is dead too. We are vulnerable, Ninshubar. We need to be patient and clever."

"Put out the barrel," I said.

The sun had not moved much in the sky when I caught sight of a sharp white sail.

"That looks like a temple skiff," I said. "Indeed it looks like a skiff from the White Temple at Uruk."

"I don't know where it's from," said Nanna. "I've never asked them."

The skiff was coming straight for the island with four people on deck.

As they drew close, the figures resolved into four young men. They were bringing the boat in fast towards our beach.

"Hah!" I said. "I know those boys."

I stood up and lifted a hand to them. All four lifted a hand to us and even at a distance, I caught the gleam of four bright smiles.

Moments later they rode the boat up high onto the beach and leaped out onto the sand as the sail fell neatly onto the deck. It was an extraordinary display of sailing prowess.

The boys bowed low to the moon god and then low to me, but with grins. "Lady Ninshubar!" said the largest of them. "We have been waiting for you. We have kept this skiff safe for you, just as you requested."

"You know each other?" said the moon god, slowly standing.

"They once took me to Eridu." I smiled at the boys. "And later, when the Akkadians began their attacks on Sumer, these boys came south with a message for me and Inanna. I asked them to stay here and keep the skiff safe."

"And we did," said the smallest boy.

"Sailors, what say you to some food?" I said.

We sat beneath a palm to eat and talk. There had been three-quarters of a pig left when the moon god and I had finished eating the night before. Now in a matter of some half an hour, the pig, sprinkled with salt, was entirely consumed.

"We knew you were waiting here for a reason," the leader of the boys said to the moon god. "Now Ninshubar is here, it can begin."

"Soon Ur will be free," said the smallest boy.

"It makes sense that you would come now," said the boys' leader. "King Akka was foolish to leave the guard so thin here."

The moon god and I caught each other's eyes for a moment.

"Where is King Akka?" I said to the boys.

"Gone north," said the leader. "With many barges and most of his army. This is the ideal time to attack Ur."

Of course, it was not the plan. There was no way that we could free a city with an army of two gods, of sorts, and four young boys. But it did not seem the right moment to explain that to them.

"So you have been here in the river mouth since I said goodbye to you?" I said.

"At first we only hid, since we knew no one here," said the boys' leader. "We fished, we found fresh springs. We hid very well. But then the mast broke."

We turned to look down the beach at the skiff and its elegant oak mast, golden against the sea.

"Of course, any small problem with the boat, we can fix ourselves," the boy went on. "But we needed tools then that we did not have access to. So we began to get to know people in the ten thousand islands. We began to barter. Now we have contacts all over the gulf and we run messages and cargo. We even work for the Akkadians now, so that they do not think anything much of us, except that we are useful."

The smallest boy clapped his hands together. "But now you are returned and the Akkadians will be ousted!"

"I cannot tell you the exact nature of our business," I said, frowning.

All the boys grinned even wider at that and raised their eyebrows at each other.

"We need you to get word into the city," I said. "Word to the man you always go to, with messages from this fisherman here. We need the man to let us into the city at a certain place and at a certain time."

All four boys nodded solemnly.

"We will carry that message for you," said their leader.

Late that afternoon, in the highest heat of the day, the boys left for Ur.

"You give over the message and you get out of the city

immediately," I said as they pushed off. "Do not be waiting for any answer or any result. Is that all clear?"

All lifted cheerful hands to me and then they busied themselves with their sails.

"Time to get ready," I said to the moon god, "if we're to be at the walls of Ur at midnight."

He seemed to have sunk into a deep gloom. "This plan is terrible," he said. "So many things can go wrong."

I watched the skiff's clean white sail growing smaller on the water.

"One step and then the next," I said to the moon god, clapping him rather hard on the shoulder. "We get into the city, we get Gilgamesh's boy, and we get out. That's the plan." I smiled, thinking of Harga. "Quickly in and quickly out."

"A terrible, terrible plan," said the moon god, but mostly to himself.

CHAPTER 15

GILGAMESH

In the inbetween

The five of us met in council in the dark caves that lay between the realms.

We were a strange collection.

I sat on a wide, round rock with the queen of the underworld next to me, enveloped by the protective light ring of one of her *mees*.

Inanna and her tall, red-headed companion were perched opposite us on a ledge, in a pool of their own light. The red-headed woman sported a coat of large golden scales; quite something. She said her name was Bizilla, and she was *sukkal* to my beloved Ninlil, and she was also so like my friend Marduk that I could not get over the surprise of it.

To complete our council, the gatekeeper Neti stood halfway between our two camps, an oil lamp in one hand.

Ereshkigal sat with her face turned towards me and away from her sister. "Inanna killed all my demons," she said to me.

"Did you know that? And she killed our brother Utu. Did you know that?"

Inanna had no eyes for her sister, but only because she was beaming at me. I had forgotten how unguarded and friendly she could be. And how very lovely, with her shining black eyes and silken hair.

"What a strange and happy meeting, in this dark place!" I said, returning Inanna's happy smile.

"A very happy meeting," said Inanna, very earnest, her whole body turned to me, her hands clasped in front of her.

We had by then established that Inanna and Bizilla had come to these dark caves directly from Heaven, with the help of Enki's magical flies. And of course, Ereshkigal and I had come directly from Abydos. Now we were all trapped in a dark cave system that Neti claimed to be outside all normal realms.

"Do you know what has happened to Ninlil?" I said to them. "We only know she went into the Kur."

"Ninlil is alive and in Heaven," said Bizilla.

"And she's safe?" I said.

"As safe as anyone is in the palace of Creation," said Bizilla.

"So what now?" I said.

"I am going to get Nergal," said Ereshkigal. "And you can show me how to get there." The last part was directed at Bizilla.

Inanna lifted her hands to her sister. "Ereshkigal, you should return with me to Earth. No good can come from any trip to Heaven. It cannot be safe for you there in your condition."

"Condition?" said Ereshkigal, very stern indeed. "My condition?"

Inanna was quiet a moment and then said: "I only meant that it cannot be safe for any of us there."

"My safety is not my concern," said Ereshkigal. She heaved

herself to standing, one hand to her swollen belly. "Bizilla, show me the way to the gate you came through."

Bizilla also climbed to her feet. "Ereshkigal, I will gladly show you the way to the gate to Heaven and I will pass through it with you." She looked back down at Inanna. "I must go back for Nergal and Ninlil."

I had a moment of uncertainty. Should I be going with them to Heaven? Nergal was only a name to me, but Ninlil was a mother to me when I moved to Nippur as a boy. She was a childlike creature, but she had been so very kind.

But then I looked over at Inanna, sitting alone on her rock ledge. She looked very small and vulnerable. Surely my duty was to her?

"Inanna," I said, "whatever you choose to do, I will stay with you."

"Thank you," she said, with what seemed to be deep feeling. She looked up to Neti. "And what about you, gatekeeper?"

"I think it is madness for anyone to go on to Heaven." He turned to Ereshkigal. "You do not know this woman Bizilla or what she truly wants."

"You are welcome to come with me and help me," said Ereshkigal. "Perhaps we will be less noisy if you are with us."

"Neti," I said, interrupting them. "I can guide Inanna back to the gate that leads to Egypt, if you would give me your lamp. That is, if you decide to follow Ereshkigal through to Heaven."

The gatekeeper stood for some moments as if frozen. "Everything is a bad idea," he said.

Inanna approached her sister, one hand stretched out. She had two small black beads in her hand. "Ereshkigal, take the flies. They are of great value, as you well know. Perhaps they can help you as they helped me."

Ereshkigal, without smiling or thanking Inanna, took the two black beads and tucked them down the front of her dress.

Neti watched the exchange with no expression, but then said: "I will go with you, Ereshkigal." He handed me his lamp.

Abruptly, we were parting, the groups reassembled. I held up the oil lamp in my right hand and took Inanna's right hand in my left.

Ereshkigal, Bizilla, and Neti, in pools of yellow and white light, began to move away from us across the dark cave floor.

"I hope to see you all again," Inanna called after them, holding on tight to me.

"I hope never to see you again," Ereshkigal called back. They were already being swallowed up by the dark.

By the small light of our oil lamp, Inanna and I made our way across the cave floor.

"I am so absurdly happy to see you," she said, squeezing my hand tighter. "I can't explain it. It's so impossible that you are here. And yet here you are, so real, so warm!"

"I am very real and very happy," I said, although my knee hurt and I was rather worried about finding the way back to the correct cave.

Inanna looked down at my left leg. "What is wrong with your knee?"

"An old injury. You have been gone a long time, moon cousin."

I had not meant to upset her, but pain flickered across her face. "I am so sorry for it." She took a deep breath in. "What news do you have of Sumer?"

I lifted my oil lamp higher to better light up the crystalline slope ahead of us. "The Akkadians have overrun every city except Sippur," I said. "Perhaps you know that."

"I did not know that."

"Yes, we are in hiding now, those of us who are left. They are the kings of Sumer."

Inanna looked down at her feet, her mouth turned down. "I did not know. So who is still alive? Tell me everything."

I took a deep breath in and a deep breath out. "My mother died at Uruk, I don't know if you heard that. And before that, Enlil died in Nippur, at the hands of Ereshkigal's beloved, Nergal. But that was all before you left for the Kur."

"I did not know," she said. "And my mother? Do you have news of her?"

"She was well when I last saw her," I said, hoping that the gloom would hide my blush. I took a deep breath in and a deep breath out. "Also, my wife and son were executed at Ur," I said. "In revenge for my escape from the city."

After a short pause, she said: "I am very sorry for your loss, Gilgamesh."

"And of course, you know about Ninshubar."

"I was there when she died," she said.

I squeezed her hand against my ribs. "We have been doing what we can to make things harder for the Akkadians. Isimud and your mother have been leading the resistance." I looked away from Inanna for a moment, remembering waking beside the moon goddess. "So your mother is well," I went on, "or was very recently. Marduk is well too. And Harga. Lilith also. And we just left Enki behind in Egypt."

"You were with Enki?"

"Yes, he's been part of the resistance. He provided a sanctuary for us in the marshes."

She frowned but said nothing.

"You have bruises on your hands," I said.

"I was not well kept by the Anzu," she said. "Do I smell foul?"

I laughed, the noise echoing around us. "You smell of your lions, just as you always have!"

"I did not know that." Her face collapsed into sadness. "I abandoned my lions."

I lifted her hand to my mouth and kissed it. "Your lions are in Egypt, in fact."

"Really?"

"With Enki," I said. "They seem very fond of him."

I was becoming increasingly worried that we might be lost, but then I saw the row of red discs on the cave wall. "It's this way," I said.

We made our way along the narrow passage and down into the cavern that Ereshkigal and I had first appeared in. Inanna looked up at the handprints at the entrance. "They look old," she said. "It all feels very old in here."

"Come, let me help you climb down," I said to her.

And then everything went black.

CHAPTER 16

NINSHUBAR

At Ur, Inanna's home city

We set off towards Ur at dusk. I made the moon god sit in the front of the canoe so that I could keep him firmly in view.

"I don't see why you are making me come," he said.

He was putting no effort into his paddling.

"Why would your contacts let me, a woman they have never seen before, into the city?" I said. "You, they will open the gates for."

"Or they will at once strike me down dead, for having betrayed them."

"Then justice will have been done," I said.

We paddled on in silence.

The moon god and I waited out in the waves until it was truly dark before pulling up onto the sandy shore. High above us, on the city walls, soldiers moved back and forth.

By starlight alone, we stashed the canoe in some low bushes.

"Even if we get to the city gate alive," the moon god whispered, "and even if my man meets us there, even then he will not agree to take us through the city to the royal nursery. It would be suicidal."

"We will see."

"Can I at least have a weapon?"

"No," I said. "Now keep low."

We crept forward through the sand dunes, almost doubled over, very aware of the eyes up on the ramparts. The sand gave way to thick tussocks of grass and not long after we were at the foot of the great walls. "This way," the moon god said, gesturing right.

With the city walls hard to our left, we walked on, slow and quiet, until the moon god turned to face the clay-brick rampart and put his hands to the wall. "Here," he said. He began pulling bricks away. "The gate is behind one thin layer of bricks."

Indeed the bricks came away easily and behind them I could feel the shape of metal bars. "I put this here as an emergency way out," Nanna said, "after the first time the city was overrun by enemies."

With the bricks removed, we peered through the metal bars into darkness.

"There is another gate in there and then a corridor leading to the barracks," the moon god said.

He put his arms through the bars and began to fiddle with the lock on the other side of the gate. As he did so, there was movement inside the tunnel.

Bright light sparked ahead: a lamp had been lit.

I could see the second gate then. A man was trying to get it open from within; an old man in a hooded cloak.

The moon god took a step back, but said to me, quietly: "It's him."

The hooded man unlocked the inner gate and then came through to unlock the outer gate with a long metal key. Three more men emerged from the dark tunnel behind him, all in hooded cloaks. Nanna put a hand out to me. "I know them."

"We have been waiting a long time for you to come," the man with the key said to the moon god. "But, my lord, we knew you would come."

Another man, even more bent and ancient than the first, came forward. "My lord, all the people are ready. The whole city stands ready."

The four men came out through the outer gate and, amidst the tumble of discarded bricks, knelt in front of the moon god and took turns to kiss the hem of his fishing smock.

"My lord," said the man with the lamp, "we stand ready to take back the city for you. Every man, woman, and child is awake and armed. We await your orders."

"No," he said. "That is not the plan."

There was a long pause.

The four men looked up at Nanna expectantly, but with a growing air of puzzlement.

I stepped forward. "You've done well," I said. "I am Ninshubar, *sukkal* to Inanna, daughter of this city. I stand at Nanna's side."

"We welcome you, my lady," said the man with the lamp.

"A new plan then," I said to the moon god. I gripped his arm hard. "Lead on, gentlemen."

The moon god and I paced down the stone tunnel with the four men ahead of us.

"You said quickly in and quickly out," the moon god hissed at me.

"Plans must bend to the facts on the ground."

We passed through a heavy oak door into a room full of men and women and children. They were all heavily armed, albeit with a mixture of traditional weaponry and kitchen implements.

All gathered sank onto their knees, as far as there was room for it, as the moon god entered.

A grizzled man in fighting leathers and a wolf-head helmet held up a bronze sword and said to Nanna: "My lord, we stand ready."

Nanna, high god of the moon, finally seemed to find himself. He stood straighter; his face grew stern. "You have done well," he said to the man. He lifted his face and voice to the room. "Together, we will take the city."

"We have killed all the Akkadians who were inside these barracks," the man in the wolf helmet said. "Eighty-five men in all."

"How many Akkadians are still alive and in the city?" said the moon god. He had a serious air to him now; he had the air of a man of both thought and action.

"There are soldiers living in the city," said the man in the wolf helmet, climbing up off his knees. "There are soldiers at the main gates. Inside the palace, there are the royals who did not go north with King Akka and all their guards and servants."

"Let us split into smaller groups," said the moon god, "and pick off all these Akkadians. I will lead a group to the griffin gate. I want every Akkadian dead by dawn."

"Is there a Sumerian boy amongst the royals?" I said, stepping forward. "A young child called Shara?"

"Gilgamesh's son is there, if that's who you mean," said the grizzled man. "Although they pretend he is one of theirs."

"Spare me a guide," I said to the moon god, "and I'll go straight to the nursery for Shara."

"We can spare you a guide," he said, quite regal in that moment.

I followed a young lad through a city that you might have thought empty, until you caught the glint of eyes in every patch of shadow.

We passed close to a city gate. Akkadians sat hunched over a board game there; a man was pouring them all a drink.

Quiet as ghosts, we scaled a wall into the palace garden and crept along an avenue between ponds and palm trees and towards the dark shape of a large building. Then we were through a small door and into the palace. Three floors up, my guide put one finger to his lips and pushed open a door onto a torch-lit corridor. Three Akkadian soldiers were standing not five paces from us, leaning against a wall. They turned as one to look at us as I threw myself forward.

I killed the first of them with an axe to the forehead. The second with a knife. The third jabbed me in the gut before I got my knife into the side of his throat.

"Are you all right?" said my companion. He had very wisely stayed back from the fray.

I put my left hand over the wound. It was bad, but I had had worse.

The three Akkadians had been guarding a heavy oak door.

I lifted the latch, and pushed open the door.

An old man with a long grey beard, dressed in shining blue, was standing just inside the room. A knife wobbled at me in his shaking right hand. There were children behind him, all sat together on a bed.

"You will not hurt these children," the old man said.

I put my axe and my knife away. "I will not hurt these children. That is the solemn promise of a goddess."

I turned back to my escort. "You may leave us now."

I was bleeding heavily and losing strength in my legs, although the pain from the wound was strangely muted. "We should push something against the door," I said to the old man, once my escort had gone. "Just until the killing is over with."

When the door had a bed across it, I sat down in an old leather chair, my hand to my bleeding gut. It was a pretty room with green shutters and beds against every wall, and candles burning on every table.

I looked over at the cluster of children and was sorry to see them so frightened.

"What's your name, old man?" I said, stretching out my legs.

"Biluda." He sat down opposite me on a padded bench.

"That's a good name," I said. "Now, Biluda, will you tell me, is Shara amongst those children there?"

"I will not tell you."

I laughed, holding my belly wound. "I hope that means he is."

"Who are you, my lady?"

"I am Ninshubar, *sukkal* to the lady Inanna."

"I've heard of her," he said. "So you fight with the Anunnaki?"

"I do."

The distinctive noises of battle rose up through the shuttered windows. Men screaming, swords clashing.

"How many men did you bring?" said the old man, his eyes on the windows.

"Only one, actually," I said.

I shut my eyes a moment and almost lost consciousness.

"May I ask you a question?"

"Certainly. If I have not bled to death before I can answer it."

"We have heard rumours of a pale-faced warrior in the marshes."

He was going to say more but I cut him off. "You speak of Marduk."

His bearded face split into a smile. "So it is really him! How is he?"

"I've not seen him for a while. But the word is that he is alive."

"I am very glad indeed," he said. He really did seem to be delighted. "I knew him in Kish," he said. "He was an impossible boy."

I accidentally shut my eyes and had to force them open again. "Biluda, will you take first watch? I am not at my full strength."

"You look to have a belly wound there," he said.

"That too," I said, and promptly fell asleep.

CHAPTER 17

ERESHKIGAL

Lost

I stood in the cave that was meant to take me to Heaven to rescue my beloved Nergal. My *mee* of protection blazed, lighting up every part of the cave.

Nothing happened.

I turned round to Bizilla and Neti. "Well?"

"I told you that this system is not simple," said Neti. He stood with his hands behind his back. "I have been in this cavern many times and have gone nowhere."

"But this is where Inanna and I arrived," Bizilla said, frowning. "I am certain of it."

"These are not so much gates as passages," said Neti. "That is the distinction I am making. And besides, the flies brought you here with a gate of their own invention."

"Perhaps we should hold hands," said Bizilla. "All three of us. We must try to stay together."

"I suppose," I said.

I took Bizilla's hard hand in my left hand and Neti's soft and dusty hand in my right.

"I think we should not be using our *mees*." I did not fully trust Bizilla, but needs must. "In case that is preventing us moving."

Bizilla's yellow light blinked out, and a moment later I let my white shield fall.

Absolute blackness fell upon us.

I had the sensation of falling and also rising up, my hard, swollen belly collapsing and then reappearing.

I was still standing, in the darkness. I was still holding hands. I let go of them and put my hands to my belly and felt my guts lurching.

I lit up my *mee*.

We were all three still there, all standing just as we had been in our cave in the middle of the inbetween realm.

"What now?" I said.

Neti put one finger to his lips. "Something has changed," he said, very quiet. "We have moved."

"This is not the same cave," said Bizilla, nodding at him. "The markings on the wall are different."

"They look the same to me," I said. But then I remembered that strange feeling of falling both upwards and downwards.

"I think we might be in Heaven," said Bizilla. "There's a musty smell that's very familiar to me."

"Even if we are in Heaven," said Neti, "we could very easily be nowhere near Creation."

For the first time, I felt profound doubt. Perhaps I was a complete fool to try to rescue Nergal. A fool on a doomed mission that would certainly end in death for me and my baby. I gave out a sort of sob.

No. I must not think like that. I took deep breaths to stop myself crying.

I could not start believing in a baby. If I started to believe in a baby, it would all go wrong. I must think of my swollen belly as sickness and deformity, so that I could not be disappointed when it turned out to be a fantasy.

"I cannot remember sleeping," I said. I began to cry.

"I will get us out of here," said Bizilla. "Stay here. I will look around."

The *sukkal* edged herself along the cavern; for a moment she was lost to view. She reappeared, looking back at us. "There's a door here."

Neti and I followed her over, me leaning on him heavily. The floor was dangerously slippery.

There was indeed a door, carved from stone and covered in inscriptions. The marks were in the same writing system as I had often found inside the Kur and they bore the same instruction as the door that led out of the Osirion: tread gently.

Bizilla put a finger to her lips and slowly pulled the door aside.

She crept forward into the light-filled space beyond, turning from left to right to look around.

"There's no one out here," she said. "I know where we are." There was relief in her voice.

Neti and I followed her into a small block-stone room with a wooden table and chairs at the centre of it. A small firebowl was burning low in one corner and the table had candles guttering upon it.

"We are in Heaven, so that at least is good," said Bizilla. "But this is Qingu's estate. I served here once."

"I told you this was a mistake," said Neti.

I jabbed him hard in the chest. "None of your gloom!" I turned back to the Sebitti.

"How far to Tiamat's castle?"

"A journey," said Bizilla, quietly. She pointed to the door at the end of the room. "The guards won't be far. There is always a squad of Sebitti on the gate to stop anyone accessing it. What they won't expect is anyone coming out of it. Both of you get up against that wall while I open the door. They may strike first and ponder later."

I did as I was told. "Neti, come here!" I said, when he did not follow.

After a short pause, Neti followed me.

"What are your powers here?" I said to him, while Bizilla fretted at the door. "What can you do?"

"So far it seems that I can be ordered around and also jabbed in the chest."

"Go back then," I said. "Go back through the gate while you can."

"It is kind of you to think of me, Madam, but I think for now I will remain in this realm."

Bizilla pulled the door to the next room open. Whatever she could see beyond, she immediately lifted both her hands into the air.

"Brothers and sisters!" she called out.

A voice from the other side: "Back away from the door."

Sebitti warriors crowded into the room, long black clubs in hand.

"Where did you come from?" a male Sebitti said to Bizilla.

"Why not take a guess?" she said.

"Oh, Bizilla," said a woman amongst the Sebitti. "I think I have died of shock."

All eight Sebitti stood looking at each other, very serious.

"We heard you had run off," the man said. "With the girl that Qingu was holding."

"I did run," Bizilla said. "Now I am returned and with friends." She gestured over to us.

Only then did the Sebitti look our way and for a moment they only stared at us.

"Weapons down," one of them said, and they all lowered their clubs.

"This is Ereshkigal," Bizilla said. "Daughter of Nanna and Ningal, of the Anunnaki. She was a girl when they fled this realm. I think the man is part of the gate system."

"That is quite rude," said Neti.

Bizilla took a step forward towards her brethren.

"I call for a full muster of the Sebitti," she said.

"What?" I said, stepping towards her. I shook my head. "What?"

"I call this muster by ancient right," said Bizilla, showing no sign of having heard me. "I call the muster in the name of the old gods, whose names we no longer know. I call it because I am the oldest amongst us and when I call to muster all must come."

I knew ritual words when I heard them.

"No," I said. "Bizilla! What is this? We are here for Nergal and perhaps Ninlil if there is really time to fetch her too. Let us go and get them and then be gone. There is no time for meetings. No time for ancient rites."

"I did warn you about her," Neti said.

"We are the only Sebitti here," the man said to Bizilla, ignoring me. "Everyone else is at Creation preparing for the exodus. We must go there for the call to be answered."

Bizilla came to stand over me. She put a hard hand on each of my shoulders. "Ereshkigal, we will rescue Nergal and Ninlil. But I am not leaving this realm without giving my brethren a chance to come with us. We have been slaves here a thousand years and it is long enough."

"But there are hundreds of you," I said. "We came to rescue two people and that was impossible. But now you want to rescue hundreds of people. Neti spoke of madness. This is madness!"

"Ereshkigal, I have spoken the words. If the Sebitti vote to leave Heaven, we will not leave without them."

I looked to Neti. "Can you not help me?"

"I told you this was a bad plan," he said.

"If we succeed, Ereshkigal," said Bizilla, "you will return to Earth with an army of Sebitti at your back."

"Well, I suppose that is a thought," I said.

CHAPTER 18

NINSHUBAR

At Ur

I passed out, wounded, in the royal nursery of an Akkadian city. I awoke, early the next morning, in a Sumerian city.

Sun was streaming through the half-opened green shutters. Biluda was asleep, his head bowed low over his chest, on the padded bench opposite me.

I winced as I tried to sit up, and Biluda at once opened his eyes, and smiled at me.

The children were too fast asleep to stir; they made small shapes beneath the flaxen sheets.

"Is Shara safe?" I said, very quiet. "Which one is he?"

The old man pointed to a bed against the far wall.

One hand to my belly wound, I went to stand over it. I could only see one plump arm, thrown out of the sheets, and a face. Dark curls, and two dark brows, like arrows. I knew him at once from those brows. It was Gilgamesh's son.

I went back to my leather chair and briefly examined my wound. It had scabbed over, but it was still a painful mess. I would certainly have been on the verge of death had it not been for the *melam* in my veins.

"The Anunnaki wants to see you," said Biluda. "Or the one who claims to be an Anunnaki. He has sent three emissaries, but I begged them to let you sleep a little longer."

"Look after the children for me while I'm gone?"

"I do not need to be told to look after the children," he said, smiling.

"Where will I find the moon god?"

"There's a tall, seven-storey building here that they call the moon tower," said Biluda. "That is at the heart of his temple complex, so you might start there."

As it was, there was no need to search for the moon god. There were two men outside the royal nursery when I opened the door. Both wore mismatching armour and helmets, and carried Akkadian swords, but they spoke to me with Sumerian accents. The city guard had changed while I slept off my belly wound.

"Goddess, I am to take you to the moon god," said the youngest of the men.

"Lead on," I said.

The palace was beautiful in the morning light. There were windows everywhere, the shutters all flung back against whitewashed walls to let the sun in.

I caught glimpses of blue ocean beyond.

"We call this the Palace of Light," said my escort.

We climbed down wide stairways to a large ornate hallway, the floor and columns all inset with mosaics. The walls were covered in paintings of the moon gods, Ningal and Nanna, in formal poses. It was strange to recognise the faces of two people I knew upon the great gods pictured.

Then we were out into the hot sunshine and an ancient garden shaded by full-grown cedars. Beyond the gorgeous swell of the trees, the mighty ramparts shone yellow in the morning sun.

"It's this way," said my guide.

He led me past reed-lined fish ponds to a high stone wall with a wooden gateway set into it. I could already hear the hubbub on the far side and we passed through the gate into a crowded, sand-covered square. At the centre of it, beneath a large leather canopy, stood the moon god.

Nanna had sat, useless and cowardly, on a beach for half a year. He had been happy to look over the city he once built and do nothing. Now he was a different creature entirely. He stood with a large wooden table before him, and a line of scribes standing to attention, their clay tablets in hand, as he oversaw the day's business.

"So, Ninshubar," Nanna said, in a voice of authority, as I approached. "You are to go to your friends in the marshes. You will tell them that I have taken Ur back and you will ask them to come here to help us defend it. In return, we can provide some proper walls to eat their dinner behind."

"And your motive in sending this message?"

"We lost this city once to Akka's forces and I do not intend to lose it again. The resistance have good fighters amongst them and detailed knowledge of Akka's movements. We must be allies now if we are to drive the Akkadians out."

I took a step closer to him and lowered my voice. "You ran away last time the Akkadians came. You were not even in the city when Akka arrived."

He waved a hand at me. "That was then and this is now." He lifted his voice. "The temple skiff and its crew are waiting for you. They will take you to the marshes."

I breathed in deep and I made my calculations. Should I take the boy Shara with me? I worried that that might not be wise, when I had no idea what lay ahead of me in the marshes.

"Keep Gilgamesh's boy safe," I said.

"He will be safe," said Nanna.

"And the old Akkadian man in the royal nursery. His name is Biluda."

He nodded. "And the old man."

"I need you to make a promise."

Nanna stiffened, but said: "I give you my promise. The sacred promise of a god."

An hour later I was in the temple skiff. The boat leaned over one way, in the hard wind, and the boys and I leaned the other. The great city of Ur and the dunes where I had been buried were behind us. Ahead of us lay the gulf of ten thousand islands and, somewhere to the north, the great marshes.

"Do you know your way into the marshes?" I said to the boys.

Their captain turned his bright smile to me. "We will take you directly to the Refuge, my lady."

CHAPTER 19

NINLIL

In Heaven

A black, glistening shape, about the size of a curled-up man, slipped from between my mother's back legs. Priests and Sebitti warriors rushed forward, only to spring back when the creature thrashed its way out of its caul.

It was a long fat serpent with a huge head and impossibly long, dripping fangs. It kept on unfolding from its folds of translucent tissues until it was the length of five men.

The chief priest fell to his knees. "It is a *mushmahhu* serpent!" he called out, in his ceremony voice. "It has poison for blood."

The black serpent reared up and bit off his head.

The priest's body went one way, the serpent the other; blood went everywhere.

All present fell silent for several long moments, except my mother, the dragon, who was groaning as if ready to give birth again.

Sebitti came forward, swords out, towards the murderous serpent. The hissing creature twisted around, its yellow eyes flashing, its long white fangs dripping crimson.

"Do not hurt it!" shouted one of the priests. "This creature is sacred."

The gold-scaled Sebitti surrounded the hissing, swaying creature, shouting out in their own language. More Sebitti entered the room at a sprint armed with long golden spears and nets.

"What fun!" said Qingu, but he quickly stepped up onto his throne. "I would keep your feet out of the fray, sister," he said. "Unless you want a nasty bite."

Amidst the chaos, my mother gave out a second roar so loud that it shook the room and another glistening bundle slipped from inside her. Another huge serpent unfurled, heavy as a man, but covered in metallic spikes. Dark sparks flew from it as it threw itself into the horrified crowd.

"An *ushumgallu* demon!" called out a priest. "Just as prophesised!"

I climbed up onto my throne with a nod to my brother. It was undignified, yes, but I did not have a death wish.

"There is a painting of this out in the central hall," I said to my brother. "I did not realise what it was before. A stream of black monsters flowing out of a black dragon."

"I always thought they were smaller dragons," said Qingu.

My mother was roaring again.

"Put the creatures somewhere safe," my brother called out to the Sebitti. "They look very useful, but I think for now let's try to minimise the slaughter."

The Sebitti, fighting for their lives against the two serpents, did not acknowledge my brother's advice.

My mother was giving birth again. Another dripping bundle, but this time something more human was inside. A human body at least, but with horns and black feathers all over it.

The creatures kept coming, another every few minutes. Eleven kinds in all. Men like lions, men like scorpions, fierce demons with horrifying, bulging eyes. Scores of each, and they kept on coming, the Sebitti wrestling them out of the audience chamber as fast as they could. How could all these creatures have been contained within my mother's belly? Yet they kept on coming.

"What is that?" I said to my brother, as a human-like creature covered in fish scales staggered to its feet, birth tissues sloughing from it.

"Your guess is as good as mine," he said. "There is one over there that looks like a bison."

Another priest was killed. Many more were badly maimed before the Sebitti could get in to protect them. The priests' blood mingled with the birthing blood upon the flagstone floor of the audience chamber.

"How can she still be giving birth?" I said. "Where are they all coming from?"

"She draws on the central power," said my brother.

He climbed down off his throne and sat down on it. "You know, thrilling as this has been, I find myself rather weary of it now."

He beckoned over a priest.

"What's your understanding of this?" said Qingu.

"I do not understand the question," said the man. His robes clung to him; wet with blood or birthing juices or both.

"What are these beasts, man?" said my brother. "And when is this going to stop?"

"They are creatures of war," the priest said. "An old tradition. That the dragon queen gives birth to her whole army."

"I've never heard of this tradition," said Qingu.

"And yet it is painted on the temple walls," said the priest, his mouth flat. "As soon as the last of them is born, then the queen will be ready for the invasion."

"And when will that be?"

"When she decides her army is large enough to invade with."

"Exodus," said Qingu. "It's not an invasion, it's an exodus."

"As you say, my lord," said the priest, with a shallow bow.

I sat down on my throne. "She means war, brother," I said. "This is not only about finding safety. She means to have her revenge upon the Anunnaki and all who serve them."

My brother bared his sharpened teeth at me. "And all because of you, little sister."

CHAPTER 20

HARGA

In the marshes

We did not make it to the marshwoman's plague-cursed island on that first day and we were forced to spend the night on a stretch of boggy ground that was barely big enough for us to all lie down on.

We had spent the day drinking the foul water we were floating in, wading through, and relieving ourselves in, but we had no food with us. Nor did we have blankets or shelters. Even if we had had wood with us, it would have been too dangerous to light a fire.

I had a simple plan: keep everyone alive, until I had a better plan.

"Lie down and try to sleep," I whispered, as I passed amongst the wet and frightened crowd.

That first evening, when I had checked that everyone was as well as they could be, it was already almost dark. "Marduk has volunteered for first watch," I said to Ningal and Isimud. They both looked strong and well, but then that is the *melam* for you. "Let's get some sleep while we can," I added. "Even the gods must sleep."

I lay down with Lilith behind me and two small children scooped into the curve of my body, my right arm resting gently over them. It might have been a restful scene if it was not for the mosquitoes and the fact I was wet through and lying in stinking mud with a grumbling hole in my belly and my shoulder pain flaring.

"Sleep well, old friend," Lilith whispered to me.

I woke to the horrifying sound of a child screaming and then a terrible growling from the dogs. I let go of the two children I was cradling, leaped up, and scrambled in the darkness over prostrate bodies towards the ungodly noise.

Isimud's red shield of protection flared, lighting up a scene of horror.

An enormous crocodile had hold of a small boy. The three dogs were on top of the monstrous creature, locked on with their jaws. Marduk was there then, running up behind Isimud. He looked as if he was going to slam into Isimud's shield and I was about to shout out to him in warning when I realised he was passing through it. Somehow, in a sinewy, sideways fashion, he slid inside Isimud's shield and out again, and then he brought down an axe into the crocodile's spine.

The beast let go of the child and thrashed its way back into the water. One of the boy's legs was missing; blood was spraying everywhere.

The boy stopped screaming and lay still, his face turned up to us.

All around us, children were screaming and crying. Lilith

appeared, covered in mud, and said: "A little girl is missing."

By the light of Isimud's *mee*, we counted everyone up. We had lost two children into the water without anyone noticing. The little boy with the missing leg was the third.

Three children dead in one night.

Marduk stood over the boy with his mouth hanging open. "The dogs started barking," he said. "I sensed nothing before that."

The light of Isimud's *mee* was already fading. He and Ningal had burned through their Anunnaki weapons in our operations up and down the river.

The marshwoman came to look down on the dead boy.

"Can you guide us through the marshes in the dark?" I said.

"Yes," she said.

"We might as well keep moving," I said. "No one is going back to sleep tonight."

Marduk's face was wet with tears. "I did not hear the crocodiles," he said.

"I should have sat up with you," I said. "This is not your fault, Marduk."

He did not look appeased.

"The dogs did well," I said, nodding at him.

He nodded back at me, but his tears kept flowing.

So, back into the water, but with everyone so terrified of crocodiles that no one wanted to be on the outside of the group. We could only go very slowly or risk being split up from the canoes. Hour upon hour went by, and even in that hot marshland, in the dead of the night and in the water for so long, I began to feel very cold.

At the first hint of dawn, we heard Akkadian voices lifted over the frog song.

We withdrew into a wall of reeds and stayed there, listening and catching our breath. The pain in my bad shoulder had worsened in the panic and exertions of the night, so I spent the time breathing through it and waiting for it to die away.

The marshwoman, Sagar, put up her hand to signal it was time to move and soon we were wading and pulling ourselves through the reeds again.

We made little progress on that second day. Every time we thought we were covering some distance, a boat of Akkadians would slide by and we would have to hide or change direction. We spent most of the day clinging to reeds, all of us very hungry by then, the babies and young ones growing increasingly upset and tearful.

"Harga, is there something else we can do?" Marduk whispered to me. He and I were floating close together at the outer edges of the group.

"What like?"

"Perhaps I could do something more," he said. "Something heroic."

"Let's meet in council," I said. I paused a moment. "Marduk, it was not your fault, what happened. No one could have done better than you did. Even if we had kept moving all night some of us would have died."

"I suppose," he said, not looking at me.

"Marduk, when the crocodile had the boy, I saw you enter Isimud's shield of protection and then step out of it again."

"It was in my way," he said. "I had to get to the boy."

"How did you do it?"

"You just have to move through the edges of it very slowly," he said. "I learnt it when I was on the front, fighting alongside the moon goddess. I could not always be inside her protection and fight well."

"Quite a trick," I said.

We met in a desperate and awkwardly arranged council, out there in the city of reeds. Ningal, Lilith, and the old marshwoman held their canoes together in order for them to be present. Isimud, Marduk, and I were in the water, hanging on to their canoes. The Uruk boys hung on in the reeds near us in order not to miss anything that might be said.

We all spoke in low whispers, for fear our words might cause panic in the group.

"Can we make it to your island before dark?" I said to the marshwoman.

She shook her head. "We are too slow."

"We need a better plan then," I said. "Or more of us are going to die out here in the mud."

Marduk raised an axe above the water.

"Yes, Marduk?" I said.

"If we see a ship again, I could attack it," he said.

I nodded, thinking. "It would certainly be better to be on a ship," I said. "Much better than in these reeds."

"Perhaps we could hunt a ship down," said the moon goddess, "rather than keeping going for the island."

"I always prefer to attack," said Isimud. "So that has my vote."

"It is a bad plan," I said. "For countless reasons. But at least they will not be expecting it."

CHAPTER 21

INANNA

Lost

It was dark but I still had Gilgamesh's hand in mine; I could smell his sweet cedar scent.

He squeezed my hand tighter. "Inanna, are you well?"

"Yes," I whispered. "Did you drop the lamp?"

"I had it in my hand, but it's gone. Don't let go of me."

I put out my free hand and it hit rock: damp, rough, rock.

Gilgamesh still had hold of me, but he was twisting around. "I think we have travelled," he said. "The cave here is different. Very narrow. The walls are wetter."

"Is this Egypt?" I said, into the total darkness.

He moved closer to me and took up both my hands in his. "It could be. I entered the main temple chamber in Abydos and was immediately transported somewhere different. But Ereshkigal told me that when she arrived there she found herself in some sort of cave and had to crawl along to get into the temple chamber. So perhaps we are in that cave and need to find our way to the temple chamber."

"I must ask you about her pregnancy," I said, "when we have worked this out."

"If she is pregnant," he said. "She keeps denying it."

We were both silent then, listening only to the drips in the cave.

"You don't have any *mees*?" he said.

"I should have asked Bizilla for one."

It was then that I shut my eyes.

To pure blue light.

The shock of it cascaded through me. I had no need of any *mees*. My power was all around me.

"Gilgamesh, we are on Earth," I whispered, my eyes still shut. "My power is returned to me."

The blue lake of light, glimpsed before in dreams, reached for in grief and anger, now lay soft all around me. Did I even need to reach for it?

I opened my eyes and without any effort or conscious thought I lit up the cave around us with iridescent aquamarine light.

Gilgamesh stood with his mouth open in surprise. "Now that is a sight," he said.

We looked about us, in the bright blue light. We were in a narrow rock gully. To our right the cavern widened out, although we could not see what was beyond it.

"Shall we try this way?" said Gilgamesh. Then he turned back to stare at me. "Moon cousin," he said. "You have blue light streaming out of you."

I stood on tiptoe and kissed him on his warm, sweet mouth. I felt such happiness in that moment, I could not stop myself.

"I am so happy to be back," I said. I felt so well in myself. The blue power was flooding every part of me, wiping away pain and tiredness and bruises. I felt young and strong and well again. "I will follow you."

He hesitated a moment, then turned and limped, slowly, along the gully. He turned back briefly to take one of my hands again. "Let us not get split up."

As I walked, I tried to make sense of the blue patterns in my mind's eye, but I could not. "Everything feels unfamiliar," I said. "But then I have never been to Egypt before."

Gilgamesh led us out into a wider section of cave. Shimmering with my blue light, it was as beautiful as any temple, with dramatic flows of rock and towering ceilings. We followed a dried-out riverbed along the lefthand side of the chamber.

I felt suffused with energy as I stepped carefully along the rock-strewn riverway. I did not need to concentrate to light up the cave. I felt so different, so much more powerful, so much more sure of my instincts.

In that moment, returned to Earth, returned to life, I felt such a pure and open love for Gilgamesh. I felt so very happy to be there with him, my hand in his large and powerful hand. Oh, the delight of simply being with him!

I glimpsed something on the cave wall to my left and pulled Gilgamesh back to me.

It was a painting of an animal. I shone my light brighter upon it.

"Is that an elephant?" I said. Its trunk seemed to be drooping along the ground and it had a red mark where its heart might have been.

"I think it's a mammoth," Gilgamesh said.

I wondered how old the painting was and who had painted it.

"I saw one once, in a high forest," Gilgamesh said, peering closer at it. "A real one, I mean."

"I thought they were all dead."

"The one I saw is certainly dead now, but perhaps there are others somewhere."

"There are other paintings here," I said, moving on. "A deer."

"Are these axes?" he said. He pointed at a series of dark shapes sketched in red ochre.

We moved on, trying to catch the shapes in the undulating rock wall, and then ahead, up a slope of scree and tumbled rock, I caught the unmistakable glimmer of natural light.

"I can smell fresh air," Gilgamesh said.

Moments later we were clambering, through a narrow gap, from the cave.

We climbed out, hand in hand, onto thick lush grass. The sky above was a bright grey; a stiff wind buffeted us. It was very bright indeed and very, very cold.

We stood on a small grassy ledge, looking down onto sharp rocks and a powerful, deep blue sea. The cliffs to our left and right, and up behind us, were cloaked in heavy, verdant forest.

I let my blue light fade, although when I had stopped reaching for it, I still felt it dancing beneath my skin.

The air was unlike any air I had ever breathed before, so wet and very cold.

"Is this Abydos?" I said, looking out over the ocean.

"The one thing I can say, and with some confidence," said Gilgamesh, "is that we are most definitely not in Egypt."

CHAPTER 22

NINLIL

In Heaven

For the second time in two days, my brother came to fetch me from my bedchamber.

"She's lost all sense," he said, from the doorway. "Nobody knows what to do."

"And?"

"The whole court stands paralysed," he said. "When we should be going through the gate. There was a thought that you might be able to reach her."

"Why not just abandon her, brother? Go through the gate. Leave her behind?"

He scratched at one of his horns. "The Sebitti control the gate. Not that I would consider going against Mother, of course."

I stood up. "I will try to help her if she will let me."

My brother's guards pulled the giant doors open but were quick to step away into the shadows.

My mother was at the centre of the huge chamber. She turned all seven heads to face me and bared her seven sets of fangs.

Dead bodies were piled on the flagstones all around her. Black-robed priests clustered in the shadows, some injured, some weeping. Anzu birds, chained to the walls, stretched their wings in panic.

My father was on the floor, still tied to his chair. One of his bony, peeling legs seemed to have broken off.

I took a deep breath and walked straight across the foul-smelling chamber towards the dragon, my hand out to her. "Do not fear me, Mother."

She reared up, her huge scaled chest heaving, her seven heads weaving over me.

I kept on walking straight towards her, stepping over the body of a dead Sebitti.

"Mother, let me touch you." I was so close then that the fire in the air around her began to burn my cheeks and lungs.

She struck at me with one powerful front leg, slicing into my side. I fell forward hard onto the polished flagstones, blood pumping from the wound between my ribs. I forced all my healing energy towards it.

The dragon moved around me. She picked me up by one arm, her claws slicing into me, and dashed me down onto the floor, hard enough to break bones.

I stopped breathing. I stopped moving. I looked up with frozen eyes upon the vaulted stone ceiling and only was.

The dragon dropped her heads down, sniffing and pushing at me. For one moment, as she shifted, her tail swung low over my face.

I put both my hands up and grabbed her tail hard, and my inner ocean, the healing sea, rushed out into the dragon.

She struggled at first, thrashing her tail and smashing me into the floor, trying to get her mouths and claws to me. I was flooded with the darkness that pulsed beneath her scales, but I clung on with all the strength I had, and my oceans crashed out into her.

In the end, when I was so broken and bloody I was almost done for, she collapsed down onto the flagstones.

We lay together. The great dragon rested her heads on the ancient floor, and I lay wrapped around her tail.

The Sebitti, my brother, all present, backed away from the two of us.

I took in a great breath and let myself feel my own pain. I let my healing sea flow out into her and I let her dark poison flow back into me. At times, I passed out with the effort of absorbing so much darkness.

When I was conscious, I whispered to her: "Let me heal you."

She fought me, but I only held her tighter.

I drank in her fear, her anger, and her shame, fury, and madness. Her terrible, dangerous fragility. I went deeper and deeper, looking for the human inside her.

I awoke to find myself still on the floor with my mother, but with priests all around us. Some held up candles; others beat on small drums and sang. My father was back on his chair. His severed leg had been tied back onto him with a strip of gold cloth and the dead bodies had been cleared away. My mother was breathing.

I realised that Qingu was in the room, although standing

well away from us, his back to what had once been the grand windows onto the gardens.

"Are you actually doing something to her?" he said.

I did not answer, but laid my head back down on the dragon's obsidian scales.

"At least she's calm, I suppose," said Qingu.

I thought for a while that she was dying and I pulled back. I only wanted to heal her, not hurt her. Then I felt a new heat coming from deep inside her: something was happening inside the dragon. Withdrawn from me, hiding from me, molten and pulsing, something fire hot was forming inside her.

I sat up. The dragon was still, but it was still alive. For now. I looked around at the haggard faces of the priests. Slowly, I stood. "I'm very hungry," I said to them. "Is there anything I can eat?"

Qingu was on his throne, sitting next to our father. "What is happening, sister?"

I took a few steps away from my mother, staggering. "I am desperate to eat," I said. "I need strength if I am going to be able to help her."

The dragon began to thrash around on the floor, its heads and tail flailing. The priests scurried backwards, taking their candles and drums with them.

"Someone get my sister food," said Qingu. "Anything will do."

"Lots of food," I said.

I lay down with her again when I had eaten, but this time with my head against her powerful chest.

I had absorbed her dark poisons. My ocean of healing lapped

gently over both of us. But what was this mass of heat that she was hiding from me, that I could not quite get sight of? Every time my mind reached out for it, it seemed to slip away from me.

The dragon gave out a low groan.

I opened my eyes and sat up. "Something is happening," I said. I pushed myself back from her and priests rushed forward to help me stand.

The dragon jerked up onto its powerful hind legs and something long and dark slipped from its hindquarters.

Qingu stood up. The priests crept forward. The Sebitti emerged from the shadows around.

The dragon collapsed as if dead, its eyes frozen open.

I stood, holding my breath, looking down upon the newborn creature as it twisted and thrashed inside its transparent caul.

"Should we help it?" said a priest.

"I don't think it needs help," I said.

Hands appeared, scrabbling through the membrane, and then a head. The dragon had given birth to a full-grown woman with pale skin and long, oily black hair.

She opened her eyes and looked straight at me as she took in her first breath.

"Hello, daughter," she said.

PART 3

"Tiamat, who fashions all things...
She bore giant snakes,
Sharp of tooth and unsparing of fang.
She filled their bodies with venom instead of blood.
She cloaked ferocious dragons with fearsome rays,
And made them bear mantles of godlike radiance."

From "Enuma Elish", as translated
by Stephanie Dalley

CHAPTER 1

INANNA

Lost

Gilgamesh and I stood together and looked out over the dark and surging sea.

"I'm cold," I said, hugging my grey cloak tighter around me.

Gilgamesh was dressed only in a short, sleeveless tunic and sandals, with his axes slung over his back in their leather straps. He stood with his powerful arms hugged to his chest. Just to see if I could do it, I threw an invisible shield of protection around us to keep the wind off.

"I am not too cold," Gilgamesh said, dropping his arms to his sides. He gave me his searing smile. "I wish I had some piece of clothing to offer you, but this tunic is all I have."

"I will be warm soon enough," I said.

High above us, in the pale grey sky, a fish eagle circled.

"I would like to shut my eyes for a while and see what I can see," I said.

"What do you see when you close your eyes?"

"A pattern of blue light," I said. "I can see everything that has *melam* in it. I can even see you." I smiled at him. "Normally I can make out the shapes of our family."

"Shall we sit?" He put a hand out to me.

We sat down on the wet grass, me cross-legged, him stretching out his legs in front of him with a brief grimace.

Oh, the joy of it, to be back in the world and sitting on some damp grass with Gilgamesh, the hero of my childhood.

He took my hands in his. "I will watch over you, while you see what you can see."

It made me smile, that he thought I needed protection. But I was very glad to give him my hands.

I shut my eyes and at once found myself on the shore of my luminous blue lake. I smiled again to find myself there.

The animals were there, lining the water's edge for as far as I could see. Jaguars standing beside hippos, elephants next to crows. All eyes upon me.

I turned to look out over the water and a pod of dolphins rose up in it, rolling their eyes at me. Behind them, great sea whales broke the surface of the shining water. All expectant, but for what I could not yet be sure.

I slowly waded into the water. I caught hold of the blue network that fed into the lake; the network that was a map of all the *melam* in the world. It all came to me so easily now, yet I could not make out the shapes around me. It was all too unfamiliar. I did not know which way to look. I sensed some familiar shapes close by, but could not make sense of them.

I opened my eyes, to find Gilgamesh still holding my hands and the air still cold and blowing, and the eagle still high up above us. "I think we are far from home."

"Let us look around. I have my axes and you have your blue light. Let us go hunting for answers."

We grinned at each other, still holding each other's hands tight.

"You know," he said, "for seven long moons I have sat round campfires with those who love you, with your mother, with Lilith, with all the others, and we have talked over and over about what might have become of you. Did Inanna go through to Heaven? Did she die in the Kur? You know we spent weeks at the Kur digging for you? We talked and talked about you, yet I think no one truly expected to see you again."

A bright yellow butterfly staggered past us in the sea wind.

"The point of my speech is, welcome back to Earth, moon cousin," said Gilgamesh. He kissed my hands.

"Wherever this is!"

He laughed his beautiful laugh. "Wherever this is."

Then I remembered about Ninshubar and the pain cut through me as fresh and raw as the first time.

"Ninshubar," I said. "I keep forgetting and remembering all over again."

He leaned over and pressed his lips to my forehead. "Harga and Marduk have kept on looking for her. Hoping against hope."

We were silent a moment.

"Come, I will help you up," he said. He took my hand and together we made our way across the grass ledge towards the steep, rocky slope that led up into the forest above. In the bright, grey light of the new world we found ourselves in, I could see that his left knee was horribly swollen and discoloured. Each time he put his weight onto it, he took a moment to recover.

"I think this is a path," he said, pointing upwards. It was only faint, but there was a track threading up through the rocks.

"I am so truly sorry about your family," I said, as we began our climb. "About your mother, about Enlil, about your wife and child."

He took another step up, before answering. "I blame myself."

"Oh, I know about blaming oneself," I said, putting my free hand upon a rock as I climbed. "I rose up to Heaven when I should have stayed and fought for my people. As for Ninshubar's death, it was my fault entirely. I should have run from Nergal, not gone towards him. Or at least, I should have done something different. I was not locked into my fate."

"I find it's easy to look back and see the pattern of one's errors," he said, "but harder to see it all clearly when it's happening." He gave me a warm smile.

"Let us start now afresh," I said. "Carve new histories for ourselves."

"I would very much like that." He tightened his grip on my hand.

At the top of the cliff, we peered into unfamiliar forest, the trees all very strange to us. Gilgamesh paced back and forth. "People come here regularly," he said, his eyes on the ground. "There's a proper path here, leading into the forest."

It was at that moment that my husband Dumuzi appeared from the trees, as if magicked up by the woods themselves. He was wearing a wolf-fur cloak and had a basket in each hand. His mouth dropped open at the sight of us. "By all the stars," he said.

"Hello, husband," I said, when I had recovered from the shock of his appearance.

Gilgamesh somehow had an axe in each hand. "Are you alone?" he said to Dumuzi.

"What are you doing here?" I said in the same moment. I had puzzled over familiar shapes in the network of blue power, but only now could I understand them.

Dumuzi put down his baskets; I glimpsed mushrooms. "As must be fairly obvious even to you two, we found ourselves in that cave down there," he said. "We were in the Kur and then we were here."

As he spoke, his sister Geshtinanna appeared behind him, a basket in each of her hands.

"Oh, Inanna!" she said. It was hard to tell if she was happy or frightened to see me. "And who is this?" she added, looking at Gilgamesh.

"You both look awful," said Dumuzi, before either of us could answer her. "Did you come here from some slave market? Have you been in some sort of fight?"

"Did you also come through the gate?" said Geshtinanna. I had forgotten how lovely she was to look at.

"Of course, they came through the gate," said Dumuzi. He turned back to us. "Do you know where Ereshkigal is? We were with her one moment and then a moment later she was gone."

"She's with child," said Geshtinanna, "and we are very worried for her."

"She was on her way to Heaven when we last saw her," said Gilgamesh. "In fact we have only just parted from her." He slipped his axes back into their harnesses. "She was intent on getting Nergal back."

"We know all about that," said Dumuzi. "She has been intent on that for quite some time."

"I am so glad she is alive," said Geshtinanna.

"But where is this?" said Gilgamesh, lifting his hands to the trees. "We don't know where we are."

"That we know all too well," said Dumuzi. "Welcome to the far north."

CHAPTER 2

NINLIL

In Heaven

In a room bright with candlelight, the priests bathed my newborn mother in hot, myrrh-scented water. I sat in a chair next to her high-sided bronze bath and watched them wash the blood from her.

She looked exactly as I remembered her. The glittering blue eyes, the long and elegant nose, the black hair which now floated in the water around her.

"How do you feel?" I said, smiling at her.

She began to retch. The priests quickly lifted her to a more upright position, so that she could vomit out dark liquid into her bath. "That's better," she whispered.

The black vomit swirled around her pale limbs.

"Mother," I said. "Let me stand at your side now."

She nodded at me, her head back against the bronze, but did not speak.

"Let us pass over to the realm of light together, but let us go in peace," I said. "I will speak to the Anunnaki and make a pact with them. They will welcome us in. There will be plenty of room for us all if we go in peace."

She closed her eyes.

"I would like to show you the Earth," I said. "I would like to show you Sumer and my home city in the north."

"I would like to see it all," my mother said.

I looked around at all the priests. "Will you leave me with my mother a moment?"

When we were alone in the bath chamber, I said: "Mother, Qingu is the one who gave me to the Anunnaki. He organised my rape and kidnap. A long time ago, yes, but I spent four hundred years trapped in the pain of what happened and I believe you have too."

I reached into the hot water to take hold of one of her hands, but she moved before I could touch her, sitting herself upright in her bath. "Go on," she said.

"The murder, the mayhem, the human sacrifices… we can make things different now. We can make a fresh start together in the realm of light. We can stand together, you and me."

She sank back into her bath. "You've grown well," she said. "Reached a good height. You will be useful to me."

A chill passed through me, in that hot, steamy room. "And Qingu?"

"Qingu is a good administrator. As for what is sacrificed to me and how I run my court, that is up to me."

I was quiet a moment. "Did you hear me, when you were a dragon, when I told you what he did to me?"

She turned her long nose to me. "I heard you and I heard him too. He says that you loved Enlil."

"Mother, I was a little girl." I saw how it was going to be. All hope had gone by then and I knew how foolish I was being.

Yet I found myself to be in tears.

"You always had a dark streak in you," she said. "You were always wilful. Whining and wilful. Refusing to do what I said and embarrassing me." She climbed out of the bronze tub. "You will stay in your room until we go."

"If you care so little for me, Mother, why send Nergal to find me? Why bring me back here?"

She began rubbing down her limbs on a stretch of cloth. "I do care," she said. "You are mine and you should be here. And now you are. Enlil took what was mine and so he is dead for it. I'm not interested in sharing."

She pulled a long black dress over her head, and tied it round her waist. "I'm looking forward to going. I've been stuck here a long time, the same patterns, the same meat. Everything dark and cold and spiralling downwards."

"Mother, what will happen to my son?"

Her blue eyes shone bright in the candlelight. "Be very good and I will think about bringing him."

"I will be very good," I whispered.

She lifted her voice. "You can come back in," she called.

The priest entered, slow and uncertain.

"Take my daughter to her room," she said.

CHAPTER 3

ERESHKIGAL

In Heaven

The Sebitti put a fur cloak around me and hurried me through the long, dark corridors of Qingu's castle. In the rooms we rushed past, I glimpsed ancient oil paintings, the pale faces dimly familiar to me, and heavy black furniture covered with candles.

The Sebitti soldiers moved at a jog with Bizilla out in front of us and Neti trailing behind. At times my Sebitti escorts held me so far off the flagstones that they were simply carrying me. How I hated to have my feet dangling!

We came to a stone staircase that wound upwards into darkness. "It's up here," said Bizilla, but as she put one foot on the staircase, two men in red stepped out of the shadows.

The Sebitti with their arms around me came to a sharp halt and I found myself back on my own feet.

One of the men in red said: "Bizilla?"

I had not seen her draw a weapon but as he spoke the man went down with blood gushing from his throat. Bizilla hit the other man hard in the throat with a black club like the one I had seen my beloved Nergal use. The man collapsed onto the body of his colleague.

Bizilla stepped over the bodies, cast a glance back at me, and then began running up the staircase, her *mee* blazing yellow at her wrist. The rest of us swiftly followed, me with my feet hanging in the air once more.

"There are men coming up the stairs behind us," Neti called up to us. "They are only a cable behind me."

"Then hurry," Bizilla called back. "Or we die here."

We burst through a door and out into the shock of the freezing night. I had not seen snow falling since I was such a little girl but now it fell thick as feathers, lit up golden in the light of Bizilla's *mee*, and spinning around me as I looked up.

And then I saw the birds there, looming up at us out of the storm. Giant birds with the heads of lions and the bodies of eagles, their feathered backs cloaked with white.

I had a rush of childhood memory, long forgotten. "Anzu birds!"

The birds bared their fangs and growled at us. They were twice as tall as any man. How wonderful they were!

"I had one as a child," I said to no one in particular. "I flew from cloud to cloud." The Anzu birds of my youth had become a dream to me, but here they were a reality. "I had forgotten what they were called."

"Five of us on each bird," Bizilla shouted. "I will ride behind Ereshkigal."

The gigantic birds growled louder as the Sebitti moved to untether them from the stone platform.

It was then that a host of men in red uniforms came crashing out onto the platform.

I was instantly picked up and deposited on the back of a bird, its hard feathers scratching my thighs through my skirts. How strong and musty the bird smelled!

A Sebitti climbed on in front of me and Bizilla climbed on behind me. She pushed herself forward hard against me, as more Sebitti climbed on behind her, and moments later our bird was lifting off, its wings beating powerfully. I gripped its back hard with my legs and threw my arms around the man in front of me.

And just like that we were flying through the snowstorm. As I turned to look back down at the roof terrace, a score more men in red rushed out onto it, their faces tipped up to us.

Far below us, bright flows of molten lava cut through the white icescape, sending up clouds of steam and lighting up the dark stone towers of Qingu's palace.

"Was Creation always like this?" I said, half-turning my head to Bizilla.

"Everything is collapsing," she said. She refolded my furs around me and then wrapped her arms around my chest, resting them lightly on my belly.

I sat with my spine straight and my knees gripping the Anzu bird's feathered back, as I had been taught to do as a girl. I rested my head on the Sebitti in front of me.

It was perilous and exciting, to be up there above the world of my childhood on the back of a creature born in Tiamat's belly. I could not truly believe it, that I was actually there in Heaven. That I was on my way to Nergal. That I might actually, pray to all the stars, see him again. My mind was racing, my heart thumping.

I immediately collapsed into sleep.

I awoke as I was lifted off the bird. It was still snowing heavily but the sky above glowed strangely pink. The two Anzu birds were released and lifted off as a pair into the night; the seven Sebitti from Qingu's estate ran off at a sprint.

Then it was only the three of us, Bizilla, Neti, and I, standing there in the snow. Bizilla lit up her yellow *mee* again so that we could see each other's faces through the snow.

"Is this Creation?" I said.

"This is the sacred games arena, just outside the palace gardens," said Bizilla. "A quiet place for our muster."

"I need to sit," I said.

Bizilla came to take my arm. "This way." She cleared the snow from a marble bench and sat me down there. Neti came to stand near me, his hands behind his back.

"Are you not cold, Neti?" I said.

"I find it an interesting experience," he said, dusting snow from his shoulders. "To feel something, I mean."

"What is your plan?" I said to Bizilla. "I thought you couldn't hurt Tiamat. That you are slaved to her."

Bizilla rubbed the snow from her face. "When we are close enough to touch her, we find ourselves kneeling before her in supplication. It is bred into us. But we can act against her non-violently. Over the years some of us have escaped." She turned her head, listening. "They're coming," she said. "Both of you stay out of things. You will only confuse it."

Sebitti began to appear through the snow, all of them wrapped in heavy furs. They gathered around Bizilla's pool of yellow light, some standing on benches to get sight of her. Scores at first, then hundreds of them.

"How long will this take?" I whispered to Neti.

He put one finger to his lips.

Finally Bizilla lifted up her voice and spoke to the crowd of Sebitti in a tongue I could not follow.

"What is she saying?" I said to the gatekeeper.

Neti frowned, listening. "That they follow a fallen god. That the time of their bondage is over. That Tiamat has broken the sacred pact. Killed some of them." He paused, frowning harder. "They need to choose their path now."

"Do sit down," I said. "It is making my neck ache, to peer up at you like this."

He sat on the bench beside me and crossed his legs. "These are fine warriors, but I'm not sure they can protect us against Tiamat. Do you still have the flies with you?"

I put one hand, surreptitiously, to my bosom. They were still safely there. "There is currently no life in them," I said. "I am not sure how to revive them."

"I'm not sure where my duty lies," Neti said. "But I would like to discuss the matter with the so-called flies."

Bizilla was standing over us.

"It is done," she said. "The Sebitti are with us."

"Just like that?" I said.

"Just like that," she said. "Our time of slavery is over."

CHAPTER 4

INANNA

In the far north

I was standing there with Gilgamesh, and my husband and his sister with their mushroom baskets, when I sensed movement in the trees. Sparks of white in my mind's eye.

I caught at Gilgamesh's arm. "We are not alone, cousin."

"Oh, that will be our hosts," said Dumuzi, very nonchalant. He looked back into the forest. "They call themselves the Sebitti."

Seven tall pale warriors stepped from the trees. Barefoot, dressed in wolf skins, and with wooden spears and stone axes in their hands, they might have been a clan of nomadic hunters. Yet with their blaze-red hair and dark blue eyes, they looked uncannily like Bizilla and Marduk, and here or there I caught the glint of a golden scale sewn into a headdress or bright against a wrist.

A female warrior stepped out in front of the others. She had a long braid of red hair over one shoulder and a scatter of ochre freckles across her nose and cheeks. "I am Enmesarra," she said. "I welcome you to our country."

"Thank you," I said. "We are glad to be here."
"Our camp is not far," said Enmesarra.

As we followed the red-headed warriors through the forest, Dumuzi frowned at me and then at Gilgamesh, his mouth turned down. "You were always sniffing at each other, you two," he said. "Mooning at each other. And now here you are together."

"You are unchanged, husband," I said.

I turned to smile at Gilgamesh.

This time, I will not let him go, I thought.

I squeezed his hand tighter.

The Sebitti's leather tents stood in a wide semi-circle around a communal fire pit. Gilgamesh and I sat on a log together in front of the fire with our thighs pressed close. Hot venison stew was swiftly produced for us, along with fresh water, and we ate and drank very gratefully with the eyes of the seven Sebitti upon us. My husband and his sister sat at the end of our log and applied themselves with some intensity to their food.

The Sebitti came to sit down opposite us, a long line of bright red heads.

"May I ask how you all came to be here?" I said to them.

"I became pregnant," said Enmesarra. "We knew the baby would be killed as soon it was born, so we decided to flee through the gateway beneath the palace at Creation." She looked around at her comrades. "We spent a long time lost in the dark."

Both Gilgamesh and I nodded at that. "We too were lost a while," he said.

"Do you know a woman called Bizilla?" I said. "We have only just parted ways with her."

Enmesarra's face, so serious a moment before, softened into a smile of true delight. "Of course, we know her," she said. "She is the best of us."

"I don't mean to interrupt," said Gilgamesh, a spoon in hand and his mouth full of stew, "but do you also know a boy called Marduk?"

Enmesarra shook her head. "Should I?" she said.

"He was once called the Potta," I said. "That was his old name."

The Sebitti had been friendly, if watchful. Now all seven of them stood up with their hands on their weapons belts and faces so serious that for a moment I thought of reaching for my blue fire.

"Do you mean in this world, or in Heaven?" said Enmesarra.

"In this world," said Gilgamesh, "although somewhere rather hotter than this."

Enmesarra crouched down at our feet. Her long pale hands were shaking. "Potta is an endearment in our language," she said. "It means a loved one."

She was looking at me so intensely that I took a moment to answer her. I did not want to be giving her false hope. "I am talking of a boy who is very tall, with pale skin just like yours, the same red hair, the same blue eyes," I said. "He was in the south of Sumer, the land I come from, when I saw him last."

"I know him very well," Gilgamesh put in. "He fights well. It's something to see."

Enmesarra took in a deep breath and sat back on her heels, her hands on her thighs. "My son was taken from this camp seventeen years ago. We have had no word of him since. We never leave this place because we hope he may one day find his way back."

"He does look just like you," said Gilgamesh. "And you know, he told me he was from the far north. He told me he had a memory of seeing his mother from the sea. In the snow, I think. Something like that."

Two of the Sebitti came forward to put their arms around Enmesarra. She was fixed upon Gilgamesh. "It was snowing when he was snatched away," she said. She nodded, her dark blue eyes brimming with tears. "It's him," she said. "It can only be him." She looked to her comrades. "Can it be him?"

"I think it's him," I said. "You give out the same white light as he does, in my mind's eye, I mean."

Enmesarra stood up. "We must go south. We must go at once."

"I've been saying we should go south," said Dumuzi.

"And now we will," said Enmesarra. Tears were streaming down her face. "We will go south and find my son."

It was agreed that we would set out the next day. The Sebitti gave me a wolf-fur cloak and leather sandals.

Gilgamesh helped them begin the process of breaking their camp, while my husband and his sister prepared the evening's food of venison, ground roots, and a great number of mushrooms.

I sat near the fire, alone in a sea of activity, grateful for the time and space to work out what was going on inside my head. I shut my eyes, breathed steadily, and slowly followed the lines of blue outwards. I had no idea which way was south, but when I found the blue light thinning and waning, I shifted direction. Slowly, I found my way back towards Sumer. The blue light began to build. I began to see sparks around me of those who shared blood with me.

A shock. A shape so familiar to me, although I could not at first identify it. An. The great god An. Faint, yet distinctive.

I moved on, further south.

And then a shape that could not be mistaken.

It was too much to take in at first.

She was in a boat, leaning over backwards. Her hair was strangely long and she was smiling at someone; she was ablaze with strength and goodness.

I put my hand over my mouth, to stop myself crying out.

Gilgamesh had me by my shoulders, drawing me back to the world. I opened my eyes, gasping. I began to weep, my body heaving with sobs.

The Sebitti surrounded us. "What is it?" said Enmesarra. "What is wrong?"

I could not stop crying. Huge, shaking sobs.

She was alive.

Gilgamesh, kneeling in front of me on his horribly swollen knee, kissed my eyes, my tears, my cheeks. "Inanna, what is it? What has happened?"

When I could finally speak, I said: "Ninshubar is alive." I put my arms around his strong neck and breathed in deep on his sweet, cedar scent. "She's alive."

CHAPTER 5

MARDUK

In the marshes

As dusk fell, everyone clung together in the reeds, many past exhaustion. I was not tired, but I was sunk in sadness and self-recrimination. I was the one who had volunteered to stand watch when the crocodiles killed the children. Harga said I was not to blame, but how could I not be?

I had to keep on doing, keep on breathing. I had to try not to think of the terrible weight of what had happened, but only of the new mission: to find an Akkadian ship and take it for ourselves.

I also tried not to think about Inush. I had seen him on the deck of the Akkadian ship, with his nose a mess of scars. I could not think of him as an enemy. What would happen if we came face to face?

Harga was right up close to me in the reeds, and he turned and must have caught my expression. "Are you well, Marduk?"

"Well enough."

Isimud pulled himself through the reeds towards us. "I will take command now," he said to Harga.

"I think not," said Harga, his mouth a flat line.

"You are in charge of the Refuge and I am in charge of the resistance," said Isimud.

The moon goddess paddled her canoe closer to us. "Lilith is in charge of the Refuge, not Harga," she said. "And I am in charge of the resistance, being an Anunnaki, and with my father Enki away."

The two men looked up at her from the water.

"Harga is in charge today," she said.

"I have more experience," said Isimud.

"I don't like your experience," said the moon goddess, her face hard and closed. "Now enough squabbling, both of you. It will be dark soon."

I saw that Harga did not like the "both of you" and nor did he like being accused of squabbling. I saw all that just from the way he tightened his mouth. But he had won his point and a heartbeat later, he said, very polite: "Very well, goddess."

We shifted ourselves around between boats and water for the new plan. Harga, Isimud, and I would be in the front canoe, with two soldiers in with us. Ningal, the Uruk boys, and more soldiers would be in the canoe behind. Next would come Lilith and the marshwoman, with my dogs and a gaggle of young dependants. And behind them: everyone else.

Harga steered us over to Lilith and the marshwoman. "When we see the Akkadians, the two front canoes will go hard at them," he said. "You stay well back, hidden, until you are sure of our success. You are in charge of keeping everyone hidden."

"We understand, Harga," said Lilith. "You need not keep telling us the same thing."

"Let's begin," said Isimud, "before it gets too dark."

As we paddled back to our position at the front of our damp convoy, I thought about Inush and my last memories of him. Of him riding off with King Akka's army in the night, leaving me at the Akkadian supply camp. It had not felt right running off that night, but then surely a slave owed nothing to his master?

Harga turned round to me. "Concentrate, Marduk. This is no time for worrying over things."

"I'm here. My mind is here." I put a hand to his shoulder. "I won't let you down."

"I know you won't," he said. "Not once the fighting starts."

When we had been trying to escape the Akkadians, the marshes had been lousy with them. Now that we were trying to find them, they were nowhere to be seen.

It was soon too dark to keep looking and the people were too weak to keep going all night. We took refuge on a small island and huddled together at the centre of it, far enough from the water, we hoped, to evade the crocodiles. I sat up all night, my axes in my hands, with Harga and the dogs beside me.

In the darkness, Harga patted the dogs and said to me: "They have let us down a few times with their incessant noisemaking, but they are good in an emergency."

I put my hand out to each of the dogs, scratching at their ears. "They are good dogs," I said. "Thank you for saying so, Harga. I know they have been a torture to you."

"No heroics tomorrow," he said. "I mean, there must be heroics. But nothing too unusual." He put one heavy hand on my arm. "I mean it. You can die as well as anyone. Look what happened to Ninshubar."

"No unusual heroics," I said, smiling for him, although it was too dark to catch each other's expressions. I took a big breath in. "Harga, you know I knew one of the Akkadians on board that barge we saw."

He was quiet for one long moment. "Do you mean Inush?"

"I was in his household, when I was a slave in Kish."

Again, Harga was quiet a moment. "I did not know that. You know we had him as a prisoner in Uruk before the fall."

I took a deep breath in. "He was good to me, in a way. We were friends, although that might sound strange."

Harga shifted next to me. "Will it be a problem?" he said.

"What do you mean?"

"If you need to kill him, will it be a problem?"

"Harga, I don't know. I don't know if he's my enemy or my friend."

There was then a long silence.

At last, Harga put a hand onto my arm again and squeezed it briefly, steady and warm. "One step and then the next, Marduk, as your mother used to say."

"I feel very foolish for complicating things. They are all bad men. I do know that."

"Things are never as clean as you hope," said Harga.

In the morning everyone was exhausted and starving but they were all alive. I counted everyone twice.

The babies and small children were finally too tired to cry or complain.

The marshwoman looked up at the sky and then smiled over at me and Harga. "I have an idea of where they are." She pointed to the pink sky to the west of us. "You see that there?"

I peered at where she was pointing but could not see much more than a slight smudge upon the pink. "The Akkadians are lighting fires for breakfast," she said. "They do not care if we see them. After all, they do not think they need to hide from anyone."

"We should leave some people behind and come back for them later," said Isimud. "It would be safer for them and quicker for us."

Harga shook his head. "We stay together."

"I will lead," said the marshwoman.

For a long hour we wound our way through reed beds, the marshwoman constantly stopping, paddle on her lap, to frown back at the crowd in the water.

And then I smelled it: smoke, with the faintest trace of roasting meat upon it. The marshwoman turned and winked at us.

On we went, very slow but silent as ghosts. Once a large cow rose up before us and I was glad I had bound the dogs' mouths. We heard children's voices close by and the sound of a dog barking. On we paddled, waiting every few heartbeats for those in the water to catch up.

Then I caught the glint of copper through the reeds ahead.

The marshwoman lifted a hand, her fingers spread wide. We made our way just a little further forward through the reeds, to get a proper view.

An Akkadian barge was anchored only a few cables from us and not far out from an ancient wooden jetty. Canoes plied back and forth from the jetty to the barge. There were some marshmen in the canoes, but most of the men were Akkadians; some of them were half familiar to me.

The ship had two anchors down, fore and aft, and its sails

were stacked on deck. There looked to be a small crowd of soldiers on board. They were clustered around something, looking down. A board game, perhaps.

I felt the shift in me, with battle close. My mind had been different since I was hit by lightning. The shape of what I was going to do unfolded naturally before me.

I put my hand on Harga's shoulder. "I can swim under water from here to the barge," I whispered. "I will kill everyone and then cut the anchors. Then you come over in canoes, very fast, with about twenty rowers."

"What about everyone else?" he said.

"We should be able to move the ship with twenty rowers," I said. "We can row straight back here, pick up everyone, then we escape."

"A lot could go wrong," said Isimud, from behind me.

"I can do it, Harga," I said.

He tipped his head to me, in assent.

I stood, careful not to tip the canoe over. And then I dived into the thick brown water.

CHAPTER 6

GILGAMESH

In the far north

As I moved around the Sebitti camp, I felt Inanna's black eyes upon me. She had the same look to her as she had had in Uruk when she set herself out to have me. The same complete openness, trust, and conviction. It seemed likely that unless I said something to her, she would ask me to her bed that night or follow me to mine.

An idea that appealed to me very strongly.

But should I say something, about the thing I tried never to think about?

I sat down on my own near the fire and pulled my borrowed wolfskin tight around me. It was fiercely cold with the sun gone down.

I did not want to say anything, but if I said nothing to her about me lying down with her mother, and she found out after, would she ever forgive me?

Inanna was a high goddess, but she was also a woman. Was it a nonsense even to think of telling her? Would it only hurt her and for no reason?

Of course, perhaps she would not care at all. Yes, perhaps it was nothing. She would laugh it off. I breathed in, and I breathed out. I wanted to live truthfully and honourably. What was more honourable: to tell her, or to never mention it?

On balance, I thought I should say nothing. When I got back to Sumer I would make sure that Ningal never mentioned it either. Why cause Inanna pain? Yes, that was the right thing.

As I sat there, deep in my thoughts, Inanna sank down next to me. She turned a bright face up to mine. "How is your knee?"

"My knee doesn't matter," I said. "I'm so pleased about Ninshubar."

"I cannot wait to get to her," she said. "Oh, Gilgamesh, I am so happy." She put a hand to my bad knee, very gentle. "I would like to try something."

"Oh?" I said, instinctively nervous.

She moved closer to me. "When Ninshubar died, or rather when I thought she was dead, I gave myself over to this blue power that I have." She looked down at the fire and took a deep breath in. "In that state, when I was one with the power, I could see everything. And I saw Ninlil and what she was capable of."

I took one of her hands in mine. "Go on."

"Gilgamesh, she could heal people." Her black eyes flickered with blue light. "I think I can heal your knee."

"Oh, really?" I found myself frowning.

"I think I need to go inside you." She laughed. "Not physically. I need to creep inside you, in my mind's eye, and heal you from the inside. I think that's what Ninlil did. I did not see her do it, but I absorbed what she was and how she worked."

I did not like the idea of Inanna creeping inside me, and I did not like the idea of someone fiddling with my knee, when it was already agony. But I also remembered what Enki had said about my walking days being over. I did not want that to be true.

"I will be very gentle with you," Inanna said, smiling wide.

"All right," I said, lifting my chin. After all, was I not a soldier? "I would like you to try."

"Shut your eyes then."

I breathed in, and I breathed out, and she put both her hands on my bad knee.

Oh, I did not like it. The feel of her seeping into me; it felt very wrong indeed, as if I was losing control of myself.

Only then, belatedly, did it occur to me that she might learn something from being inside me. That she might find out all my secrets. I turned my mind away quickly from the memory of Inanna's mother pouring me a drink. From the memory of Ningal beneath me, her wonderful curls spilling out over the bedroll.

My knee began to burn with a new kind of pain. Then I forgot about Ningal. My knee grew so hot it felt as if it would burst into flames. It was an unnatural, terrible, burning feeling, like nothing I had ever endured, and it took every scrap of strength I had to keep on sitting there with Inanna's hands on me.

And then, sudden release. Her hands were gone.

I opened my eyes.

The pain in my leg was entirely gone. Very carefully, I lifted my knee and put it down again. It was no longer swollen. It looked exactly like my good knee. I let go of Inanna and stood up. Without pain. For the first time in so long, I stood without pain. I burst out in laughter, but I also felt like weeping.

"Oh, Inanna," I said. "What a witch you are! I thought I would die with my leg in ruins. But I think you have entirely cured me."

I sat back down, with no pain at all, and kissed her on the forehead.

Her brow furrowed as I pressed my lips to it. "What are you keeping from me?" she said. "I do not mean to pry, but... I feel that you are keeping something important from me. Is there something I should know?"

There was a short silence.

I found I could no longer see any way out of it.

"Inanna, while you were gone..." I began.

"Yes?" Her beautiful, open face was fixed on mine.

"I did all sorts of things while you were away."

"Do get on with it, cousin. I am in an agony of anticipation." She laughed.

"I made mistakes." I paused again, looking down at my miraculously cured knee.

"Is this a confession?" She laughed again.

"Yes."

She squeezed my arm. "Did you murder an innocent? Conspire with Akkadians? Torture my lions?" She leaned over and kissed my shoulder. "I forgive you, Gilgamesh, whatever it is."

I laughed at that, rather nervously. "No, it was nothing like that, nothing military." I took a deep breath in, and a deep breath out. "After I heard about Della and my boy, I got very drunk."

"If you are going to tell me that you lay down with someone, do not bother yourself," she said, playful but stern. "What do I care if you have lain with every man and woman in Sumer? That is nothing to me. We are not bound by convention. I am a goddess and you are a king. And that aside, we are not bound to each other. You have made me no promises. No confessions are necessary." She squeezed my arm again.

"It was your mother," I said flatly.

Inanna removed her hands from my arm. "My mother?"

"We were on campaign together. I had just learnt about

my wife and son. We were both very drunk. So drunk I could remember nothing after."

Inanna made no discernible movement and yet, somehow, she seemed to have moved away from me. Her voice, when she spoke, seemed also to be more distant. "As I said, we are not bound to each other."

How I wished then that I had said nothing. Or that I had made something up. Why did I tell her the truth?

"I was in despair," I said. "And we were very drunk."

"There is nothing to say sorry for," she said. "You both thought me gone forever."

She was no longer the warm, shining, open girl she had been only moments before. Now she wore her temple face. No warmth, no upset, no emotion escaped her.

"I did think you lost forever, yes," I said.

She stood, pulling her wolfskin tight around her. Blue light flickered in her eyes. "I am going to destroy the gate," she said. "It needs doing before we go."

I stood up too, careful of my knee, before remembering that I no longer needed to be careful with it. "Should we discuss it with the Sebitti?"

She shrugged. "I have made my decision."

I did not want to argue with her, when I was already so firmly in the wrong, but it seemed rather high-handed not to discuss the matter with our hosts.

"What if Ereshkigal and Bizilla need to come out this way?" I said.

"They will need to find another way. We cannot go south and leave this gate unblocked." She was looking over at the Sebitti as she spoke, her face a blank.

"Should we not wait for daylight?"

"I make my own light now," she said. She did not seem sad or sombre, but there was no joy in her.

"I'll come with you then," I said.

"As you choose."

As Inanna made her way down the pathway to the cave entrance, the blue light shone brighter and brighter around her, the air transformed into burning, fizzing flame.

"Moon cousin, I am so sorry," I said, careful on the path. I was still getting used to having two good legs and walking evenly on them.

"There is no need for an apology," she said. "Everything is as it was before."

I did not need to be some great wiseman to know that that was untrue. This was not the first time I had lost the goodwill of a woman, and this had a chill and a permanence to it that made me feel very sad indeed.

"Stand back," Inanna said, when we reached the low grass ledge outside the cave. With no further warning, she unleashed a storm of molten blue fire at the cave entrance. Rocks crashed down from above; the whole hill moved beneath us. Where there had been the dark of a cave entrance, there was only heaped-up rock with dust rising off it.

Inanna was still surrounded by a whirling spin of blue light.

"Inanna," I said. "I am very sorry."

Without turning her head, she said: "Gilgamesh, it is all over between us, if there ever was anything to be over. I am not angry with you. I am not going to try to punish you. I am simply making things simple for us."

"Simple, how?"

She turned to face me, a sheen of blue light still clinging to her. "I will never lie with you again and more than that I will never yearn for you again. There, that is a promise, the sacred promise of a goddess."

I shook my head at that, frowning. "Do not make that promise. Please, Inanna. I was crazed with upset when it happened."

"The promise is made," she said, impassive.

"Do not make such a promise when you are upset."

"I was upset when you told me," she said. "You knocked me over like a cup of water and I felt myself splashing out everywhere. But I am recovered."

"So quickly," I said. "How can anyone recover so quickly?"

"A high goddess recovers quickly. And makes decisions for the higher good."

She turned, without saying anything more, and began her journey up the cliff.

I followed on behind her but did not try to say anything more to her.

CHAPTER 7

ERESHKIGAL

In Heaven

As a young girl I heard wondrous tales of the Palace of Creation. It was a castle full of gold and mirrors, elaborate feasts, garden parties, and royal chambers so vast they must surely have been built by the old gods themselves. How I dreamed of going there!

The palace was no longer beautiful. Moreover, it was bitterly cold and dark. As I was hurried through it by my two Sebitti, I could not make sense of the geography of the place or even what was happening around us, with people huddled in every dark alcove. Bizilla was ahead of us, Neti behind, but I had seen groups of Sebitti peel off and disappear down dark corridors. "Where are they going?" I said to Bizilla.

Bizilla turned and set her jaw at me. "Ereshkigal, be quiet."

In the next corridor I was briefly set onto my feet as the Sebitti struggled to open the rusting metal door in front of us. When I turned to face Neti, I felt the flies vibrate between my breasts. A moment later, I felt a pulse of energy pass through my *mees*. *Mees* that I had thought near finished had come alive again.

I said nothing about it to Neti.

"Everything is out of balance here," he whispered to me. "It cannot be much longer until this world collapses in on itself."

The door was finally opened, and I was picked up again without ceremony and carried along the freezing corridor at a terrifying pace.

I could only see darkness ahead, but the Sebitti abruptly came to a halt.

"It's Tiamat," said Neti, his voice low.

The darkness ahead of us was moving, resolving. For a moment it looked like a huge dragon, but then I could see that it was only a woman.

She was tall and willowy, and she was dressed in a suit of black scales very like the one my Nergal had worn when he descended to Earth. I had studied that suit and knew what it was capable of.

She shone very pale against the darkness of the corridor.

Bizilla moved to stand between me and the woman in black.

My Sebitti escorts began creeping backwards, carrying me with them.

But then the woman lit up with a strange black light. She pulsed with it.

Bizilla stopped moving. The Sebitti on either side of me let go of me and I fell forward onto the flagstone floor, landing painfully on my hands and knees as I struggled to protect my belly.

My baby moved over in my belly and I put both my hands to it, breathing through my tears. How awful, to have kept it alive so long, to have so nearly carried it long enough, for it to die here and me with it.

I had fallen with my back to Tiamat, but her regal voice rang out down the corridor.

"I should have killed you when you lost Ninlil," she said.

Her words made no sense until I realised she was speaking to Bizilla.

I heard a noise like someone being kicked. And then someone falling hard and heavy.

"You were responsible for her on the day she was taken," said the woman.

"I spent a thousand turns in prison," Bizilla said. Her voice did not sound right, as if her throat was damaged. "A thousand turns for obeying your son that day."

Tiamat sighed out. "Who is this strange little creature you are with?"

Could she possibly mean me?

I very slowly pushed myself up to sitting and turned to face Tiamat.

The queen was standing with one black boot on Bizilla's gold-scaled flank. Bizilla's face was turned to me; a mess of blood.

"I see we have a gatekeeper here," said Tiamat, looking past me. "A gatekeeper is always useful."

Then Tiamat was looking down at me. A crown of living black flame played around her head. "Well, who are you?"

"I am here for Nergal," I said.

I tried to will Enki's flies and my *mees* into life, but they did not respond.

"Whose child is that in your belly?" said Tiamat.

"There is no child," I said.

"If it is Nergal's child, it is my great grandchild." She gave me a ghastly smile, black flames licking around her. "That would be something. The only babies I have these days are monsters."

She guffawed, as if she had said something very funny.

The queen looked back down at Bizilla. "First you and the Anunnaki girl flee to another realm. Now you return with another Anunnaki. And you seem to be leading an insurrection."

She took one step back from Bizilla, then stamped down hard on her head with her right foot. Bizilla's eyes rolled backwards in their sockets.

Tiamat walked past me to one of the Sebitti standing frozen behind me. She took something dark from the man's belt and shook it out.

A long black knife.

Tiamat walked back past me and brought the knife down on Bizilla's neck.

"Better to be sure," she said, grunting with the effort of it.

I turned my face from the sight of Bizilla's severed head. The blood was already spreading out towards me.

"You really are a funny little thing," Tiamat said, coming to stand over me. When she moved to push her hair back, she smeared blood across the side of her face.

"Take off your *mees* and put them on the floor," she said to me. "And take out those creatures you are hiding between your breasts and put them on the floor too."

I took off my *mees* and felt for the flies. I piled everything together on the bloody stone in front of me.

A man appeared behind Tiamat; a man in a long white fur coat with huge horns on his head like a bull's.

Tiamat picked up my *mees* and the flies, and then lifted her head to the man with horns. "Is the gate secure?"

The man drew closer. "The gate is secure, but there are gangs of Sebitti everywhere."

"Such a waste of good soldiers," said Tiamat. "But it is not the first time I have had to start anew."

"What's this?" said the man with the bull's horns, looking down at me.

"She says she is here for Nergal," said Tiamat. "It's all very strange."

Then I think she kicked me in the head.

CHAPTER 8

GILGAMESH

In the far north

I had enjoyed a short summer in the warmth of Inanna's love and friendship. Now I faced a long winter bathed in her cold disfavour.

We left the Sebitti camp and walked for three days and, league after league, Inanna's disapproval showed no sign of abating.

The Sebitti paced out in front, each carrying a leather backpack. Dumuzi and his soft-spoken sister, with basket panniers strapped to their backs, walked behind them. Next came Inanna, walking empty-handed, and finally there was me, no longer limping as I walked, but with sad eyes on Inanna's firm back.

I wished, over and over, that I had not told her the truth. Yet it was done. Irrevocable.

I was glad about my knee; more than glad. But I had messed up horribly.

On the fourth day we reached a torrent of a river that crashed out over a wide stretch of sand into open sea. On the far side of the river, set with its back to cliffs, stood a large, wood-built village. On the beach below the village, three wooden ships stood high on the sand.

"We need to cross the river," said Enmesarra, falling back to speak to us. "There is a rope bridge just upstream."

Inanna walked past the Sebitti woman without speaking. She made no particular movement, but a wave of blue fire surged out in front of her as she walked towards the river. It burned up the water into heavy clouds of steam and kept on burning it up.

Inanna, without looking back at us, walked across the wet sand of the riverbed as the water continued to boil all around her.

I saw the look on Enmesarra's face as she watched the goddess. "I know this magic," she said to me. "That is bad magic."

Inanna waited for us all to make our way across the riverbed before allowing the river to crash back into life. She turned and walked on towards the village, blank-faced.

Dumuzi was very cheerful, as we made our way across the sands. "What have you done to my wife?" he said.

"What do you mean?"

He laughed. "You no longer limp. Did she cure you? Yet she is furious with you. She was never this angry with me even when she sent me to the underworld."

"I do not know what you mean," I said.

"You must have done something," said Geshtinanna, coming to join us. "She seemed happy and cheerful when we first met you. Now she is boiling rivers!"

"I do not know what you mean," I repeated.

The ships were long and sleek, each with one mast and standing high at the stern. I had seen ships like them a long time before in the seaport outside Eridu, in the very south of Sumer.

As the people of the village came down to speak to us, wrapped in their sealskin cloaks, it began to rain.

The Sebitti stood at the front of our group, speaking to the villagers in a local tongue. Inanna stood just behind them, silent. I realised that the rain was not falling on her.

As the negotiations dragged on, the rain grew heavier and blue lightning streaked across the sky. Was Inanna calling down the weather on us?

"Can you understand what they are saying?" Geshtinanna said to me. I had not noticed her standing so close. She was very pleasing on the eye, even in her rough, handsewn clothes and with her hair scraped back into a knot. I had not properly looked at her before. I swiftly turned my mind from such thoughts. I was in enough trouble for two lifetimes as it was.

"I have no idea what they're saying," I said. "I don't even recognise the sound of it." I looked at her again. "Have we met before, Geshtinanna?"

"I met you when you visited Eridu as a boy," she said. "I must have seemed like some very ancient lady to you then and you paid no notice to me."

"Yes, how we mortals do age," I said, "while the gods go on the same."

I remembered then that she had been tortured by my men when we were looking for her brother. It felt like an age had passed since then, but it felt odd not to mention it. "I hope you know I had nothing to do with what happened to you, when we were hunting for your brother," I said.

She stiffened for a moment. "That is all over now." She smiled at me again, softening. "I find it better not to think of it."

"I know that feeling," I said.

The rain fell heavier upon us, streaming off my wolfskin

cloak, and then the blue light began to dance around Inanna. Abruptly, the whole sky above us was lit up cobalt blue.

All present turned to look at her, the villagers with their mouths open.

"Tell them to give us the ship or I will kill all of them, even the children back there in the huts," Inanna said to Enmesarra.

After that the ship was quickly ours and six seasoned sailors with it.

"The sailors will bring the ship back when we are done with it," said Enmesarra.

She was about to hand over a handful of gold scales as payment when Inanna shook her head.

"You do not have to pay them," said Inanna. "I am Queen of the Earth. The ship was mine before they gave it to us."

"Goddess, we may come back here," said Enmesarra. "We would like to leave goodwill behind us."

"As you choose," said Inanna, without any apparent emotion. "Which way will we sail now?"

"We will sail west first," said Enmesarra, "and then when we have cleared the land mass there, we will head south."

The rain stopped falling. The skies cleared. A firm warm wind began to blow in steady from the east.

"Let us head west then," said Inanna.

We stood upon the deck of the ship, beneath a square sail stitched from hide, and watched the shining green coast disappear into the mist. Geshtinanna stood beside me, holding her furs tight around her. We both had our eyes on Inanna, who stood at the front of the ship with loops of blue fire burning around her.

Dumuzi and the Sebitti had made seats for themselves in

the stern, well out of the way of both the sailors and Inanna's flickering power.

"It seems too good to be true," Geshtinanna said to me, lifting her voice over the wind. "That Inanna can call down infinite power with no harm to herself. With no apparent effort."

"I had heard of this power," I said. "Heard of her calling it down during the battle for the Barge of Heaven. And people said she had done it again after Ninshubar was killed. But I had never seen it until now."

Inanna was too far from us to have heard us, yet now she turned to look back down the ship at us. "The power is mine," she called to us. "And I will use it to do my duty."

"And what is that?" said Dumuzi, coming past us towards Inanna. "What is your duty, wife?"

"To protect this realm," she said to him. "That is the beginning and the end of it."

She turned her back on all of us to look out over the rolling ocean.

CHAPTER 9

MARDUK

In the marshes

I took one last glance at the Akkadian barge and then I made my dive. The water was so warm, even early in the morning, that I might have been swimming through blood.

My eyes adapted quickly to the dark greens and browns that I swam through. The shapes of canoe hulls formed ahead of me and I pulled myself down deeper. As I swam, my mind, unasked, played out the shapes of what might happen when I climbed up out of the water. If this man went this way, this is what I would do. If he went that way, that would be the shape of the weave.

The great oak hull of the barge loomed up before me. I felt my way along the slippery planks to the stern, keeping myself well below the surface of the water, and slowly rose up beside the ladder at the rear.

I came up only as far as my lower eye lashes, so that I could look around. No eyes were on me. I lifted my mouth up and took in a delicious gasp of air.

Well, my mother always said to me, if you are going to do something, better to do it quick.

I swarmed up the narrow ladder and onto the boat. With my two wet feet firm on the wooden deck, I drew out my bronze axes. It was Gilgamesh who taught me about axes. Up close, they kill. But the trick is that you can also throw them, and they kill just as well that way once you get the trick of doing it right.

A young man stood with his back to me, three paces away; he had not yet seen me. I leaped forward and put an axe in his neck and wrenched it out again as I spun around.

There were two men behind him, caught in the blood spray. They turned to face me, their faces slick with red, their mouths hanging open, as their comrade fell. They had no weapons in hand, only bowls.

I crossed over my axes and killed both of the men with one double-axe swing, and then I leaped away with both axes free and sheets of blood flying.

The others had all seen me. I counted eight men on board and alive.

I ran hard at the four on my left, taking out one man with an axe as I went past and then leaping over the rowing benches to attack a man on the far side of the ship. He went down with an axe in his back and I lost a moment dragging it from his spine.

Two men with spears were coming at me from the front of the ship. Long copper-tipped spears, raised as if to be thrown. I did something then that I had never tried before although I had traced the shape of it in my mind.

I dived forward onto the deck, as if diving into water, but turned my dive into a fast, tight roll in the final heartbeat, unfolding myself almost beneath the men.

I planted an axe in each of their guts. Then I hurled myself upwards, taking their spears from them as they fell, and I landed, behind their screaming bodies with a spear in each hand.

On shore, they had caught sight of what was happening. The jetty was boiling with men.

I threw one spear hard and pinned a man to the central mast with it. I threw the second spear just as hard at another man, but he threw himself down and the spear went overboard.

I drew out my two knives from my weapons belt.

There were three men left to kill and more coming over the water in canoes. The men on board had had time to grab their weapons; they approached in one wide line, a sword and a spear per man.

Behind them, out in the reed beds, two of our canoes were coming at the barge. I had told Harga that he should wait for me to cut the anchors, but there he was and Isimud too. Ningal was in the boat behind. Their faces were all fixed on me and very grim.

My mind flicked back to the Akkadian soldiers coming at me. They were heavy-set and all looked to be seasoned men. I did not know them personally, but their armour, their smell, their weapons, everything was familiar to me from my time in Kish. Unbidden, the shapes formed in my head of the dance steps that would leave the men dead.

A movement to my right; someone was climbing over the side of the ship.

It was Inush. His hands were empty, stretched out to me. "Marduk," he said.

The shock of seeing him again, of him saying my name, of him being there, took my mind away from the dance.

Something hit me hard in the gut. It was a spear. I fell, forward, and the shaft of the spear twisted agonisingly inside me.

I heard Inush shouting: "No!"

I was on the deck, my hands on the spear, but I could not shift it out of me, even with two hands. There was blood everywhere, blood under my head, blood all over my hands. Was it my blood?

Inush was there, kneeling over me. His sweet, familiar stable scent. I could not be sure where I was. Were we in Kish, in the dog yard? "Look after Moshkhussu," I said to Inush. "Will you?"

"Of course, I will," he said, his hands on my shoulders.

"Thank you, Inush," I said, but I was already falling fast into the darkness.

CHAPTER 10

INANNA

On the high seas

The ship left a track of churning white behind us as we cut across the ocean, heading south.

At first, I had to focus on smoothing out the water ahead of us and bringing the wind true and brisk upon our stern. Only at first. After a while it was no effort to me to hold the wind steady behind us and to press out the energy from the waves ahead. Also, to keep myself dry and warm as I stood there on the front deck of the sailing ship with my hands folded behind my back.

Sometimes I felt the eyes of the sailors and my companions upon me, but if I looked back at them they would quickly look away.

I kept my heart and head clear and steady too. When doubt or emotion threatened to rise up, I used the blue flames to press the disturbance away.

There must be no lurching over waves, no careering around wildly. The more I practised, the stronger I was, the steadier the wind blew, and the calmer I felt inside myself.

Dumuzi gave up on his satirical smiles at me. Geshtinanna

only cast me worried glances. Gilgamesh kept away.

The Sebitti looked upon me with no emotion except wariness. But then what was I to them? Nothing at all, except the path to their lost child.

Days passed, nights. I stood on deck, upright, centred, calm, and the ship cut through the ocean. Great whales lifted up to roll over and cast their eyes at me. Whales far larger than I had ever imagined existing. Strange birds with pale grey, round chests arced over our mast or for a few minutes would come to sit on deck, their pointed beaks turned up to me.

Every day, the air felt a little warmer, the sky looked just a little bluer, and at last we left the dark, swelling ocean and passed into waters as flat and unrippled as a Sumerian canal. Day after day, we cut through that soft water with no need for me to exercise dominion over it.

I looked down into the turquoise depths and my old friends the dolphins rose up towards me, spiralling up through the light, their eyes all upon me.

We sailed past wooded islands, the forests a luscious green. We passed small, whitewashed ports, and markets offering up fresh fish and ripe fruits. It did not occur to me to stop, but my companions campaigned for us to take on provisions. Sometimes it would occur to me that I would need strength for what lay ahead, and so sometimes I agreed.

When we threw down our anchor the Sebitti would go ashore for food or fresh water. I would strip naked and dive into the sea. I dived in just as Ninshubar had taught me to do, with my ankles together and a light hop as I jumped.

I swam fast and true through those turquoise waters, stronger all the time, the blue power surging through my limbs. The dolphins would come to swim alongside me and I no longer feared the looks they gave me. I knew what they wanted. What they expected. They wanted me to protect the realm from darkness and that I could do, and I would do. The Earth expected and I would deliver. Everything I had struggled to understand was clear to me.

One crystal morning, Enmesarra swam over to speak to me as I lay upon the rocky shore of a small island. I was lying face down, letting the sun turn my back mahogany brown.

She hauled herself out of the water and sat beside me, her long, wet red hair free upon her back. "Inanna, this power you are accessing, I have seen Tiamat doing the same thing and it has been a disaster in the realm I was born into." She spoke with great calm and seriousness. She was not a woman to be lightly ignored; I could see that. But she did not carry my burden.

I did not answer her.

"At first it seemed harmless," she went on. "But it was dangerous and not only for her personally."

Enmesarra had red, peeling patches all over her face and arms; I had not noticed before. The sun did not suit her and her brethren.

"Do I look like a dragon to you?" I said to her.

"It is too much power for one person. It burnt out her humanity."

I smiled. "Shall I let the wind die then, Enmesarra? Shall I stand back and let Tiamat invade this realm, for fear of this power I have?"

"I only seek to counsel you," she said.

I sat up. "I thank you for your counsel, Enmesarra. I do further assure you that I will do what is necessary to protect this realm. That is where my duty lies."

She gave a nod, stood, and dived back into the turquoise sea.

A few bright, blue days of sailing later, Gilgamesh took his turn to come to speak to me as I stretched myself out naked on a beach.

"Are you well, Inanna?" He sat down next to me on the sand in one easy movement. The knee was fully healed, then.

"Do I not seem well?" I said.

"You do look very well."

I sat up, pushing my hair back from my face. I examined his beauty without being moved by it. "What do you want?"

"I would like to be friends again." He looked as if he meant it.

"We have never been friends," I said, without any animation. "Indeed, I do not think a man like you could ever be friends with a woman."

"Oh?" He picked up some sand in his right hand and let it run through his fingers.

I kept on going. "Yes, I have been thinking, you know, about what kind of a man you are and indeed I have been thinking about all the men in my family and what kind of men they are. For example, I have been thinking about Enki, who you have so recently been travelling with."

Gilgamesh nodded and raised his left eyebrow but said nothing and did not look at me.

"You know Enki raped his step daughters, when his wife Ninhursag left him? It is taught in temples everywhere, is it not?"

I left a pause there.

"I don't know the truth of any of that," he said, his eyes meeting mine.

"My father knew what Enki did and yet my father handed me over to him, when I was so young I had not even started to bleed. And then Enki handed me on to his son. You knew the story and yet you were happy to share a tent with Enki and have great adventures with him. Good old Enki, such a useful man."

"Inanna, one never really knows what another man has done," he said, his eyes turned from me. "In war, you cannot be too choosy."

I had a burst of future-memory. Of the priests closing Gilgamesh's beautiful eyes and placing stones upon them. Of the grave goods I would choose for him. Of the dykes that would be built to stop the Euphrates flowing, so that his grave pit could be dug beneath it.

I pushed my hands into my eyes to push the memory away.

"I have been thinking too," I went on, when my mind was neat and hard again, "that really there is not that much difference between you and Enki."

"How so?" said Gilgamesh. He sat back from me then, the softness draining from him.

"You are famous for lying down with young girls. For catching them before they go to their wedding ceremony. For creeping into attics. Even as a hostage in Akkadia, you lay with the king's sister. All this I already knew before I met you and yet I did not really think about it as pertaining to me because I was young, ignorant, and selfish. I thought how you treated other girls didn't matter. That it only mattered how you treated me."

"Now you think different," he said, his voice stiff.

"Now I think that those girls you lay with may have said yes, but what choice did they have? Della, your wife, let us just take her as one example. Did she want to get pregnant? Did she have any way of protecting herself from that? Did any of those girls? Do you know if I did?"

"I suppose at the time, I never thought about it." He was looking out to sea and did not turn his head to speak.

"But even setting aside the babies you might have had, you have preyed upon young girls, and young boys too, with your fame and charm and power. You have pushed things as far as they could ever go without someone shouting rape at you. They say that the people of Shuruppak sent the wild man Enkidu to you to stop you despoiling a maiden. That the father of the maiden was begging you in tears to leave his daughter alone and that you refused to stand down. Only a fight with Enkidu ended your lust."

He said nothing.

"And then of course there is Enkidu, who died because of what you did to King Akka's sister. That everyone agrees on."

He turned to face me. "Almost everything you say is true."

"You no longer look so beautiful to me, Gilgamesh. I have been inside you now and I understand that you are all surface. The strength I thought I saw in you, when I was a foolish young girl, was an illusion. Beauty masks so very much and in your case, it covers over emptiness and selfishness. You are a bag of meat and impulses."

He stood up. He paused a moment and then said: "Your eyes are shining with that strange light of yours."

I looked up at him, shielding my eyes from the sun. "Because I have lectured you, do you now lecture me?"

"I thought you might want to know."

A laugh burst out of me. "Because you are beautiful, because you are brave in battle, because you know how to raise a cup of wine to a man and give a toast and slap him on the back after, people want to know you, be with you, follow you. People mistake all this, the valour, the comradery, the beauty, they mistake it for substance. For true worth. I am no longer going to make that mistake."

"I will leave you alone," he said.

I turned my head and looked out to sea as he walked away. A few cables out from the shore, a huge rock thrust itself out of the sea. I realised I wanted to be in the water again.

As I dived into the liquid blue, I thought: *The sea is mine now too.*

I broke the surface, and realised for the first time, that I had dreamed of this exact beach. A dream of prophesy. I would one day lie on this beach again, with the surf washing up over my body. A man would stand over me in armour.

"Aphrodite," he would say to me.

I shook my head, to clear my mind of the future-echoes. I would worry another time of what was to come when I walked the world with a different name.

For now, I was Inanna, and my duty was to the realm.

CHAPTER 11

HARGA

In the marshes

Marduk went down with a spear in his gut when we were only halfway across to the barge.

My rule for all engagements was simple: quickly in and quickly out.

This was not quickly in and it would not be quickly out.

I should not have let him go off on his own. He had never been badly injured in battle before, but there is always a first time and there is not always a second time.

I strained at my paddle, despite the flare of pain in my bad shoulder. Behind me Isimud and the soldiers matched my strokes.

We reached the barge just as a host of Akkadian canoes touched to on the far side of the ship.

I was up on deck first, Isimud and the others close behind me, but a moment later there were Akkadians flooding up onto the barge. To my right, Marduk was down on the deck with the Akkadian prince, Inush, leaning over him.

Marduk looked dead but I could not be thinking of that.

There was no hope now of taking the ship. I must retrieve Marduk's body and then we must all get away into the reeds.

The Uruk boys appeared at my elbow.

By unspoken assent, I went right, with the boys behind me, to get to Marduk. Ningal and Isimud went left, a small pack of our soldiers with them, to kill the boarders and discourage others from coming up the side.

I took the first man out with a pebble to the forehead. People think you cannot kill up close with a catapult and small stones but, believe me, you can when you have fired as many as I have.

I met swords with the second man and for a moment we grappled each other before Shortboy put a knife through the man's neck.

Inush was still kneeling over Marduk when I got there. He had the look of a man in shock. I kicked him as hard as I could in the head and he went over backwards.

To my left, Isimud and Ningal were deep into it but outnumbered badly and there were more Akkadians coming over the side.

Marduk looked dead, but there was no time to be sure. It can kill a man when you pull a spear out, but I could not manhandle him as he was, so I put my foot onto his hip, gripped hold of the spear, and wrenched it from him. Fresh blood pumped onto the deck.

"Let's get him straight into the water, boys," I said to Shortboy and Tallboy.

We dragged and wrestled Marduk's long body over the side of the ship, bashing him this way and that as we did, and then in an ugly tumble the four of us went over the side.

We sank deep, thrashing and flailing. I had Marduk's robe in my hands; Shortboy and Tallboy clung to my back.

I kept sinking, although I was trying to kick upwards.

I thought, *I wish Gilgamesh was here.* He was a monster of selfishness, but he was good in a fight. No one could say any different.

Somehow, I got my bad arm to a rope. I desperately strained upwards, my lungs screaming for air. I got my mouth above water and gasped for air.

There was a boatload of Akkadians almost upon us. A line of copper caps. The man at the front had a spear lined up for my head.

In that moment, I could not see a way out. Marduk's head was still underwater. On my back, dragging me down, the two Uruk boys were taking ragged breaths. I was holding us all up with the last strength in my bad shoulder.

I could not see a way out.

As the Akkadian drew his arm back to throw his spear, I let go of the rope and sank back under.

My eyes were open, looking up through the filthy marsh water at the hull of the ship on one side and the canoe hull on the other. The boys behind me were panicking and struggling, and it only served to pull us down faster.

Marduk's red hair fanned out in front of my face as we sank.

CHAPTER 12

GILGAMESH

Heading south towards Sumer

Enmesarra, mother of Marduk and leader of our new Sebitti friends, pointed to the desert shore and the low town that lay there. "The sailors say that this town is the closest we can get to Sumer by sea." She had wrapped her long red plait around her head a few times; an unusual sight, to Sumerian eyes. "From here we must go over land."

"What does Inanna say?" I said, lifting my chin towards the goddess, who stood at her usual post at the front of the ship, silent and unmoving.

"She says she can see the way south," said Enmesarra. "She says she herself is the map." The Sebitti disapproved of Inanna's use of her power, but there was no doubt that they respected her. Or feared her; perhaps that was more accurate.

I had been angry and upset after Inanna's words to me. Now those feelings had dulled into a familiar disappointment: a disappointment firmly directed at myself.

Dumuzi and Geshtinanna, both stripped down to light tunics

in the heat, came to stand beside me, and we looked out together to the town. As we sailed closer, we made out a set of wooden piers on the eastern side of the town.

"We should find ourselves mounts," Dumuzi said. "Ideally horses or mules, but I will put up with a camel if not."

"I hate camels," I said, but then I remembered that with two good knees a camel might not be too bad.

"If indeed they have animals for sale here," said Enmesarra.

In the event, it did not matter if they had animals for sale.

The sailors brought our ship in very lightly against one of the wooden piers. Docksmen reached out to steady us; ropes were being thrown by our crew.

In the midst of this activity, Inanna jumped down onto the pier and let the blue light spill out from her. Even in full sunlight, she shone very bright indeed.

The seamen on the jetty knelt down, silent, and bowed their heads.

Inanna seemed to choose one man at random. She leaned over to him, lightly touching him on the shoulder. "I need horses or mules," she said. "Or camels if not."

Whether the man knew anything at all about the getting of animals seemed not to matter. He ran off very smartly and a short time later a train of mules came trip-trapping along the pier towards us in the care of a pack of children.

The animals were all a ruddy brown in colour, except one white-coated mare. Inanna went up to the mare and said: "I will not need the bridle or the saddle." When a boy had stripped the mare of its tack, Inanna said to Enmesarra: "Lift me up."

Inanna, settled upon the white mare, at once set off. The animal seemed to need no guidance except the weight of the goddess on her back, and Inanna rode along the jetty, through a hushed and kneeling crowd, looking neither right nor left.

I barely had time to collect my few possessions from the ship in the scramble to catch up with her. As soon as we were all mounted, the sailors from the far north dropped rope and slipped to sea. They raised their hands towards the Sebitti and the red-headed warriors raised their hands in reply.

Then we were on our way, pushing our animals to catch up with Inanna. Even at distance we could see the blue fire dancing over her shining brown skin and along her mare's curving neck.

"All hail Inanna," Dumuzi said to me, bringing his mule up next to mine. "Queen of all the Earth."

I turned round in my saddle to speak to Enmesarra. "All these people we are passing by, could we ask some of them to march with us? Would an army not be useful when we reach Sumer?"

"She says she is the army," said Enmesarra.

I did not have to ask who "she" was.

"Let's hope she is as powerful as she thinks she is," said Dumuzi.

A bolt of blue lightning hit the sandy ground only cables in front of us, sending up dust and sheets of flame.

We pulled up our mules, all shocked. A fraction closer and we would have been killed.

The dust cleared to reveal Inanna with her mare turned to face us. "I am power itself, husband," she said, her eyes on Dumuzi.

Her mule turned, apparently without instruction, and Inanna rode on.

And how Inanna did ride on, never stopping for food, drink, or sleep. She rode on through searing sun and air that scorched our lungs. At night she lit up the desert around her, turning darkness to chill blue.

"You are all half-gods or otherworldly creatures at least," I said to Geshtinanna, as we rode across a plain of sparse scrub on the second morning. "For you, riding all day and night with no respite, and having to leap from your mule for only moments when you need to relieve yourself, for you all this is no doubt a pleasure."

"It is not a pleasure, I assure you," she said. "I fell off my horse last night when I went to sleep."

I learned to survive on snatched naps on my horse's back, but the days stretched out very miserably into the nights.

"Enmesarra, can't you speak to her?" said Dumuzi, riding up beside the Sebitti in the oppressive heat of the third day. "I just want to lie down flat for a bit. This is all too much."

But there was no need for Enmesarra to say anything.

Inanna's horse slowed to a halt and she turned to look back at us, frowning. "I'm hungry and thirsty," she said. "I would also like to lie down a while." She looked down at her hands, as if surprised to find them there. "I had not noticed how I felt."

The seven Sebitti went off to hunt, while Dumuzi and Geshtinanna gathered wood for a fire. Inanna sat on the ground amidst our small muddle of bags and blankets, and for the first time in a long time seemed somewhat human, perhaps even approachable.

I sat down next to her, but not too near, and offered her my waterskin. She took it and drained it. She did not thank me, but nor did she tell me to go away.

"May I ask where we are heading?" I said.

Her black eyes turned to mine. "Sippur," she said, a little impatient, as if she had given me the information many times. "My brother's city is still under siege and An is there." She shut her eyes just for a moment. "Your father is there too."

"Is he well?" I said, a burst of joy coursing through me.

She did not answer.

I was not sure then that she was truly, properly awake. "Inanna, I do not mean to press you, but do you know if my father is well?"

She shut her eyes for a moment. "He's weak," she said.

"My father?"

"An is weak." A silence, then: "I only met him once. When I was a baby and he came south to see me."

"I remember it," I said. "I remember him sailing south from Uruk. I waved him off from the quay and I remember him returning and declaring you a goddess of love."

She smiled at that. "Akka is there too."

"At Sippur?"

"Yes," she said. "He has travelled north to break the siege."

"Will you tell me your plan, Inanna? Let me understand your thinking."

"It's a simple plan," she said. "We must sweep King Akka and the Akkadians out of Sumer. Then we must make sure that Tiamat cannot follow us through to this realm. All the gates must be found and permanently blocked."

"Do you know where all the gates are?"

Her smile faded and she looked down at her hands in her lap. "I'm going to sleep," she said. She eased herself down onto the sandy ground, shut her eyes, and immediately appeared to be unconscious.

I was still sitting there, watching over her, when Dumuzi and Geshtinanna returned with blankets full of sticks.

Geshtinanna put down her load and came to look at the goddess. "She was always strange," she said. "Do you not think so?"

"I thought so at first, but then for a while I found her delightful," I said.

"I remember that you abandoned her," Dumuzi said, as he knelt down to start on the fire. "You crept off in the night from Uruk without warning her that you were going. That is how I remember it. So you can't have found her that delightful."

That I said nothing to.

Instead, I looked down at the sleeping goddess and thought, How I wish I had not ruined it.

CHAPTER 13

NINLIL

In Heaven

I had been locked in my room all morning and no one had come with food or water. The coal was finished, the fire out, and my last candle was almost gone.

I banged on the door, but to no response.

Bizilla had told me to wait in my room if things went bad, but Bizilla was gone now; she had disappeared with Inanna. So I sat in bed, in my fur cloak, listening to the sounds of the storm outside my boarded-up window. Listening for something that would tell me what was going on.

They had said to wait in my bedchamber, but what if my son was in trouble?

I took up the bronze fire poker and walked over to the boarded-up window. I tried to get the end of it between the wooden boards, bashing at the cracks between them. Finally, I got a little purchase, and then, putting every scrap of strength I had into it, I wrenched one board off. It fell with a huge cracking noise and a bang as it hit the stone floor. I froze a moment, listening, but my door remained closed and I could hear nothing outside in the corridor.

I removed two more boards from the window. How glad I was in that moment to be large and strong.

The window behind the boards was completely clogged with snow and I could see nothing out of it. I tried to force it open and it would not budge. Not knowing what else to do, I lifted my poker and smashed it through the window. I paused for a moment, unsure what would happen next, and then a huge drift of snow, spiked with broken glass, cascaded down onto me.

I leaped backwards, shook myself, picked the worst of the glass off my fur, and then I pulled over my old rocking chair, stood on it, and climbed up onto the windowsill.

It was snowing heavily; the sky was a dull pink. It was so cold that my eyes felt like they would freeze. But there was nothing for it. I leaped out into the snow and the night, landing heavily on my side.

And I was out. I had only one thing on my mind: I must find my son.

The snow lay so thick upon the terrace outside my window that it was hard to walk. To my right a new river of molten lava had formed only a few cables from the walls of the palace, casting pink light out as it cut, steaming, through the snow.

The snow seemed to be heavily trampled everywhere I looked. Here or there I saw dark stains that might have been blood.

A shout to my right and on instinct I crouched low. There were people on the far side of the river of lava, out on what had once been the palace lawns. A burst of white fire: a *mee*. People were fighting out there in the storm.

There were more shouts behind me, so I stood up and kept on going through the heavy drifts and down icy steps.

When I reached the door that Bizilla had taken me through, I found it standing open.

There was a body on the floor inside the door. Someone in a coat of gold scales. I felt for a wrist, but they were dead.

I took the *mees* from the Sebitti's right arm and pushed them onto my own wrists. *Mees* of protection. It was a long time since I had worn a *mee*, but the feel of it at once came back to me, and I lit up the corridor with white light.

It was a male Sebitti on the floor. His face had been burned away.

I stepped over him and hurried down the corridors to my son's room, my heart in my mouth. There were two Sebitti outside his door and I let my *mee* light die away.

"Is Nergal here?" I said.

The Sebitti man pushed the door open and called in, quietly: "Nergal."

My son came to the door of the brightly lit room and wrapped me in his arms. "I was about to come for you. It is all uproar. Ereshkigal has come here to rescue me."

I pulled away from him. "She's here?"

He laughed. "She is truly mad. Brave, too. She has come back with Bizilla, and all of the Sebitti have decided to rise up. We are all going to Earth together. Right now."

"Where is Ereshkigal?"

"Bizilla is taking her straight to the gate," he said. "Come, we are almost ready here."

He handed me a baby wrapped in black fur. I looked down into its pale face and dark blue eyes and held it gently to me. I was suddenly terribly, terribly afraid. "Ereshkigal should not have come here," I said.

Nergal picked up two children, one under each arm. "The plan now is to get to the gate and get away. We will meet the others there."

"There is fighting outside," I said, holding the baby to me.

My son came over to me and kissed my forehead. "We'll stay inside," he said. He grinned at me. "She came here for me," he said. He laughed. "I am told she is pregnant."

Again, I was stricken with dark dread. "Let's get to the gate quickly," I said.

Torches raised, we hurried through the palace. I jogged along with the baby tight in my arms. Nergal followed close behind me, two young children hugged to him. The rest of the children were either on foot or being carried by our Sebitti escorts.

We ran through the vast hallway in which painted dragons fought and released their streams of monsters. Then we passed through a small servants' doorway into a narrow corridor. "A back route down to the gate," said my son.

The Sebitti ahead of us drew to an abrupt halt. There was something ahead, in the gloom.

My mother was there in the narrow corridor, pacing towards us with blood on her face. She was dragging something.

Qingu was just behind her, his horns gleaming dark, his white fur wrapped around him. I pushed past the Sebitti in front of me, handed the baby to one of them, and walked to meet them.

My mother had Ereshkigal by one foot and was dragging her along the ground. Ereshkigal's belly was huge and she was moaning in what sounded like pain.

"It's Ereshkigal," I called back to my son. "She has Ereshkigal."

Bizilla was nowhere to be seen and a terrible suspicion rose up in me.

"Mother, whose blood do you have on you?" I said. "Where is Bizilla?"

My mother, a soft smile on her face, stopped walking and dropped Ereshkigal's foot.

And then a lot of things happened at once. My mother lit up her *mees*; I lit up mine. My son ran past me and grabbed hold of Ereshkigal, lifting her up off the floor. Qingu engaged with two Sebitti.

In the melee, I hurled myself at my mother. As our shields of protection met, I grappled my way forward, absorbing the pain and the heat.

Nergal was shouting for me.

My mother's attention was caught for a moment. In that thin fraction of time, I wrapped myself around her chest and held her tight as a snake.

The black flames licked at me, but they did not burn me.

"How could you?" I said, as I crushed her with my arms. I let my inner ocean surge into her, but this time I did not seek to heal. I sought to scour, to punish, to ruin.

"How could you," I said again, holding her harder. I did not care what I did to her. I only sought to destroy. "I tried to help you," I said. "I thought there was good in you. Bizilla was my family."

My mother tried to pull away. "I will kill you if I have to, daughter."

The black flames licked at my arms. They began to burn my skin. I could hear Nergal shouting, but I could not catch his words. By then the corridor was a seething mass of Sebitti and soldiers.

My mother got a hand to my throat and began to squeeze it. As I stopped breathing, I realised that I could no longer see gold scales; all the Sebitti had gone.

My brother loomed into view, a black club raised.

"Enough of this silliness, sister," he said. And then he hit me very hard indeed.

CHAPTER 14

HARGA

In the marshes

I was sinking fast with Marduk heavy in my arms and the two Uruk boys clinging to my back. The boys were panicking and in their struggling dragging us deeper.

Somehow, I took in a breath of water and choked on it.

And then I was drowning.

A vision of Ninshubar rose up from below us. An apparition so vivid it might have been real.

She was floating in the water, her red robe lifting up around her, a bronze axe in one hand. Her hair was strangely long, a halo around her head.

Had I not been drowning, I would have smiled to see her so. A ghost, a delusion, a hallucination, but so real.

The ghost of Ninshubar grabbed Marduk from me, wrestling him away. She powered herself up towards the surface, her feet beating, dragging the pale boy with her. A moment later she swam back down to me, took hold of my robe and with incredible strength pulled me upwards to the surface, the two Uruk boys still clinging to my back.

There were many hands on me then, hauling me upwards and out into the air. I found myself convulsing and vomiting out water onto a wooden deck.

The ghost of Ninshubar crouched down next to me. "Harga," she said. "Will you live?"

How real she seemed, for a ghost. She had two *mees* on each of her wrists.

"How is Marduk?" I whispered.

"Alive."

The vision that was Ninshubar stood up and as she did two Akkadians in copper helmets appeared over the side behind her. She lifted one wrist at them and, with a blast of bright white light, sent the two of them screaming overboard.

"Ningal, you look after Marduk," said the ghost of Ninshubar. "Isimud, cut the anchors."

I turned over onto my back and watched the ghost give out her orders.

How heavy she stood upon the deck, and how loud her voice was, for that of an apparition.

She lifted both wrists and a bright, fizzing shield arched out around the whole ship. She stooped down then and prodded Tallboy. "Are you alive?" she said.

"Yes," he croaked.

"Are you all there are?" she said. "Are there more of you, from the Refuge?"

"There are many more of us, hiding in those reeds over there," whispered Tallboy, one finger pointing out to the reeds.

"All right, let's get to them," said the ghost Ninshubar.

I realised that the deck was thronging with marsh children. A face appeared above me. It was the boy Tilmun, son of the marsh leader, sporting a vicious-looking black eye.

"I have broken with my father," he said. "My sister has joined me and all those from our initiation bands. We are fifty swords in total."

He held up his own sword to me. It was almost as long as he was. "We met the lady Ninshubar as we were looking for you. To pledge our help to you."

"You've done well," I whispered. "I honour you for it."

Ninshubar, who seemed so very, very real, came to look down at me. She put out one strong hand to me.

I felt that her hand was impossibly far from me, although it was so close I could easily reach for it. Slowly, hesitatingly, I reached up my right hand to meet hers. I found I could not bear to touch her hand in case the dream I was in suddenly ended.

"Take my hand, Harga," she said. "We don't have much time."

I clasped her hand.

The shock of her solid warmth ran through me.

"Are you a ghost?" I said. Even as I said the words I knew that I had never sounded so foolish. But I was half-drowned and it made no sense at all that she was there.

"I am no more a ghost than you are," she said, holding my hand tighter.

She pulled me up onto my shaking legs. For a moment we stood there together, our right hands still clasped between us, so close we might have touched noses. I was momentarily overwhelmed with nameless, shapeless, overwhelming emotion.

"Help Isimud with the back anchor," she said, dropping my hand and stepping back. "And then come help me with the sails."

I walked, as instructed if rather unsteady, towards the stern of the ship, weaving my way through the marsh children. The

Akkadian prince, Inush, was lying near the door to the cabin in a tunic now entirely soaked with blood.

As I crouched, careful to keep his hands in view, to feel for his pulse, Shortboy and Tallboy came to stand over me.

"My lord, we are sorry we dragged you down in the water," said Shortboy.

"I will teach you to swim when this is over." I stood up. "For now, I want this one kept alive." I pointed at Inush. "Tie him up and stow him in the cabin."

I continued my slow progress to the stern.

"You look well for a drowned man," said Isimud. "Now help me with this anchor."

CHAPTER 15

INANNA

Heading south to Sippur

In a stone village, in a cool, stream-cut highland, I accepted a hot bath from the villagers.

While we waited for the bath to be ready, I sat on someone's neatly made bed with two children holding my hands, one on each side of me. The girl on my right had a bright smile, but one of her feet was twisted and ruined. I smiled at her, and then at the women who sat cross-legged before me on the floor of the simple hut.

"What kind of a god are you?" the oldest woman asked me.

"A god of war," I said.

I did not mention love. That part of me was dead.

When the wood-plank bath was ready, they stripped me of the bedraggled black dress I was wearing and helped me into the water. I lay in it, my eyes shut, and let the warmth seep into my bones. I let my mind rove out south, looking for gateways to other realms. The gate at the Kur was buried deep in the mountain. I had made sure of the gate in the far north. I let my mind rove east. There was a gate in Egypt that still stood open. That was something I would need to deal with.

I circled wider and wider, but could see no other gates.

"Are you ready to get out now?" said a villager, and I opened my eyes, pulling myself back into the light.

They dried me, rubbing me very gently. The cloth they brought out for me must have been the best in the village. The linen was undyed, but it had small blue butterflies embroidered all over it. I remembered how, an age before, a lifetime it felt like, a flock of butterflies had landed on me on the banks of the Euphrates.

I was confused for a moment, about what was then, and what was now, but as they cut the cloth and sewed it into a simple dress for me, I had time to smooth out my thoughts.

They combed the knots out of my hair and brushed it flat upon my back. They polished my feet with rough stone and rubbed almond butter into them, and then tied soft leather slippers to my feet. The linen dress dropped cool and light over my head.

"We wish we had a crown for you," said the young girl with the twisted foot. "You should have a crown."

I traced a line of flickering blue around my head with one hand and let it burn there for her. "Here is my crown." She hobbled close to me, and I kissed her on the nose.

All present knelt at the sight of my blue flame, pressing their foreheads to the stamped-earth floor. The girl was last to go down, because it was harder for her to kneel.

"Do you plan to take back Sumer?" the eldest of the women said.

"I am taking back the world."

Afterwards, the villagers lifted me onto my mule and I set off again. The faint path took me down a ravine, crossing scree-strewn slopes, dipping here or there for a mountain oak, but the blue light led me on true.

"All hail Inanna!" The chant lifted up, high above me. The people had come out to line the top of the ravine. "Queen of all the Earth!"

The young girl with the twisted foot blew me kisses.

I lifted one palm to her and then turned back to the path of blue before me.

Moments later, Dumuzi came to ride alongside me on the narrow path, our knees jostling. "You're madder than your sister," he said, sounding quite angry. "I hope you realise that. Ereshkigal is quite normal now, relatively speaking. You are going the other way."

I took in his high-cut cheekbones and the scatter of dark freckles upon bronze. His skin had deepened in tone in all these weeks outside and his eyes and teeth flashed white as he remonstrated with me. That beauty spot beside his mouth. Perhaps I would have him serve me in temple, if I decided to resurrect the rites.

"How do I seem mad to you?" I said, genuinely curious.

"Well, to take one example, why did you not tell us when you were about to leave the village? Why have us scrabbling after you like fools?"

I thought about his question. "I'm not thinking about any of you. I often forget you are here. I did not have you in my mind when I left the village."

"That sounds honest, but very mad indeed."

"It's only important that I go south. It doesn't matter if you go south."

"And why is that?"

"I don't need your help. I can do what needs to be done on my own. I am alive with power now. Your swords and *mees* will not change the outcome."

Dumuzi looked down the ravine to the rock-strewn plain that opened out below.

"Enmesarra has told you that this power you are drawing on is going to kill you from the inside out. And yet you ride along here, even now with no crowds in attendance, with that blue crown burning on your head. What possible need can there be for that blue crown?"

"What do you care, husband, about what hurts or kills me, or what is sustainable for me?"

"I suppose I care about the realm," he said. "About this land. And you know I never hated you, Inanna. I thought you very odd, but I did not dislike you. I did not even dislike you after you banished me to the underworld. I thought you a woman of honour, I suppose. Now I wonder what kind of hero you are becoming."

"Leave me alone," I said.

"What about that little girl with the twisted foot, who I saw you blowing kisses at? I saw you making a pet of her in the village."

"And?"

"You healed Gilgamesh's knee. Could you not have helped her?"

"Do you want me to heal every child along the way? We will never get to Sumer."

I urged my lovely mule to move faster, to put Dumuzi behind me.

"I rather think this is all just a sulk," he called after me. "A sulk because Gilgamesh has done something you don't like. We need you to be better than that."

"Go ride with your sister," I said, turning to look back at him. "Follow me, don't follow me. It makes no difference."

The girl's face rose up before me, and the memory of her hobbling beside me.

I pushed the thoughts aside.

Soon enough I had stamped out the sparks of upset and doubt, and all was strong and bright and steady again. The words of a man like Dumuzi, the actions of a man like Gilgamesh: these things were nothing to me.

On the sixth day I glimpsed a looping turn of the Euphrates in the distance. We had been travelling overland east from the sea. Now we would go south to Sumer and we would travel by river.

When I reached the edge of the river, I slipped down from my mule.

Two large coracles were passing down the river, loaded with sacks, donkeys, and merchants. The donkeys and merchants turned to look at me with wide eyes.

I had known boats just like these coming to Ur when I was a girl. They came south from the mountains, letting the current take them, and then in the south they sold their goods, folded their boats into pieces, and travelled north again on foot and donkey-back.

"I need your boats," I called out to the merchants. I did not raise my voice over the roar of the river, but I knew they heard me.

As they unloaded their donkeys and wares, the three Sumerians and the seven Sebitti arrived next to me at the river's edge.

I nodded to Enmesarra. "Help me get my mule onto a boat," I said.

I sat on a pile of bags in the lead coracle, with my very unhappy mule lying next to me.

By concentrating hard, I could bring the whole power of the river into the pushing along of our coracles; no other steering was necessary. My eyes shut, my hands in my lap, I learned to push away the logs and mats of reeds that lay ahead of us and might have slowed us down.

When I opened my eyes and stood up, careful not to tip over, the land was familiar to me. Palms, fields, and reed-hut villages. Clouds of swifts wheeled above us in the sky and crocodiles lay stretched out between the reeds, ready to slip into the river.

I was on my way home.

"It's so hot," said Enmesarra. "So hot, so strange. So many fields. So many canals. Where are all the people?"

"They are hiding from me," I said. "The word has run ahead of us."

All was well with me on the river, with the power running through me, at least when I was awake.

Yet dark dreams plagued my sleep. Dreams of oil-black feathers, spread wide over a mountain. Of Ninshubar lying in grey rubble, her mouth and eyes open. Of a serpent crawling towards me, its mouth and fangs impossibly huge.

I took to sitting up all night. My dreams were frightening, so I would no longer dream them. The power would sustain me. I would put sleep behind me.

On the third morning on the river, as the sun lit up the reeds, I guided our coracles onto a stretch of pale sand.

"Where is this?" Gilgamesh called over from the coracle behind. "Is this Sippur?"

He had found himself armour and a long bronze sword on the journey south. He looked like the soldier that he was.

I had no need for a soldier.

"We are close to Sippur," I said to them all. "Two Anunnaki gods, An and Lugalbanda, are here. Their enemy King Akka is here too, besieging the city. I am going to end the siege."

I jumped down onto the sand and gestured for the Sebitti to carry my mule ashore.

It was Gilgamesh who led the animal to me.

"What is your plan for lifting this siege, Inanna?" he said, frowning.

"I am the plan," I said. The blue light began to dance around me, faster and faster. "You do not have to come, cousin."

"We're going to come," Gilgamesh said. "Of course, we are going to come. We are with you, Inanna. All of us."

I looked up at the sky. Storm clouds were gathering, where moments before there had only been the pastels of dawn. I sent down a bolt of lightning into the river and watched as it sent steam billowing in all directions.

"Stay well back from me then," I said to Gilgamesh.

I let Enmesarra help me up onto my mule.

And I rode on towards Sippur.

CHAPTER 16

NINSHUBAR

In the marshes

We loaded up the barge with the refugees hiding in the reeds. I let my shield drop to allow them to clamber on board, and Harga and Ningal climbed down and balanced on various canoes in order to help the most vulnerable and to wrestle with the scrabbling dogs.

Ningal was so changed; so lean, so hard-looking. It was so strange to see Harga with his hair shorn.

When it became obvious they did not need my help, I made my way to the stern, through the crowds of priestesses and children. They were stripping the Akkadian dead of clothes and weapons, and I was glad to snatch up a bow and a quiver of arrows from them.

The Akkadians had lost their barge to us, but they still had canoes and they were coming across the water at us as fast as they could, each canoe packed with copper-capped soldiers.

I raised my bow and began to pick off the men holding paddles. Isimud stood next to me, hurling spears at anyone who brought a canoe close enough. It felt unnatural to be standing together as comrades.

"That's everyone on board," called out Harga.

I lit up the sky around us with the moon god's *mees*.

"Oars!" Harga shouted out, as he made his way over to us. "Anyone who can, get on an oar." He pointed to an old woman wrapped in black. "Can you guide us out?" he said to her.

The woman was familiar to me, and indeed, as I frowned at her, she gave me a smile. "I know you, Ninshubar," she called out. "Do you remember me from my floating hut? When you were bleeding from every part of you?"

I laughed. "I remember you. You are the one who saved me when I escaped from Enki's dungeons."

"And you told me you were a hero," she said. "Now I see that you spoke the truth."

And then we were moving off towards an open waterway. The Akkadians came after us in their canoes, but kept well back from the edge of my barrier of protection.

I went over to check on my son the Potta, or Marduk as he now was. He was being cared for by a shaven-headed woman in a priestess's robes and he lay with three dogs lying next to him on the deck. I remembered the large brown dog from the day when I was cut down.

It took me a moment to recognise the woman with the shaved head. She looked so very different without her hair. "Lilith!" I said.

"Hello, Ninshubar," she said. "He will be so very glad you are alive. He has never stopped looking for you."

I sat down next to her and took my son's cool right hand into mine. The moon goddess, with a baby in her arms, came to sit with us, and leaned over to kiss me.

"Marduk's doing well," she said to me. "The Sebitti heal well."

"What does that mean?" I said. "Sebitti?"

"We have a lot to tell you," the moon goddess said.

"Have you heard anything of Inanna?" I said to her.

"Only that she went into the Kur and we have heard nothing of her since."

We smiled at each other, in sadness. I thought about telling her about her husband, but could not see a good reason for mentioning him. "I should help with the ship," I said.

I was hauling the sails out of their leather bags, with the help of several marsh children, when a cry went up from the lookout. I made my way forward, followed closely by Harga and Isimud.

There ahead of us, its sails pristine white against the green reeds, was the skiff from the White Temple.

"They're with me," I said. "They brought me here from Ur."

"From Ur?" said Isimud.

He and Harga both turned to look at me.

I am a humble woman and have never in all my life boasted. Yet I found myself happy enough to amaze those two men.

"Yes, we took Ur," I said. "I left it in Sumerian hands."

"Who is we?" said Harga.

"Me and one other," I said. "The moon god Nanna. He is waiting for us there."

The two men, open-mouthed, turned back to look at the skiff.

"What have you been doing these past few moons?" I said.

"What we could," said Isimud, frowning.

"How did you take Ur?" said Harga.

I gave a casual shrug. "The people rose up," I said, "when we arrived." I smiled at them both. "I will make a story of it later. The sailor boys there can lead us back to Ur in their skiff."

As I turned to go, for a few heartbeats Harga and I stood close.

"I am glad you are back," he said, his voice low.

I had a strong urge to kiss him, but of course I did no such thing.

"I will get on with the sails," I said.

CHAPTER 17

GILGAMESH

At Sippur

We rode up onto a high dyke and from there we had a perfect view of the ancient city of Sippur. It was a small town but with impressively large mud-brick ramparts. I had been there once or twice and nodded at the walls, but found it otherwise unremarkable.

Now a sprawling army surrounded the city; a sight you would not forget. The land in all directions had been trampled dark by Akkadian boots. Every tree had been cut down, every path churned to mud.

On a low rise to the south, a fine tent rather larger than all the others had been put up, with a strip of bright blue flying from the highest tent pole. That would be King Akka's tent.

I brought my mule up alongside Inanna's. "If we can see the Akkadians, then they can see us, Inanna," I said to her.

She did not acknowledge my words. The blue flame rippled over her like thin cloth sculpted from fire, and she seemed at that moment to be very distant from me indeed.

Far off, perhaps half a league distant, I caught a streak of azure amidst the dark of the Akkadian army. "Perhaps that's the king," I said.

"It's him," said Inanna.

The sky above us darkened into grey, blue lightning flashed across it, and rain fell like a waterfall upon the land.

Yet it did not touch those of us who rode with Inanna.

The goddess's white mule moved off, straight down the dyke towards the besieging army. As Inanna rode across the muddy, rubbish-strewn plain, the blue light played over her dress and sparkled through her hair.

I hastened after her. Aside from anything else, I was keen to remain within the penumbra of her rain shelter. Dumuzi, Geshtinanna, and the Sebitti were quick to follow my example.

Inanna turned her head to me when we were almost at the outskirts of the Akkadian camp. "Your father is there on the walls," she said.

I peered through the heavy rain at the city ramparts. "I cannot see him."

"He's in his armour," she said. "Near the tower to the left." Only then did I catch the dull sheen of his bronze chest plate through the rain.

"And An?" I said.

She shut her eyes briefly. "Deep inside the city somewhere. He's weak."

Cobalt lightning forked across the sky above us.

Astonishingly, the Akkadians were not looking towards us as we rode up to their rear guard. Some were looking up at the sky. The rest were looking over towards the city.

Akka, their king, was riding his mule along the front line. Even in the heavy rain, he had the animal in a canter; he looked to be making some sort of show for the men. Were they about to attack in force?

Inanna's mule came to a halt a few cables from the enemy's rear lines. I drew up beside her, looking to her, but she said nothing. Her blank eyes were on King Akka as he rode across the empty ground in front of the city, almost close enough to have been brought down by an arrow.

When he was half a cable from us, the land, the entire sky, lit up in a blast of ice-blue light. The rain was gone. Only the strange, cold, blue light surrounded us.

The Akkadians, to a man, turned towards us.

And saw Inanna.

She sat on her white mule, small and plain and unremarkable except for the crown of turquoise flame that blazed upon her head.

I suppose it might have been argued as a trick, that crown. But the waves of invisible power that rolled from her could not be denied. No one there, on that day, could have thought her anything less than a god.

The Akkadians did not run, at first, but they began to back away.

A path opened out before us. King Akka came at us through the ranks of soldiers at a trot, one hand on the reins of his animal. He seemed unchanged; the same long black beard, the same thin gold crown pressed down into his black hair. His kingfisher blue robes clung wet to his belly.

He was a brave man that day, for the way he rode straight at us.

Inanna waited for him there at the outer edge of the army, impassive.

When he was close enough to speak to us, Akka pulled up

his animal. He was about to say something, but Inanna spoke first.

"Akka," she said, without any passion or particular interest in her voice. "This is not your land. This is not your city. I command you to go home."

King Akka looked over at me, took in the Sebitti, and then turned back to Inanna. "Take your lightshow tricks elsewhere, little girl," he said. "We know what they are worth."

He looked back at me then. "Hello, woman killer," he said. "Hello, rapist. I thought you would like to know how much I enjoyed your wife before I had her thrown from the moon tower."

Inanna, beside me, made the smallest movement of one hand.

A bolt of blue lightning forked down from the sky and struck the king through the heart. He tumbled from his horse, his chest black and smoking.

Panic rippled out through the Akkadian army as they began to understand what had happened.

The men closest to Akka's smoking body began to run.

"I want you to go home," Inanna said to the Akkadian soldiers. She spoke in an ordinary voice, but in the strange quiet that had fallen over the army, her voice carried in every direction. "All of you Akkadians, lay down your arms and walk away. Go back to your own land. Hurt no one on your way back. Do it quickly before I hurt you."

The army scrambled away from us in disorder.

All those months of war, loss, devastation, yet on that day not one Akkadian raised a weapon at us. Not one of them let off an arrow.

It seemed they did fear the gods after all.

The muddy wasteland, studded with army tents, was quickly left deserted. Only Akka's body remained as the last fleshy remnant of the army that had fled.

The bright blue light faded, the clouds above cleared. I felt the strange sensation upon my skin of ordinary sunshine, on an ordinary Sumerian summer's day.

Only Inanna's flaming crown of light gave a clue to what had just happened.

Ahead of us, the city gates opened and my father was the first to walk out. I was astonished by how old and thin he looked as he made his way across the muddy ground to us, a huge smile on his face.

The great Lugalbanda, *sukkal* to An, dropped down stiffly into the mud in front of Inanna's mule.

"The city is yours, high goddess," he said. He stood up again, slowly, both his knees caked in mud. "All praise, Inanna," he said. "Truly queen of all the Earth and first amongst the Anunnaki."

It must have cost him something, to call her that, when his own master, so long the first amongst the Anunnaki, lay ill behind the city walls. But you would not have guessed it from the way he smiled up at Inanna.

The goddess looked down at my father, apparently without interest or recognition. She glanced up at the walls of Sippur and the men lining the ramparts.

Then her mule turned and took her away, back towards the river. All without Inanna saying a word.

"Wait there, Father," I said to him.

I squeezed my mule on and quickly overtook Inanna, planting myself in her path. "Where are you going?"

"The Barge of Heaven is here," she said. "I'm going to take it south."

I put a hand out, and caught hold of her reins.

"Inanna, we will all want to go south with you. You may need us. Please, be just a little patient and we can all go south together."

For the first time she met my eyes. "Time is running out."

"Because of Tiamat?"

"I will wait a few minutes," she said.

I cantered back to my father and the others. "Inanna is going south and she is going now," I said to them all. Then I turned to my father and said: "Will you come?"

"An is too ill to move," he said, glancing back at the city.

"Father, I want you to come anyway. Leave a guard with him. Come, please. I would like you at my side now."

"I'll bring half the guard with us," he said. "That should be enough to move the barges."

I looked over at Dumuzi and Geshtinanna, and the Sebitti behind them.

"If you are going to come, come now," I said.

CHAPTER 18

HARGA

Heading for the Euphrates

I had never been so happy about anything in my life as I was to have Ninshubar on board the barge, alive and giving out orders. Yet I found myself strangely unsure of myself. When she passed me she would pat my arm, very companionable, and cast me an uncomplicated smile. A smile no different from the smiles she cast at all her other shipmates.

I found myself keeping busy, just for the sake of it.

In the filthy heat of the day, Marduk's war dog was sitting with her snout pressed to the door of the barge's small wooden cabin. "What is that dog doing?" I said to Shortboy, who was standing guard.

"She wants in, at that Akkadian."

"To kill him or lick him?"

"We are not sure, my lord."

I remembered Inush kneeling over Marduk's body. He had been trying to staunch the blood.

"Keep him alive if you can," I said to Shortboy.

I took the oar for a while, but the pain in my shoulder overcame me. I went to sit with Lilith, Marduk, and the two black dogs while the pain died down.

"Is he any better?" I said.

"I think he is coming back to us," said Lilith. "The wound is healing cleanly."

"By rights he should be dead," I said. "Any ordinary man would be dead." I watched Ninshubar as she hoisted the main sail, the rope passing through her hands without apparent effort.

She had spoken to me about us, a long time before. I had told her the idea was a bad one, me being mortal, and very old and ugly, and her being immortal, and very young and beautiful. Now I was only older and uglier, and if anything, she was more beautiful and more powerful. No doubt she had long ago moved on from that moment.

"Why not speak to her?" said Lilith.

"Speak to who?" I said.

Lilith shook her head at that in mild irritation. "Harga, I loved a goddess. In the end I lost her, but I am not sorry for the time we had."

"What is your point, old woman?" I said.

She looked over at Ninshubar, lifting both her eyebrows at the goddess. "Oh, I have no point at all, old man."

"I will go help with the sails," I said.

By the time I reached Ninshubar, the main sail was already up and billowing out cleanly above us. Behind us, the last of our Akkadian pursuers downed paddles to watch us go.

Ninshubar let the shield around the barge fade and disappear.

"How is he?" she said.

"Lilith says the wound is healing cleanly."

We were stood very close.

A hoot from the boy on the mast; the hoot that meant enemy sighted. We looked up to see which way he was pointing.

Ninshubar and I made our way over to the left side of the boat as fast as we could, stepping between marsh children and clusters of refugees. For long moments, we could see nothing except reeds and water. Then one, two, three huge barges hove into view, coming straight at us under oar. All crowded with Akkadian soldiers.

"How long can that shield of yours last?" I said to Ninshubar.

"Not long," she said. "We need to outrun them."

The Akkadians had seasoned rowers on their oars. We had what you might call a mixed crew. Our enemies were no doubt well provisioned. We had what had happened to be on board that morning when we took the barge. The wind favoured us, at first, then turned to blow upon our prow.

All day, through the heat and the biting insects, running with sweat, hungry, we rowed. There was no time to be fussing over the pain in my shoulder. I shared an oar with Tallboy and Shortboy, and took my fair share of it.

Ninshubar and the other seasoned archers stood to the rear of the ship. We did not have many arrows on board, but those we did, they aimed at the black beards on the barge closest behind. When she had to, Ninshubar would lift up her white fire around the ship, to protect us from projectiles, or send bolts out across the water, in order to discourage the barges from closing with us.

As dusk fell, the reeds began to thin and I caught the fresh, sweet smell of the open river. We passed out into the delta with the dark shape of Eridu's towers to our right, and ahead of us, the land of ten thousand islands. The Akkadian barges assumed a new formation behind us, three abreast, and then they began to spread out, the outer barges creeping up past us.

"They mean to surround us," I said to the Uruk boys.

Ninshubar remained at the stern, standing, her eyes on our pursuers.

When it was almost dark, and we were well out into the river, I went to stand by Ninshubar and I offered her a waterskin. She took it and drank without looking away from the Akkadians.

"You called me a ghost," she said.

"You were something of a surprise."

She looked at me a moment and then back at the Akkadian barges. "I was dead," she said. "I was in a grave, buried." She nodded, still not looking at me. "Somehow, I woke up and climbed up out of the grave. So perhaps I am a ghost of sorts."

"When did this happen?"

"The climbing up? A few days ago. I am freshly returned to the world."

I put both my arms around her. After a moment, she put her arms round me.

For a few heartbeats, we stood there together, with her very warm against me and the scent of salt and citrus filling my lungs. "You are not a ghost."

She nodded into my neck.

Then because I did not know what else to say, I said: "It is strange to see you with your hair grown."

She let go of me, took a firm step back, and passed me back my waterskin. "We cannot let them catch us," she said. "You should get back to your oar."

CHAPTER 19

ERESHKIGAL

In Abydos, Egypt

I awoke in a bed, lying on my side, surrounded by white linen curtains.

My hands went to my aching belly. The skin felt bruised, but with a surge of relief, I felt the baby move inside me. I thanked all the stars then, and all the gods, ancient, real, and false. I thanked everything and everyone, for the feel of the life within me.

I was thinking about how to sit up when Nergal lifted up one of the thin curtains and sat down next to me, tipping the whole bed towards him. He smelled of heat and dust. He seemed so huge and real, after so long imagining him. His dark, snub-nosed face was so close, so handsome.

"You chased me to Heaven," he said. "You crossed realms to rescue me."

"Help me sit up," I whispered. My throat felt as if someone had stepped on it. "But then you rescued me," I said. "You saved me from Tiamat."

He lifted me up into a sitting position and, leaning in close to me, arranged the pillows behind my back. I almost bit his neck, he smelled so good to me. "I did not have enough time with you," I said. "I am so happy, so very happy, to have you back here."

I noticed that he had the master *mee* on his right wrist.

"Is this Abydos?" I said.

"It is." He was thinner than when I had first met him, but his head no longer had its terrible wounds, and his hair had regrown over what had once been open flesh and skull.

"I am going to kiss you on the mouth," I said.

Oh, how I kissed him. My beautiful, beloved Nergal. I kissed his mouth and nose and eyes and cheeks and neck and then I kissed him on the mouth again. "I only want to kiss you now," I said. "That is all I am ever going to do now." I kissed him and kissed him.

He kissed my bruised face and neck very gently.

"May I ask?" he said, dipping his head, very delicately, towards my belly.

"It is your child," I said to him. In fact, it could just as well have been Dumuzi's, but that did not matter. It would be our child now.

Nergal lifted his chin, his eyes shut, tears spilling down his smooth-shaven face. He leaned over and kissed my huge belly. "Goddess," he said. "I never expected such a gift."

Deep inside me, I felt the baby move. Perhaps it really was Nergal's; I hoped so.

"Tell me what I have missed," I said. "Who crossed over with us? And what is happening now?"

"Around two hundred of us passed through the gate," he said. He gave a deep sigh out. "My mother did not get through."

I sat up straighter and put my arms around him. "I am sorry, my love."

"We were separated in the fighting. I last saw her with her arms around Tiamat. Then I was focused on getting through the gate." He wiped more tears from his eyes. "She never came through and then the gate closed."

"And Neti?"

"I didn't see him again after I went to grab you."

He put his two strong hands on my belly and I felt the child respond to the pressure. "I can feel it moving," he said. "I am so very sad about my mother, but I am very happy about this baby."

"The baby is a fighter, just like me," I said.

"Or perhaps just a little like me," he said, smiling.

"I would be a marvellous soldier, if I had ever taken any interest in it," I said. "What happened to the rest of the Sebitti?"

"There was a back-up plan. That those who could not make it through the gate would go to Qingu's estate and try the gate there. So perhaps they will find a way through to safety."

"But they will not have the master *mee*," I said. I put my hand to it. "May I have it, my love? There is a great deal I could learn from it."

He paused a moment, but then took the dark bracelet off and handed it to me. "My queen," he said, bowing his head over it.

"I need to work out what is happening," I said, as I slipped the iron-grey bracelet onto my left wrist. "I want our baby born in Sumer. I need to know that all is secure there."

"Before you use the *mee*," said Nergal, "perhaps you could come down and speak to your grandfather Enki."

"Oh?" I said.

"We are at war, downstairs, about what to do next."

"Very well," I said. I looked down at the master *mee*, with my grandfather in my mind, and thought about all the different things that it could be used for. "I will go downstairs with you."

In the main courtyard of the palace, around a pretty tiled pond, the two warring armies were drawn up. On one side my beloved Nergal and the leaders of the Sebitti. On the other, my grandfather Enki, his lions, his daughter Isis, the goddess of Abydos, and a strange man with heavily scarred skin. The scars were red and raw, tracing a grisly pattern upon his neck, face, and hands.

"Who is this?" I said, pointing at the scarred man as I made my way into the courtyard.

Isis turned her sullen face to me. "My husband and brother, Osiris."

The scarred man seemed about to speak, but then shook his head, his hand to his throat.

I sat down at the edge of the pond and put my swollen feet into the water. "Well, what are you warring about? Get it over with."

My grandfather, Enki, came forward and sat down on his side of the pond, cross-legged, the lions on either side of him. "We must block up the gate," he said.

Behind him, both Isis and the strangely scarred man, Osiris, nodded.

"Why have you joined with my grandfather?" I said to Isis. "I thought you hated him."

"He helped me while you were gone," she said. She turned to her husband-brother. "Osiris was killed and Enki helped me raise him again."

Enki leaned forward to me. "If Tiamat gets through the gate and accesses the power that Inanna uses here, there will be nothing we can do to stop her. It is our duty to shut the gate now."

To my left, my beloved Nergal stepped forward. "Ereshkigal, my mother may come through at any moment. Hundreds of Sebitti may also need to come through. We must give them just a little more time."

I shut my eyes for a moment and followed the lines of blue power outwards. In the far, far distance, I saw the brilliant blue star that was my sister Inanna.

I could not tell much but I saw that she was frightened.

I looked up at my darling Nergal, very sad. "The gate must be closed now," I said. "I am very sorry for your loss, my love. But it must be closed now."

"Tiamat does not have the master *mee*," he said. "We cannot be sure that she can reach Earth now."

"But she may," I said. "She is a queen with all the resources of Heaven. She has my flies, she has the gatekeeper. If we delay, you may not only lose your mother. You may also lose the baby in my belly and all your Sebitti friends. The gate must be shut."

Nergal took in a deep breath. He looked at those about him, and then looked back to me. What a good man he was, and so beautiful and handsome.

"Very well, my love," he said. "We will trust you."

Enki stood up, with a great sigh out. "Finally," he said. "Now who will help me do it?"

CHAPTER 20

INANNA

Heading south down the Euphrates

I stood on the deck of the Barge of Heaven, my breathing steady. One hundred oars bit into the river and flashed bronze as they lifted high again. Three blood-red sails billowed taut against the blue summer sky.

I cleared logs and rafts of matted reeds from the river ahead of us and I turned the wind to blow directly upon our sterns and drive us neatly south to Uruk and beyond.

But my mind was not on the sails, or rogue logs on the river, or the barge's splendid sweep of deck, ten cables long. Over and over, the dark thoughts rose up.

Ninshubar was somewhere ahead, to the south. I wanted to see her more than I had ever wanted to see anyone. But once she was with me she would want to help me.

The dreams came to me now when I was wide awake. Dreams of Tiamat spreading her black wings over the Earth. Dreams of me being devoured by her seven sets of fangs.

Everyone who tried to help me would die. I had dreamed it now, over and over.

For a moment I staggered, lost beneath my old confusion, lost beneath so many memories of the times that had gone and the times that were yet to come.

I grasped for the blue flame and let it pour into me, strengthening me, pulling me upright, calming my troubled heart.

Gilgamesh was at my elbow, frowning at me. "You are all lit up blue again," he said. "Why is it necessary? Let the river take us south. Let the sailors and the oarsmen do their work. Come back to us a moment, Inanna." He took a step closer to me. "Everyone is worried about how much power you are using. I do not mean to harass you, Inanna. I do not mean to question you. But they are all in my ear, full of warnings. The Sebitti especially, because they have seen Tiamat be changed by power of this kind. But my father also warns against this. He has seen how it went in Heaven."

It took something of an effort not to shut him up with a blow.

"You no longer look the same," he said. "The whites of your eyes have gone. Find something to look in, if you do not believe me. Your eyes are a solid black."

I turned away from him, focusing harder on the river surging beneath us and the warm wind on my back.

He was still standing there. "Inanna, I know you think you are doing your duty, but you are not alone in this."

I pushed down an upsurge of sadness and upset and let the blue calm spread in me.

"I must clear out the Akkadians," I said. "Right down to the sea."

"Are you worried that Tiamat is here already? Or that she might be here soon? Why not speak, Inanna?"

"Let me be," I said.

I turned my face from him until he went away.

We came to Uruk at dusk on the second day. It had once been so beautiful, sitting glorious and golden on a turn of the Euphrates. Now there were gaps in its ramparts and wild animals roamed the streets.

I did not want to stop there. I kept the wind blowing and threw an invisible line of fire around the oarsmen to keep them rowing evenly.

Lugalbanda, Gilgamesh's father, came to stand next to me at my place on the foredeck.

"Inanna," he said. "Let us leave a small force here to start the work of rebuilding. The people will start to come in from the land if we garrison the city. It would be better for all to leave it secure."

The bats dipped down, ahead of us, to kiss the river. Were they drinking or catching flies?

"If we stop only for a few moments, we can unload enough soldiers to do the job," Lugalbanda said.

I turned to look at him. The *melam* was fading in him and I wondered how long he had left. In my dreams now he died on the back of a lion-headed Anzu bird.

"I don't care," I said. "Leave soldiers if you want to. But do not take long about it."

I thought of my own father, for the first time in a long time. I shut my eyes and followed the faint blue threads south to Ur.

Blessed Ur, that I had once loved so much.

My father was in his old bedchamber, high up in the palace. He was kissing a young girl.

I pulled away fast. Some things I did not ever want to see, goddess or not, blue power or none.

"Inanna, we cannot stop the barges unless you loosen your grip on them," said Gilgamesh.

I opened my eyes.

"My father is at Ur," I said.

"I thought he had fled," said Gilgamesh.

I let the wind on our stern die. With some deliberate effort, I began to slow the fleet.

"He's in his old rooms," I said. "It seems he is King again there."

"I thought Akka had the city."

"If we survive this," I said to Gilgamesh, "I will give the city to Ninhursag. Enki's first wife. She was kind to me when I was at Eridu. Have you ever met her?"

He shook his head. "I think I did as a boy, but I don't remember her." He took a deep breath in, and a deep breath out. "Inanna, please tell me, is Tiamat already here? Is that what has you in such a hurry?"

I lifted my chin to the ruined city of Uruk. "You can use the oars now to steer us in. But be quick."

He looked hard at me a moment but then nodded and spoke gently to me. "As you say, goddess."

When we were underway again, the broken ramparts disappearing around a bend in the river, my husband Dumuzi came to stand beside me.

"They are saying that you can see where all the Anunnaki are," he said.

"What of it?"

"I wonder if you can see Ereshkigal. We would like to know that she is safe."

"None of us are safe."

He moved round to block my view of the river, his head bent to one side, his chin tight with irritation.

"Can you tell me if she is in this realm?"

"What do you care, Dumuzi?"

"Actually, I care about Ereshkigal very much. She has been very good to us both, and especially to Geshtinanna. Indeed, she has shown more kindness to Geshtinanna than any other relative. So we would like to know she is well and that the baby is well."

I shut my eyes with a sigh, and turned my attention to the web of blue. Very quickly, I found her there. "She's in this realm," I said. "In Egypt. The baby lives inside her."

"Thank you, Inanna," he said.

I went deeper into the web of blue.

"They have blocked up the gate at Abydos," I said. I had not expected that.

"Does that mean all the gates are blocked or buried?" said Dumuzi.

I blinked my eyes open. "The Kur is buried and the gates in Egypt and the north are closed," I said. "I cannot find any other gates."

"This is good news," said Dumuzi. "I will tell the others. This is very good news, Inanna."

I stood alone then on the deck. I stood alone in the great power. The hippos turned their eyes to me. The crocodiles, lined up upon the shore, turned their eyes also. Above my head, eagles gathered, in larger and larger numbers.

So, was it over?

I had to grip the rails hard to stay upright. I had been waiting for Tiamat to come for so long that I could not believe it might be over.

Elephants appeared through the reeds. A family of them, all looking at me.

I no longer knew what they wanted of me. If I did not exist to battle Tiamat, what was I good for?

CHAPTER 21

NINLIL

In Heaven

My father sat in his rusting chair beside a pile of packing crates. Up close, I could see that he was tied to the chair with old pieces of leather which had cut deep marks into his desiccated skin.

I sat next to my father, amidst the chaos of the exodus, in my own metal chair, and I was chained to it at the neck, elbows, and ankles. My skirts were wet with urine, but that was really the least of anyone's problems.

The gatekeeper, Neti, lay at my feet, very well trussed and with a so-called bolt around his neck.

All around us, courtiers and soldiers made their final preparations for our flight through the gate. My mother's monster-spawn had been put into separate metal cages to avoid them killing each other, and very probably us, on the way through. These cages were now stacked all around us, and they shook violently as the demons threw themselves back and forth inside them, screaming their horrifying screams.

Every now and again the heavy-fanged creature in the cage jammed up closest to me would almost get a wriggling arm or snout or tongue to me and begin screaming even louder, and spraying me with dank fluids.

My mother appeared, in her close-fitting black suit, and she kicked at Neti with one black-booted foot. "Stand him up," she said.

Two black-robed footmen rushed forward to drag Neti onto his feet.

The gatekeeper peered up at my mother, silent, his skin ashen.

She tapped his chest with one armoured finger. "You are going to show us through to Earth," she said.

"My lady," said the gatekeeper, "without the master *mee* we may end up trapped in dark space between the realms. Or we may end up in a realm entirely unsuitable for you. One with no breathable air, for example. I cannot guide you without the master *mee*."

My mother drew back her gloved right fist and punched Neti hard in the nose.

Thin lines of black liquid slid down from his nostrils towards his mouth.

"So you do bleed," my mother said, smiling. "You can be hurt." She put a hand to the heavy black weapons belt around her waist. "I wonder who else can be hurt?"

She held out her palm to Neti, to show him the two obsidian beads sat gleaming upon it. The so-called flies.

"I can destroy them both, very easily," she said. "They have so little energy left, that I could crush them under the heel of my boot."

"What do I care?" he said. "What does this have to do with me?"

"Oh, stop pretending," said my mother. "I know who you serve. You are going to take us through the gate and if I do not find myself on Earth on the other side of it, I am going to grind these two into dust."

The gate, in a cave-like room at the bottom of the palace, stood open when I was carried to it, a rectangle of brilliant rainbow light. "Do not do this," said Neti, as my mother pulled him along by the metal bolt around his neck. "Do not disturb the old gods."

My mother walked straight through the door of life, dragging the gatekeeper with her. My father and I were carried through behind her on our chairs.

There was the briefest moment of confusion; the sensation of falling but also rising.

And then I was through.

Into the strangest scene.

The gateway behind us still blazed with light, lighting up the world around us as it disgorged its flow of footmen, soldiers, wooden crates, and heaving metal cages.

Before us lay a steep, tumbled mountainside, a mess of fallen rocks. The sky above was pitch black, with no stars showing. My mother's servants were stood all about in confusion, looking around. I was set down on my chair with a view of the gate, and my back to the slopes below, and so it took me a few moments to understand where we were.

My mother, quite naturally, was slower to understand.

She held up Neti in the air, his feet dangling, her face very close to his. "This is not the realm of light," she said.

Neti seemed unable to speak.

She lowered him onto his feet and let go of his metal ring. "We are on Earth," he whispered, one hand to his throat. "This is the realm of light. Or rather, we are somewhere beneath the realm of light. This is the Kur."

My mother looked around her, peering into the far distance. Behind her the arrivals from the old world continued to flow.

"Why bring us here?" she said. "To this underworld?"

"The other gates have been blocked off with heavy stone," said Neti. "This is the only gate it was possible to walk through. But we are buried beneath a mountain."

My father's chair tipped over and he went sprawling into the rubble of the mountainside.

"Someone pick him up," said my mother.

My brother appeared beside her, his horns gleaming in the sparkling gate-light. "Was that an earthquake? I felt the ground move."

"The gate should not be opened when the Kur is on the Earth," said Neti. "With the gate standing open as it is, we will no doubt be sinking further into the ground. The Kur may completely collapse in on itself."

Qingu yawned. "It's hard to get a breath in here," he said.

"That is because the air is running out," said the gatekeeper.

Meanwhile I sat there in my chair, ignored, hungry, desperately thirsty, and increasingly struggling to take a breath.

I found I did not mind too much.

My son had escaped through the gate. He was gone and he was not here. It was highly likely that he had found his way to the world of light, with the woman he loved.

I found that was enough for me.

If death in a chair was good enough for my father, then it was certainly good enough for me.

CHAPTER 22

MARDUK

On the Euphrates

In my fever dreams, my mother Ninshubar was alive. Truly alive. Her hair was long and standing tall on her head.

"I have your ivory star somewhere," I said to her.

"You do?" The whites of her eyes were so bright against her skin.

"I wish you were alive," I said. "I thought I would find you. I kept looking."

"First Harga accuses me of being a ghost, now you," she said to me in my dream.

"I did not stop looking," I said.

"I am here, Shub-son," she said to me. "You are burning up."

I dreamed that I was lying on my back, beneath a clear cobalt sky. My belly was aflame with pain. My mother, Ninshubar, was speaking to someone close by, her voice low. "He doesn't know what is real and what is not," she said.

Harga was hovering over me, his shaven face blocking out the sky. "I struggled to believe it, at the time that she was saving us from drowning," he said to me. "But it's her. She's real. She came back."

I turned my head on the wooden deck, trying to see my mother. The two black dogs thrust their faces into mine.

"Moshkhussu is trying to get to your Akkadian friend," Harga said.

"What friend?"

"Inush. He is tied up in the cabin."

I slept.

Ninshubar hovered over me, smiling, her hair a dark halo.

"Your hair has grown," I said.

"I must shave my head," she said. "When I have more time." She put one hand up to it. "When we do not have three Akkadian barges moving to surround us."

"I cannot believe that you are here."

She leaned over, kissed my nose, and then slapped my face, hard.

"Ow!" I said. "There was no need for that."

"Would a ghost slap you?"

"I don't think so."

Slowly, very slowly, she helped me sit up. "I also have a belly wound," she said, "but yours is a great deal worse than mine."

We put our arms around each other and for a long time only held each other.

My tears came. "You are alive," I said. "I had started to lose hope."

She kissed my forehead. "I had to, I will tell you."

I felt in my jerkin and drew out her eight-pointed ivory star on the new piece of leather I had strung it on. I had been carrying it with me since her death.

"Hah!" she said. "I was missing it."

She tied the star around her neck and it gleamed very bright there.

"Marduk, you have found me," she said.

I put my arms back round her, and wept like a baby. It was not very manly of me, and I knew what Harga would think of that, but she was the only family I had ever had, and being with her was the only home I had known.

I woke and it was night. I had my head in Lilith's lap.

"Did someone say Inush was here?" I said. "Or was that a real dream?"

"The Akkadian prince? He's in the cabin."

"Alive?"

"I think so," she said. "How are you feeling?"

"My belly is on fire, but I think the pain is dimming."

"My strong boy," she said.

I woke again, in early light, to find everyone standing up around me. They were all looking out at something; all silent. Something very serious was happening.

I stood up slowly, holding my belly, leaning with one hand on the side of the ship.

We were out on open water. There was an Akkadian barge close behind us; one just ahead of us; another on our right flank.

And coming down river at us, on our left flank... An entire fleet.

The lead ship was lit up gold in the early sun. Great crimson sails burst at us from the low mist.

My mother Ninshubar came over to stand with me.

"That's the Barge of Heaven," she said. "It's King Akka's fleet."

It would have been obvious to the smallest child that there was no way that we could outrun them.

And then I caught sight of something, on the Barge of Heaven.

I put a hand on my mother's shoulder, but she had already seen it.

"Hold a moment," she called out, shading her eyes to see better.

On the prow of the Barge of Heaven, there stood a small figure in a pale yellow robe.

A girl with black hair.

"I see her," my mother said, standing very still, a wide smile forming on her face. "I see the goddess." She lifted up her voice to all on board our barge. "It is Inanna!" she cried out.

I was no longer looking at the goddess. Behind her, on the Barge of Heaven, stood a small crowd of pale-skinned warriors. Pale-skinned and red-haired.

All looking straight at me.

PART 4

"You flash like lightning over the highlands;
you throw your firebrands across the Earth.
Your deafening command,
whistling like the South Wind,
splits apart great mountains.
You trample the disobedient like a wild bull;
Heaven and Earth tremble.
Holy Priestess, who can soothe your troubled heart?"

From *Inanna, Queen of Heaven and Earth*,
by Diane Wolkstein and Samuel Noah Kramer

CHAPTER 1

NINSHUBAR

At Ur

There was then a great hubbub and a hullaballoo in which Inanna made short work of the three Akkadian barges that had been chasing us; one bolt of blue fire, one mast in flames, and they at once submitted. Inanna's fleet then made for the dock, as did we on our barge, and in the happy chaos of it all, she and I both stepped down onto the smooth stones at exactly the same moment.

I went at once to her, picked her up, and kissed her. She felt very small and slight in my arms. "My heart is full," I said.

Above us, in the morning sky, a flock of kites circled.

I put her back down onto the quay and only then did I realise that her black eyes were bright with a strange blue light, but that there were no whites to them.

"I thought I would never see you again," she said, looking so happy despite her blacked-out eyes.

I laughed. "I was dead, Inanna. I wandered upon a grassy plain of dreams, looking for you. I dug a hole!"

She put her arms around my waist and squeezed herself against me, her head to my chest. "Oh, Ninshubar. I have been lost without you."

I looked around at the growing hurly-burly on the quay. Why was Dumuzi, who we had sent down to the underworld, now climbing ashore? As I watched, two black dogs slammed into him, almost knocking him to the quay in what seemed to be pure joy. Harga was watching me, but he turned away when he caught my glance. Gilgamesh leaped down off the Barge of Heaven, a hand up to Harga.

My son the Potta, who everyone now called Marduk, stood as if frozen, watching the red-headed warriors who were climbing off the Barge of Heaven behind Gilgamesh. I already knew, in my bones, what their red hair and pale skin might mean for my son.

There were so many forces in motion; all of them seismic. I felt myself divided. But when I looked back down at Inanna's dark head, I knew she needed me most.

"My goddess," I said. "Shall we walk up to the city?"

"Yes," she said. "Let us walk together." Blue flames began to burn around her head: a crown of living flame.

She took my left hand in her right hand, her face turned up to mine. "What happened here? What happened to the Akkadians?"

"I ran into your father," I said. "After I came back to life, I mean. And then your father and I came back here. But it was not us who freed the city. It was these people you see around you who took it back for you. They had had enough of the Akkadians. They risked their lives to oust them."

"Did my father behave well?"

"With some encouragement," I said.

The heat of the day was beginning to build as we made our way, through the growing crowds, along the sandy road to the great city. Those closest to us knelt and gradually all followed suit, even the soldiers watching from the high ramparts.

The blue flame danced higher upon Inanna's head. It was the same blue light she had given off, so long ago, when we fought off Enki at the Battle of the Barge. Then, she had used it to save us all. Now the sight of the flaming crown on her head felt wrong to me.

"I am not entirely well," Inanna whispered to me, as we climbed up towards the city gates.

"How so?" I said.

"I am strong in my body, but I have dark dreams." She turned her blacked-out eyes up to me. "Everyone says it is the power. That I have used too much of it. But I had to free Sumer. And I have to guard against Tiamat."

I put my arm around her shoulders. "You are here with me now. You are safe. Let the power go awhile. Set it aside just for now."

She stopped walking and looked up at me. "I'm not using the power, Ninshubar."

She seemed in earnest, but even as she spoke, the flames burned brighter around her head.

"Perhaps you are still using just a very little of the power," I said. "Perhaps you will feel better when you've rested."

We passed through gates guarded by two huge stone birds, and into Inanna's home city. The crowds knelt in the streets.

"All the gates to Heaven are shut now or buried deep," said Inanna. She seemed not to see the people around her. "Yet I find I cannot stop worrying."

I leaned over and kissed her head. "Goddess, you have earned some rest."

"Yes, perhaps, before I do anything else, I should lie down.

I have been stopping myself falling asleep. I can't remember being asleep."

She swayed a little, as if about to fall.

"Let's get you to bed," I said. "Everything else can wait."

Inside the palace, priests and servants rushed to and fro with piles of linen and jugs of water. An old man approached and knelt before us. "Inanna, you will not remember me, but I was a priest in your mother's temple," he said.

"I remember," she said.

"Your father is here," he said. "He is preparing to come down."

"I don't care about that," she said. "I don't want to see him. I am going to take my mother's old rooms."

The man stood, head bowed. "Of course. We will just need to prepare them."

"I'll take them as I find them," she said. "I know the way. Come, Ninshubar."

Her mother's old rooms must have been occupied by some princess of Kish, until the night we ousted the Akkadians from the city. I wondered what had happened to the woman. Now there were only piles of clothes to show for her, and a cluster of make-up pots under the shuttered window that looked out onto the Euphrates.

Inanna lay down upon the unmade bed and I went to sit next to her. There were red blood marks on the sheets she was lying on, and dark, damp stains upon the mud-brick floor next to the bed.

"Go," she said. "I am only going to sleep now."

"Someone should watch over you."

Her eyes were already shut but she smiled. "Go, Ninshubar."

When I was sure she was asleep, and had enlisted a squad of soldiers to guard her door, I made my way out into the city to find Gilgamesh.

I found him in the barracks, taking stock of the city guard.

"You look very well for a dead woman," he said. He put his arms around me and I breathed in his cedar-wood scent.

"Has anyone told you?" I said.

"Told me what?"

So, he did not know.

"Will you come with me, Gilgamesh?"

His fine brow creased into a frown; I could see that he felt his business in the barracks was more urgent. "You seem so serious. What is it?"

"Walk with me," I said, smiling. "Trust me, you will want to walk with me."

"Well, all right," he said, nodding to the men he had been talking to. "Although I accuse you of being mysterious."

I led him to the main gate into the royal palace complex. The soldiers at the gate smiled at me and stepped aside to let us through.

"I am in an agony of suspense, Ninshubar," Gilgamesh said, as we passed through into the palace gardens.

"Patience."

I followed the route I had followed on the night I first came to Ur, entering the palace by the same door.

"So, you have seen Inanna," he said, closing the door behind us. "What did you think of her?"

I turned to face him for a moment. "I think she will be better for sleep," I said. "I think she's made herself sick with exhaustion."

He shook his head. "I think she's hiding something. Or planning something. There's something that's frightening her."

"I think I would know if she was hiding something. She is still worrying about Tiamat, just as she was when I last saw her."

"You knew the old Inanna," he said. "This is the new Inanna. I think she is hiding something."

I paused a moment longer, nodding. "I'll ask her later. Now, come."

There were two men on guard outside the royal nursery, but they stood aside, with smiles, when they saw me.

Biluda answered my knock, just his head and long grey beard appearing. "You again!" he said. He looked to Gilgamesh then. "Come in both."

The boy Shara was sat on a bed, playing with a clay donkey. He looked up to smile at us.

"Your son," I said, turning back to Gilgamesh.

He stayed where he was in the doorway to the nursery.

"They told me he was dead," he said.

"A lie," said Biluda.

Gilgamesh walked slowly over to his son's bed and sat down an arm's length from the boy.

"I do not recognise him," he said, lifting his eyebrows at me. "How can I know it is him?"

"He's yours," I said. "Any fool can see it."

Biluda sat down on the bed and shifted Shara into his lap.

"Shara," he said to the round-cheeked little boy. "This is your father. His name is Gilgamesh."

CHAPTER 2

MARDUK

At Ur

The Sebitti woman and I sat together in the shade of a full-grown cedar in the palace gardens. Moshkhussu lay at my feet; I could see she was upset and confused by the departure of the other dogs.

"This is Moshkhussu," I said, scratching her behind the ears. "I have two other dogs, but they seem to have abandoned me for their old master..." I realised I was babbling. "Well, that's not important."

I could not think what to say to this stranger who was not a stranger. "Do you have dogs in the north?" I said, not knowing what else to say.

"We have wolves," she said, her voice low and deep, and so familiar. If anyone had asked me that morning, "What did your long-lost mother sound like?", I would have told them I had no idea. Yet now she spoke and I knew her voice and I knew her. This was no stranger, putting her hand out to Moshkhussu.

She had thick, bright red hair, just like mine except it fell full and heavy to her waist. She was as tall as I was; the same wiry muscles. Her skin was burned from the sun, but beneath the burn it was the same colour as mine.

"You don't find the sun hard on your skin?" she said.

"I used to, but then I was hit by lightning," I said. "By Inanna's blue lightning, or so we think now."

"I have seen a great deal of her blue lightning," she said. Her eyes were on my bloodied shirt. "May I look at the wound?"

"My friend Harga just checked it," I said. "He says I am healing well."

She smiled and that too was shocking to me, in how familiar it was. "We Sebitti heal well."

"I've been told I am a Sebitti," I said. "But no one can really tell me what that means."

"I can tell you." Her eyes were suddenly full of tears. She wiped her eyes dry on one of her sleeves. "I can tell you everything you need to know." She took a shuddering breath in. "I want to put my arms around you, because you are the little boy that I lost. You are my whole life. And yet you are a man now. So I do not know what to do or say."

I put my arms around her, and after a moment, she leaned into me and put her head on my shoulder. I could smell her hair; I recognised the scent. I had to take deep steady breaths then to control what I was feeling.

For a while we sat there like that, her against my shoulder, me with my arms around her. When I first lost her I had been so very alone and so very frightened. I had spent years putting that all behind me. Now it all came crashing back down on me.

I felt her take a deep breath in. "What happened to you, after they took you? Do you remember?"

"It does not matter," I said, sitting up.

"Did they hurt you?" Tears were spilling down her cheeks.

I took her hands in mine. "Never," I said. The lie came strong and confident. "I have always been treated with kindness."

She began to sob. I put my arms around her as she wept. "Oh, by all the stars," she said. "I have not had a moment of peace since you were taken, worrying what might have happened to you, imagining it."

When she had stopped sobbing, I said: "When I was ten years old, or thereabouts, I was adopted by a woman so good and so true to me. When you meet her, you will know how lucky I have been."

"We've heard about Ninshubar," she said. "Inanna has praised her to the stars to me, as has Gilgamesh. I feel more grateful than she will ever know, and I also feel bitterly jealous of what she had that I did not."

"In truth, she was only a girl, no older than me, when she adopted me. She has never been a normal sort of mother."

"I'm still jealous, although I have no right to be, when it is me that lost you."

We sat there a while in silence, holding hands.

"I would like to know what happened," I said. "Although I know already it was not your fault."

"We were attacked and I thought someone had you," she said. "But no one had you. You were alone in the tent." She sat up straight and wiped her eyes; a soldier once more.

"I don't know your name," I said.

"Enmesarra," she said.

"My name is Marduk."

"I named you Bel," she said. "Do you remember that?"

I wanted to, but I could not. "My other mother called me the Potta, but I don't remember anything before that."

"We never stopped looking for you," she said. "Even though I knew you must be dead, I never stopped looking for you."

"Bel," I said, trying it out. I leaned over and kissed her cheeks. "You must call me Bel. That will always be my name when I'm with you."

But that only made her start crying again.

Later, I slowly made my way through the heaving, excited city to the barracks. I at once ran into Gilgamesh. He put his arms out to me.

"Careful of me," I said, as he gripped me. "I caught a spear with my belly."

He let me go, but stood on tiptoes to kiss my forehead, his beard scratching my skin. "Go back to bed then, terrible slave boy. Why are you staggering around with a belly wound?"

"I wanted to see Inush."

Gilgamesh smiled at that. "What do you want with him?"

"He was good to me in Kish."

The hero's smile faded. "You come to visit him as a friend?"

"I want to see how he is," I said.

All the warmth in Gilgamesh was gone. "If you had come to torture him, I might have understood it."

"No." I smiled at him but received no smile in return.

"Do you know what they did to the priestesses at Uruk? By his orders, Marduk. Mass rape. The slaughter of civilians. Do you know what they did to my wife?"

"I know."

"Inush is in chains in the dungeons. He will stay there until he is executed. And no, you may not see him."

A burst of anger rose up in me. "Gilgamesh, I am not a child to be told yes or no. I have fought alongside you and risked as much. I have done my part and I think I can choose whether to see a prisoner or not. I have earned that right."

"Not this prisoner," he said, his mouth a flat line.

I took a step closer to him. I was taller than him and I knew, very well, that in a fight I could take him.

"What crimes did you commit in this war, Gilgamesh? How clean has your own conduct been?"

He caught me by the neck with one strong hand. In the same heartbeat, I had both my knives out and their tips pressed into his throat.

Moshkhussu, at my knee, bared her teeth and let out a deep growl.

For a few heartbeats, Gilgamesh and I stood locked together.

"They cut my mother into pieces," he said.

He let go of me and walked away, his fists clenched.

It was then that I remembered that Biluda was in the city.

"Impossible boy!" he said, opening the door of the royal nursery to me. He seemed unchanged; the same bright blue robes, with kingfishers stitched on them. His long beard still grey and silken. He reached up one crooked hand to pat me on the top of the head, and then looked down at Moshkhussu. "And your horrifying dog. I am not sure she should be inside a nursery."

"She will be very good."

We sat in the window seat together and looked down at the beautiful palace gardens. The royal children of Kish gathered in a circle around Moshkhussu, reaching out very bravely to pat her.

"Inush is in the prison block," I said.

"I heard," he said.

We smiled at each other.

"Do you think Inush is a bad man?" I said.

"I don't really know what that amounts to, in war."

"I don't know either. But when we met again, in the marshes, he didn't want to kill me. He didn't feel like an enemy to me."

"You look very tired indeed," said Biluda.

I realised he was right; indeed I could barely hold myself upright.

"May I lie down and have a sleep here?"

"I will watch over you," he said.

I picked out an empty child's bed and lay down on my back, careful of my bandaged belly, with my feet hanging over the end of the mattress. Biluda threw a thin sheet over me.

"I am glad to see you again, Marduk," he said.

He sat next to me on the bed, with one hand on my right hand, as I plunged down into sleep.

CHAPTER 3

NINLIL

Inside the Kur

The eighth gate stood open, its light blazing out over the dark mountainside of the underworld. Footmen and soldiers continued to stream through carrying boxes and screeching cages between them.

"We should start moving," said my mother.

"Where are we going?" I said, but no one answered me.

I was carried along on my chair by two footmen in red, my brother's house colour. They carried me backwards and so I could only see the shining gate and the crowds descending the mountainside behind us. The men carrying me cursed between them at how my chair cut their hands as they manoeuvred me over rocks and rubble in the near-dark. The further we got from the bright square of light of the gate, the darker it became.

Now and again, I glimpsed my father's drooping head amidst the procession behind us.

My brother, wheezing, for a while walked next to me.

"You do not seem to be suffering with the air," he said.

"I am used to it, I suppose. Also, sometimes I choose not to breathe."

"There is no need to show off," he said. "Your Anzu gifts were given to you, not earned, in case you have forgotten that. Had I been drenched in *melam* and other medicines in the womb, as you were, no doubt I could do more than grow myself horns."

When I had last crossed this dark landscape, there had been stars. Now they were all gone. "What is the plan, brother?"

"Well, it's interesting," he said. "This huge landscape used to be one small room. The gate room, to be precise. But the Anunnaki fiddled with it, so we perceive it as this great space."

"That is interesting," I said.

"Neti says that if we can just get out of this gate room then things will become simpler."

"But the Kur is buried under a mountain?"

"Buried under a pile of stones and earth," he said. "Quite how deep we are remains to be seen." He stubbed his toe on something, swore, and then lit up the ground around us with the red light from one of his *mees*. "Come on, come on," he said to the men carrying me.

The gate was still alight, in the distance now. "Are you just leaving it open?" I said to my brother.

He turned his great horns round to look at it. "I thought it made sense to limit numbers, but our mother thinks differently." He smiled over at a rattling cage with a monster writhing within it. "She thinks our very strength will lie in how many we are, and in our monsters of course."

We passed through the remains of the Dark City. Ereshkigal's Black Temple stood dark over the streets, but its roof and spires had collapsed in on it. I looked up at the steps where I had been reunited with my son when he came to fetch me between realms.

I did not want my mother and her ghastly monsters unleashed upon the Earth, but I could not think how to stop their progress. By then we were a great horde, flooding the rubble-strewn streets.

Once we had left behind the city, we reached another hillside covered with rubble. My mother lit up a *mee* on each wrist, spilling out hard black light.

My chair was briefly set down. Someone had left a set of homemade shovels and lamps at the edge of the rubble, and I wondered what had happened there.

My mother was pointing upwards. "There," she said.

I craned my head around to see what she was pointing at.

High above us, bright with my mother's black light, stood the remnants of the stone walkway that had once led from the seven gates down to the Dark City. The walkway ended mid-flight; the section closest to us had entirely collapsed.

"Is that the bridge, gatekeeper?" said my mother.

Neti was dragged forward by the bolt around his neck. "If we can get up onto the walkway," he said, "then it will lead us to the gate system that leads out of the Kur."

"And to the controls to the Kur," said my mother.

"Yes," said Neti, very sombre. "And to the controls."

"We will build a ramp up to the stairway," said my mother. "If we all do our part, it will not take very long."

CHAPTER 4

NINSHUBAR

At Ur

We ate out on the terrace of the Palace of Light that night, surrounded by firebowls and candles, and it was to my mind a glorious affair. We were sat at a huge cedar banqueting table and the food was delicious and plentiful. Roast venison and boiled greens, and fried fishes and spiced bean dishes, and peaches afterwards. A full moon rose silver over the sea beyond.

Yet pools of tension and disquiet seemed to ebb and flow around the table. Some of it made sense to me, but most of it did not.

It was no surprise that the two moon gods, Nanna and Ningal, sat well apart and kept their noses turned from each other. Their marriage was known to be in ruins and I knew for myself how much, or rather how little, Nanna was worth.

It made sense also that both of them might feel awkward at seeing their young daughter now their superior and sat at the head of their shining cedar table.

Inanna, meanwhile, sat and ate with a living blue crown upon her head, her strange black eyes on her food. Her afternoon's sleep seemed not to have left her rested. More and more, I began to think that Gilgamesh was right: she was hiding something. She had Lilith on her left hand and Sagar, the marshwoman, on her right, but she ate without speaking to either woman.

Meanwhile Gilgamesh, who was sat beside me, seemed tense and unlike himself. He recounted the long story of his journey into an in-between realm, and back again, and questioned me, intense and interested, on my resurrection. Yet his normal good humour was nowhere in evidence.

He had just been reunited with his son. The Akkadians were being driven from Sumer. He was back with his friends. Was he still in mourning for his wife? Could it be her death that cast clouds across his beautiful face?

My son Marduk sat opposite me, his pale face turned to his new mother. He should have been happy, but instead he looked so sombre, so turned in on himself. His two black dogs were sat at the far end of the table, their chins on Dumuzi's thighs. The dogs had chosen Dumuzi from the moment they caught sight of him on the quay at Ur. But surely it could not be dogs that my son was worrying over?

Dumuzi was sat next to his sister, Geshtinanna. They had come south with Inanna; they seemed at ease with the Sebitti. They seemed to have been welcomed to Inanna's table, despite their troubled history with her. Yet they both looked very grim as they ate.

I turned to Gilgamesh and said to him, quietly: "How serious everyone is."

He looked up from his food. "Who do you mean?"

"Dumuzi, for example."

Gilgamesh lifted his chin a fraction, towards Inanna. "They

think she's going to blow up the world. That she is out of control."

"Why do they think that?"

"We've spent a lot of time watching her, these past few weeks." He went back to his meat.

There was one person at the table that I did not look at, although I was more keenly aware of his presence than of anyone else's. He was sat next to Lilith on the far side of the table from me. It was foolish, the way I sat with my eyes turned from him, yet longed to feel his eyes on me. Foolish and childish.

Very deliberately, since I was not a child, I turned to look full at Harga. Feeling my eyes on him, he at once turned to look back at me.

"How long since you ate at a table?" I called over.

"A long time," he said. He lifted both eyebrows to me, as if expecting me to say more.

Since I could think of nothing more to say, I turned my eyes back to my plate.

That night I showed Inanna to the bedchamber she had chosen for herself. In her absence the rooms had been cleaned and the bloodied linens and floor stains removed. I made doubly sure there was a proper guard upon her door and that they would be staying there throughout the night. I could not think what would hurt Inanna, while she was so soaked in power, but it made me feel better to see the guards there.

"I could sleep next to your bed," I said to her as she lay down.

Her eyes still shone with her blue light and every heartbeat or so a line of blue flame flickered over her head. "I thank you," she said, into her pillow, "but you must go and get some proper sleep."

"You are still shining with your blue flames," I said.

"I am weaning myself off it." She lifted her head. "Tell them not to let my parents in."

"As you wish," I said. "I will tell the guards."

"I cannot be bothered with them now," she said, and closed her eyes.

I thought it an odd thing to say, and out of character. Her father, I understood. But why would she not want to see her mother?

Yet she was already asleep, so I said nothing, and left her.

I went over to the royal nursery to check on Marduk. He had decided to sleep there with Biluda and the children. "What is playing on your mind?" I said.

He shook his head at me. "Nothing, Mother, all is well."

"Is it the Sebitti woman?"

He smiled. "It's a shock to see her. A huge shock. But I am glad of it. She is a stranger, but also not a stranger."

"Are you upset about the dogs?"

That he laughed at. "Actually I am! But I will get over it." He kissed me. "I am all right, Mother."

At last, rather tired, unusually ill at ease, I made my way to the room that had been allotted to me by the palace servants. I had asked to be near Inanna, but in the event my bedchamber was many flights of stairs away, along some guest corridor.

As I turned into the corridor in question, I saw Harga ahead of me, standing outside my room.

We stood there a moment, looking at each other, both frowning a little.

"This is my room here," he said, pointing to the door opposite mine.

"That is mine," I said, pointing to mine.

We continued to look at each.

"I have wine," he said. "If you want to talk over the day." When I did not answer immediately, he said: "But I imagine you want your bed."

"No, I would like to talk things over," I said.

"Good," he said, his voice neutral, and he led me into his room.

There was a candle lit next to the small bed. His leather knapsack was neatly set upon a wooden chair.

Harga walked past the bed, pushed open the tall wooden shutters beyond, and led me out onto the small terrace there. There were three chairs set out, in the moonlight, and a small table with a jug and three cups on it. "Were you expecting someone?" I said.

"Ningal and Lilith were here earlier," he said. "Oh, I will get you a clean cup."

He was briefly gone.

I looked down at the three cups and for the first time understood that I had not only lost time when I was in my grave. I had also missed out on experiences. Missed out on many moons of Harga and Lilith and Ningal living a life I would never really know about now. Of moons and moons of Harga's mortal life.

We each took a seat, looking out towards the sea.

He poured us wine, and lifted his cup to me. "To your resurrection," he said.

We touched our cups together.

The moon looked huge and very beautiful, hanging over the ocean.

"I am going to sound like a fool now," he said.

"Yes?"

There was an urgent rapping at the door to the rooms and a few heartbeats later the moon goddess, Ningal, came bursting out onto the terrace. She was wearing a simple white tunic, barefoot, with her hair down around her shoulders. "Inanna has gone," she said.

I put my cup down and stood up, checking for my weapons. "I saw her into her rooms. Perhaps half an hour ago."

Ningal put her hands on the terrace wall and leaned out, looking east. "They saw her from the walls. She has taken a horse and she is moving fast."

I stood up and in the far distance I could see something moving, glowing bright and blue.

"I think she's heading for the Kur," said the moon goddess.

CHAPTER 5

HARGA

At Ur

We gathered in the torch-lit hallway of the palace at Ur. Ninshubar and I were both still dressed and armed. The moon goddess, Gilgamesh, his father Lugalbanda, and Marduk were in their bed clothes.

"Why would she go?" said Marduk.

"Perhaps because she has lost her mind," said Lugalbanda.

Gilgamesh shook his head. "She was having nightmares about Tiamat appearing through a gate. About her being here on Earth and killing people. She must now sense something."

"Or she's lost her mind," said Lugalbanda.

"Well, she's heading for the Kur," said the moon goddess. "Or she's heading east, anyway, and there is no other gate in that direction."

"I will go now on foot," said Ninshubar. "Either to get her back or to help her in whatever she is trying to do."

"I will run with you," said Marduk.

"We will all come with you," I said, looking at Ninshubar.

"We could also take soldiers," said the moon goddess.

"We could also take my Sebitti family," said Marduk. "I believe they are valuable soldiers."

"We must leave now or we may not catch her," said Ninshubar.

I nodded to that. "I agree."

"Six is an unlucky number," said Lugalbanda, looking around our small group.

"We will be seven when we catch up with Inanna," said Ninshubar, in a manner meant to end any debate.

It was then that Isimud arrived in the hall, his chest plate on, a sword in his right hand. "Is she headed for the Kur?" he said.

The moon goddess assumed her temple face and turned to face the *sukkal*. "Isimud, you will hold the city for us."

"What about your husband?" he said.

"Do you see him here?" said the moon goddess. "The city is in your hands."

Within twenty minutes we were out on the sand dunes and heading east after the faint blaze of blue on the horizon. Ninshubar and Marduk ran out in front with the Akkadian dog of war at their heels.

The rest of us were on fine horses, after a plundering of what had recently been King Akka's stables. "These horses were all mine once," said Lugalbanda.

We swam and waded the canal that bounded the city to the east, and then rode up onto a raised road that gleamed white in the moonlight. There I manoeuvred my horse beside Gilgamesh's. I had not had a chance to speak to him since our groups were united.

"All this is your fault," I said to him. I kept my voice low, since Ningal and Lugalbanda were riding not far behind us.

"What do you mean?" he said.

"You know exactly what I mean."

He took a moment before answering. "Are you talking about what happened with the moon goddess?"

"You know very well that I am."

He turned his face away from me. "You are always blaming me for everything," he said, sounding genuinely angry, "but it is nonsense this time. Inanna is a woman, a high goddess, and she is drawing on great power for which no one has a good explanation. I am not to blame for her riding off alone in the darkness."

"I think you are to blame," I said. "You found a way to make things worse and you followed it."

"Go ride with someone else," he said.

"Why don't you go and ride with someone else?" I said. "Why don't you go ride next to the moon goddess? You must have a lot to talk about. Or why don't you ride with your father and explain to him what has happened and your part in it?"

Gilgamesh kicked his horse on and rode ahead of me but then he turned back to hiss at me: "I am a man, Harga, not a boy, and you need to stop treating me like one."

"A man?" I said, kicking my horse on to draw level with him. "What sort of man are you?"

"Well, what about you?" he hissed at me. "Too frightened to speak to Ninshubar? What sort of man are you?"

We both rode on, along the moonlit road, in furious silence.

By the time the first light appeared in the sky ahead of us, I was bone tired and thoroughly wet, us having been forced to wade or swim across so many canals and rivers during the night.

I found myself brooding and worrying. I had not said goodbye to the Uruk boys. Who knew what they would do when they awoke to find me gone? And what about the boy Shara? Who would be looking after him with us gone? We should have told Lilith we were going. We had been comrades, she and I, for more than half a year, and I had ridden away without a thought for her.

"Harga?"

It was the old Anunnaki general, Lugalbanda, his kind face turned to me. "Is all well?"

"As well as can be." I sat up straighter in my saddle. "What should we expect of Tiamat, if Inanna is riding east to meet her?"

"Tiamat has been fighting wars and winning them for a thousand years," he said. "You must prepare yourself, Harga. I know Tiamat, I have met her, and more than that I know all the histories of Creation. If she is coming with her armies, then Inanna may blaze very bright indeed, but it may not be enough to stop Tiamat."

"You cannot know for sure," I said quietly. I glanced ahead at Ninshubar, running smoothly and steadily out ahead of us.

"I don't know for sure," he said. "I also hope that this is all a mistake. I hope Tiamat is not coming."

"It is the hope that kills you," I said.

"Do not let me cast you down," Lugalbanda said. "We are the Seven of Battle, or we will be once we catch up with Inanna. In the old stories, there was always a Seven of Battle. Who knows what we might conquer?"

"That is comforting," I said, although I was not comforted.

And so we rode, we Seven of Battle. Six of us, anyway, in pursuit of a mad woman burning up with blue fire, and with who knew what ahead of her.

CHAPTER 6

ERESHKIGAL

Heading home to Sumer

The gods of Abydos came to the edge of town on their gold platform to wave us goodbye. They sat side by side on their golden thrones and waved little flails at the townsfolk who had come to watch. Osiris was as heavily made up as his sister and without the scars being so obvious, he did look rather handsome.

"You know you can come with us," I said to Isis. I was sat upon a basket saddle atop a camel, and not very happy about it, but we were obliged to cross a desert before shifting ourselves onto the sea. "I will not let that man hurt you again," I said, and waved my nose towards Enki, who was sat on a camel close behind me.

Isis turned to look at her brother. "My story is here now," she said.

"Well, you will suit yourself," I said.

The journey across the desert was a torture to me. Enki and Nergal said they did not mind their camels, but then neither of them had an enormous baby in their belly.

The Sebitti children had been put onto the few mules that were to be had, and the rest of the red-headed warriors simply walked across the dunes, their faces blistering in the desert sun. Only Enki's lions seemed happy as they patrolled ahead for enemies and game.

At the sea at last, the young boy Userkaf proved worthy of our trust. Four fine sea ships lay waiting for us in the dusty port.

After that things were much more pleasant. I lay upon deck beneath a shade with Nergal feeding me sips of water and sweetmeats.

Meanwhile gangs of Sebitti slouched on the deck around us, all looking very unhappy.

"What a lot of fuss they are making," I said, "about the air and light and heat. I am sure I never made such a fuss, even though I was only a little girl when I first came down to this realm."

"You know the air and light almost killed me when I first descended to this realm," said Nergal.

Deep inside me, the baby turned over. "I'm so huge now," I said, closing my eyes.

He kissed my forehead. "Have you decided where you want to go?"

"Ur," I said. "Everyone has gathered there. They will want to see the baby when it comes."

I followed the master *mee*'s network of blue light towards the east. I liked to try to work out what was happening ahead of us in Sumer.

I did not like what I found there.

My sister had moved away from Ur, heading east. I followed her blazing trail of power. At the heart of the Kur, a new black light was shining.

I opened my eyes again. "Trouble," I said. "More trouble."

We met on the foredeck in a council of war. Nergal, my grandfather Enki, the three most senior survivors of the Sebitti, and Userkaf, our captain, stood about, while I sat in the one deck chair with the lions beside me.

"Tiamat is inside the Kur," I said. "But I cannot tell much more than that. What if she is touching all my things?"

Nergal took hold of one of my hands and kissed it.

"I should have kept digging there," said Enki. "And made sure the gate was blocked up."

"Even if she is through, won't she be stuck under the mountain just as you were?" Nergal said to me.

I put my hands on my belly. "My sister is heading for the Kur," I said. "Others follow her. My mother amongst them. We must go straight there." I turned to Userkaf. "We must be dropped off as close to the mountains as possible."

"I agree," said Enki, and the others all nodded in agreement.

Nergal came to speak to me in private afterwards.

"We will be passing close to both Eridu and Ur," he said.

"What of it?"

"My love, you should get off the ship there. You can rest, think only of yourself and the baby, while we go deal with Tiamat."

I squeezed his hand tight enough to hurt him. "No," I said. "No. We will not be separated again. Do you understand me?"

"I do," he said, and kissed me on the mouth.

"Besides, I cannot trust my sister to deal with Tiamat. Yet again," I said, "it must be me that saves the day."

CHAPTER 7

INANNA

Heading east towards the Kur

In my mind's eye, the Kur was lit up a brilliant blue.
Tiamat was through the gate. Hordes of her soldiers and monsters were still passing through it.

The Kur was deep beneath the ground. So, in theory, Tiamat was trapped.

Yet every fibre of my body rang with alarm and foreknowledge. She was coming. She was going to pass through the seven gates of the Kur and out into the world.

I had seen myself living for millennia. I had also seen myself dying upon the mountain, torn apart by the dragon queen. I had no idea what lay before me.

But I made two resolutions on my journey to the underworld.

First, if I survived Tiamat, I would make my life mean something. I was never going to have children or a husband who meant anything to me. I had seen a host of possible futures and I had seen enough to know that I would never be a mother goddess.

I must create a legacy of another kind.

In every city under my rule, I would turn my temples into sanctuaries. They would be a place where the weak could be free of their oppressors. I would welcome in wives abused by their husbands, children fleeing cruelty, slaves. Anyone cast out and abused for being themselves.

Everyone will be welcome in my temple.

There would be new laws to protect the oppressed from their oppressors. The temples would not only be a means to power. They would also offer hope.

That was my first resolution.

I stopped walking and realised I was in a forest.

On foot. Where was my horse?

I had been so wrapped up in my thoughts, I had not noticed leaving the riverplains and I did not know where my horse was.

Had I already passed through the Tigris? I had no memory of it.

I was wearing a linen dress embroidered with blue butterflies. I could not remember putting it on. For a moment, the world seemed to tip in towards me.

I sat down on the forest floor and shut my eyes.

Once again, I stood on the edge of the gorgeous blue lake. I put my ankles together neatly, as Ninshubar had taught me, and I dived into the pearlescent blue.

I found myself, in the blue, steadying. Calming.

I opened my eyes again, and looked around me. The trees were full of snakes, birds, weasels, and squirrels. In the pine cones and twigs underfoot, a host of bright eyes looked up at me. Voles, frogs, a plethora of small, creeping things. On the higher branches, owls shuffled to get sight of me.

I sat down there, on a seat of pine needles, and for a while only existed. I breathed in the sweet smell of the pines. I listened to the tumble of a mountain stream. I looked up to glimpses of pure blue sky.

I took a deep breath in, stood up, and kept on walking.

In the dappled light, I made my second resolution. It was a thought that had come to me before; now I embraced it in earnest.

I am stronger without the love.

When I was a young girl, my parents warned me not to get attached to humans, because they would be gone so soon and it would only break my heart. I realised now that it was not only humans I must keep my distance from. All those around me were going to die long before me. Ninshubar had been given back to me, but I had had a vision of her dying with Tiamat's black boot upon her chest. In another vision, she had died of poison. I had seen Gilgamesh dying in a number of spectacular ways.

I breathed in deep.

Even if my friends survived this conflict, they would die soon enough. I would outlive them all. I must keep myself apart to stop myself going mad again. To keep my balance in the power.

If I survived Tiamat, I must walk the Earth alone. Walk through the centuries, the ages, smiling out at those who loved me, but keeping my heart safe from them. I would be Ishtar, soon enough, and after that Aphrodite. One day, I would be Venus. I had seen that path laid out and it had been laid out for me alone.

The love I must give out now, must be equal for all... but dosed out in careful moderation, to protect me for the future.

To do my duty, I must let the blows, the deaths, wash over me. I must breathe in deep and let all the pain go.

I had been focusing on what lay ahead of me. On myself. For the first time, I turned my mind's eye to what lay behind me.

I realised I was being followed.

Ninshubar was there, running. Oh, her good, strong, steady heart. Her clear resolve. But I had not asked her to come. I had seen her death, a dozen versions of it, if she came to the Kur with me.

The Potta, who was now called Marduk, was running along just behind her with his dog at his heels. His light was very bright and white.

Gilgamesh was there. He had joked once about being a mayfly and me being the sun. It had been the truth. He would live longer than most men, but he would still be dead so soon, even if he survived Tiamat. His father was there too. The great Lugalbanda, hero of so many temple stories, fading now.

My mother was there. She was trying to remake herself; to become a person in her own strength. She had wanted to speak to me, when we saw each other again at Ur, and I had said I was too busy.

Harga was there, good Harga. An old man, a human. I had seen Tiamat's serpents biting his head off at the neck.

I wondered whether there was a way to stop them following me, but I could not think of how to do it without hurting them.

Far behind Harga, I saw the shapes of the seven Sebitti from the north. It seemed they were coming to the Kur too, if they could reach it in time. And further away, off the coast south of Sumer, I saw my sister. Still pregnant. As I looked at her, she seemed to sense me, and I quickly slid away.

I walked on faster, in my full power, with the blue light spilling from me.

I am stronger without the love.

CHAPTER 8

NINSHUBAR

Heading to the Kur

In the foothills of the Zagros mountains, I ran surefooted up narrow rocky gullies and through twisted pine forest. I said to myself, over and over, the running words.

One step and then the next.

Marduk ran close behind me, matching my pace and my breaths.

A shout behind and we turned to see Harga pushing his horse forward to us.

"The animals are exhausted," he called out.

I paused a moment, thinking. Inanna would not be stopping. I could keep running and leave the others behind. But then we were the Seven of Battle, or would be when we caught Inanna. We should be together.

"Let's stop to eat," I said.

We sat in a circle amidst the trees with the horses grazing nearby. Only Harga had had the common sense to bring food, but he shared his dried fruit and nuts out equally between us. He had also, it now emerged, been killing birds along the way, and these were now roasting over a fire.

I put my hand to my hair. It stood out so far from my head now. "Does anyone have a knife that would cut hair?" I said.

"I can do it for you," said the moon goddess. She moved over to sit on a rock behind me and I turned to find her with a bronze knife in hand.

"You want it shorn?"

"To the skin," I said, just a little nervous.

"I can do that," she said.

In fact, she could not do that. After some long minutes of my scalp being pulled about very roughly, Harga said: "Ningal, you tend to these birds. I am used to shearing heads."

Harga swapped places with the moon goddess, took my head firmly in his hands, and began to work on my hair. "I've been doing this for Gilgamesh and Lilith," he said. "I have become quite the master of it."

I liked the feel of his hands, sure and confident, on my skull. The shockwave of each movement he made reached down through my body and up again.

"So you shave your heads for a year after the death of a loved one?" I said, trying to sound very cool and calm.

"Not in stone country we don't," said Harga. "But when in Uruk, as they say."

My hair fell onto my shoulders and chest, black and glistening, as he cut it away.

"Was it Enlil you cut your hair for," I said, in part to hide what I was feeling, "or Ninsun?"

"For both of them," he said, his voice low. "And others who died."

I sat silently then as Harga finished the job. The rest of the group talked; of where we were, of how long the horses would last. Harga said nothing though, and I said nothing. Now and again he would rub my scalp to clear the loose hair away. I liked all of it: his fingers touching my head, cheeks and neck, and the feel of him so close to me, one of his knees against my back.

What a creature I was, what a greedy childlike creature, to sit there so secretly happy just to be touched.

At Ur, Harga had started to say something, on the moonlit terrace. He had said to me that he would sound like an old fool when he spoke, but then the chance to speak had been taken from him.

A long time before that, in what seemed like another life now and perhaps actually was, I had spoken to Harga and he had refused me.

It seemed likely to me that he regretted that decision. At least it seemed so. That is what my head told me. That meant he might speak to me again at any time.

I was not sure how I felt about that, although it was not like me to be cowardly.

The truth was, and it was a thing of not much import and yet it was the truth: I had never lain down with anyone.

In my home country, the girls were with child as soon as they could bleed. From that day on they were with child or breastfeeding until the day of their death. And it was often a baby that took them in the end.

I had not wanted that for myself.

It was not that I had never thought about it. I had looked at men and thought about kissing them. Thought about pressing myself down on them. But I had known where it would lead and it was not a future I wanted.

Since then, in Sumer, there had been no time for wishing and wanting. The only time I had ever spoken to a man it had been Harga and he had refused me.

I lifted my chin a little.

No doubt I would be excellent at it once given the chance to learn the basics.

I had seen Enki lying down with his limp wife in the Temple of the Aquifer. Would it be like that? Of course, there would be no drums and dancing girls. But perhaps it would be something like that.

"Ninshubar," said the moon goddess, breaking in on my thoughts, "you are looking so worried. What are you thinking about?"

The four around the fire were all looking at me in expectation. Harga's hands paused on my head.

"I'm worried all of this is taking too long," I said.

What a liar I had become!

"And that we should be moving on soon."

Harga took his hands from me and moved his knee away. "I am all done," he said.

"The birds are ready," said Ningal. "Let's eat and get going."

I watched Harga as he moved over to the fire, putting his knife back into its sheath, but I could not read his expression.

CHAPTER 9

NINLIL

Inside the Kur

My mother's army built a huge ramp of boulders and earth so we could climb up onto the walkway that led to the Kur's seven gates.

Neti was dumped down on the ground next to me as the ramp neared completion.

"Why are you here, gatekeeper?" I said.

He opened one ashen eye, and peered up at me, but said nothing.

"Were you with Ereshkigal?"

"Yes," he said, in not much more than a whisper.

"If you were with Ereshkigal, why are you helping my mother?"

He shrugged his crimson shoulders. "If only things were so simple."

"She brings death with her," I said. "How can it be right for you to help her?"

He turned his strangely indistinct face to me. "My purpose is not to decide what is right or wrong. That is not what I am for."

"What are you for then?"

"A servant serves," he said, turning his face into the dust.

"Who do you serve, gatekeeper?"

"The gods who are older than the old gods," he said. "Pray you never meet them."

I had many more questions for the gatekeeper, but then I was being picked up and carried along the heaped-up ramp and onto the narrow walkway that led through darkness. I was again carried facing backwards, this time with an excellent view of both the abyss below us and my brother walking close behind me.

He peered down, his horns above the drop. "It's a clever effect," he said.

At the end of the fly-over walkway, I was carried through a hatch and into the blue-lit space, and set down next to Neti. We were in a metal room with more rooms leading off in different directions. "This is where we lived, when we were coming down in the Kur," I said to Neti.

"I remember it," he said. His head was pressed against a metal cage and the creature within flicked a tongue out to get a taste of him.

"Ugh," he said, and shuddered.

I could not see my mother, but I could hear her. "There is no point, Qingu, in passing through the seven gates. That will only lead us to a wall of stone and mud."

I was picked up and moved again, and this time set down next to an old metal bed. Was this the bed I slept in when we lived on the Kur?

The local people who saw us descend from the sky called the Kur the "Thunderbird".

Bits broke from the vessel as we came in to land. We looked down on snow-capped mountains far below and watched pieces of the Kur tumble down into the green valleys between them. We were terrified. We barely made it down.

For the first time the thought occurred to me: could the Kur fly again?

Qingu's great horns appeared before me. "Let's tie their chairs to this bed," he said.

Soldiers pressed in, moving me, tying me to the bed frame. My father was pushed right up next to me, and his chair tied to mine.

"It might get rough," said Qingu, giving me a big wink and a grin. "Don't you move!"

I sat there then, frightened, trying to make sense of the voices around me. I tried to remember what was in this set of rooms between the sixth and seventh gates. I knew we were at the heart of the Kur here; that it could be controlled from here.

And then my mother dropped down onto the narrow metal bed next to me. She sat in a crouch, looking hard at me.

"I am struggling to make the Kur work," she said. "Even with Neti apparently helping me."

"It was damaged on the way down to Earth," I said. "Enki said it would never fly again."

"Well," she said. She lit up a *mee*, filling our cabin with her hard, black light. "I have just one question for you, daughter. When Inanna drew down great power. When she attacked the demons inside the Kur. When she chased you through to the eighth gate. What colour light did she give out?"

She smiled at me.

"I don't know," I said.

"If you do not tell me," she said, "I will track down your son and everyone you have ever cared for and kill them all. That is the promise of a goddess."

I looked into her face and I believed her.

"The light was blue," I said.

She nodded and shut her eyes, her lashes dark upon her cheeks.

A smile began to play across her face. A flame of blue light snaked through her hair.

"There it is," she said. "There you are."

CHAPTER 10

INANNA

Heading east towards the Kur

I walked in the power and I understood that there was *melam* in every living thing on Earth if you were only able to catch the gleam. In the living things but also in the rocks and streams. The whole world was connected through this net of power and I walked at the heart of it. When I picked up my foot, the whole realm felt me do it. When I placed it down again, every creature, every tree, every drop of water felt my heel touch down.

Our time was running out, though.

The gate through to other realms, deep inside the Kur, was bright with light again.

I saw Neti's face there, at the Kur, amidst the shadows. Sculpted from pressed ash. He said: "This far but not further, Inanna. There is too much noise." But then he was gone, only dust falling to the floor.

Neti did not know what I was capable of. The outcome was not certain. I would press on, faster and faster.

When night fell, I kept moving but I let my mind rove back to the warriors following on behind me.

Marduk, a white wraith, stretching out his legs and arms at the front of the pack. He was so like the Sebitti, in the light he cast out, but he was also something unique. A child of two realms, just as I was.

Behind him came my Ninshubar, running so effortlessly. I loved her so completely. Yet if she died again, I would survive it; I would not go mad as I had the last time. She and I had had our time together and if that was all there was, then so be it.

Behind Ninshubar, Gilgamesh and Harga rode together as a pair. I smiled to myself, at how upset I had been, like a child, at the idea of Gilgamesh lying with my mother. What did it mean? Nothing.

I turned my attention forward, towards the Kur. I could see Tiamat in there. A tall, pale-skinned woman with black hair tumbling down her black-scaled body suit.

Tiamat looked straight at me: "Did you think this was all yours?" she said. "Did you think this was all yours to play with, Inanna?"

The blue light went out.

I reached for it and it had gone.

"No!" I screamed into the mountain air.

I knelt on the rocky path and shut my eyes. I reached out, blindly, for my power. For my blue lake and for Tiamat. For a moment, I saw her there, standing on the shore of the lake, with animals all about her. She turned her head to smile at me.

And then the vision was gone. The blue was gone. My network was gone.

She had taken every drop of power for herself.

And I was nothing without it.

CHAPTER 11

NINSHUBAR

Heading up to the Kur

We came upon Inanna at dusk. At first I thought it was a wounded animal on the path. She was sunk down on all fours, in a narrow ravine, her hands pressed to the rocky path before her. But then I made out her flax-coloured dress and the fall of her black hair.

It took me a while to understand, as Marduk and I climbed up to her, that she no longer burned with light.

Close to, her lungs were heaving, her mouth open. Marduk held his dog back from her. I knelt beside her and put one hand onto her right shoulder. "Inanna it's me," I said.

She turned dull eyes to me.

"Tiamat is inside the Kur," she said. She looked back down at the rocky path beneath her. "I thought I could fight her, but it is already over."

I sat down next to her. "What can we do, Inanna?"

She frowned down at the path.

Gilgamesh and Harga were there then, swinging down from their mounts.

"Is she hurt?" said Gilgamesh.

Ningal and Lugalbanda arrived and dismounted.

"Back away a little," I said to them all. "Leave me with Inanna a while."

The five of them retreated to a stand of fir trees.

"Come lie with your head in my lap," I said to Inanna. I helped her rearrange herself, and then I sat looking down on her lovely, worried face.

"You are going to give me a fine speech," she said with a soft smile. "You are going to tell me to take one step after the next. But I am done, Ninshubar. I can barely lift my head up."

I stroked her fine black hair from her forehead. "Do all your visions come true, Inanna?"

"Some do."

I kissed her forehead. "I have not told you this but after I died, they threw me in a grave pit outside Ur."

"I am so sorry, Ninshubar."

"I lay there deep beneath the earth, in a soup of mud and rotting bodies, for half a year or more."

"I so regret leaving you. I should have searched for you. I should not have gone through to Heaven."

"I had to crawl up and out, but it took me a long time to understand that." I took in a deep breath, pushing down the dark memories. "So yes, this is a speech, but let me finish it."

"I am listening," she said, very soft.

"My mother was not kind to me, but she taught me that in life it is not about getting back up once. You have to get back up every time. You have to climb back up and keep climbing back up."

Inanna smiled, her face pink with the sunset. "Ninshubar, I don't know where to start. When I reached for the power, it was always there. Now it has simply gone."

"So," I said. "What happens if you let this woman keep this power? If we retreat to Ur, and let Tiamat be free to pursue whatever she wants to pursue?"

"Terrible things," she said. "It must not happen. All my life the animals have been looking at me, to stop just such a thing happening."

I squeezed her shoulders. "Then find a way to take the power back. She took it. There is a way to take it. You are Queen of all the Earth. Take it back from her and you will be Queen of Heaven and Earth."

"Just like that, I must take it back." She smiled up at me through tears.

"Just like that, you must try."

She turned her head, to kiss one of my hands. "I will try, Ninshubar. For you, I will try."

"And keep on trying," I said.

Gilgamesh insisted on taking Inanna on his horse. He put his right arm around her waist, holding her to him, and rode with his reins in his left hand. Inanna seemed to instantly go to sleep, slumping sideways against him.

Lugalbanda looked up at them, before himself mounting. "Now we are seven," he said.

He looked around at the rest of us, at the darkening sky, at the mountain peaks all around and said: "And seven is a good number."

Marduk and I walked with the riders from then on; the horses were slower now we were climbing and I did not want to leave Inanna behind. I walked with one hand up on Inanna's left thigh.

"So what is the story of the Seven of Battle?" my son Marduk said to Lugalbanda.

"It is just a story from the old days," said Lugalbanda. "It's a story from a war so old that even I wasn't alive when it happened. But I'm certain the Seven win. They always do. It's why the Sebitti always serve in groups of seven. An old superstition."

We climbed in silence for a while after that, gaining the top of the ravine and passing out onto a plateau. The moon was rising, offering light enough to walk by. For a moment there was a burst of blue; the blue flame was playing over Inanna again, although she still seemed to be unconscious.

"Ninshubar!" said Gilgamesh, although of course I had already seen what was happening.

But then the blue fire was gone.

"Is that good?" Gilgamesh said to me.

"I think so."

We crossed the plateau, jumping from one patch of tufted grass to the other. It was hard on the horses, who sank into the mud in between.

Then we were in another rocky valley, climbing up between oaks.

Inanna slumped lifeless for long periods, but would wake when the blue light began to creep over her in waves, lighting up our whole group. Heartbeats later she would moan in what sounded like pain, then it would be dark again and our eyes would have to readjust to climbing the mountain by moonlight alone.

"Lugalbanda," I said to the old general, "did you know Tiamat when you lived in Heaven?"

"Ah," he said. "She was a cousin to my mother. An ordinary girl to look at but then the Anzu are never truly ordinary."

"So what powers does she have?" I said.

"It's four hundred years, more, since I saw her," said Lugalbanda. "She has *mees* at her disposal. She has her Sebitti. If she now has access to this power Inanna has been accessing…"

"What?" I said.

It was then that the mountain began to move beneath our feet.

CHAPTER 12

NINLIL

Inside the Kur

My chair was vibrating. My father, beside me, was vibrating too. Something fell soft and feathery from his head into his lap. The animals in the cages began to screech and thrash.

I could hear a distant, growling rumble.

The small metal room we had been stowed in lit up in brilliant blue as the Kur began to shake with increasing violence.

The dim and distant growling noise began to build, escalating into a screaming roar all around us.

I was tossed back and forth between the metal bed and my father, my chains cutting into my skin.

The Kur was moving again, or trying to move. The room seemed to lurch around me. The screaming noise intensified.

It felt as if we were grinding our way through rock.

One final upwards lurch, sending my belly into a somersault, and it felt as if we were aloft. I heard my brother's laugh.

And then we crashed down hard and everything exploded around us.

When I opened my eyes again, I thought that the lights inside the Kur had failed, and that my mother's blue light had died.

Then I saw the moon.

A glorious full moon, ringed with blue.

I was looking up at a night sky. The Kur had split open around me.

My mother climbed into my eyeline, brilliant in her blue light, brighter than any moon.

"Unleash the demons," she said.

CHAPTER 13

NINSHUBAR

Near the site of the Kur

The rock beneath me shifted. I knew the feeling; it had happened to us once in Uruk.

"Earthquake!" I cried out.

There was the most terrible, bone-rattling noise of rock wrenching or falling. Rocks and huge boulders began tumbling past us down the slope.

The whole mountain seemed to shift again, and I was on my back and falling.

A horse screamed.

I had no idea where Inanna was.

For a heartbeat, everything went black.

I could not breathe and all the old feelings from the grave pit returned to me. Something was pressing down on me, clogging my mouth. In pure panic, I pushed and fought until, finally, I could breathe.

Moonlight, and a mouth full of dust.

My body was covered with rocks and rubble. Slowly, too slowly, I uncovered myself, one rock at a time. I lit up my *mees* of protection, throwing out pure white light all around me. I had blood on my dust-covered hands and blood running down my face and filthy arms.

Everything seemed changed.

I was stood on a slope of scree. The oak trees were gone. The valley we had been climbing in... was gone. My companions were all gone.

Then the dog came rushing at me, making small but deep-throated yelps. I let my shield fall and rise again, to allow her into it. I put a hand to her then, rubbing her head. She lifted her snout to me then darted off to my left and began licking at something in the scree. I followed close behind her and crouched next to her. She was licking a dust-covered hand.

I began to work slow and steady to uncover the hand and the person beneath the scree. My whole heart was in my mouth, but I tried to breathe steady and work slowly. Panic and hurry would not help me.

One step and then the next.

Carefully, carefully, I began to dig down to find the owner of the hand.

A face. I wiped the dust from it. Ningal. She was breathing. "Stay there," I whispered. "I'll be back."

Moshkhussu was just to my left, again letting out her short yelps. I went to her, felt around in the rubble, and there, leather. A man's back. I resisted the urge to rush and slowly cleared the rubble from him. It was Gilgamesh. He was alive.

"Have you got her?" I said to him, when I had uncovered his head and he had opened his eyes.

"I don't think so," he said. "Help me free my legs."

My son slid into the pool of my white light, half-carrying Lugalbanda with him. "I think I know where Harga is," he said. His pale face was covered in blood.

We found Inanna last. She was lying on her back beneath fallen dust and rock, her hands folded neatly over her chest. Her face was badly battered but her eyes were open, dark slits. "You need to kill all the creatures," she said.

"Inanna, there was an earthquake," I said to her, as we uncovered her limbs. "You are safe now."

I was not sure she was fully conscious as we worked, all six of us, to free her. When she was free of rock, I helped her sit upright.

"It was not an earthquake," she said. "Tiamat raised the Kur up out of the mountain. She has set it down on a plateau just to the south of us. Her creatures are pouring out of it. She has an army of strange demons."

"Can you guide us to the Kur?" I said.

"Due south," she said. "It's not very far. They will be on you soon." She looked up at me. "Ninshubar, be very careful."

"We will be careful, Inanna."

She shut her eyes again. "Even one of them could kill you all."

CHAPTER 14

INANNA

Heading for the Kur

I came to myself for a while. It was night-time and I was being carried in Ninshubar's arms.

Her face, lit up white by a *mee*, was caked in dust and mud. She smiled down at me. Her very beautiful, steady smile.

"You are covered in dirt," I said.

"A mountain fell on us."

"I remember. I have been dreaming of her."

"Of Tiamat?"

"She looks like a woman now. But she has the heart of a dragon."

Ninshubar leaned down to kiss my forehead. "Have you worked out how to take the power back?"

"I don't know what I'm doing. But I'm trying."

I slipped down into heavy darkness. I was in a dark cave, feeling my way along in the blackness. Was I back in the space between the realms?

I thought I could see, in the far distance, the gleam of a blue lamp.

I hurried, but I could not catch up with it.

I dreamed the Kur had broken into two halves. Strangely shaped creatures twisted and reared out of the wreckage, the moonlight glinting off their metallic skin.

There were men and women amongst them, more ordinary in form, but very bright in my mind's eye, shining with a hard, dark light.

I was back in the dark cave. There was almost no light, but in the far, far distance, I could see the glint of that blue lamp. It bobbed up and down, as if someone was carrying it.

I went as far as I could towards it, bashing my shins on pieces of rock; sometimes slipping forward hard onto the cave floor.

Was I catching up with them? I was certain now that it was a lamp, in the darkness, being carried along by someone.

At last I was close enough to make out the shape of the person.

A man.

He turned to face me, lifting the blue lamp higher.

It was Neti.

"Hurry, Inanna," he said.

I stood on the shore of my blue lake, with my feet in soft sand. The infinite, liquid power stretched away from me.

I had thought of it as mine and only mine.

But there, only a stone's throw away from me, stood Tiamat, naked, with her long black hair tumbling down her back.

She was looking straight at me. She had high, round breasts and a black triangle of hair between her legs; she looked human. Yet she had the brilliant blue eyes of the dragon.

"You think this is all rightfully yours." She did not need to raise her voice for me to hear her. "Because you got here first, you think it yours. But why should that be so? Why is that fair?"

She began to wade into the water, the blue light circling around her.

On an impulse, I ran at her.

I ran as hard and fast as I could, although my feet sank in the sand and they sank deeper as I reached the water. I threw myself at the dragon queen, my hands hooked into claws. But she was already gone and I landed with a heavy splash in shallow water.

I was back at the lake, though. That was something. I had found the lake.

I dreamed of the Kur, lying split open in the moonlight, creatures twisting out of it. Tiamat was there, climbing up and out of the vessel. She shone more brightly in my mind's eye than anything I had ever seen before. She was wearing a suit made of tiny scales, and sometimes it looked black, and sometimes it looked like the surface of a clear, fast-flowing river.

Tiamat looked at me, a smile upon her face, through the web of light that connected us. "You are already slipping away again," she said. "Yet the struggle only makes me stronger."

She turned away, to look down at her son Qingu, who was still down in the wreckage of the Kur. He was wearing his huge bull horns; he was sitting down; he seemed to be struggling to breathe.

Tiamat turned back to me. "I am going to kill all your friends," she said.

I opened my eyes and I was still in Ninshubar's strong arms.

"Tiamat is wearing Nergal's suit," I said. "Will you tell everyone? You cannot get a weapon through it. But her face is uncovered. Will you tell them?"

"They are right here with us, Inanna," she said. "They can hear everything you say."

I shut my eyes again.

When I came to myself again, I had my head on Gilgamesh's lap as he sat leaned against a rock. I sat up and could barely see the others through the blue fog that surrounded us. The sky above was a haze of pale grey.

"Is it day?" I said.

"It's about midday," said Gilgamesh, his eyes very bright in his filth-covered face. "But we cannot see to the end of our arms in this fog."

I looked around at the others; they were all covered in mud and dust.

"We fear to wander further in this fog, when we could go off a cliff at any moment," said Gilgamesh.

"We must be close to the Kur now," said Marduk, "but then again we may be completely lost."

I looked about me at their dear faces. I had seen them all die on this day and yet somehow I had contrived to lead them all here.

I wiped sudden tears from my eyes.

"I am making this fog," I said. I smiled and nodded at them. "Tiamat has made a threat against you all and this is my attempt to hide you. I cannot hide myself from her, but perhaps I can hide you. Perhaps that can give us some advantage."

"Do you know where we are?" said Harga.

I nodded, looking around at them, trying to think clearly. I had access now to the blue network, but I was hanging on to it by the frailest of threads.

"I should tell you what lies ahead," I said. "Tiamat has access to the same blue power that I do. She certainly has Nergal's suit and it has *mees* set into it. Her son Qingu is with her. He has all kinds of *mees*, so do not get too close to him. There are courtiers and soldiers there with them, but I don't know their names or what weapons they carry."

"Sebitti?" said Lugalbanda.

I shook my head. "The Sebitti from the far north have followed us from Ur. They will be here in a few hours. And there are Sebitti with Ereshkigal. She came back through the Egypt gate. Did I not tell you that?" I turned to Ninshubar. "Did I not tell you all this?"

"You are telling us now," said Ninshubar. "Go on."

"There are no Sebitti with Tiamat, but there are the demons."

"I fought alongside Tiamat, a long time ago," said Lugalbanda. "She brought strange demons into battle and they had poison for blood. It sprayed out onto anyone who attacked them and it ate away their skin and eyes."

All present were silent a moment as they absorbed this information.

I let the blue fog thicken around us. It was cool and damp upon my skin.

"Inanna, do you have a plan?" said Ninshubar.

"I'm afraid it is a simple one."

"That is no bad thing," she said, smiling at me, encouraging.

"We need to get to Tiamat and kill her. Only that will end this. That is my plan in full."

"A trick might be useful," said Harga. He was looking over at Gilgamesh.

Gilgamesh nodded slowly. "Can she be killed like any woman?" he said. "As my mother was?"

"If you can get to her," I said. I looked around me at the fog. "I have never seen it like this. In all my dreams of the futures to come, I never saw the mountain like this. And I never saw us talking like this."

I was losing my grip on the present once more. I put a hand onto Gilgamesh's warm arm. "Beware the bull."

"What bull?" he said.

I tipped over onto my right side and would have hurt myself if Gilgamesh had not caught me. "The Bull from Heaven," I said.

CHAPTER 15

HARGA

In the high mountains, close to the site of the Kur

Gilgamesh and I led the Seven of Battle through the thick fog. Lugalbanda and Ningal took the rear.

"Beware the bull," Gilgamesh said to me, taking careful steps forward through the blue mist. "Do you think one of Tiamat's monsters is a bull?"

"I think we will know soon enough."

It was tremendously unsettling to be walking downhill with no idea of what you were about to step on and with little idea of what lay ahead, except for the scattered account of one very confused god, of course. I glanced round at Inanna, lying limp in Ninshubar's arms.

"I don't think I've ever killed a bull," Gilgamesh said to me. He had an axe in each hand and despite the playful tone to his voice, I could tell that he was nervous as a cat.

I had three stones in my right hand and my sling in my left, but I could see nothing ahead of us except, here or there, a great pile of rocks looming up out of the fog.

"I killed a bull in temple once, for Enlil," I said to Gilgamesh. "It was not a job you would volunteer for."

"No, I don't mean a temple bull or a farm bull. I mean a wild bull."

"I'm not sure I have even seen a wild bull."

"Well, I hope to know it when I see it today."

"It is not going to be an ordinary bull, Gilgamesh. That much is obvious."

He lowered his voice. "What do you think to our chances?"

"I think our chances against a bull are fairly good," I said, "but I cannot say the same about the deadly monsters that have been spoken of."

"I have half an idea for a trick," he said. "Not even half an idea."

"Tell me then," I said.

"I am still thinking it over." He cast a look over his shoulder at Inanna and then dropped his voice even lower than before. "Do you think I'm no better than Enki?"

"An odd thing to ask," I said, peering down through the fog.

"Someone suggested it to me. That there might be no difference between me and Enki."

"I suppose there is some difference."

"Not very comforting, Harga."

"I would never try to measure the worth of another," I said, earnest for a moment. "The enemy should die and everyone else should live. Does it need to be more complicated?"

Gilgamesh nodded, swinging his axes. "If I die here today, will you make sure of my son?"

"If you die here, I will die here."

"Maybe. Or maybe you'll be hanging back, trying to get a good stone throw in, while I'm out there in the action."

"Are you accusing me of hanging back?"

"I accuse you of nothing, Harga. Although generally when I am captured in battle, as has happened a few times, you do somehow seem to slip away."

"And then I come back to rescue you. Risking everything."

"No one ever remembers Uruk," he said, sounding rather cross for a moment. "When you were lying there like a sick baby on the floor of that prison cell with your head in Ninshubar's lap. No one ever mentions that." A moment later his ill temper had evaporated. "I am not ungrateful, Harga, for all that you have done for me."

Somewhere in the fog ahead, Moshkhussu let out a short bark of warning. There was something on the ground, only half visible in the thick mist that cloaked the mountain.

A huge creature, laid out on its side. Alive, but not by much.

We formed a half circle around it, none of us eager to get close. It seemed to be patched together from different creatures; some mythical, some real. A bear perhaps, crossed with a dragon. Dark blood streamed from its swollen eyes and its fanged mouth gasped for breath.

"They do not like the air here," said Inanna. She spoke as if she had been wide awake all this time. "Please put me down, Ninshubar."

She looked strangely aged, her face harshly lined, as Ninshubar set her down. She might have been older than the marshwoman. Her hair, so black before, shone silver in the fog.

"They have poison for blood," Inanna said, looking down at the creature. "Like acid. It will burn you." She stumbled a little, as if about to fall. "Tiamat has backed away," she said. "She is doing something, but I cannot see what."

She looked up at Gilgamesh then as if seeing him there for the first time.

"Beware the bull," she said to him. She put a hand onto his arm. "The Bull from Heaven."

"You have already warned me," he said. "Trust me, my eyes are on stalks for the sight of a bull."

Inanna turned and began to walk down the mountain, taking small, determined steps, her spine hunched over.

Ninshubar turned to me. "Harga, I have the front," she said, with a nod.

"Gilgamesh and I will take the rear," I said.

We crept down the mountain in silence, following Inanna. The strange half-dead creature moaned in the fog behind us. We clustered tighter together, glancing ahead, glancing round to our rear, unsure of where the enemy might come from.

Ahead I could see a stacked column of rock, slicing upwards through the fog.

"Oh, no," said Inanna.

She looked up, her mouth open. A moment later the sky above us went dark and I was knocked over by a blast of downdraught. Another moment, and Inanna was lifting up away from us in the huge claws of a bird with a head like a lion. She let out a sharp scream of shock and pain.

I glimpsed a pale-faced woman, with long black hair, on the creature's back.

Ninshubar threw herself into the air after the bird, but missed its tail as it lifted. I let a stone fly and hit one of its clawed feet, but half a moment later the lion-bird was high above us, with Inanna dangling from its claws.

And then they were simply gone.

We stood, the six of us, frozen in horror.

And then the first of Tiamat's raging monsters was upon us.

CHAPTER 16

GILGAMESH

At the Kur

I gripped Marduk by both shoulders. "I know how fast you can run," I said. "Try to follow the lion-bird."

"I can't leave you all," he said.

I gripped him harder. "Get to Inanna," I said. "Get to Tiamat. You are the only trick that we have."

"Keep my mother safe," he said. Then he was gone, the dog at his side.

I turned to find a spiked, black serpent coming at me, throwing off sparks of black light as it writhed across the rocks.

I got an axe into its spine, but in the doing of it, I got its blood on my leg and my skin burned, agonisingly, wherever droplets had landed on me.

It took me a while to wrestle my axe from its spine, while trying to stay well back from the spurting, burning blood.

I had lost sight of my colleagues in the melee in the dense mist.

I thought I heard something up ahead of me, straight up the slope, and so with an axe in each hand, I began to run up the hill.

I saw the horns first, emerging from the mist.

Beware the bull, Inanna had said. *The Bull from Heaven.*

It was a man. Or a god perhaps. Either way, he had a bull's horns attached to his head.

I smiled at him. In the chaos of the morning, I had understood Inanna to mean an actual bull. Or rather some monstrous, fantastical form of one.

This was only a man, albeit a man in a huge white fur, preposterous on a summer's day, even up so high in the mountains and with a magical mist twisting around us.

The man in bull's horns had very black hair and his brilliant blue eyes were rimmed in red; he seemed also to be struggling for breath.

I swung around my axes, to make sure of the weight of them.

"Hot, isn't it?" said the man. He shrugged off his white fur, revealing red fighting leathers and pale bare arms stacked with *mees*. I caught the distinctive shimmer of a protective *mee* around him.

"Welcome to our realm," I said, giving him my full smile and lifting my axes to him. "I'm sorry the air doesn't suit you."

"Yes, it's rather ghastly," he said. He had a strange, unfamiliar accent, each word icily distinct. "The light too. I thought my *mees* might provide protection." He smiled at me. His teeth had been sharpened to points. "Who are you then?"

I kept up my confident smile.

I needed a trick.

I looked up at the sky. Nothing. Not even a vulture. Just pale, grey cloud.

I lowered my chin. "It will not be much of a fight for you," I said. "I have no *mees*, no special tricks. Only these two axes. I am only a human, not some great god like you."

"I can see you also have a knife on your hip," the man said.

In fact, I had two knives upon my person: the one on my hip and the one hidden against my left ribs.

"I am a great fighter here, you know," I said. "But I cannot compete with your Anzu trickery. It's a shame you use trickery, because I have heard you called the Bull of Heaven and I would have liked to fight you man to man."

The man laughed. "Do you attempt to draw me into a duel?"

"Does the idea frighten you?"

He laughed again. "You know, I have not had a fight for an age. I can't even remember the last time I struck someone." He smiled at me. "I'm not sure I can even remember being in battle. Not viscerally. Not raw memory." For a third time, he gave a belly laugh. "Come on then, Earth creature. Let's see what you can do with those axes."

Astonishingly, astoundingly, the shimmer around him was gone.

"Let us have a fair fight," he said. "I'm quite excited for it."

Then he charged at me, horns down.

He was much faster than I expected. I had planned to throw an axe at him; no one likes having an axe thrown at them. But there was no time for the throwing of axes.

The last thing you need in battle, I will tell you, is a fair fight. But it seemed there was no way round it.

I raised both axes to meet him. It was surely folly the way he was running at me, horns first. How could he even see where he was going? I thought I had the measure of his movement and a plan for getting an axe into his neck.

At the last moment he shifted his run, ducking lower. As I moved in for my attack, he shifted upwards and somehow twisted under and around, stabbing one of his horns into my gut.

I saw it but I did not feel it at first.

He had run me straight through. He was jammed up against me, with his right horn piercing me.

I no longer had my axes. Blood surged out around the piercing horn. I put a hand to my back and there was his thick horn, emerging from me.

In that moment of horror, while I was still understanding what had happened, I grabbed for my chest knife and stabbed it repeatedly into the man's neck and spine.

My reward, for this frenzy of stabbing, was that the Bull of Heaven collapsed dead onto the mountain, taking me down with him.

For a while I lay immobilised beneath him, his horn still through me, the pain and shock building. I could see what needed to be done. I had to pull myself off his horn. But it took a while before I had the courage to do it, and then, in the absolute agony of it, I made the wound even bigger.

I had had gut injuries before, but nothing so likely to kill me.

I climbed onto my feet, one hand to my wound. One of my axes gleamed at my feet. I picked it up and swung it hard down on the Bull's ruined neck, just to be sure he was dead, and his head tumbled out into the fog. The horns really did seem to be growing directly out of his skull.

For good measure I then fished around in the fog for his horned head, lifted it up, drenching myself with even more blood in the process, and hurled it off the mountain.

With great difficulty and in great pain, I then took off my armour and my tunic, and did what I could to bind the tunic tight around my midriff, covering my gushing wounds front and back.

Ahead, a noise. It was another serpent monster, coming straight at me.

CHAPTER 17

INANNA

At the Kur

The Anzu bird dropped me from its claws and I fell through empty air.

I landed, with a bone-shattering blow, on my back, my skull cracking against rock. I had to force what I had of the blue power into my bones, to stop myself drowning in the agony.

Vast wings spread out above me, against the grey sky, as the lion-headed bird settled itself beside me on the mountain top. Tiamat sat astride it, her long black hair floating in the breeze.

"I have nothing personal against you, Inanna," she said, as she climbed down from the bird. "You will die here with honour. Death at the hands of a greater, wiser, older queen. There is no shame in it."

I wanted to speak, but could make no sound.

Tiamat was dressed in Nergal's tight-fitting suit of black scales. She took in a deep, ragged breath, and said: "The helmet on this suit doesn't work. It used to work before I lent it to Nergal." She smiled down at me. "But the blue power helps me strengthen and change myself. Soon I will breathe easy in this new realm."

I again tried to speak, but could not.

She looked about her, frowning up at the grey sky. "It is very bright here. Very garish. The colours so bright. I will get used to it, I suppose. I will belong soon enough."

I shut my eyes and focused on the power that I had once thought of as mine.

It twisted and burned between us. When I felt I might be able to wrestle it from her, she would somehow snatch it back. And all the time I was weakening. My blood was spilling out around me onto the rock. I had tried to numb the feelings, but pain was dragging me downwards.

With my eyes shut and my mind in the network of blue, I could see the Kur, far below us on the mountainside. It had broken into two pieces and as I watched, huge creatures reared up out of the wreckage and slithered away. Further down the mountain, there were pockets of intense fighting. For a moment I thought I saw the light that was Ninshubar, and then she was lost in the fray.

I felt Tiamat sit down next to me, and I opened my eyes to look up at her.

"I see you are self-righteous," she said. "You think your fight a noble fight and I an evil invader. But your family stole my daughter from me and brought her here. I would never have turned my attention to this realm, had they not shut themselves up here, hoping to get away with their crime. Why should this be Anunnaki land? Why should it not also shelter the citizens of Heaven when their own world is falling into ruin?"

For a few long moments, Tiamat was still. "My son is dead," she said. "I do not understand how." She shook her head. "I will resurrect him," she said. "He wronged me, a long time ago, but he did it in order to triumph over another and that is something I have always respected."

I shut my eyes.

I stood on the shore of the blue lake. The sand beneath my feet was hard and cracked. Tiamat appeared, perhaps five cables from me, standing with her feet in shallow water. I thought, *What would Ninshubar do?*

Yes, what would she do?

She would act and act quickly.

I ran towards the dragon queen. She took a step back from me, but I leaped forward and grabbed her left arm. I held on to it with all my strength.

Tiamat pulled away from me but for the first time looked a little rattled; a slight frown formed upon her brow.

Then I saw the animals. They were still there, in the distance, lining the lake shore. Their faces all turned to me. In expectation, yes, but also, I saw, in offering.

For a long time, I had been seeing the animals there, when I entered my mind's eye. Seen the hippos standing by the elephants and the gazelles by the leopards. They were there to help me. They too were guardians of the realm. Every living creature.

How had I not understood that before?

I opened my eyes to the world of light. High above us an eagle soared. I smiled up at it. The eagle at once plunged, wings tucked, hard down at us. It landed, screaming, claws out, on Tiamat's head. She screamed as she fought it off. Moments later she had lit up a dark shield of light around us.

Blood poured down her face. "Was that your doing?" she said.

Another eagle came plummeting out of the blue and exploded into flames on Tiamat's shield. A harrier plunged down at us and was instantly burned up. A mass of black crows came barrelling down on us, all burning up useless. Next came mountain ravens and a flock of doves, then came crickets and mantises and dragonflies. All burned up upon Tiamat's shield wall.

"What a waste of flesh and life," said Tiamat, her face suddenly close to mine. "This costs me nothing, Inanna."

A mountain leopard landed hard against her shield, exploding through the insects, bursting into flames as it fell back. Tiamat flinched. Then came a herd of high-mountain gazelle and after that the small creatures came, the mountain hares and the weasels. All burned up alive against the dark fire of Tiamat's protective shield.

"How keen you are to throw life away," Tiamat said. "Is this some foolish attempt to waste time?"

The bodies no longer burned up; now they only sparked against the shield and then lay, twitching, in a huge, mounting, pile of death all around us.

"All of the animals are coming, small and large," I said. "The people too. It will take them time but they will all come and give up their lives to stop you."

Two eagles slammed into Tiamat's shield and fell dead upon the carcases of the other animals.

The Anzu queen shook her head at me. "Very soon the last of your power will be gone and I will kill you and then the animals will stop coming." She took a deep breath in. "I have done all of this before, silly little girl. An eagle cannot save you. Your friends cannot save you now. Take your rest now, Inanna. Your time as guardian of this realm is over."

CHAPTER 18

NINSHUBAR

At the site of the Kur

I ended up back-to-back with Harga in the fight. By then we had not only lost Inanna to the lion-bird; we had also lost track of the rest of the Seven in the melee and the thick fog.

Four of Tiamat's glittering-black scorpion monsters squatted around us, each the size of three men, each with a pair of vicious clawed arms and a lashing, spiked tail. The monsters took turns to take a run at us, hissing at us, slashing claws and gaping black jaws extended. They had care for themselves, and they were methodical, taking turns to harry us.

Each time one came at us, clicking and hissing, we were slower and weaker.

"I'm out of arrows," I said to Harga.

"This is why I always carry a catapult," he said. "No one brings an arrow back to you. But you only need look down and you can find another stone."

"I thank you for the advice," I said, "and next time I am fighting for my life against giant scorpions, I will be sure to bring a catapult."

"What do you have?" he said, his shoulder blades against mine. "Is there anything left in your *mees*?"

"I have nothing. My *mees* are dead."

"Can you turn and take a knife from my belt?"

As he spoke a monster leaped forward and dragged its black, metallic claws down my chest.

The monster staggered away with Harga's axe in it, but I immediately began to feel nauseous and dizzy. "Poison," I said, sitting down hard on the rockface, chin deep in the blue fog.

Harga moved to stand over me. He cast one quick glance down at me, before lifting his chin back up at the monsters.

"How bad is it?" he said to me, taking more stones from his leather pouch.

"My legs and arms are jelly."

"Let me think," he said.

Two more monsters came to join the fight; now six encircled us.

It was then, by some curious feature of the mist or the early mountain air, or perhaps the shape of the mountain itself, that a woman's voice floated to us, very clear, on the morning wind.

"I am more of a literary queen, than a fighting queen," the woman said.

She sounded so very close, but I could only see the monsters, shifting around us, their tails raised, and Harga's leather-clad legs.

Yet I was sure I had heard the woman. Was it the venom working on me? "Did you hear that, Harga?"

"Hear what?" he said, without looking down at me.

I fell over, hard onto my left shoulder, and I found I could do nothing to help myself. I began to struggle to breathe.

All I could see was the blue fog.

Inanna, I tried to say. *We must help Inanna.*

But I was long past making sound.

CHAPTER 19

NINLIL

At the site of the Kur

Two soldiers stood guard over me amidst the wreckage of the Kur. "Please unchain me," I kept saying, but the soldiers would not turn their ears to me.

In the early morning, one of the fish-man creatures came sliding over into the wreckage and killed my protectors. The demon looked at me for a moment, the gills on its necks opening and closing, before bounding away.

For a while I was alone. Shouts came to me, through the thick blue fog. Once, I saw an Anzu bird flying overhead. My father was no longer next to me. Had he been thrown out onto the mountainside?

And then at last, came the miracle. A face appeared above me, peering down from the walls of the Kur. It took a moment for me to recognise her with her hair pulled off her face and a knife in one hand.

"Ningal!" I said. It was the moon goddess.

She laughed. "Ninlil, how you have grown!" She climbed

down to me, glancing around warily as she did. "No monsters in here?"

"I think they're all gone," I said.

She hacked away at my bindings and helped me stand. "Can you fight?" she said.

My knees were weak, after so long sitting, but I nodded. "I can fight," I said.

She led me back over the jagged rock walls of the Kur and down into the fog that clung to the mountain. "Be careful where you step," she said. She turned to smile at me again. "You have doubled in size, Ninlil!"

A man appeared out of the mist, bare-chested and very bloody, his midriff wrapped in a cloth. He had an axe in one hand and he was so covered in blood that it took me a moment to recognise him. "Gilgamesh!" I ran to him and he at once gave me his weight.

It took all my strength to hold him up. "He's badly injured," I said to the moon goddess.

Ningal rushed over to help me lower him to the ground. "I need to put my hands on him," I said. "I can heal him, but it will take some time."

The moon goddess looked out into the fog with a frown. "Do it then. Be as quick as you can."

I let my healing sea flow into Gilgamesh. I had watched him grow up, and loved him like a son. As I went to work on him, I realised he had been gored by my brother; I could taste the marks of Qingu's horns in Gilgamesh's gaping wounds. I let myself flood, absorbing his pain, mending the flesh, soothing his fright.

"Ninlil," said the moon goddess, in a temple voice. "There is a creature here."

I opened my eyes, pulling myself away from the healing.

The creature was a demon in the shape of a bison, but with skin like a serpent. It stank of sulphur as it stood pawing at the fog, its horns lowered at us.

The moon goddess raised her knife at the creature. I held Gilgamesh tight to me.

I suppose I thought we were all about to die. But then a golden spear pierced the bison-creature's forehead. After a few long moments, the horned demon collapsed down into the fog.

There were suddenly Sebitti everywhere, their gold scales shining blue with the light from the mist. Ereshkigal was there too, looking down at me from a horse. And then Nergal, my son, was squatting down next to me.

"Thank all the stars," said my son. "How are you?"

"I'm well, but this man is dying," I said. "I need to heal him now."

"I will watch over you while you work," he said. "And when you've finished we have another patient for you. A woman who has been poisoned."

"I will do what I can for them," I said.

My son locked eyes with me. "It's Ninshubar, Inanna's *sukkal*. I very much want her to survive."

"I will try," I said, and closed my eyes again to focus on my healing.

In the end, it did not take me long. Gilgamesh had always been strong; after all, both his parents were Anunnaki.

As soon as he was fully himself again, he said: "I should get to Inanna."

Ereshkigal was still sitting on her horse, frowning down at her belly. "Inanna is locked in combat with the dragon," she said, lifting her chin. It was not at all clear who she was talking to.

Gilgamesh moved onto all fours, and then stood, letting out a groan. "My lady Ereshkigal, that is the master *mee* on your wrist," he said, once upright. "I should take it to Inanna. It is her weapon and perhaps it could help her now."

Ereshkigal shook her curls at him. "My sister has so much power already, much greater than this."

I stood up, and put a firm hand to Ereshkigal's horse. "Hand the *mee* over, Ereshkigal. You know it is the right thing to do."

"Why should I?" she said. But even as she said it, her eyes were turning to Nergal, and I could see that she was thinking through how this little scene might look to him.

She took off the *mee* and handed it to me, with her mouth turned hard down. "It is always me who has to be the hero," she said.

CHAPTER 20

MARDUK

At the site of the Kur

I ran uphill through the thick fog with Moshkhussu at my heel. I had glimpsed the Anzu bird, once or twice, ahead of me, Inanna hanging from it. I had an idea that they were heading for the very peak of the mountain.

I stopped just once, to gape at the sight of a corpse tied to a rusting metal chair. I looked the ancient, desiccated creature in the face for a moment, and then, shaking my head, I ran on past the strange relic.

I ran as I had been born to run, as the child of two warriors of Heaven, and as the adopted child of Ninshubar, a warrior of the plains. I truly felt it then: the two realms running through me, joined by Inanna's lightning, as I bounded up that mountain.

Ahead of me a lion-bird came in to land, turning its jawed head to me. I lifted up an axe and kept running, but then I recognised the shape of the man on the huge bird's back: it was Lugalbanda.

"You are too slow," he said to me, as the bird bucked beneath him and stretched out its wings.

"Where did you get the bird?"

"I found it tangled up with a serpent. Get on. You will not reach them in time." Lugalbanda had hold of leather reins that disappeared into the animal's feathered neck. "Come up behind me."

"What about Moshkhussu?" I said.

The lion-bird bared its fangs at my dog. Lugalbanda reached out one callused hand to me. "Marduk, we must leave her. She will survive."

I looked up at the bird. It was the same animal that I had once had tattooed on my arm, before Inanna's blue lightning hit me. I could not ignore the sign.

I leaned over, kissed Moshkhussu's head and said to her, very firm: "I will find you, girl." Then I leaped up behind Lugalbanda, gripping the bird between my knees, and a heartbeat later we were lifting into the air.

I watched Moshkhussu, her head tipped up to me, getting smaller and smaller beneath us, upon the fog-cloaked mountain.

"I think I know where they are," said Lugalbanda. He kept on talking, but the words were snatched out of his mouth by the wind as we soared higher. I put my arms around Lugalbanda's waist, and it was a few moments before I picked up the courage to look down again at the mountain below us.

I had never seen the world from the air before. "Oh!" I said. How different it looked from on high, like some gorgeous pattern laid out just for me. The high peaks that stuck up clean out of the fog, and in the distance, the vibrant, shimmering green of the river lands and beyond, the blue of the ocean: it was beautiful.

"There," said Lugalbanda, pointing to what at first I thought was a mound of earth.

It was a huge heap of dead bodies, made up of hundreds or even thousands of animal corpses. At their centre, I caught the gleam of the light of a *mee*, and within that, two shapes. Tiamat, standing, and Inanna lying flat on her back on a rock.

As I watched, two mountain leopards surged over the dead bodies of the other animals to burn themselves up on the outside of the protective shield.

Lugalbanda moved his hands forward onto the Anzu bird's wings and the bird plunged downwards. We dropped so fast that I thought we were going to collide down hard onto rock, but at the last moment the bird tipped backwards, landing gently on its hindlegs.

Heartbeats later, my legs shaking, I climbed down from the giant bird.

The old Anunnaki warrior nodded at me. "May the stars be with you," he said, very formal.

"Please go back for the dog," I said. "Make sure she is safe."

"There are people dying. I will do what needs to be done."

"Please go back for the dog," I said.

"Marduk!" he said, apparently quite angry.

"Promise me, Lugalbanda." I clasped my hands before me in supplication.

The old warrior clenched his jaw. "I will go back for your dog, but I curse you for it."

"Thank you," I said, and then watched the Anzu bird lift up, its enormous wings flapping, with Lugalbanda upon it.

The ghastly hill of dead animals loomed over me.

Well, if you are going to do something, better do it quick.

I ran full pelt ahead, across rock first, then up the mountain of warm bodies, crushing bones and feathers beneath me. Soon I was climbing up the grotesque hill of horns, fur, and upturned hooves on all fours. As I climbed, more creatures ran or flew ahead of me, burning themselves to death on Tiamat's shield.

When I reached the top of that ghastly mound, and the edge of the shimmering shield, I had a clear view of Tiamat. She was stood at the centre of the hollowed-out pile of dead animals with the goddess Inanna laid out on a rock, as if for sacrifice.

Now the secret to getting behind a shield is to glide in very slowly. I had done it many times, to Ningal and the others, when I wanted to share their protection with them. Or sometimes to annoy them, or because they were in my way and battle simply required it.

This time was no different.

I crawled forward, oh, so slowly, crushing dead and burned animals beneath me, and then my head was through the shield and I was looking straight down on Tiamat. Her mouth was open, as she looked up to me.

With a slow twist born of long practice, I lifted my feet and swung them slowly through the shield. And then I dropped down like a cat.

I stood face to face then, with the Anzu queen. We were about the same height; we had the same pale skin.

Tiamat straightened herself up. Behind her, Inanna turned black eyes to me.

"Sebitti," said Tiamat, without any sort of surprise. "Did Ereshkigal send you?"

A wave of unexpected feeling swept over me: I felt a strong urge to kneel. A *compulsion*.

Tiamat frowned. "Kneel then. Make your obeisance."

Oh, I wanted to kneel to her. I wanted to throw myself on the ground before her and promise her everything. I knew then that kneeling before this woman was my destiny. I had been born for it and if I did it, I would be her loyal soldier. I would be looked after; rewarded. I could fight to keep my family safe from within her protection. There would be honour in it.

I knelt, and was flooded with relief.

Tiamat smiled at me. "I will build up the Sebitti. I will make brothers and sisters for you. But you were the first to return to me. So, you will be the first amongst the Sebitti."

Tiamat turned back to Inanna and blue light flickered between them.

"Is this what you've been hiding from me, Inanna, with your useless fog? A Sebitti cannot hurt me. This man will serve me now. I will make him a great man. A leader of armies."

I had known love on Earth. I had known friendship. But in my very core, I had never felt at home. Kneeling there, in that pit of dead animals, with the black-scaled dragon queen standing over me, I felt a deep sense of being where I ought to be.

I could imagine myself running out across a wide plain with an army of Sebitti behind me. All of us dressed in golden coats and with gold spears raised in one arm. All of us running as one, for our queen Tiamat.

"What is your name, my son?" said the dragon queen, turning back to me.

That pulled me back to reality. The woman standing over me was many things, but she was certainly not my mother. Indeed, I had two mothers, here on Earth, and both of them were women of honour. This woman had no right to call me "son".

Yes, I was Tiamat's creature, but I was not only that. I had been raised on Earth. Born to an ordinary Sebitti, not the dragon queen. I had been struck by Earth's lightning, brought down by this goddess dying before me. And more than that, I wanted to be able to choose. Slavery had taught me that: the extraordinary gift that it is, to have a choice.

I do not want to kneel. The thought came to me ice-clear. In that instant, I knew that if I wanted to, I could stand.

For a moment I knelt there with my hands crossed on my chest and my fingers resting very light on the leather straps that held my axes to my back.

Well, what was I waiting for?

With Tiamat's eyes back on the young goddess, I sprung from kneeling to standing in one move, twisting around as I did so.

I brought a bronze axe down hard on the top of Tiamat's skull. I did it with a feeling in me that my whole life suddenly made sense, and Tiamat's head split down the middle into two halves. Even Harga would have praised me for the neatness of it.

As she staggered, blind, towards me, through a deluge of her own blood, I spun around and, with my other axe, cut her head off at the neck.

Her head spun away in two pieces, blood spurting and black hair tumbling, and the shield around us collapsed. The corpses of gazelle, jaguar, and a thousand mountain creatures crashed down on us.

For long heartbeats, I could not move beneath the weight of the corpses and panic threatened to overwhelm me. I could not even move a foot, to kick myself free. But then something was lifted from my face; a dead dove, its wings stretched wide. And then there was Inanna.

She was slick with blood, but somehow she was on top of the dead animals, and standing, looking down on me.

"I did it," I said. "I did it!"

"You killed her," she said.

"It was Gilgamesh's idea," I said. "He knew that I might be different from the other Sebitti, but that Tiamat might not see the difference."

Inanna frowned at me, but then smoothed out her face, and smiled.

"Marduk the hero," she said.

CHAPTER 21

INANNA

Near the Kur

When Marduk suddenly moved, a blur of movement, to attack the dragon queen... everything froze.

Yes, so this is the part that Marduk would never remember.

Kurgurrah and Galatur appeared amidst the frozen tableau, both with their heads politely bowed to me and their hands behind their backs.

All around them, everything was still. Marduk was caught in the action of leaping, axes half out of their straps, one foot on the floor, the other raised. Tiamat stood with her mouth open, caught in the moment of speaking to me. The birds overhead, intent on battering themselves against Tiamat's shield, hung in the air mid-plunge.

I reached out to the blue power and found it to be all mine. I pulled down hard on it and used it to help me sit up, battered and broken as I was. "I am pleased to see you, old friends," I said. "I have damaged my skull and I remember how you once helped me fix it."

Kurgurrah, the blue shadowman, now a real, vivid man, wearing a cloak that only hinted of blue, pulled back the hood from his handsome brown face. "Hello, again, Inanna."

Galatur pulled back his hood also. "Hello, young queen."

"How are you here?" I said.

Kurgurrah smiled. "The dragon queen carried us here in her belt."

"And straight to you," said Galatur, "although of course that was not her intention."

"Do you see what is about to happen here, Inanna?" said Galatur, his hand out to the frozen figures before us.

"Marduk is attacking Tiamat," I said. "She does not expect to be attacked by a Sebitti. He appears to be about to kill her."

Kurgurrah shook his head. "In fact, she has been attacked many times by Sebitti over the millennia. She has a suit packed with *mees* and she will turn and obliterate him. She has already sensed him moving."

I could not tell, from the way Tiamat was standing, what the truth was. But why would the flies lie to me?

"So, are you going to help him?" I said.

Movement to my right: Neti was suddenly with us, grey-faced and terribly aged. "Hello, Inanna. How dreadful you look."

"I might say the same for you," I said. I looked from him to the shadowmen. "So, is this some sort of council?"

"Yes," said Kurgurrah. "Exactly that. A council of guardians."

"I am bleeding heavily," I said. "And holding a fog upon this mountain. Perhaps we could get straight down to business."

"To business then," said Galatur.

The three of them found rocks to sit on, and we four sat in council, amidst the frozen tableau.

"My lady, you have made too much noise," said Neti. Now

he no longer looked at all like himself. He looked like a creature far heavier, larger, more ancient. "Not only you, others too. But you and Tiamat are the loudest. There has been too much back and forth between realms by creatures with no idea how to walk lightly. Too much drawing down of power that should not be drawn. First by Tiamat, then by you." He lifted his heavy chin to me. "There are far worse predators out there than Tiamat. You are going to bring them down on us."

He spread his grey hands out to the dead animals all around us. "Sanctuaries like this are more precious than you realise."

"What do you ask of me?" I said. "Tell me."

Kurgurrah pressed his hands together before him. "We will let Marduk move for a few heartbeats before we allow Tiamat to move. He will kill her and the dragon queen will be vanquished. This battle will be over. And then we will make sure that the gates will never open again."

"In return," said Neti, "you must give up your hold on the power."

I let his words sink in. "You mean, give it up forever?"

Neti nodded. "Let it go. You will never be able to get to it again."

"I will just be an ordinary woman," I said slowly. "With some *melam*."

"You must do it now," said Galatur.

"I will no longer be able to protect myself and those I love." I was still thinking it through. "Why not make this offer to Tiamat?"

Neti shook his head. "She would never agree to give up the power. There is no one she would do it for. If a deal is to be made, it must be with you."

"You must choose right now," said Kurgurrah.

"What happens if I say no?"

"Tiamat will kill Marduk and then you and she will battle it out for control of this realm," said Kurgurrah. "We think in fact you will win. But then there will be repercussions. Your friends will die. And one day very soon, the creatures we speak of will come to have their reckoning."

I shut my eyes. I looked out over the electric blue of the lake of power.

It had been something indeed, to be able to walk down any path in the land and not fear for myself. To know I was stronger than all those around me and that I could protect anyone I chose to. To know I could heal.

Yet of course it was no choice at all. I pushed myself backwards, away and away from the glorious blue. "I relinquish it," I said to the council on the mountain top. "I give it up."

Moments later, Tiamat's head was in two pieces, and her blood was everywhere. The shadowmen were gone, Neti was gone, and dead animal carcases were tumbling down towards me. A moment of panic, but then I found myself lifted up and I was standing on top of the heap of bodies. A last piece of help, by the agents of the old gods.

My head was whole and I was strong again. The fog all around was gone; the mountainscape revealed. A mess of stone.

I shut my eyes a moment. To the ordinary sparkle of sunlight through eyelids.

The blue power was gone.

I was nothing more than an ordinary woman, as I dug my way through dead animals to find Marduk. I would live a long time, yes, but that was all there was left to me.

I felt tears on my cheeks and wiped them away.

"I did it," Marduk said, when I freed him. He shone with happiness.

"Marduk the hero," I said.

I already knew that for all of history his name would ring out as the slayer of Tiamat.

He knelt up, lifted my hands, and kissed them both. "Queen of Heaven and Earth," he said. "That is what they will call you now."

I looked about at the stretches of grey rock around us, strewn with the bodies of Tiamat's creatures. On the mountainside far below us, the wreckage of the Kur gleamed red in the sun.

"Do you think more of them will come through the gate?" he said.

I smiled at him. "The gate is closed," I said. "Some friends of mine have closed it forever."

I was glad that Tiamat was dead. I also, without my power, felt lumpen and useless. When everyone found out that my power had gone, what would I have to offer? What would stop the likes of Enki taking whatever they wanted from me once more?

That was when I saw Gilgamesh, coming up the mountain towards us. He frowned at the sight of all the dead animals, but then smiled when he saw us sitting on top of them.

"Where is the dragon queen?" he said.

"Dead!" said Marduk.

Gilgamesh's smile was so beautiful; I had forgotten. It threw everything around him into the shade.

"I have a gift for you, Inanna," he called up. "A small peace offering, I hope." He held out a *mee* to me. It was the master *mee*.

I climbed down to Gilgamesh and accepted the *mee*. "Where did you get it?" I said, slipping it onto my left wrist. It tightened, cool, around my skin.

"Ereshkigal had it," he said. "She's here with an army of Sebitti. Oh, and the Sebitti from the far north are here too. They are trying to sweep up all the creatures. But I thought you might still need this against Tiamat."

My plan came to me in that moment, fully formed. I realised something very straightforward. Neti was gone. The flies were gone. Tiamat was gone. The gates were shut forever. There would be no more visitors from other realms.

Only someone wearing this master *mee* would ever be able to tell that I no longer had my blue power. And that master *mee* was now on my wrist.

So, I would wear the master *mee* again. And I would simply pretend to have my old powers. It was not much of a plan, but it was a plan, and Ninshubar had taught me the value of a plan.

This would be the secret that I would keep until the end of my days.

I looked up from the *mee*. "Thank you, Gilgamesh," I said. "It has sentimental value for me."

He kissed my left hand, his short beard scratching my skin. The touch of him sent an old yearning through me. "Queen of Heaven and Earth," he said. He knelt down before me and kissed my hand again.

Yes, I was Queen of Heaven and Earth now. A good story, and who would choose to test me on it?

PART THE LAST

"Who can challenge a queen who raises her head higher than the mountain tops? When she speaks, cities turn to ruins – homes for ghosts – and temples become deserts."

From the "Hymn to Inanna" by
Enheduana, as translated by Sophus Helle

CHAPTER 1

ERESHKIGAL

At Ur

I paced back and forth around the bedchamber, naked, my fists clenched, sometimes moaning out loud.

None of them understood how brave I was being.

I had borne babies before and watched them die. It meant nothing at all that I could feel this one moving inside me between bouts of pain. I could not count on any good outcome.

At times the pain was so bad that I leaned against a wall and cried.

Geshtinanna was the only one I could bear to have near me.

She fanned me and was always close but not too close with her soft hands and kind eyes. "Come outside," she said, when I had been labouring all night.

She led me out into a small courtyard and helped me sit down at the edge of the pool with my feet in the cool water and the morning sunlight on my swollen breasts and belly.

"There is a queue of priestesses outside," she said. "They say they should be in here for the birth of a god."

"*If* it is a god," I sobbed. "*If* it survives."

Geshtinanna sat down next to me, her bare feet in the water, and ran a bone comb through my hair, over and over, scratching at my scalp. "Inanna, who sees everything, says the baby shines very bright with Anzu magic. She is certain that this baby will survive and thrive. I know you cannot believe that, but I believe it."

"I wish Namtar was here," I said. "I love you very much, but Namtar knew how to make my pain go away."

"I know he did," she said. "Now I am going to pour you some mountain tea and put a little honey in it."

"And you know my sister does not see everything," I said, as she stood up. "She sits there with her nose in the air, better than everyone, but she does not see everything."

I breathed through a new bout of pain but could not get any comfort and ended up on all fours in the water, weeping. "If you can see this, Inanna," I shouted out, "I hope you are enjoying it!"

Geshtinanna came back outside with a clay cup, smiling kindly at my joke. "Why don't you lie on the bed again? There is a clean sheet. I could prop you up a bit. Then you can sip your tea while I fan you."

"All right," I said, and held on to her tight as she helped me out of the pool. "You are a very good daughter to me, Geshtinanna."

One tear ran down her right cheek, as she led me back into the shade of the bedchamber. She wiped it away on her arm. "Ereshkigal, you are the only mother I have ever had and I am so very glad to have you."

"Silly, sentimental girl," I said, as she put down my tea, and carefully lowered me onto the cool sheet.

"What will you call the child?" she said.

"If it lives."

"If it lives, what will you call it?"

"It's a girl," I said. "I will call her Tadmustum."

"That's a lovely name."

"I shouldn't have said it. There are old gods that snatch away babies. I have heard of them in temple!"

"I'm going to fan you," she said.

"Oh," I said, with the pleasure of it, as she waved a fan of feathers over my damp skin. "Oh, you are a very good girl. Where is Dumuzi today?"

"He is making his case to Inanna."

"Ah," I said. "He had better make his case from his knees."

Geshtinanna laughed. "And kiss each of her toes! And grovel and grovel and grovel!"

I was quiet for a while, as my belly grew rigid again with the most horrible pain.

"Keep fanning me," I said at last. I reached out and squeezed Geshtinanna's hand. "If Inanna says no to him, then you and your brother will always have a home with me wherever I go. That is the promise of a goddess." I burst into tears. "I am in so much pain!"

"No, no," she said. "Only think of the cool air on your skin. Think of how much we all love you." She leaned over and kissed my knee. "You are bathed in our love, Ereshkigal. You are truly our queen."

"Oh, you are a good girl," I said. "I do feel much better when you speak to me like that."

CHAPTER 2

INANNA

At Ur

I sat in state in the whitewashed temple that had once been my mother's. The Akkadians had stripped the room of furniture, but a small wooden chair had been brought in for me and I sat with my feet on a cushion.

I was dressed in a magnificent new gown cut from kingfisher blue cloth. The Akkadians had left behind treasure when they went north.

My lions sat on either side of my makeshift throne, in their gold and carnelian collars.

Ninshubar stood behind me, tall, severe, in a borrowed white robe, the light from the shuttered windows playing over her.

Behind my *sukkal*, in a semi-circle, stood all the priests and priestesses of Ur who had somehow been left alive. They also wore white, the colour of the city.

My husband, Dumuzi, meanwhile, knelt before me on the mud-brick floor.

"So go on then," I said. "Say you are sorry and then tell me what you want."

He looked up at me. "I suppose I am not entirely sure, Inanna, what I ought to be sorry about." Indeed, he did not sound sorry. "Perhaps I did wrong you when we were first married," he went on. "Perhaps I could have helped you when you were murdered by your sister's demons. But have I not already been punished for that? So, what am I meant to be sorry for? Besides, I was very helpful to you in the far north, and I did everything I could for you on the journey south, as did my sister. You cannot argue with that."

"You threatened to cut my arm off," I said, "when your father sacked my bedchambers in Eridu."

"I did not mean it, Inanna."

"I think you did. Also, you lied to me over and over about my mother. You said she was being well treated, but she was not. Also, you married me when I had no choice in the matter and no liking for you. And then you brought your sister to Uruk and lay with her in private."

He stood up. I saw he had been emboldened by his time with Ereshkigal; that he had gained strength in the light of her favour.

"I married you because I was frightened of my father," he said, polite but firm. "And, Inanna, you lay with the boy Gilgamesh in private and I do not remember making a fuss about it."

"You can kneel," I said.

After only the smallest moment of hesitation, he knelt back down.

"I suppose I don't really care what you did or didn't do to me," I said, which was the truth of it. I glanced around at Ninshubar, but she was standing like a soldier at sentry; she gave no sign of listening to us. "You asked what you might apologise for and those are some things you could apologise for. But anyway, what is it you want? Make your case."

He folded his hands before him. "I ask that, as your husband, I have a place in Uruk when you return there. And my sister too."

"And why would I agree to that?"

"I would only propose a marriage in name. We would never appear in the rites together unless you thought we should. You know I love Uruk. I would help rebuild it and I would help administer it once rebuilt. I could help with the building of your new sanctuary there. I am a good worker, and very detailed, you know I am. And the people would like it. We were a popular pairing and we could be so again. It would be celebrated all over the river lands."

I stretched my legs out in front of me, admiring my beautiful, shining blue skirts, and then set my bare feet back on my cushion. "It would annoy Gilgamesh," I said, which was also true. "I suppose I ought to consider it."

"Thank you, goddess," he said, bowing his head.

I remembered about Ereshkigal.

"How is my sister?" I said. "We hear her screams and moaning even here."

Irritation flickered across his face. "Your sister has reason to be so frightened," he said. "But she is doing well since you ask. My sister is with her constantly."

I found it rather sweet, his loyalty to Ereshkigal.

"You will go now," I said. "I have Enmesarra waiting to see me."

CHAPTER 3

MARDUK

At Ur

My mother from the far north, Enmesarra, was in the waiting room outside Inanna's audience chamber. She was wearing the same leather clothes that she had come south in, but she had tied gold scales into her long red hair. I was in my new blue velvet robe, a gift from Biluda.

I did a little bow for her and kissed her on each cheek. "Waiting to see the high goddess?" I said.

She leaned down to greet Moshkhussu. "How is your belly?" she said, standing straight again.

"Good," I said, putting my hand to the wound. It ached, but it was healing well. "I've heard a rumour that all the Sebitti might be going north."

She frowned at that. "I wanted to know Inanna's mind before speaking to you."

"I understand."

"We could have our own land in the far north," she said. "We could find an island and make it our own. Fashion our own laws. Be our own people."

"I can see it."

We smiled at each other.

"There is a question over the Sebitti children," she said. "Will they come north with us? I think they should. But Nergal does not want to be parted from them and Ereshkigal wants whatever Nergal wants."

"So what will happen?"

"We may ask Inanna to intervene." She glanced at the door to the temple chamber.

We stood quiet together a moment.

"Will you come, Marduk?" she said, her voice soft. "Will you come north?"

I let the question settle between us.

"I will come north, but not yet," I said. "That is a promise."

She took the blow well, with no hint of emotion. "Is it because of this city you have been given?"

"No, it's not about Eridu," I said. "There are things I need to do here." I was going to say more, but the doors opened, Dumuzi was brushing past us, and a priest was stood before us, waiting to speak to my mother.

She smiled at me. "You look very fine in that velvet."

"I have someone to visit," I said. "A formal thing."

I made my way into the barracks. I saw men about to ask me my business, but then biting down on their questions. I was a prince of Sumer and the slayer of Tiamat. My name was being written on tablets in every temple.

They bowed their heads to me and hurried to open doors and gates.

They had put him in the prisoner cells at the top of the building.

"You can go out," I said to the guard who was sat outside the cell.

"Are you sure, my lord?"

"Quite sure."

I pulled the bolts of the door and opened it to darkness and the stink of a cell with no bucket. Then I made him out, a shape on the floor.

"Hello, Inush," I said.

There was a small, barred window in the room outside the cell. We sat beneath it, on a brick bench, him in his filthy blue robes and me in my very clean blue robes.

He sat with one hand over his missing nose.

"You know, I looked and looked for you," he said. "I thought the goddess Ninsun had snatched you from the supply camp outside Uruk. I did not know what they might have done to you."

"The scar is not so bad," I said.

He dropped his hand, lifting his chin. "It's a mess."

I smiled and shook my head.

"So why are you here?" he said.

"I've been thinking about what I owe you for saving my life in Kish and saving Moshkhussu's life too. When you could easily have had us both killed."

He gave the faintest of shrugs. "I wanted you in my bed, Marduk. You owe me nothing."

"Yet still, to sit and do nothing, while they execute you, does not feel right to me."

He glanced up at the barred window. "Do you know how they are going to do it?"

"They intend to throw you off the moon tower, as so many Sumerians were thrown off it. There are those who blame you for everything that happened here."

"I was not my uncle," he said, "however I will not make excuses. We waged war as the Akkadians have always waged war and I did nothing to change the pattern of it."

I took a deep breath. I had not been sure what I was going to do, on my way up the stairs to his cell. But I knew then what felt right to me.

"I am here to set you free," I said.

He gave out a laugh. "That seems unlikely."

"I am quite serious," I said. "I am going to ride you north to Kish. It will be a great deal safer for you than trying to go alone. We could take the dog and Biluda with us."

"And they will allow this? Inanna will allow it?"

"Inanna will not care what happens to you," I said. "Indeed, I doubt she knows you are here or even who you are."

"So we will simply walk out?"

"Well," I said. I tipped my head from one shoulder to the other. "Inanna will not care. But some others may make a fuss. Harga and Gilgamesh, for example. They may not be happy about me releasing you. They have a different sort of outlook on the thing. They are quite fastidious in some ways, sticklers for stuff, if you know what I mean. So if by any chance we run into them, I do encourage you to keep out of sight."

"I see," he said.

"What I am saying is, we will have to slink out. Avoid too

many eyes. But do not worry. I can do this."

"And Moshkhussu?" he said.

"They wouldn't let me bring her in here," I said. "Silly rules. She's waiting outside. I doubt anyone will try to run off with her."

He smiled at that, his scars creasing across his cheeks.

"You do not owe me this," he said.

"And yet I choose to give it," I said.

CHAPTER 4

HARGA

At Ur

Gilgamesh and I floated on our backs in the warm sea, our faces turned up to the lapis lazuli sky. He spoke but I did not quite catch it with my ears under water.

I stood up, sand underfoot. "What?" I said.

"I've never thought of you as a swimmer," he said, turning his head to smile at me.

"Of course, I'm a swimmer. I'm a stone man. I grew up in and out of boats. I am half fish."

He stood up also, peering down at the sand through the translucent water. "Well, I'm not sure I have ever seen you in water. Of course, yes, wading or swimming a river or somesuch when we've been travelling on foot. In necessity, yes, you are a swimmer. But never for pleasure, I mean."

A heron flew overhead, trailing long legs, and we both tipped our faces up to watch the bird pass.

"Perhaps you are right," I said. "Perhaps swimming is a new thing for me. It's good for my shoulder."

"Can you not ask Ninlil for some help with that?"

"She has more important things to worry about."

I sank down to my neck in the water. "Where is your boy?"

"With my father," he said.

"You won't let them take him north?"

"How little you think of me, Harga! Of course, my son will stay with me. Here and then in Uruk, when we start to rebuild. I will devote myself to raising him."

That seemed very unlikely indeed, but I said nothing.

"So what did Inanna say?" Gilgamesh said. We began to make for the shore and I noticed, as he waded naked through the shallows, that he walked like a young man again.

With the ramparts of Ur behind us, we sat upon the beach to dry off a little.

"Inanna says I am to have the town of Girsu as my reward for my part in the war," I said.

"I heard."

"She wants it built up into a great city and she wants one of her sanctuaries established there. I will be a god and king there rolled into one, to start at least, and my name will be Ningursu."

"Nin-gurrr-sooo," he said. "I don't mind it."

"Perhaps in private you can still call me Harga."

We both laughed.

"How very gracious of you, lord god Ningursu!" said Gilgamesh. "So, when will you leave?"

"I need to gather up my boys and a few troops. Lilith will come, to help me set up the temple. We'll build a shrine for your mother there."

"That's good," he said. "I thank you for it." He looked out over the water. "All this time such a point was made of me not being a god. But now it seems that anyone can be a god if Inanna chooses."

"I would not have chosen it," I said.

He shook his head, smiling. "Look, I might come with you. You should have an honour guard."

"Should I?"

"A new god, or god elect, arriving at his city for the first time. Yes, I think there should be some fuss, some fine armour. At least one person who looks the part. And what could be more awe-inspiring than the King of Uruk escorting you in?"

"Nothing that you personally can think of, I'm sure. But aren't you needed here?"

"It's not far. Three days there do you think?"

"Maybe two if the paths through the marshes are dry."

"I would like to make the trip. And before I come back, I thought I'd head north and see what's left of the house at Shuruppak. I feel bad about the dogs, and also the priestess Shamhat. I suppose the Akkadians might have razed it all, but I think I ought to at least check."

"Any waifs and strays, you must send them south to me."

"I will," he said, nodding. He looked me in the eye. "Did you ever speak to Ninshubar?"

"I speak to her all the time."

He rolled his eyes, most elaborately. "You told her the gap between you was too wide. But is it too wide now? I mean, you are an ancient creature, but you are a god in name. You will have your own city. Why not speak, if you are still mooning for her?"

After a long pause, I said: "It is hard to know what to say to her."

Gilgamesh put one warm hand out onto my shoulder. "Harga, she is a woman of vast honour and total straightforwardness. Surely any words will do?"

"I'm not sure," I said, shaking him off. "Is there word of Ereshkigal?"

"Only that she labours."

"May all the gods look kindly on her," I said. The phrase did not mean what it once had to me, now that I myself was being entered into the god lists. But habit is a hard thing to kill.

"Just speak to her, Harga," Gilgamesh said, clapping me on the back. "Allow yourself to hope, just this once."

CHAPTER 5

NINLIL

At Ur

I sat with my feet neatly together on the floor and my hands on my knees. My son Nergal paced back and forth in the waiting room outside Ereshkigal's chambers.

The walls of the room were lined with the priests and priestesses who believed they should be in attendance at the birth.

"She should let me in," Nergal exclaimed. "I should be in there." He turned to me. "You could be helping her with the pain."

I smiled at him. "I am sitting here in case she asks for me. She knows I am here."

The door to the bedchamber sprung open.

Geshtinanna came out, quickly shutting the door behind her. "Lord Nergal, she says you can come in if you say nothing at all, and you must not breathe loudly."

My son's broad face split into a smile. "Thank you, Geshtinanna." He cast an apologetic look at me.

"Go," I said. "I will be here if she calls for me."

I sat quiet for a while, listening to the priests whispering around me, and thinking of my mother, the dragon queen. I was glad she was dead. Yet it felt wrong that there had been no ceremony for her.

Ningal, the moon goddess, dropped down beside me on my bench. I had not noticed her enter the antechamber. She seemed so very distant from Ereshkigal that I sometimes forgot they were mother and daughter.

"Any news?" she said.

"She has let Nergal in," I said, smiling at her. She was a lovely looking woman. "What are your plans, Ningal? What will you do when the baby is born and Inanna goes north?"

She was about to speak, but then did not.

We sat a while in silence.

A tear rolled down Ningal's cheek. "I failed all three of my children," she said.

"Surely you did the best you could?"

She wiped away her tear. "Ereshkigal was a hard child for me to love. I am ashamed of myself, but it is the truth. I did love Utu, but he had no use for me. Inanna was the love of my life, she still is, but there is such a breach between us now."

"I could put my hands on you," I said.

She shook her curls at that. "It's right I feel this pain." She smiled. "What will you do now?"

"I am going north, home to Nippur. I will rebuild the city and I will rebuild my husband's temple. I have many of his memories within me, his talents too. I will hold the north for all of us. I will put walls around the city. I have even wondered if I might be able to regrow my husband in my belly."

"Could that be done?"

"Perhaps. I am an Anzu, after all. But what about you?"

Ningal smiled but shook her head. "I have not spoken to Inanna about this yet, but I have thought about going north with the Sebitti for a while. I have a yearning to look out on snow and wear heavy furs and see high mountains."

"Like the view from the Thunderbird," I said. "When we were coming down."

"Yes," she said. "I would like to step out into that view and see what it's like to walk there." She was very beautiful when she smiled. "But I must ask Inanna first."

"All hail Inanna," I said, and kissed her on her soft cheek. "And all hail the mother of the high goddess, Ningal of the moon, and only at the start of her adventure."

"I wish Inanna needed me here, but the truth is she does not," she said.

She looked very sad indeed.

"Did you know that your father Enki has come to bend his knee to her?" I said.

"Hah," she said. "That is something I would like to see."

CHAPTER 6

INANNA

At Ur

Enki climbed down onto his knees as my traitorous lions frothed around him, purring and rubbing at him.

"Everyone seems to be getting younger and more lithe," he said. "All except me."

"You will address me as 'high goddess'," I said, frowning down at him.

"High goddess," he said, bending his head.

I felt a strong compulsion to use the master *mee* on him, but then there was no point in draining its energy.

"I've already had your son in here today," I said. "So what is it that you want?"

He turned his leopard eyes up to mine. "You know how much I love Eridu. I would like to see out my days there." He bent his head again, clasping his hands together. "I am begging you for your mercy."

It was a good impression of a loyal subject begging a favour.

"As it happens, you are in luck," I said. "I will allow you to return to Eridu. The city is Marduk's now, as you may know, but you may hold it for him in his absences and serve there in any way that pleases him. I do not think him much interested in the running of a city, so perhaps you will be useful to him."

I watched anger pass over his features, to be replaced by a veneer of politeness and then a smile.

"High goddess, I am forever grateful to you," he said.

"Your gratitude is meaningless to me," I said, sitting up straighter on my wooden chair. "I have a list of tasks for you to perform if you do indeed wish to return to Eridu."

"A list?" he said.

Ninshubar leaned forward and passed me the clay tablet. I held up the tablet to my face to read it carefully.

"You do indeed have a list," said Enki.

"First," I said, "you will go to Egypt and clean out that rat's nest in Abydos. I am told they sacrifice children there. All that will stop. It's your fault that Isis and Osiris are there, so take responsibility for it."

"Very well," he said, after half a moment's pause.

"When you have finished your work in Egypt, you will go north to Kish and fetch your mother, Nammu of the Anunnaki."

"I believe she is dead."

"Not quite. They have released her from their dungeons, since they have decided she is an Akkadian war hero and she is still creeping about there. You will take her to Eridu with you and put her back in the Temple of the Waves." I turned my head and nodded at Ninshubar. "The priestess there, Dulma, has been tasked with keeping a close eye on her. But you will also be responsible for her."

"Egypt, and then my mother," said Enki.

I turned back to my tablet. "Your former wife, Ninhursag, has vowed to kill you for your crimes. If she does, I will not punish her for it. But whatever she does, you will never raise a hand against her. I task you with living in peace with her and offering her any assistance she may need here in Ur."

"In Ur?" he said.

"I am giving her Ur."

He paused before speaking. "You are giving her this city?"

"Fourth," I said, looking back to my tablet, "should Marduk see fit to let you rule in his stead, you will rule Eridu with kindness and compassion. You will side with the oppressed over the oppressors."

"The oppressed," he repeated flatly.

"Fifth, you will protect the sea borders of Sumer and face execution for any failures in that regard."

"Very well," he said. Any pretence of good humour had evaporated. "Anything else?"

"Also," I said. "If your current wife Damkina resurfaces, you will be good to her. Seventh, Ninshubar will be coming west soon to visit you and to set up a sanctuary where the slave market is now. You will run that sanctuary to my exact specifications."

Enki made to speak, but then closed his mouth without doing so.

"I could send Dumuzi to Eridu instead of you," I said. "He has just been in here convincing me of his dedication and his administrative strengths."

"I am very pleased to receive this list from you," he said. "Delighted, in fact."

"I am only halfway through the list," I said. "Perhaps you could stay quiet until I am finished."

CHAPTER 7

GILGAMESH

At Ur

"Why are you wet?" Inanna said to me. She was sat on a wooden chair, in a blue robe that was very fetching against her sun-darkened skin and black hair. She might have looked very grand except her feet did not reach the floor, and were instead balanced on a cushion.

"I've been sea swimming with Harga," I said. "Most refreshing on a day like this."

Inanna shifted in her seat but said nothing.

There was a silence.

In the midst of that pause, I smiled down at Inanna's lions, both unconscious on the brick floor.

"You asked for this audience," Inanna said at last.

I looked back up at her and gave her my smile.

"I hear that you are restarting the temple rites," I said. I had not planned to mention it, but the blue against her skin had made me think of it.

"The rites will restart," she said, sombre. "I want the city to know that the Anunnaki are here forever. That we rule as we always have. That we are doing everything we can for their crops and their livestock and for the sun to keep rising steady upon the river lands. But not until I am back in Uruk."

"But when we are back in Uruk, I was thinking that if the high goddess of Uruk were to lie down with the King of Uruk, then it would send a strong message of strength and continuity."

"Yes," she said. "That is one idea." She lifted her eyebrows. "I may also choose to lie down with my husband Dumuzi. He has asked to return to Uruk and we are accustomed to doing the rites together. I think that would give the message of strength and continuity that you are speaking of. Do you not agree?"

I tipped my head from side to side, as if considering the topic very seriously. "I have more history there," I said. "The child of Lugalbanda and Ninsun, who founded the city with An." Somehow I found myself rather far from the point I had been trying to make, and perhaps doing myself no good at all.

Inanna frowned down at me. "I do not mean to be petitioned about the temple rites. Is this your reason for asking for an audience? You might have asked Lilith about this. She is in charge of temple business."

I pulled down my damp linen shirt and then held out my open palms to her in friendly supplication.

"Inanna, I did not ask for an audience. I came to your door this morning and knocked on it and was told that if I wanted to see you, this was the way to do it." I gave her another smile. "What I wanted to ask you was, do you want to come swimming? You said you would come swimming with me once, but I never took you. There's a lovely beach not far from the city walls. The water is perfection."

For a moment, her icy demeanour seemed to thaw a little.

"I do love to swim."

"I know you do," I said. "Think of all those beautiful swims on the journey south."

"I am quite the dolphin," she said, and she turned to smile at Ninshubar. "Really I am, Ninshubar. I swam and swam on my way south."

Ninshubar returned her smile, and a bolt of jealousy shot through me, at how close they were. But as Ninshubar would say, one step and then the next.

"If there's time later," Inanna said, turning back to me, "then I will come swimming with you. I think I would like that."

"Thank you, high goddess," I said. I winked at her.

"If you wink at me again, there will be no swimming," she said.

I was about to laugh out loud, but instead I lowered my head almost to the floor. "No more winking, high goddess, I promise."

Yes, as Ninshubar would say: *One step and then the next.*

CHAPTER 8

NINSHUBAR

At Ur

In a gap between audiences, I climbed up onto Ur's famous ramparts to stretch my legs and look out again on the site of my resurrection. I had it in my mind also, half-admitted to myself, to see if I might find Harga. He had tasked himself with overhauling the city guard and I had seen him up on the walls earlier, his head tipped in council with local men.

The ramparts were ten strides wide and with glorious views of the ten thousand islands and in the far distance, the haze that was Eridu. I soon found Harga. He was stood at the highest point along the ramparts with the two boys he always kept about him, and he appeared to be remonstrating with them.

When he caught sight of me, he lowered his voice, and spoke again to the two boys, but more gently. They ran off, each with a hand raised to me.

His hair looked damp.

"Swimming with Gilgamesh?" I said.

He gave me his careful smile. "Are you running a spy network now?"

"Not yet," I said. "Perhaps I should though."

He nodded, and looked out over the view of the river, and then rolled his shoulders. "Any news of Ereshkigal?"

I shook my head.

He nodded again, and rolled his shoulders once more.

"Ninshubar," he said. He rolled his shoulders a third time and took a pebble from the pouch at his belt.

"Yes," I said.

We were both about the same height and for a moment we looked into each other's eyes.

Then he looked down at the pebble in his hand.

"Ninshubar," he said. "You said some kind words to me once I think and I was an old fool and I said the river between us was too wide, or something like that."

"I remember."

He put the pebble back into its pouch and lifted his chin, as if at parade. "The river is even wider now," he said. "I am only getting older. I have a shoulder that is always getting worse."

"I am sorry for that," I said, keeping my face free of emotion.

"To get to the point of this, I am leaving soon for Girsu," he said. "And I wonder if you would consider riding out with me when I go. Lilith is coming, and Gilgamesh too. You need not be gone long. I would appreciate your advice in Girsu, in the setting of the temples and so forth."

"I do not know much about temples."

He stood, looking very serious, contemplating that, and then laughed. "You are not as kind a woman as people think."

"Say it plainly," I said. "Or it is not said."

He took a deep breath in. "Ninshubar, please will you come

with me? I would like to spend some time with you."

I thought over what I was feeling. My heart was beating faster than normal; I felt both excited and frightened, but also rather nauseous. I did not like the feeling of not being in control. But I wanted to be closer to him.

Well, if you are going to do something, better do it quick.

I stepped forward, took Harga's clean-shaved face in my hands, and kissed him on the mouth.

The shock of it ricocheted through me.

After half a heartbeat, he put his hands to my face and kissed me back.

One heartbeat later, I let go of him and took a step backwards from him.

"I will ask Inanna if she can spare me," I said.

I turned and walked away from him.

"Ninshubar," he called after me.

I composed my face before turning to him.

"Is there anything you're not good at?" he said.

CHAPTER 9

INANNA

Many moons later, in Uruk

I felt An's sandalled foot upon the White Quay as he was helped from his barge. I felt him draw closer as he was carried up through the newly built city precincts, past the young palms and fresh-dug ponds, into my pristine sanctuary. I felt his slow and heavy tread upon the steps up to the temple chamber where I sat waiting.

I was sat on a throne that was not much more than a simple chair, except it was cast from some unknown, black metal. And except for the fact it had once had Apsu, high god of Creation, strapped to it. What was left of Apsu and his wife, Tiamat, was buried beneath the floor of my new temple. Indeed, I sat directly above their remains in my metal chair. I sat upon them as reminder that I was high goddess of Heaven now, and not only the Earth.

I wore the kingfisher blue of Kish that symbolised my triumph over my human enemies. Upon my head, pressing down heavy upon me, I wore the famous shugurrah, the gold crown of the steppes, that spoke of my ancient heritage. It had been found amongst King Akka's looted treasures. My skirts were embroidered with the black scales of Tiamat's suit as a reminder of my dominion over all other gods.

Wings had been found for me and upon my chest I wore the bronze breastplate that the goddess Ninsun wore into battle on the day of her triumph over the Akkadians. I had had to change the story of Ninsun; I could not have an Anunnaki dying on the battlefield.

Now here was An, his eyes on my wings.

I had seen him in my mind's eye, in the days when I was all-seeing, as a man close to death. But Ninlil and her healing hands had been at work on him. Now he walked towards my metal chair, slow, but tall and strong. As he bent his head to me, I saw that although the ends of his curls were white, the roots were black.

"Great-granddaughter, it is good to see you," said An, as he, very slowly, knelt.

I nodded.

"Goddess of love and war," he said, his voice deep and commanding, and very familiar to me, although I had not seen him since I was newborn. "You did not forget the second part."

I lifted my right hand to him. He climbed up onto his feet, and advanced to take my hand and kiss it. As his beard scratched my skin, old memories of my future self, my future lives, swept over me. Being washed up in the warm, foamy surf of an island called Cyprus. The memory of Troy and how I was blamed for it. Legions flowing out from Rome, as I stood on the steps of my stone temple there.

But in this moment, here I was, with An's mouth pressed to my hand.

"I'm told you can call up storms," he said, letting my hand drop. "That you can bring down lightning upon your enemies. That you can see where we all are at all times and even what we are doing.

That you can turn gold to silver, and men to women, and back again."

"I am the change," I said, unsmiling.

"That is quite a story," he said quietly. "You still wear the *mee* I gave you," he added, his eyes on the master *mee*. "I'm surprised you still need it, with all the power flowing through you."

I threw out a loop of invisible blue fire around him, and then another. He took two, careful, steps back from me.

"Perhaps I like the look of it," I said.

Behind me, Ninshubar stood statue-still in her armour, her eyes on An. All around us stood the priests and priestesses of my new temple, with Gilgamesh and Lilith amongst them.

I shut my eyes for a moment and imagined diving into the Euphrates. I imagined bursting up out of the water, and seeing Gilgamesh there, stripped to the waist and dripping wet. How astonishing his smile was. I would go swimming with him again when the day's ceremony was over with.

I blinked open my eyes.

The light from the high windows fell upon An's two-tone curls. He got back down on his knees, groaning a little with the effort of it, and kissed each of my bare feet.

"Queen of Heaven and Earth," he said, lifting his head, and his voice. "All hail the great goddess Inanna."

Yes, in Athens, they call me Aphrodite now.

In Babylon, they call me Ishtar.

But in the first days I had only one name.

Inanna.

THE END

A NOTE FROM THE AUTHOR

Those of you who have read my notes at the end of the first two books in this series will know that this novel was inspired by the ancient mythology of Mesopotamia, the oldest recorded stories in existence. As with the first two books, this novel also follows the archaeological evidence where possible in its depiction of the lost world of Sumer, which is the first civilisation known to have risen up in what is now modern Iraq, and also arguably the world's first ever civilisation.

All that said, these are novels, not history books. If I want my characters riding horses (which may only have existed in Asia at the time), I have them riding horses. If I want them to have pockets (apparently not a Sumerian thing, as far as we know), I give them pockets. I have also had to make a million choices, along the way, about which parts of which myths to stick to and which to completely ignore, because the stories from Ancient Mesopotamia are contradictory, fragmented, and often recorded thousands of years apart. Some are only a few lines long; some of them long and repetitive, and full of echoes of other myths. Some of the myths were rewritten over the ages, with gods' names swapped out and new ones put in, for religious or political purposes, or both. They absolutely do not fit into any sort of a neat whole.

Moreover, as in any novel, once my heroes had risen up on the page and become real people in my mind, then they became my primary guides as to what would happen next. I may have always had an end point to each book in mind, based on some key piece of mythology, but Ninshubar, Inanna, Gilgamesh, and the rest of the gang were my guides as to how the story would get us to that end point.

In case you are interested in finding out more about the mythology, here are some details about which ancient stories I absorbed into these novels, wholly or partially.

In *Inanna*, the first in the series, I wove together the famous *Epic of Gilgamesh* with the less well-known stories of Inanna's descent into the underworld and her battle to free a "huluppu" tree from its poisonous guardians. I also wove in the poems about Inanna's passionate courtship with the sheep god, Dumuzi, although in my version, it was not very courtly and not at all passionate.

Parts of the *Epic of Gilgamesh* and "Inanna's Descent", by the way, are amongst the very first pieces of literature ever recorded. The Descent may be a version of a prehistoric story that existed as an oral tale long before writing began to be invented in Sumer in about 3,500 BC.

In *Gilgamesh*, the second in the series, I wove together another of the great myths about Inanna, her theft of the *mees* from Enki, with the story of Ereshkigal's love affair with the war god Nergal, and the chillingly nasty story of Enlil and his young wife Ninlil.

I also used "The Envoys of Akka", an old fragment of story very popular amongst schoolchildren in ancient times, as the basis for King Akka's siege of Uruk. I also began to properly weave in the elements of the key Mesopotamian creation myth known as "Enuma Elish", something that I only began to hint at in *Inanna*.

Which brings me to this, the final book in the trilogy, *Ninshubar*. As with the other books, it is heavily threaded with fragments or inspiration from many Mesopotamian myths (for example, the story about Lugalbanda and the Anzu bird). But the underlying architecture here is the previously mentioned "Enuma Elish". This important creation myth (the oldest surviving creation myth that we have), in which Tiamat is finally slain by Marduk, is a Babylonian story, but it may have been based on a much older Sumerian story that has not yet been discovered.

A new translation of "Enuma Elish" by Sophus Helle was recently published, by the way. The book, from Bloomsbury Academic, includes essays from leading Mesopotamian scholars that dive deep into the meaning of the myth, and I heartily recommend it.

Other books I recommend to you, if you are interested in reading further:

Sophus Helle's book about Enheduana. She was a priestess of Inanna and is probably the world's first named author. Helle's translations of Enheduana's poems about Inanna are simply gorgeous.

The *Epic of Gilgamesh* as translated by Andrew George. A classic, but updated not too long ago. The updating is important because new scraps of Gilgamesh stories continue to be found on a regular basis. Some of these scraps come up fresh from archaeological sites and others are found hiding amidst old museum collections.

Inanna, Queen of Heaven and Earth by Diane Wolkstein and Samuel Noah Kramer. As I have said before, this book made me realise that Inanna's stories could be pieced together into an epic.

Myths from Mesopotamia translated by Stephanie Dalley. This is my most heavily thumbed and scribbled upon book about the region and its literature.

Between Two Rivers by Moudhy Al-Rashid. This is a lovely new history of the region, as told through the prism of the ancient writings and objects found there. I found the human stories she pulls out from the archaeological record very moving.

ACKNOWLEDGEMENTS

Thank you to this book's first reader, Jack Absalom, who is an excellent judge of plot.

Thank you to Chloë Wilson and Sapphire Jones Medeema for their thoughtful critique of character, language, and scene blocking.

Thank you to Esther Addley, another superb reader. Esther, whatever I write next, I promise that it will *not* involve a whole fleet of goddesses all beginning with the letter N.

Thank you to Catherine de Lange, who is far too busy to be reading unfinished novels and yet is kind enough to do it for me (and what an amazing reader she is).

Thank you to my editor at Titan Books, Daniel Carpenter, who commissioned this series and has edited all three books in it, earning himself an encyclopaedic knowledge of Ancient Mesopotamia (or at least my version of it) along the way. He has both sense and sensibility, and his editing instincts are absolutely first class.

Thank you also to everyone else at Titan Books who has

worked on this book, including the cover artist Julia Lloyd, copyeditor Louise Pearce, typesetter Richard Mason, publicist Bahar Kutluk, proofreader Paul Simpson and editorial assistant Rachel Vincent.

Thank you to Tim Absalom for the map of Ancient Sumer.

And finally, thank you to Jon Absalom and Aldo Absalom for their steadfast support on the home front.

ABOUT THE AUTHOR

EMILY H. WILSON is a full-time writer based in Dorset, in the south of England. *Ninshubar* is her third novel. Emily was previously a journalist, working as a reporter at the *Mirror* and *Daily Mail*, a senior editor at the *Guardian* and, most recently, as editor-in-chief of *New Scientist* magazine. You can follow her on X (formerly known as Twitter) @emilyhwilson or on Instagram @emilyhwilson1, and you can find her website at emilyhwilson.com.

For more fantastic fiction, author events,
exclusive excerpts, competitions, limited editions and more

VISIT OUR WEBSITE
titanbooks.com

LIKE US ON FACEBOOK
facebook.com/titanbooks

FOLLOW US ON TWITTER AND INSTAGRAM
@TitanBooks

EMAIL US
readerfeedback@titanemail.com